ANDY McDERMOTT

THE COVENANT OF
GENESIS

headline

Copyright © 2009 Andy McDermott

The right of Andy McDermott to be identified as the Author of
the Work has been asserted by him in accordance with the
Copyright, Designs and Patents Act 1988.

First published in Great Britain in 2009 by
HEADLINE PUBLISHING GROUP

1

Apart from any use permitted under UK copyright law, this publication
may only be reproduced, stored, or transmitted, in any form, or by any means,
with prior permission in writing of the publishers or, in the case of
reprographic production, in accordance with the terms of licences issued
by the Copyright Licensing Agency.

All characters in this publication are fictitious and any resemblance
to real persons, living or dead, is purely coincidental.

Cataloguing in Publication Data is available from the British Library

Hardback ISBN 978 0 7553 4551 9
Trade paperback ISBN 978 0 7553 4552 6

Typeset in Aldine 401BT by Avon DataSet Ltd,
Bidford-on-Avon, Warwickshire

Printed in the UK by CPI Mackays, Chatham, ME5 8TD

Headline's policy is to use papers that are natural, renewable and recyclable
products and made from wood grown in sustainable forests. The logging
and manufacturing processes are expected to conform to the environmental
regulations of the country of origin.

HEADLINE PUBLISHING GROUP
An Hachette UK Company
338 Euston Road
London NW1 3BH

www.headline.co.uk
www.hachette.co.uk

For my family and friends

Prologue

Oman

For all that the Arabian desert was traditionally supposed to be devoid of life, there was far too much of it for Mark Hyung's liking. A cloud of flies had been hovering in wait as he left his tent just after dawn, and now, three hours later, they had seemingly called in every other bug within a ten-mile radius.

He muttered an obscenity and stopped, removing his Oakleys and swatting at his face. The flies briefly retreated, but they would resume their dive-bombing soon enough. Not for the first time, he cursed himself for volunteering to come to this awful place.

'Got a problem there, Mr Hyung?' said Muldoon with barely concealed contempt, pausing in his ascent of the steepening slope. The bear-like Nevadan was a thirty-year veteran of the oil exploration business, tanned and leathery and swaggering. Mark knew Muldoon saw him as just some skinny fresh-from-college Korean kid from California, and rated him little higher than the desert flies.

'No problem at all, Mr Muldoon,' Mark replied, replacing his sunglasses and taking out a water bottle. He took several deep swigs, then splashed some on his hand and tilted his head forward to wipe the back of his neck.

Something on the ground caught his attention, and he crouched for a better look. The object was familiar, yet so out of place it took him a moment to identify: a seashell, a fractal spiral chipped and scuffed by weather and time. 'Have you seen this?'

'Yeah,' said Muldoon dismissively. 'Find 'em all over. This used to be a beach, once. Sea was higher than it is now.'

'Really?' Mark was familiar with the concept of sea level changes due to climatic shift, but until now it had only been on an abstract level. 'How long ago?'

'I dunno; hundred thousand years ago, hundred and fifty.' Muldoon gestured at the low bluff ahead, their destination. 'This woulda been a nice resort spot. Cavegirls in the raw.' He chuckled lecherously.

Mark held in a sigh. No point making his relations with the old-guard oilman any worse. Instead, he returned the bottle to his backpack. 'Shall we go?'

Sweating in the hundred-degree heat, they trudged across the sands for another half-mile, finally stopping near the base of the bluff. Muldoon used a GPS handset to check their position, then spent a further minute confirming it with a map and compass as Mark watched impatiently. 'The satellites are accurate to within a hundred feet, you know,' he finally said.

'I'll trust my eyes and a map over any computer,' Muldoon growled.

'Well, that's why we're here, isn't it? To prove that computers can do a better job than anybody's eyes.'

'Cheaper-ass job, you mean,' Muldoon muttered, just loud enough for Mark to hear. He folded up the map. 'This is it. We're two thousand metres from the spike camp, just like you wanted.'

Mark looked back. Barely visible through the rippling heat haze were the tents and transmitter mast of their encampment. Two other teams had set out at the same time, also heading for points two kilometres away, to form an equilateral triangle with the camp at the centre. 'In that case,' he said, taking a quiet relish in his moment of authority, 'you'd better get started, hadn't you?'

It took Muldoon an hour to prepare the explosive charge.

'No way this'll be powerful enough,' he said as he lowered the metal cylinder containing fifteen pounds of dynamite into the hole he'd dug. 'You need a couple hundred pounds, at least. Shit, you'll be lucky if any of the other stations even hear it.'

'Which is the whole point of the experiment,' Mark reminded him. He had set up his own equipment a safe distance away: a battery-powered radio transmitter/receiver, connected to a metal tube containing a microphone. 'Proving that you *don't* need a ton of explosives or a drilling rig or hundreds of geophones. All the simulations say this will be more than enough to make a detailed reflection map.'

'Simulations?' Muldoon almost hissed the word. 'Ain't no match for experience. And I'm telling you, the only results you'll get will be fuzz.'

Mark tapped his laptop. 'You would – without my software. But with it, four geophones'll be enough to map the whole area. Scale it up, Braxoil'll be able to cover the entire Arabian peninsula with just a couple of dozen men in under a year.'

That was hyperbole, and both men knew it, but Muldoon's disgusted expression still said it all. Traditional oil surveys were massive affairs involving hundreds, even thousands, of men, laboriously traversing vast areas to set up huge grids of microphones that would pick up the faint sonar echoes of explosive soundwaves bouncing off geological features deep underground. Mark's software, on the other hand, let the computer do the work:

from just four geophones, three at the points of the triangle and the fourth in the centre, it could analyse the results to produce a 3-D subterranean map within minutes. Hence Muldoon's displeasure: long, labour-intensive – and very well-paid – surveys would be replaced by much smaller, faster and cheaper operations. Not so good for the men who would have to find a new line of work, but great for Braxoil's bottom line.

If it worked. As Muldoon had said, everything was based on simulations – this would be the first proper field test. There were hundreds of variables that could screw things up . . .

Muldoon carefully inserted the detonator into the cylinder, then moved back. 'Okay, set.'

'How far back should we stand?' Mark asked. 'Behind the radio?'

Muldoon let out a mocking laugh. 'You stand there if you want, Mr Hyung – I won't stop you. Me, I'm gonna go all the way up there!' He indicated the top of the bluff.

Mark's own laugh was more nervous. 'I'll, ah . . . defer to your experience.'

The two men climbed the hillside. The bluff wasn't tall, but on the plain at the southern edge of the vast desert wasteland called the Rub' al Khali – in English, the Empty Quarter – it stood out like a beacon. As they climbed, Muldoon's walkie-talkie squawked with two messages. The other teams had also reached their destinations and planted their explosives.

Everything was ready.

After reaching the top, Mark gulped down more water, then opened his laptop. His computer was linked wirelessly to the unit at the foot of the bluff, which in turn was communicating with the main base station at the camp, and through it the other two teams. The experiment depended on all three explosive charges detonating at precisely the same moment: any lack of synchronisation would throw off the timing of the arrival of the reflected sonar waves at the four geophones, distorting the geological data or, worse, rendering it too vague for the computer to analyse. 'Okay, then,' he said, mouth dryer than ever. 'We're ready. Countdown from ten seconds begins . . . *now*.'

He pressed a key. A timer on the screen began to tick down.

Muldoon relayed this through his radio, then dropped to a crouch. 'Mr Hyung,' he said, 'you might want to put down the computer.'

'Why?'

''Cause you can't cover both ears with only one hand!' He clapped both palms to his head. Mark got his point and hurriedly fell to his knees, putting down the laptop and jamming his fingers into his ears.

The charge exploded, the noise overpowering even with his eardrums protected, a single bass drumbeat deep in his chest cavity. The ground beneath him jolted. He had involuntarily closed his eyes; when he opened them again, he saw a plume of smoke rising from the base of the bluff. In the distance, two more eruptions rose above the shimmering haze in seeming slow motion. After a few seconds, the thunderclaps of the other blasts reached him.

A fine rain of dust and tiny pebbles hissed down round the two men. Mark picked up the laptop again, blowing dirt off the screen. The first results were coming through, the geophones confirming that they were receiving sonar reflections. It would take a few minutes to gather all the data, then longer for the computer to process it, but things looked promising so far.

Muldoon peered down the slope. 'Too close to the surface,' he grumbled as he wiped sand from his face.

Mark stood beside him, examining the incoming data intently. 'It's working just fine.' He flinched as another tremor passed beneath his feet. 'What was that?'

'Can't be the other charges, they weren't powerful enough . . .'

Muldoon tailed off, sounding worried. Mark looked up, concerned. The shuddering was getting worse—

The ground under his feet collapsed.

Mark didn't even have time to cry out before the breath was knocked from him as he dropped down the slope amidst a cascade of stones and dust. All he could do was try to protect his face as he bounced off the newly exposed rocks, pummelled from all sides—

Something hard hit his head.

The first of his senses to recover, oddly, was taste. A dry, salty taste filled his mouth, something caking his tongue.

Mark coughed, then spat out a mouthful of sand. The back of his head throbbed where the stone had hit him. He tried to sit up, then decided it was probably a better idea to remain still.

A muffled sound gradually resolved itself into words, a voice calling his name. 'Mr Hyung! Where are you? Can you hear me?'

Muldoon. He actually sounded genuinely concerned, though Mark's faculties had already recovered enough to realise the sentiment was professional rather than personal. Muldoon's job was to look after the specialist; an injury on his watch would reflect badly upon his record.

'Here,' he tried to say, but all that came out was a faint croak. He spat out more revolting dust, then tried again. 'I'm here.'

'Oh, thank Jesus.' Muldoon clambered over loose stones towards him. 'Are you hurt?'

Mark managed to wipe his eyes. He grimaced at the movement; he was going to have some real bruises tomorrow. 'I don't think so.' He turned his head to see the slope down which he'd tumbled. 'Wow. That's new.'

Muldoon looked up, surprise on his face as he registered the change in the landscape. The landslide had exposed a large opening in the side of the bluff, a deep cave. 'Lucky you didn't fall straight down into it. It'd probably have killed you.' He held up a water bottle. 'Here. Can you move?'

Mark gratefully took the bottle, swallowing several large mouthfuls, then gingerly moved his legs. 'I think I'm okay. What about the computer?'

Muldoon held up the screen, which in addition to being cracked was no longer attached to the rest of the machine. 'I don't think the warranty'll cover it.'

'Damn,' Mark sighed.

Muldoon helped him up. 'Sure you're okay?'

'My knee hurts, but I think I'm fine apart from that.'

'I dunno.' Muldoon examined the back of his head. 'You've got a big cut there, and if you were knocked out you might have a concussion. We could call for the chopper to come pick you up, get you to hospital in Salalah.'

'I'm fine,' Mark insisted, even as he spoke wondering why he wasn't taking Muldoon up on his offer of an immediate trip out of the desert. 'Can you see the rest of the laptop? I might be able to recover the data on the hard drive.'

Muldoon snorted, but turned to hunt for it. Mark looked the other way, towards the cave entrance. It was hard to believe that the relatively small explosive charge could have opened up such a large hole.

Unless the gap had been there all along . . .

That thought was brushed aside as he spotted the rest of the broken laptop just inside the cave entrance. 'Here,' he told Muldoon, limping towards it. It looked battered, but unless the hard drive had actually been smashed open it ought to be salvageable.

He crossed into the shadow of the cave and picked up the computer. Eyes adjusting to the low light, he examined the casing. It was more or less intact, dented but not actually broken. The experiment might not be a total loss after all.

Cheered slightly by the thought, Mark glanced deeper into the cave . . .

And was so surprised by what he saw that he dropped the laptop again.

Muldoon clapped Mark on the back. 'Well, son, I had my doubts about you . . . but you're gonna make us all very rich.'

'Not quite how I planned, though,' said Mark.

'Doesn't matter *how* a man gets rich, just that he does!'

Muldoon had joined him in the cave, and been equally stunned by what lay within – though he had recovered from his amazement rather more quickly, radioing the rest of the survey team to demand a rendezvous *right now*. One of the other men had a digital camera; once they too had overcome their astonishment and obtained photographic proof of their discovery, they returned to the camp to send the images back to Houston via satellite.

Mark couldn't help thinking events were moving too fast for comfort. 'I still think we should inform the Omanis.'

'You kidding?' said Muldoon. 'First rule of working out here: never tell the Arabs about *anything* until the folks at home have okayed it. That's why the company has all those high-powered lawyers – to make sure our claims are one hundred per cent watertight. And that's just for oil. For *this* . . . Jesus, I don't even know where to start. We're gonna be famous, son!' He laughed, then ducked into the tent housing the communications gear.

'Maybe.' Mark drank more water, not wanting to get his hopes up. For a start, he was sure that Braxoil would take full control of his discovery. The Omani government would certainly also lay claim to anything found within their borders.

But still, he couldn't help fantasising about the potential fame and fortune . . .

He finished the water, then followed Muldoon into the tent.

The survey team's six other members were already inside, flicking through the digital photos on another laptop. Debate about exactly what they had found was still ongoing, but the overall consensus was much the same as Muldoon's: it was going to make them all very rich.

'Of course,' said one of the men, a New Zealander called Lewis, 'since it's my camera, that means copyright on the photos is mine.'

'Company time, company photos, fellas,' said Muldoon.

'Yeah, but personal camera,' Lewis insisted.

'Guess we'll have to let the lawyers work that out.'

'If anyone ever bothers getting back to us,' said a laconic Welshman, Spence. 'I mean, we sent the things three hours ago.'

'What time is it in Houston?' Mark asked.

Muldoon looked at his watch. 'Huh. After ten in the morning. Still no reply?'

Lewis switched to the laptop's email program. 'Nothing yet.'

'Check the satellite uplink,' Mark suggested. 'There might be a connection glitch.'

Lewis toggled to another program. 'That explains it. No connection.'

Mark raised a puzzled eyebrow. 'Wait, *no* connection? You didn't log off, did you?'

'You kidding? Soon as we get an answer, I want to read it!'

'Weird. As long as we're logged into the Braxoil network, we should be getting *something*. Here, let me . . .'

Lewis gave up his seat to the computer scientist. After a minute Mark leaned back, more puzzled than ever. 'Everything's fine at our end; we're still transmitting. But we're not getting anything back. Either the satellite's down, which is pretty unlikely . . . or someone at the other end's blocked us.'

Muldoon frowned. 'What do you mean, blocked us?'

'I mean, cancelled our access. Nothing we're sending's getting through, and nobody can send anything to us.'

'The hell they can't.' Muldoon picked up the satellite phone's handset. He entered a number, listened for several seconds, then jabbed with increasing anger at the buttons. 'Not a goddamn thing!'

'Try the radio,' suggested an American, Brightstone. 'Call Salalah. The guys there can patch us through to Houston.'

Muldoon nodded and moved to the radio, donning a pair of headphones. He switched the set on – and yanked off the headphones with a startled yelp, making everyone jump. *'Jesus!'*

'What?' Mark asked, worried.

'Beats the hell out of me. Listen.' He unplugged the headphones. An electronic squeal came from the radio's speaker, the unearthly sound making Mark's skin crawl.

'Oh, shit,' said Spence quietly. Everyone turned to him.

'You know what it is?' Mark asked.

'I used to be in the Royal Signals. That's a jammer.'

Muldoon's eyes widened. *'What?'*

'Electronic warfare. Someone's cutting us off.'

That prompted a minor panic, until Muldoon shouted everyone down. 'You're sure about this, Spence?'

The Welshman nodded. 'It's airborne. The pitch is changing too fast for it to be on the ground.'

There was a sudden rush for the door, the eight men spreading out to squint into the achingly blue sky. 'I see something!' yelled Brightstone, pointing north. Mark saw a tiny grey speck in the far distance. 'Is that what's jamming us?'

'Where are the binocs?' Muldoon asked. 'Someone—'

An ear-splitting roar hit them from nowhere. Mark had just enough time to see a pair of sleek, sand-brown shapes rush at him before the two aircraft shot less than a hundred feet overhead, sand whirling round the men in their barely subsonic slipstream. In what seemed like the blink of an eye, the two planes had shrunk to dots, peeling off in different directions.

'What the fuck was that?' Muldoon yelled.

Spence stared after the retreating aircraft. 'Tornados! Those were Saudi Tornados!'

'But we're forty miles from the border!'

'I tell you, they were Saudi!' They watched as the two fighters came about. One them appeared to be turning back towards the camp. The other . . .

Mark realised where it was heading. 'The cave!' he cried, pointing at the distant bluff. 'It's going for the cave!'

Even as he spoke, something detached from the fighter, two dark objects falling away. Then another, and another, arcing down at the bluff—

The hillside was obliterated, the explosions so closely spaced that they seemed to have been caused by a single giant bomb.

'Jesus!' someone shouted behind Mark as a churning black cloud swelled cancerously across the face of the bluff. The sound of the bombs hit them, shaking the ground even from over a mile away.

The Tornado banked sharply north, afterburners flaring to blast it back into Saudi airspace at Mach 2.

The second Tornado—

Mark whirled to find it.

He didn't have to look far. It was coming straight at him, bombs falling from its wings—

The encampment vanished from the earth in a storm of fire and shrapnel.

Black smoke was still coiling from the bluff the next morning.

The four thousand-pound bombs dropped by the Saudi Tornado ADV had caused a good part of the hillside to collapse into the cave beneath it. But the opening remained, a dark hole rendered more sinister by the soot streaking the surrounding rock.

Men stood round it.

Though they were all armed and in desert battle fatigues, none wore the insignia of any military force. In fact, they wore no insignia at all. Despite the identical dress, however, there were divisions within the team. Whether by order or by instinct, the soldiers had formed into three distinct groups, touching at their edges but never quite mixing: oil and water beneath the desert sun.

The intersection point of all three groups was marked by a trio of men, all watching the sky to the south. Even without rank insignia, it was obvious they were the leaders, experience evident in every line on their faces. One was an Arab wearing a black military-style beret, a dark moustache forming a hard line above his mouth. The others were both Caucasian, but even so the differences in their backgrounds were clear at a glance. The younger, a tanned, black-haired man with a cigar jammed in the corner of his mouth, was Jewish; the oldest of the three had thinning blond hair and eyes of as intense a blue as the sky.

The blond man raised a pair of binoculars. 'Here he comes,' he said in English.

The Arab frowned. 'About time. But I don't see why we need him at all. Our airstrike destroyed the site – bury it and be done.'

'The Triumvirate voted, two to one. Majority rules. You know that.'

The Arab's expressive face clearly revealed his displeasure at the decision, but he nodded. The blond man turned back to watch the approaching helicopter.

It landed beside the choppers that had brought the soldiers to the site. Visible in the cockpit were two people: a man in his early forties wearing a pristine white suit, and a young woman in sunglasses.

'What is this?' snarled the Arab on seeing her. 'He was supposed to come alone!'

The blond man's face briefly betrayed exasperation at the new arrival's indiscretion. 'I'll handle it,' he said. They waited as the suited man emerged from the helicopter and strolled towards them. At least his passenger was remaining in the cockpit.

They wouldn't have to kill her.

Once clear of the rotor blades, the pilot donned a white Panama hat, then approached the trio, smiling broadly. 'Ah, Jonas!' he said to the blond man. 'Jonas di Bonaventura, as I live and breathe. Marvellous to see you again.' Though his accent seemed at first a precise upper-class English, there was a faintly guttural undercurrent that revealed his Rhodesian origins.

'Gabriel,' replied di Bonaventura as they shook hands. 'You flew here yourself?'

'As you know, I prefer to be in control.'

They shared a small laugh, then di Bonaventura looked pointedly towards the helicopter. 'I see you brought a . . . guest. That was not something we were expecting.'

'A life without surprises would be terribly dull.' He smiled over his shoulder; the woman smiled back. 'She's a former student of mine. Her father hired me to take her on a tour of various African anthropological sites. We were in Sudan when I got your call for my help.'

'You shouldn't have brought her here,' said the Arab, scowling.

A Cheshire cat smirk spread across the new arrival's face. 'Oh, I couldn't leave her behind. She gives me much more than just money.' It took a moment for the Arab to get his meaning; when he did, he looked disgusted. 'So, Jonas, are you going to introduce me to your compatriots?'

'Gabriel,' said di Bonaventura, indicating the Arab, 'this is Husam al Din Zamal, formerly of the Saudi General Intelligence

Directorate.' He nodded at the cigar-smoking man. 'And Uziel Hammerstein, previously of Mossad.'

The suited man raised a faintly mocking eyebrow. 'A Saudi spy working with an Israeli spy? To say nothing of *your* background, Jonas. The Covenant of Genesis really does make for strange bedfellows.'

Di Bonaventura ignored the comment. 'Husam, Uziel,' he went on, 'this is Professor Gabriel Ribbsley from Cambridge University in England.'

The men shook hands. 'And don't forget,' added Ribbsley, chest swelling smugly, 'the world's leading authority in ancient languages. Whatever that amateur Philby in New York might think. And as for Tsen-Hu in Beijing . . . hah!' He looked past Zamal and Hammerstein at the cave mouth, voice becoming more businesslike. 'Which is why you need me here, I imagine. So, what have you found?'

Hammerstein spoke first, voice low as if to keep what he was about to say a secret even from the wind. 'Our friends in the American NSA alerted us to a photo intercept from an oil company survey team. Their computers had performed a routine analysis of the images – and identified the language of the Ancients.'

'Oh, please,' said Ribbsley mockingly. 'You're still calling them that? How tediously prosaic. I use "Veteres" myself – I'm sure Jonas can appreciate at least the Latin.'

Hammerstein drew impatiently on his cigar. 'As soon as we realised what they had found, we arranged for a computer virus to be introduced through an NSA back door into the company's servers to erase the photos, then locked out the survey team's satellite link to isolate them. After that—'

'We destroyed them and the site,' cut in Zamal bluntly.

Ribbsley looked towards the darkened opening. 'So, you just decided to bomb the site. I see.' A pause, then he wheeled about on one heel, voice dripping sarcasm. 'And what *exactly* did you expect me to learn from a smouldering crater?'

'We still have copies of the survey team's photographs,' said di Bonaventura. He beckoned a younger man, another blond European, to approach. The soldier held up a manila envelope.

Ribbsley dismissed it. 'Happy snaps taken by oily-thumbed roughnecks are hardly going to be helpful.' He reached under the brim of his hat to knead his forehead with his fingertips. 'Do you know why translating this language has been so hard? Why it took eight years for me to work out even the basics?' He lowered his hand and glared at Zamal. 'Because every time the Covenant finds even the tiniest scrap of anything new, they blow it up and kill everyone in the vicinity!'

'That is the Covenant's purpose,' Zamal said angrily.

'Yes, if you take the most literal, block-headed interpretation possible.' Ribbsley let out a theatrical sigh. 'Flies, honey, vinegar, catch . . . can anyone rearrange these words into a well-known phrase or saying?'

'You can catch more flies with honey than vinegar?' offered the soldier with the envelope, a Germanic accent to his clipped English.

Ribbsley clapped his hands. 'Top marks! Jonas, who is this prodigy?'

'Killian Vogler,' said di Bonaventura. 'My protégé.' A note of challenge entered his words, as if daring Ribbsley to continue mocking him. 'I will soon be retiring from the Covenant for a new position in Rome – Killian will take my place in the Triumvirate.'

Ribbsley backed down, slightly. 'A new position? Still *in pectore*, I assume . . . Well then, I hope this young gentleman keeps the saying he just recited in mind once he takes your place.' Vogler gave him a sardonic look. 'The next time you make a discovery like this, Mr Vogler, perhaps you might consider allowing me to examine the site *before* you blow it to pieces? If I can decipher more of the language, I may be able to locate other sites – before they're stumbled upon by random passers-by whom you then have to kill.'

'I will bear it in mind, Mr Ribbsley,' said Vogler with a humourless smile.

'*Professor* Ribbsley, thank you very much,' Ribbsley snapped. He snatched the envelope from Vogler's hand and riffled through the contents. 'Well, it seems consistent with the other sites – the *remains* of the other sites, that is. And the characters on the tablet in this photo do match the Veteres alphabet. But there's nothing I haven't already seen.' He looked back at the cave. 'What else is in there?'

Di Bonaventura nodded to Vogler. 'Killian will show you. You may as well get to know each other – I'm sure you will be working together again in the future . . .'

Ribbsley emerged from the cave just ten minutes later, disappointed and angry.

'Nothing,' he said, shooting an accusing glare at Zamal. 'Absolutely nothing worthwhile was left intact. Just more scraps.' In one hand he had a clay cylinder about two inches in diameter, fine grooves encircling its length – up to the point where it ended in a jagged break. He dropped it to the ground at his feet; it shattered. 'A complete waste of my time.'

'For which you are being very well rewarded,' di Bonaventura reminded him. 'And you still have the photographs of the site.'

'I already told you, there's nothing new on them. I'll be able to translate the text properly once I can check my notes, but I could read enough to know it's nothing of interest.' He looked at his helicopter. The young woman was still in the cockpit, clearly bored. 'Well, since there's nothing more for me here, I'll be going. I do hate the desert.' He irritably brushed some sand off his white cotton sleeve.

'I'll walk you to your helicopter, Gabriel,' said di Bonaventura. Ribbsley started towards the aircraft without even looking back at the others, di Bonaventura beside him. 'What were you *thinking*?' said the soldier in a quiet growl once they were out of earshot.

'About what?'

'Bringing your – your *girlfriend* with you. Are you mad? Zamal would have shot her without a thought just for being here, and Hammerstein would not have tried to stop him.'

Ribbsley smiled. 'Ah, but I knew you'd be in charge, Jonas.'

'Not for much longer. Once I go back to Rome, all I can do is advise. Killian will be making the decisions in the Triumvirate. And despite my teaching, he is still young enough to see the world in absolutes. And one of those absolutes is that anyone who could reveal the secret of the Veteres to the world is a threat to be eliminated.'

'Don't even think about hurting her,' said Ribbsley, a sudden hardness in his voice.

Di Bonaventura regarded him with mild surprise. 'She's that important to you? Interesting.'

'Meaning what?'

'No threat intended, Gabriel, I assure you,' di Bonaventura said with a placatory smile. 'She just seems younger than I expected.' He took a closer look as they approached. 'How old is she? Twenty-one?'

'Twenty-*two*.'

'And you are now . . . ?'

'Her age isn't the important issue,' snapped Ribbsley defensively, forcing the older man to hide his amusement. 'What matters is her personality.'

By now di Bonaventura could see that Ribbsley's passenger was extremely beautiful, with a toned body to put many a model to shame. 'But of course.'

17

'She's quite incredible, actually,' Ribbsley continued, his tone softening as he gazed at her. 'An exceptionally cultured and refined woman. And as you know, I'm a man of very refined tastes.'

Di Bonaventura caught the scent of over-liberally applied Bulgari cologne. 'And expensive ones.'

'Which is why I put up with you calling me across continents at a moment's notice. The Covenant pays far better than Cambridge!' Both men chuckled, then shook hands as they reached the chopper. 'Well, good luck with the new post, Jonas. Maybe I'll pop in to see you next time I'm in the Eternal City.'

'I look forward to it.' Di Bonaventura stood back as Ribbsley climbed into the cockpit, quickly and expertly running through the pre-flight sequence. The rotors groaned to life, rapidly picking up speed. The soldier moved back out of the whirling sandstorm.

'Goodbye, Cardinal!' shouted Ribbsley, giving di Bonaventura a jaunty wave. The helicopter left the ground, wheeled about and headed south.

Di Bonaventura watched it go, then returned to the cave, looking in the direction of the ragged craters marking what had once been the survey camp. There was still clean-up work to be done; the bodies of the men at the camp, or whatever was left of them, had to be found and buried, all evidence of the camp itself removed. Anything that could expose the Covenant had to disappear. Without trace.

Without exception.

'Why did you call him Cardinal?' the young woman asked.

'Private joke,' Ribbsley told her.

'So who were they?'

He paused before reluctantly answering. 'They're ... archaeologists. Of a sort. I occasionally help them with translations of ancient texts.'

'I had no idea Cambridge professors made house calls for translation emergencies.'

'They're very competitive about their work. Cut-throat, you might say.'

'Really?' She arched an eyebrow and smiled wolfishly. 'I'm intrigued.'

Ribbsley huffed. 'They're hardly your type . . . Lady Blackwood.'

Sophia Blackwood grinned. 'I suppose not. Can you imagine what my father would say if I spent time with some bit of rough trade? He's suspicious enough of you as it is.'

'Now, for what *possible* reason could his lordship be suspicious of a Cambridge professor?'

Sophia leaned closer, her long dark hair brushing his shoulder as she slipped her hand between his legs. 'I don't know. Maybe because you're secretly fucking his daughter?' She cupped her fingers round his groin and squeezed gently.

He made a muffled noise deep in his throat. 'That might be one reason, yes.'

She laughed, then tightened her grip slightly. 'So, you aren't going to tell me any more about those people?'

'I'm afraid not,' said Ribbsley, smiling back at her.

Tighter still. 'Really?'

The smile vanished. 'Ngh! No. Believe me, Sophia, this is one of those very rare occasions where ignorance really is bliss. Or at least safer.'

She withdrew her hand, turning away in feigned offended disappointment. 'I see, *Professor*.'

'Oh, don't be like that, *my lady*,' said Ribbsley, playing along with her game. 'I'm sure I can make up for it somehow.' He thought for a moment. 'I recall that you have a reasonable ability with languages . . .'

'Don't go out of your way to praise me, Gabriel,' she said sarcastically.

'Compared to me, I meant. But you could help me with the translation – it'd save me a lot of time if you took care of the drudge work.'

'Oh! Thrilling.'

'You'll find it interesting, trust me. The language is . . .' He smiled. '*Unique*. Then afterwards, since we're in Oman, a meeting with the Sultan, perhaps? I've met him before; I'm certain I can arrange something.'

Her perfect smile returned. 'You know, that might do the trick.'

'I thought it might.'

Her hand slid between his legs once more. 'Although . . . I'm still terribly hurt that you wouldn't tell me who those men were.'

He tensed for a moment, before her touch made it clear she was joking. 'Some things in life have to remain mysterious, Sophia.'

Attention divided between flying the helicopter and the movement of her hand, Ribbsley didn't pick up her low words over the clamour of the cabin. 'Not for me, Gabriel. I *always* get what I want. Eventually.'

1

Indonesia:
Eight Years Later

' Shark!'

At almost a hundred feet beneath the Java Sea, daylight was diffused to a dusky turquoise cast, but there was still more than enough illumination for Nina Wilde to see the predator turn towards her. 'Shark!' she repeated, voice rising in pitch. 'Eddie, do something!'

Eddie Chase swept past her, using the thrusters of his deep suit to place himself between his fiancée and the shark as he brought up his speargun. He aimed the .357 Magnum cartridge forming the spear's explosive power-head at the approaching creature . . . then lowered it again.

'What are you doing?' Nina asked, green eyes wide with fear. 'It's coming right at us!'

'It's only a thresher. Don't worry, it won't do anything.'

'But it's *fifteen feet long*!'

'It's not even six. I know the helmet magnifies things, but Jesus!'

The shark came closer, mouth gaping to expose ranks of sharp triangular teeth . . . then turned its head almost dismissively and powered off into the murk.

'See?' said Chase. 'Nothing to worry about. Now if it'd been something like a tiger shark, you'd know about it.'

'How?'

''Cause I'd be shouting "Shit, it's a fucking tiger shark, aargh!" and firing off spears as fast as I could load 'em!' The balding, broken-nosed Englishman turned so that the lights on his deep suit's polycarbonate body lit up the redhead's pale face through her transparent bubble helmet. 'You okay?'

'Yeah, fine,' Nina answered, with a slightly embarrassed smile. She had undergone dive training off the coast of Long Island, near her native New York, and was still getting used to the enormously more varied marine life of Indonesia. 'It's just that to me, "shark" equals "severed head popping out of a boat".'

Chase chuckled, then a hint of concern came into his voice, even through the distortion of the underwater radio system. 'How's your leg?'

'It's . . . okay.' It wasn't technically a lie, as the bullet wound she had received to her right thigh four months earlier, now more or less healed, wasn't actually hurting, but it had definitely stiffened up during the dive.

'Uh huh.' He didn't believe her. 'Look, if you want to go back to the ship . . .'

'I'm fine, Eddie,' Nina insisted. 'Come on, let's carry on with the survey.'

'If you're sure.' Chase managed an approximation of a shrug through the deep suit's bulky casing.

She gripped the flexible control stalk on her suit's chest and used the thrusters to lift herself off the sea bed, using her finned feet to bring herself to a horizontal position before zooming away, Chase behind her.

★

Their survey took them along a circular route, taking twenty minutes to complete. Nina was disappointed that she failed to discover anything new – but that feeling vanished as they returned to the centre of the circle.

Almost a year earlier, a local fishing boat had, by chance, dredged up a handful of wood and stone artefacts from the sea floor. The Indonesian authorities quickly realised they were very old and hence potentially extremely valuable; the lucky fishermen had received a payment to persuade them to 'forget' exactly where they had made their discovery, so the site could be properly examined before opportunistic treasure hunters picked it clean.

The job of exploration fell to the United Nations' International Heritage Agency. Nina, at the time the agency's Director of Operations, had already been engaged in a project to chart in detail humanity's expansion across the world in pre-history; the Indonesian find had the potential to pinpoint a date with great accuracy. It had taken several months for everything to be arranged, but now they were here.

And had made a discovery.

'Nina, look at this!' called Marco Gozzi over the radio. He and another scientist, Gregor Bobak, were using a vacuum pump to clear away the layers of sediment and vegetation that had built up over millennia.

'What is it?' Nina asked. She switched off the thrusters and swam the last few metres to join them: stirring up the bottom would wipe out visibility and cost them valuable time. The deep suits could operate underwater for longer than traditional scuba gear, but still had their limits – and on an operation like this, time was money. The research vessel anchored a few hundred metres away, the *Pianosa*, was privately owned, other clients waiting to use it after the IHA.

Gozzi aimed a light at what had been exposed. 'It's a net!' said the Italian.

'It is,' Nina said in awed agreement. 'Wow, this is incredible!'

Chase, hanging back, was less impressed. 'Ooh. A net. Just like the thing that found this lot in the first place.'

'*Eddie*,' Nina chided. 'This isn't exactly a nylon drift net we're talking about here.' She reached out with a gloved hand, gently brushing sand off the crudely knotted strands. 'Looks like they wove it from the local rainforest plants. Palm strands, maybe?'

'Or vines,' said Bobak in his strong Polish accent. 'Strangler figs, perhaps. There are many on the islands.'

Gozzi dug a finger into the grey sediment. 'The mud must have buried it and stopped it from rotting. Could have been caused by a tsunami, or a volcanic eruption.'

'Mark the position,' Nina told them. 'If it's a fishing net, they would have kept it close to the shore.' She checked the little display in her helmet to get their exact depth. 'Ninety-eight feet. If I put that into GLUG, I'll be able to work out exactly how long ago this spot was last above water.' She saw a yellow mesh bag on the ground nearby. 'What else have you found?'

'Stone tools, we think,' Gozzi told her. He pointed to a spot behind Chase. 'We found them there.'

Chase turned in place. An orange-painted stick marked where the other divers had been working. Near it, a little mound of round-edged stones stood out above the sea floor.

He looked back at Nina, who was using a smaller version of the vacuum pump to clear silt away from the net. Quickly becoming tired of watching her work, he swam to the stones, the deep suit's neutral buoyancy letting him hover just above them. 'Anything under these?'

'I don't know, we didn't look,' said Gozzi.

'Mind if I do?'

24

'Wait, you want to do some actual archaeology?' Nina asked, amused. 'I guess my influence is finally rubbing off on you.'

'Nah, it's just that if you're going to keep oohing and aahing over a bit of old net, I'll need something to keep me occupied. It gets boring just watching out for sharks.'

Bobak spun in alarm. 'Sharks? Where are sharks?'

'There aren't any sharks, Gregor,' said Nina as Gozzi suppressed a laugh. Still, Bobak surveyed the surrounding waters with deep apprehension before finally returning his attention to the find.

'We have catalogued there,' Gozzi said. 'Go ahead.'

'If you find anything, tell us,' Nina added.

'If it's just some stone knife, then yeah, I'll tell you,' said Chase. 'If it's a pirate treasure chest, I'm keeping that to myself!' Quickly scanning for sharks or other potentially dangerous marine life – despite his earlier jokiness, part of his job was to look after the rest of the team, a responsibility he took very seriously especially where Nina was concerned – he prodded at the nearest rock with his spear gun. Satisfied that a moray eel or similarly nasty surprise wasn't going to spring out, he pulled the stone free of the sediment.

While the exposed end had been smoothed off, the rest of it was flat-faced and hard-edged, reminding him of a large brick. Putting it aside, he aimed a light into the new hole. It was sadly lacking in pirate treasure, or even stone knives: nothing but thick sediment and the chipped corners of more blocks.

He extracted another brick, which came stickily free of its home of untold centuries like a bad tooth from a gum. A couple of colourful fish came to investigate the resulting hole, but like Chase they too were disappointed to find only more bricks.

'No treasure chest?' Nina asked as he rejoined her.

'Narr, me hearty. Didn't find anything except some old bricks.'

Nina exchanged shocked glances with the other two archaeologists, then slowly faced Chase. 'You found *what*?'

★

The brick sat on a table in Nina's lab aboard the *Pianosa*. Slightly over a foot in length and about five inches to a side in cross-section, slightly curved, there seemed little remarkable about it.

Except for the mere fact of its existence.

'It's a *brick*,' said Chase, not for the first time since Nina, Gozzi and Bobak had raced past him to the pile of stones. 'What's the big deal?'

'I'll tell you,' said Nina, turning round the Apple laptop on which she had been frenziedly working to show him. On its screen was a map of part of Indonesia and the Java Sea, Sumatra and its myriad surrounding islands on the left side. 'This is the sea level today, right?'

'Okay. And?'

She zoomed in on one area. 'This is us, here. The depth of the site is ninety-eight feet below sea level. But if I wind back time to show the last time the site was *above* sea level . . .'

The program she was using was called GLUG, for Global Levels of Underwater Geology – its full name contrived after the developers had come up with the jokey acronym. Using the most up-to-date radar and sonar maps, the program allowed members of the IHA and its sister agencies to see the topography of the entire planet, above or below the waves, with an accuracy previously only available to the best-equipped militaries. But GLUG could do more than simply show things as they were in the present: using data gleaned from geological and ice-core surveys, it could also raise or lower the sea level on a map to match that at any point in the past . . . or, by a simple reversal of the algorithm, list all the times when the sea had been at a specified level.

Which Nina had done. 'This is what Indonesia looked like when the sea level was ninety-eight feet lower,' she said. As Chase watched, the map changed, new islands springing up around the coast. She pointed at a yellow marker on the edge of one of the freshly revealed land masses. 'See? That's the dig site, right on the coast – sixty thousand years ago.'

Chase scratched at his thinning, close-cropped hair. 'So? I thought that's exactly what you were trying to prove, that early humans spread along the coastlines way back when. The whole Palaeolithic migration hypothesis thing.'

Nina gave him a surprised smile. 'You've been reading my research?'

'Hey, I don't spend *all* my spare time watching action movies. Okay, so sixty thousand years ago, Ig and Ook used to live here, catching fish and making bricks. Isn't that what you expected to find?'

'More or less – except for *that*.' She lifted the brick. 'You know when the earliest known bricks date from?'

'A week last Tuesday?'

She smiled. 'Not quite. The earliest known fired bricks were found in Egypt, and dated from around three thousand BC. Even plain mud bricks only date from at most eight thousand BC. Kind of a gap between that and *fifty*-eight thousand BC.'

'What if it's more recent? Maybe it fell off a ship.'

'You saw how rounded the exposed parts of the other bricks were. That's not centuries of erosion, that's millennia.' She turned the anachronistic object over in her hands. Though battered, its surface still retained the vestiges of a glaze, suggesting a relatively advanced and aesthetically concerned maker. Neither concept fitted well with a Palaeolithic origin.

She put down the brick. 'I think we need to expand the survey parameters.'

Chase raised his eyebrows. 'Oh, you do, do you?'

'Hey, I'm the Director of the IHA. It's my job to decide these things.'

'*Interim* Director,' Chase reminded her. Nina had assumed the role four months earlier, following the death of her predecessor Hector Amoros, and the UN's decision on the permanency of her appointment was pending. But it was a lock, she was sure; not bad for someone who had only turned thirty that year.

'Whatever. But I still think we should do it. Proving a theory is one thing, but making a discovery that could change everything we thought about early man . . .'

Chase stepped behind her and wrapped his thick arms round her waist. 'You just want to be on the cover of *Time* again, don't you?'

'No. Yes,' she admitted. 'But just think about what it would mean! Current theory believes that *Homo sapiens* didn't develop anything but the most basic stone tools until the upper Palaeolithic period fifty thousand years ago, but if they had kilns able to bake bricks . . .' She tailed off as Chase's hands made their way up to her breasts. 'Eddie, what are you doing?'

'You get so turned on when you're talking about archaeology,' he said, a gap-toothed, lecherous smirk on his square face. 'It's like your version of porn. Your nipples pop up like grapes.'

'I do *not* have grape nipples,' Nina told him in a faux-frosty tone.

'Well, they're still nice and tasty. We could just nip – fnarr, fnarr – to our cabin . . .'

'Maybe later, Eddie,' she said, pulling his hands away. 'Come on, I need to talk to Captain Branch and start a sonar survey.'

Chase rolled his eyes as she strode from the room. 'Right. Because there's nothing sexier than a sonar survey.'

Nina leaned against the railing on the *Pianosa*'s deck, watching the red and white de Havilland Otter floatplane nudge up to the L-shaped floating pontoon dock extending out from the ship's starboard side. Chase waved at her from the co-pilot's seat.

She waved back, then headed for her lab. It had taken some time to persuade Captain Branch – a stickler for adhering to the exact letter of a contract, nothing more, nothing less – to allow the floatplane to be used for anything other than its agreed purpose of bringing in fresh food from Jakarta over the course of the ten-day expedition. But she eventually got her way . . . with the promise of some extra money from the discretionary budget going *his* way.

The Otter had been outfitted with a small 'dunking' sonar array, then spent the next few hours making short hops along a rough spiral course out from the ship. At each landing, Chase lowered the sonar into the water to scan the surrounding sea bed. In theory, if any of the results matched the reading from the dig site, there was a good chance they would find more of the mysterious bricks, perhaps even their source.

In theory. There was an equal chance that the search would uncover absolutely nothing.

Chase entered, carrying the tubular sonar array. Behind him, holding the sonar's data recorder, was Bejo, one of the Indonesian members of the crew. He was still in his late teens, and growing up on one of the vast archipelago's many islands meant that he had spent almost as much of his life in boats as on land.

'How was the trip?' Nina asked as Chase returned the sonar to its large metal box.

'Pretty good. Hervé even let me hold the controls. For about a minute.'

'I *thought* I heard terrified screams,' Nina joked as Bejo put the recorder on a table. 'Thanks, Bejo.'

'No problem, Mrs Nina,' Bejo said cheerily.

'Please, I told you,' she said as she connected the recorder to one of the lab's computers, 'I'm not "Mrs" anything. Not until next May, anyway.'

'Ah! I see, then you will be Mrs Eddie?'

'No, nonono.' Nina wagged a finger. 'Then *he'll* be Mr Nina.'

Bejo erupted with laughter. 'Mr Nina!' he cried, pointing at Chase. 'I like that, that is funny.'

'Yeah, hilarious,' Chase rumbled. He joined Nina at the computer. 'See you later, Bejo.'

'And you . . . Mr Nina!' Bejo left the lab, his laughter echoing down the corridor.

'Cheers for that,' said Chase, batting Nina lightly on the back of her head. 'Now I'm going to be "Mr Nina" for the rest of the bloody trip.'

'Ah, you don't mind really. Because you *lurve* me.' She nudged him playfully with her hip.

'Yeah, I need to get my head checked sometime. So what've we got?'

Nina was already working. 'Let's see, shall we? Okay, this is the dig site.' An image appeared on the screen, blobs in various shades of grey against a black background. 'It's a composite of four readings – only objects that stay stationary in all four show up, so we don't have to worry about fish confusing things.' She zoomed in and indicated one particular group of objects. 'These are the bricks you found.'

'We didn't dig up that many,' Chase noted. 'How deep can the sonar read?'

'Up to two feet – it depends what's on the sea bed. If it's just sediment, any more bricks should show up clearly. Okay, let's see what you found.'

The first composite image came up. Nina examined it, zooming in on everything that gave a strong sonar return, but found nothing resembling the regular forms of the bricks. By the time she had finished, more images had been processed, ready for inspection. She opened each up in turn.

'Oh, oh,' she said excitedly as the eighth reading appeared. 'This looks promising.' A jumbled swathe of sonar reflections showed up strongly, like a handful of tiny diamonds cast across black velvet. 'Wow, it looks like some of the readings we got from Atlantis, remember? Like buildings buried under the silt.' She zoomed in. While the objects were scattered, many of them revealed regular, clearly artificial shapes. 'The place looks trashed, though. It'd take a massive earthquake or a tsunami to scatter everything that widely.'

'Or people.' They exchanged looks. 'How deep is it?'

'It's at . . . whoa, a hundred and fifty feet. So it's not from the same period as the original site.' Nina brought up the GLUG program on her laptop, entering figures. The map changed, sea level falling still further. '*Definitely* not the same period. If this is right, then . . . about one hundred and thirty-five thousand years ago.' She turned to face Chase, eyes wide. 'Jesus, that would completely re-write *everything* we think we know about pre-history. According to current theories, humans didn't even leave Africa until at most seventy thousand years ago.'

'Maybe it's not humans,' Chase said with a grin. 'Maybe aliens built it.'

Nina frowned. 'It's *not* aliens, Eddie.'

'Yeah, you say that now, but when we find a crystal skull . . .'

'Can we be serious, please?' She magnified the sonar image still further. The image pixellated, but individual objects were still discernible, strewn across the sea floor. 'We have to check this out. As soon as we can.'

'It's about five miles away,' said Chase, comparing the image's GPS co-ordinates to a chart. 'Bit of a trudge to get the boats there and back.'

'We'll move the ship.'

'I don't think Branch'll like that. You had a hard enough job getting him to let us use the plane.'

Nina gave him a determined grin. 'I dunno. I'm feeling pretty persuasive today.'

★

With very poor grace, even after the promise of another payment to cover the unplanned use of fuel, Captain Branch did eventually agree to move the *Pianosa* to the new site. It took a couple of hours to bring the pontoons back aboard and get the vessel under way, but after that it didn't take long to reach its destination. Once anchored, the crew reassembled the floating dock while the IHA team prepared for the dive. Nina had used the transit time to explain why she had changed the mission so drastically; both Gozzi and Bobak were startled by what she thought she had discovered, but quickly became caught up in her enthusiasm.

Chase was more pragmatic. 'We can't stay down there too long,' he said as the team went through the involved process of donning their deep suits. 'There's only a couple of hours before sunset. It'll be darker anyway because we're deeper, but any daylight's still better than none.'

'This'll just be a preliminary dive,' Nina assured him. 'I just want to be sure there really is something down there. If there is, we'll dive again tomorrow morning, and if there isn't . . . well, we'll go back to the original site.'

'Bet you won't find a bit of old net as interesting now, will you? Okay, arms out.'

Nina raised her arms. Like the other divers, she was wearing a modified drysuit, metal sealing rings encircling her shoulders and upper thighs. The ones round her legs had already been connected to the lower body of the deep suit, which Bejo was supporting from behind. She shifted uncomfortably as Chase mated the watertight rings on her arms to their companions in the heavy suit's shoulder openings, then closed its polycarbonate front section around her and shut the latches one by one.

'Oh, I hate this bit,' she muttered as Chase picked up the helmet.

'Be glad you never wore the old model,' he said. 'The helmet was even smaller.' He had used the first version of the deep suit three years earlier; it had been designed as a way for divers to reach depths impractical for working in traditional scuba equipment, while hugely reducing the risk of the bends. The suit's hard body let them breathe air at normal surface pressure, while still leaving their limbs relatively free to move. This updated design also allowed its wearer to turn and bend, if only slightly, at the waist, an improvement on the earlier rigid shell, but it was still a cumbersome piece of equipment, especially above the water.

'I'm always worried about getting something in my eye while I'm underwater,' said Nina, making sure her ponytail was safely clear of the suit's neck. 'Or sneezing inside the helmet. That'd be truly gross.'

'Or if you fart in the suit.'

'I don't fart, Eddie,' Nina insisted as he lowered the helmet over her head and locked it into place.

'She does, she just never owns up to it,' Chase said in a stage whisper to Bejo, who laughed.

'What was that?' Nina asked suspiciously, voice muffled and hollow through the helmet.

'Nothing, dear. Okay, check your systems.' Chase examined the gauges on the suit's bulbous back, where the air tanks and recycling systems were contained, while Nina peered at the repeater display inside the helmet. 'Seal is good, pressure is good, mix is normal, battery is at full. You're all set.'

Nina waddled to the ladder on the dock's edge. Gozzi stood beside it making the final check of his suit's systems, while Bobak was already bobbing in the lapping waves. He waved at her, inviting her in. For a moment Nina considered jumping in, then took the more prudent course of climbing down the ladder, the fins on her feet flapping against each rung.

Chase donned his own deep suit with Bejo's help, then fastened the belt holding his knife and other gear round his waist. 'All set, Mr Nina,' said the Indonesian. Chase gave him a look. 'Mr Eddie,' he quickly corrected.

By now, Gozzi had also entered the water. Chase dropped into the sea beside him with a huge splash. 'Show-off,' said Nina as Bejo tossed him the speargun.

Chase cocked the weapon, then looked at the others. 'Everyone set?'

'I certainly am,' Nina replied. 'Let's see what's down there.'

2

Though only fifty feet deeper than the original site, the new location was far darker, shrouded in perpetual dusk. All four divers had their suit lights on at full power, but even that failed to make much impact on the gloom.

Nina held a laminated sheet up to her lights – a printout of the sonar image of the area. 'This is it. Anyone see anything?'

Gozzi swung one flippered foot at a rounded stone. 'This might be another of those bricks.'

'Eddie, give him a hand.'

Chase joined the Italian, and together they pulled it up. Beneath the sediment, protected from erosion, was indeed another of the crisply edged, slightly curved bricks. 'Looks like the right place.'

'We'll do a survey,' Nina decided. 'We'll each take a quadrant, starting from here, out to . . . fifty metres. Anyone finds anything promising, make a note and we'll collate everything when we meet back up.'

'Make sure we stay in sight of each other,' Chase added.

They moved apart. Nina swam rather than using the thrusters, examining the sea floor as she moved slowly over it. A half-buried rock turned out to be another brick, larger than the others she'd seen. She made a note of the block's position, then thought about the nature of the bricks as she moved on. The mere fact that they were curved would limit their utility; the earliest example of that kind of architectural thinking she knew of was that of the Atlanteans, whose empire had risen – and fallen – about eleven thousand years earlier.

Quite a gap between eleven thousand and a hundred and thirty-five thousand. Could there possibly have been a civilisation that pre-dated even Atlantis?

A change in the terrain: the ground ahead dropped away quite steeply. She was just able to make out where it rose again through the murk. If the rest of the area had once been a hilly coastline, this had perhaps been a small gully, marking the point where a stream or minor river reached the sea.

Which would make it a good place to search for more traces of the mysterious brick-builders. To any primitive society, a supply of fresh water was a key factor in the location of a settlement.

She swam into the gully. Chase would probably yell at her for going out of his sight, but she could handle that. Bringing up her torch, she shone its powerful beam over the sea floor.

There was something there, a row of stone stumps rising above the silt and gently swaying plants. A *regular* row – too much so to be natural. She looked at the laminated sheet again. A line of five similarly sized blobs *there*, matching the five real-life objects *here* . . .

And more, stronger, sonar reflections just a short distance further up the gully. Her heart jumped with the rush of discovery. Something more intact – a building that hadn't been completely destroyed?

She swam towards the spot, aiming the light ahead. There *was* something there. As she got closer, she saw that while it wasn't intact, the curving wall broken up into shark-tooth shapes, nor had it been reduced to scattered rubble. Somehow, it had survived whatever had laid waste to the settlement, the deluge as the seas rose, the ravages of time.

'Guys,' she said excitedly, 'I think I've found something. It looks like the remains of a building.'

'Where are you?' Chase asked. 'I don't see your lights.'

'I'm in a little dip.'

'You *are* a little dip,' he snapped. 'I told you to stay in sight!'

'Yeah, yeah.' Now almost at the ruined wall, she slowed, tracing its shape with her flashlight beam. Whatever the structure had once been, it had apparently been circular.

The more she looked, the odder it became. Although the tallest remaining point was only a few feet above the sediment, it was enough to tell that it sloped inwards as it rose. It wasn't a result of damage, either; the bricks had been crafted and arranged quite deliberately to produce just such a shape. Extending the arc would produce . . .

A *dome*.

She tried to picture it. A brick igloo, fifteen feet high, maybe more. Domes weren't unknown in ancient civilisations . . . but *this* ancient?

She swam over the top of the wall and looked down. Slightly off-centre of the circle was a pile of rubble, fronds of seaweed wafting languidly from it. A small shoal of fish glinted through her torch beam, edging closer to the plants before flitting away as one.

The fallen bricks were probably part of the collapsed roof. If so, then whatever the building had housed could still be beneath them. Nina dropped to the sea floor and squatted as best she could in the cumbersome deep suit to investigate. 'We're definitely going to need the pump,' she said, brushing seaweed strands aside. 'If we clear out the sediment, we might be able to find—'

Something erupted from a hole between the bricks.

Nina shrieked and jerked back reflexively, losing her balance and falling on to her butt. A hideous face lunged at her, a huge mottled moray eel with its spike-toothed mouth agape.

Its long body twisted, fangs snapping at her outstretched hand—

Something shot past Nina in a trail of bubbles. There was a deafening *bang*. The next thing she knew, a swirling pink-tinged cloud of froth and shredded flesh was spreading through the water. The front half of the moray, mouth still open in what now looked like frozen surprise, bumped lifelessly against her before sinking to the sea floor.

'What did I bloody tell you?' Chase's voice said in her ringing ears. 'Don't go off on your own!'

'Jesus, Eddie!' said Nina, caught somewhere between fear, relief and anger. 'Are you trying to kill me? You almost blew out my eardrums!'

'You'd rather that thing'd bitten a hole in your suit?' He swam past her, the speargun in one hand. 'Big bugger, though. Must be twelve feet long, easily. Although a power-head was probably overkill.' He loaded another explosive-tipped spear, then tugged the severed tail end of the eel from the hole.

Nina breathed deeply in an attempt to calm herself. 'What are you doing?'

'Getting rid of this thing. Don't want floating shark-bait right where you're working.' He clipped the gun to his suit's belt, then picked up the moray's other half. 'Seen this?' he asked, waggling its head in Nina's face. 'It's got two sets of jaws, one inside the other. Like the Alien.'

'Just get rid of it!' said Nina, cringing in revulsion.

'So much for the search for knowledge,' Chase said, turning the eel to face him and moving its mouth like some awful ventriloquist's dummy as he spoke. 'And she calls herself a scientist!' The two pieces of the moray trailing from his hands, he swam off into the gloom.

'Are you okay, Nina?' asked Gozzi as he arrived, Bobak behind him.

'Super fine,' Nina growled.

'At least it was not a shark, yes?' Bobak said hopefully.

'Yes, thank God. Although I have a horrible feeling I'm going to have to put up with a load of stupid eel jokes when we get back to the ship.'

'I'd never do that,' Chase said from somewhere out of sight. 'Besides, I've got a DVD I want to watch tonight.'

'What is it?' Nina sighed, bracing herself for the punchline.

'An *Eel*-ing comedy!'

If Nina could have put a hand to her forehead, she would have. Instead, she groaned, then composed herself before turning back to the job in hand.

After she photographed the ruin, the team carefully lifted the fallen bricks. It was a slow process, Chase offering increasingly frequent reminders about the dwindling amount of daylight remaining.

But it paid off.

'Look at that!' Nina exclaimed. The collapsed roof removed and some of the sediment cleared away with the small vacuum pump, new treasures were revealed. 'We've definitely struck gold.'

'That's not gold,' said Chase. 'Looks like copper to me.'

'Metaphorical gold, I mean.' She lifted the first object. It was a sheet of copper about ten inches long, almost as wide at one end but much narrower at the other. It had obviously been crushed when the roof fell, but she guessed it had originally been conical in shape. She turned it over. 'It looks like a funnel.'

'Wow, kitchen utensils? That's even more exciting than a net,' said Chase.

Nina snorted and handed it to him to put into a sample bag, then looked at the item Bobak was holding. 'What's that?'

'I don't know.' It was a clay cylinder – or rather part of one, one end roughly broken off. The other had a hole roughly the width of

Nina's little finger at its centre. The cylinder was marked with narrow, closely spaced grooves running round its length. Bobak poked at the little hole, tipping sand out of it. 'To hold a candle?'

Gozzi guided the pump's nozzle along what appeared to be a stout wooden pole. 'Look here!' he cried. More of the pole was exposed as he moved, revealing it to be six feet long, ten, twelve . . . 'I think this is a mast!'

'It can't be,' said Bobak. 'The site is too old. Maybe the boat sank more recently.'

'So how did it end up *inside* a building that's been underwater for over a hundred thousand years?' Nina asked. No suggestions were forthcoming. She ran her fingertips through the sediment, finding the flat face of a plank. Probing further, she felt its edge. She followed it, trying to work out the length of the buried vessel.

Something moved when she touched it.

'Found something?' Chase asked. 'Not another eel, is it?'

'I don't think so.' Nina pulled her new find free of the muck. It was a clay tablet, roughly the size of a slim hardback novel. One corner had been broken off, but apart from some chipping and blotches of microbial growths the rest of it was intact. Several lines of text had been inscribed into its surface, but the elegantly curved script was completely unknown to her. 'Gregor, Marco, look at this. Do either of you recognise the language?' Neither did.

'Tick tock,' said Chase, pointing towards the surface. The level of illumination had visibly fallen. 'We need to get back upstairs.'

Reluctantly, Nina put the tablet into the sample bag. 'Mark the spot,' she told Gozzi. 'We're definitely coming back here tomorrow.'

Chase entered the lab. 'You coming for dinner? It's after eight, and I'm starving!'

'Shush,' said Nina, flapping a hand. 'I'm on the phone.'

'Is that Eddie?' asked an Australian voice from the speakerphone on Nina's workbench. 'How are you, mate?'

'Hey, Matt,' Chase replied, recognising their friend and colleague Matt Trulli. 'I'm fine. How about you? I thought you were going to the South Pole or something.'

'Yeah, in a week. Just got a few last-minute glitches to fix on my new sub; I'm waiting for the spare parts to arrive. Good job I caught the problem now – it'd be a bugger to fix in the Antarctic!'

'I thought I'd take advantage of our tame nautical expert,' Nina explained to Chase. 'I was just asking him about the boat we found.'

'Well, I looked at that photo you sent, and it's definitely a lateen rig,' said Trulli. 'Triangular sail, invented by the Arabs. Something like the sixth century.'

'BC or AD?' Nina asked.

'AD. Why, how old's the site where you found it?'

'Older.'

Trulli made an appreciative noise. 'Another world-shattering discovery by Dr Nina Wilde, is it?'

'Could be,' said Nina, smiling. 'Thanks for your help, Matt – I appreciate it.'

'No worries – I'll look in on you in New York when I get back. Oh, and consider this my RSVP to the wedding, okay?'

'Will do.'

'See you,' said Chase as Trulli disconnected. 'So, dinner?'

'In a minute,' Nina said, returning to her work. She held the clay tablet under a large illuminated magnifying lens, using a metal pick to remove the algae that a wash in distilled water had failed to shift. One particularly recalcitrant piece resisted even the pick; she used a spray can of compressed air to blast it with a fine astringent powder before switching back to her original tool. This time, the offending lump came free. 'What're they cooking?'

'Eels.' Nina shot him a dirty look. 'How's it going?'

'Pretty well. I've almost got it cleaned up.' She indicated the expensive digital SLR camera beside the waterproof camera she had used on the dive, a cable connecting it to her laptop. 'I already sent some underwater pictures back to New York by satellite, but I thought it'd be easier for someone to identify the language if it wasn't covered with crap.'

'So you really don't know? Guess you'd better withdraw that application to be the full-time boss of the IHA.'

'It might be easier if I did.'

'Really?' Chase put a hand on her shoulder. 'Hey, I was only joking. I thought you wanted the job.'

'I do. But there's just been so much bureaucratic and political garbage, especially over the last couple of months. It's like everybody's decided to gang up on me at once. Assholes.' She let out a sigh.

'I know what you mean. Every time I go through US customs now, I get the third degree from the immigration officers. Doesn't matter that I've got a Green Card and a UN work permit – they treat me like the bloody shoe bomber!'

'Yeah, you'd think they'd be more grateful, considering we saved the world.' Nina took several photos of the tablet. 'Maybe I should remind everyone of that, take up that offer to write my autobiography.'

'You need to ask for more money,' Chase told her. 'Tell 'em you want one meellion dollars.' He raised his little finger to the corner of his mouth.

'It's definitely tempting.' She turned to him, then flinched as she put weight on her right leg. 'Ow!'

'I kept telling you not to push it, didn't I? You never bloody listen.'

'It's fine, it's fine . . . no, it's *not* fine, ow, *oww*, son of a bitch!'

Nina hobbled to a nearby chair, rubbing her thigh. 'Oh, dammit, it's cramped up. I must have been standing on it for too long.'

'That and, you know, *swimming* for hours,' Chase said, with not nearly as much sympathy as Nina had hoped. 'What if that'd happened a hundred feet down? That settles it. There's no way you're going in the water tomorrow.'

'I could still use the suit's thrusters,' Nina suggested plaintively, but she could tell from Chase's expression that he wasn't going to give way on this occasion. 'Crap. I hate watching through the remote feed. Nobody ever points the camera at what I want to look at.'

'We do eventually. After you moan at us for five minutes.' He held out a hand. Nina took it and tentatively stood up, trying to straighten her right leg. 'Does it still hurt?'

'No,' she squeaked untruthfully.

'Come on, hold on to me. I'll take you down to the mess.'

'Just a sec – let me send these pictures to the IHA.' She hopped to the table and tapped at her laptop. 'Okay, done.'

'You're pushing yourself too hard,' said Chase, putting an arm round her waist to support her. 'I know this is what you do and that it's really important to you, but if you're not careful you might get hurt. Like with that bloody eel. How far are you willing to go for this stuff?'

'Far as it takes.' She smiled at him. 'Okay, let's go eat.'

Half a world away, banks of supercomputers analysed the photographs Nina had just emailed, breaking down the digital images and scanning them for patterns matching any of a vast range of criteria in just a fraction of a second.

No human had been involved in the process, yet: the machines of the National Security Agency in Maryland routinely examined every piece of electronic communication that passed through the networks of the United States, hunting for anything that might potentially be connected to crime, espionage or terrorism. All but the tiniest fraction of the constant deluge of data was deemed to be harmless. Of the remainder, most were passed on to human NSA analysts to make a proper determination.

But there were some search criteria that were kept secret even from the NSA itself, only a handful of people in the entire country – the entire *world* – being aware of them.

Nina's pictures matched one of those criteria.

The supercomputers processed the images, picked out the strange characters, compared them against a database – and raised an alarm. Within minutes, three men in different countries had been informed of the discovery.

The Covenant of Genesis had a new mission.

A new target.

3

'Good morning, Captain Branch!' said Nina brightly as she limped on to the *Pianosa*'s bridge.

Branch, an angular, tight-faced American, acknowledged her with a sullen nod. 'You know the currents are stronger here than at the original site?' he began, not wasting any valuable complaining time with pleasantries. 'I'll have to run the thrusters to hold position. That means I'll be using more fuel than I expected.'

She forced a polite smile. 'The IHA will cover any overages, Captain.'

'It better. And I'd like that in writing sometime today, Dr Wilde.'

'It's at the top of my to-do list,' said Nina, making a mocking face at him as he turned away. The other crew member in the room grinned. 'How about you, Mr Lincoln?' she asked him. 'What's the weather forecast for today?'

'Well,' said Lincoln, a handsome young black man from California, 'it's gonna be a very pretty morning, with about a five-knot easterly wind and a thirty per cent chance of rain in the afternoon. Although I foresee a one hundred per cent chance that our guests from the IHA are gonna get wet.' He gestured down at the pontoon dock, where the day's diving preparations were under way.

'Not me today,' Nina said. 'Got to sit this one out.'

'Damn, that's a shame. Still, if you need something to do, may I invite you to take advantage of the *Pianosa*'s extensive range of leisure activities? By which I mean a deck of cards with the aces marked, a box of dominoes and the PlayStation in my quarters. I got *Madden*!'

'That's enough clowning around, Mr Lincoln,' Branch snapped. 'Go make yourself useful and check the galley inventory. I'm sure somebody's been helping themselves to the canned fruit.'

'Yes, *sir* !' said Lincoln, giving Branch an exaggeratedly crisp salute and winking at Nina as he exited. She smiled back at him, then looked through the windows. The ship was about six miles from the nearest island, a low shape at the head of a chain stretching off into the distant haze. The sea was calm, the only other vessel in sight a white dot rounding the island. Away from the shipping lanes, the *Pianosa*'s only company over the course of the expedition so far had been the occasional passing yacht or fishing boat.

Although it meant negotiating several steep sets of stairs and ladders, she decided to head down to the dock; anything was better than hanging around with Branch. Compared to other survey vessels Nina had been aboard in the past, the *Pianosa* was relatively small, a 160-foot piece of rust-streaked steel that was a good decade older than she was. But while Branch was far from the most charming ship's master she had ever met, he knew his job, and his ship was up to the tasks the IHA needed of it, even if it lacked creature comforts.

'How's the leg?' the drysuited Chase called as she reached the bottom of the steep gangway running down the ship's side to the dock. Only one of the *Pianosa*'s boats was in the water today, the other hanging from its crane on the deck above.

'Oh, just fine. Y'know, I think I feel up to diving after all.'

He eyed her right foot, on which she was conspicuously not putting her weight. 'Sure you do.'

'Oh, all right, it still hurts like hell. It sucks when you're right.'

'But I'm always right!' Chase said smugly. 'Your life must just be one crap thing after another.'

She gave him a sly smile. 'You really want me to go down that road?'

'Maybe not, then. Did you get the weather?'

'Yeah. Looks like it's going to be fine – maybe some rain later, but nothing serious.'

'Suits me. Oh, here we go.' Bobak and Bejo made their way down the gangway, carrying a plastic case between them. They put it down and opened it to reveal a bright yellow pod the size of a large pumpkin, a spotlight and a bulbous lens cover giving it a lop-sided 'face'. Bobak connected one end of a long cable to it. 'At least you'll be able to watch.'

'If you aim the thing at anything worth seeing.' The remote camera unit had no manoeuvring abilities of its own, and was reliant on the divers to move it around. 'We should have got Matt to make us one of his little robot subs. At least that way I could control it myself.'

'Yeah, it's not like you buzzing an ROV round my head would get annoying.'

Gozzi lumbered down the gangway carrying the larger of the two vacuum pumps. 'I'm ready,' he said. 'Have we got everything?'

Chase nodded at the equipment lined up along the pontoon. 'Yup. All the suits are charged and gassed up.'

'Okay,' said Nina. 'I'll get back to the lab and set up the remote. Now . . . you *will* remember to take it with you, won't you?'

'Ah, get moving, Hopalong,' said Chase, waving her away. Nina grinned, then started back up the gangway as Bejo and two other crew members began helping the IHA team into their suits.

She paused on the main deck, surveying the ocean. As Lincoln had promised, it did indeed look as though it would be a beautiful day. The sun was steadily rising into a deep blue sky, and the only hints of cloud were mere wisps above the island chain. The white boat she had noticed earlier was now out in open water and seemed to be heading in their general direction, but apart from that everything was quiet. Perfect for a day of potentially world-shaking archaeological exploration . . . even if she would have to experience it second-hand.

Taking a last look at the glittering sea, she entered the ship.

'What do you see?' Chase asked a few minutes later.

'I see . . . some English guy with a funny face,' Nina replied into her headset. On her monitor screen in the lab, Chase was holding up the remote with the camera pointed at him, the fish-eye lens ballooning his features.

'Can't be me, then. I'm devilishly handsome.'

'Devilish I can agree with.'

He made an amused noise, then put down the remote on the dock, pointing out to sea. The horizon tilted at an angle.

Two dots were visible against the blue water, small boats heading side by side towards the *Pianosa*. But Nina, setting up the rest of her equipment, barely registered them.

On the bridge, Branch *had* noticed the two boats, and another one besides. The pair off the starboard bow, he saw through binoculars, had five or six people in each, but they were too far off for him to make out any details.

The other, larger vessel, off to port, was a motor yacht, an expensive-looking white and blue cruiser. He had spotted it earlier, but paid it little attention until now. Someone was standing on the forward deck, leaning against something covered in a colourful sheet of fluttering cloth, and he caught a glimpse of others moving about in the raised bridge.

It only took him a moment to realise that all three boats were on approach courses. He looked back along their wakes. They were travelling in subtle zig-zags, tacking to disguise their movements, but were definitely converging on his ship.

His immediate thought was: *pirates!* But that didn't make sense. Even before the Indonesian, Singaporean and Malaysian governments had cracked down on the menace, most attacks had taken place in the Strait of Malacca between the three nations, hundreds of miles away. And a forty-year-old tub like the *Pianosa* was hardly a prime target.

He glanced at the radio, for a moment considering alerting the Coast Guard, but decided that was paranoia. They were still a mile away, and their appearance at the same time could be mere coincidence.

But he kept watching them, just in case.

Chase rocked uncomfortably, trying to shift the deep suit's weight. Out of the water, the casing was supported almost entirely on his shoulders. It wasn't unbearably heavy, even for someone of Nina's modest build, but it was cumbersome enough to be annoying.

Bobak climbed into the water. Gozzi was having difficulty with his helmet, so Bejo had gone to help secure the heavy bubble, leaving Chase waiting to don his own headpiece. He looked out to sea past the moored floatplane, which its pilot Hervé Ranauld was refuelling, to see two boats heading in their general direction. One was a speedboat, the other a larger RIB – a Rigid Inflatable Boat, a staple transport of his time in the Special Air Service.

'There!' said Bejo as Gozzi's helmet finally locked into place. 'I can help you now, Mr Eddie.' He padded back across the dock to Chase and picked up his helmet.

'Great. My ears were starting to get sunburnt.' The boats had changed course, Chase noticed, and were now definitely heading for the *Pianosa*. 'Who're this lot?'

★

The cruiser was turning towards the *Pianosa*, Branch saw through the binoculars. A man clambered down to the foredeck, carrying what looked like a golf bag.

He panned back to the two powerboats, trying to get a clearer look at their occupants. No nets or poles, so they weren't out fishing—

Fear clenched at his heart. One man had just raised a gun, the unmistakable shape of an AK-47 silhouetted against the blue water.

His companions did the same.

Branch whipped round, looking back at the cruiser. One of the men on the foredeck pulled the coloured sheet away to reveal a machine gun on a stand. The other had taken a tubular object from the bag and was hefting it over his shoulder as he kneeled, aiming it directly at the watching American.

A rocket launcher.

Flame and white smoke burst from its muzzle.

Branch hit the button to sound the ship's alarm, then grabbed the radio handset—

Too late.

The missile, an Iranian-made copy of the American M47 Dragon guided anti-tank missile, slammed into the *Pianosa*. Its warhead, over five kilograms of high explosive, obliterated the bridge, Captain Branch . . . and the ship's radio masts, which toppled like blazing trees into the water.

The shock pounded through the ship, knocking Nina from her chair in the lab.

'Jesus!' she gasped as she pulled herself up. A loud alarm wailed. What had caused the explosion? And had anyone been hurt?

She looked at the monitor. The remote's camera still showed the view from the dock. Bobak was in the water, burning debris raining around him. Beyond him, two boats were roaring towards the ship.

She stabbed at one of the camera controls, zooming in. The men in the boats were all holding guns, aiming them at the dock—

Encumbered by the bulky deep suit, all Chase could do was throw himself to the deck behind a stack of equipment cases as the pirates opened fire, the flat thudding of AK-47s rolling across the water. Some of their shots fell short, little geysers kicking up from the waves.

Others found targets.

The inside of Gozzi's bubble helmet was suddenly painted with a gruesome splash of red as a bullet pierced the transparent polycarbonate. Darker, thicker chunks of bone and brain oozed down the inner surface, then the dead Italian keeled into the ocean.

Bejo landed beside Chase, yelling in fear as more shots punched into the boxes beside them. Chase looked along the dock. Ranauld threw down the fuel hose and jumped into the Otter's cockpit. A scream, closer – one of the crewmen had been hit. Through a gap in his minimal cover, Chase saw Bobak in the water, flailing a hand at something burning on his suit.

Dive, you idiot, get under the water—

A line of angry waterspouts snaked towards the Pole. Found him. Shattered fragments of the deep suit's casing spat into the air. Bobak stiffened, then slowly dropped beneath the surface in an expanding circle of red.

The firing continued as the boats closed in. The pirates were barely aiming, Chase realised – just hosing the dock with machine-gun fire, relying on sheer weight of lead to hit their targets. They weren't professional soldiers, but amateurs intoxicated by the rare chance to rock 'n' roll with automatic weapons. In one way, that was good – they lacked training and tactics, which might give him an opening to fight back.

In every other way, it was bad . . . because it meant they were here to kill every single person on the *Pianosa*.

The video feed from the remote jolted, then went black. The camera pod had been hit.

'Dr Wilde!' Nina looked round as Lincoln opened the lab door. 'Are you okay?'

'Yeah, but they're shooting at the people on the dock! We've got to help them!'

'We don't have any weapons aboard,' he told her grimly. 'Come on, I've got to get you out of here.'

'To where?'

Lincoln didn't have an answer as he pulled her to the exit.

The Otter's engine spluttered, the propeller blurring into motion. Chase saw Ranauld leaning from the cockpit door, desperately fumbling to untie the mooring rope. Bejo rose to a crouch, about to make a run for the aircraft.

A hissing roar from one of the boats, horribly familiar to Chase . . .

He shoved Bejo back down. 'Duck!'

The Otter's left wing exploded, hit by a rocket-propelled grenade. Shrapnel tore through the plane's aluminium skin. What few of the windows remained intact were splattered with Ranauld's blood.

Chase opened his eyes. The Otter's engine was still running, but fire was licking up its ravaged port side.

Another engine started up, an outboard. The other crewman on the pontoon dock had leapt into the *Pianosa*'s boat. He revved it to full power, turning as hard as he could to swing round the burning plane—

He barely got twenty feet. Another RPG lanced from the

speedboat and hit his craft square in the side, flipping it over and reducing him to a red haze amidst a storm of splinters.

More bullets smashed into the boxes. Chase fumbled for the catches of his deep suit. 'Get me out of this thing!'

The cruiser closed in, dropping another speedboat from its stern hoist into the water with a frothing smack. It leapt away from its parent vessel, heading round the survey ship's stern.

The pirate manning the heavy machine gun on the cruiser's bow took aim at the *Pianosa*'s superstructure, pulled the trigger—

Lincoln led Nina along a passageway, seeing another crewman ahead wielding a fire extinguisher. Black smoke billowed round him. 'Shit!' Lincoln said. 'We'll have to go back around—'

The crewman's chest exploded in a spray of gore as a .50-calibre round tore through him.

The passageway echoed with a rapid-fire metallic *bam-bam-bam* as more thumb-sized bullets punched a line of holes straight through the hull and inner walls, searing across the corridor and ripping out again through the other side.

The holes got closer, advancing with frightening speed—

Nina dived to the deck. She tried to pull Lincoln down with her, but too late. A bullet hit his upper arm – and blew it off below the shoulder.

Chase and Bejo had managed to unlock the deep suit's shoulder fastenings and some of the clips on its side when the sound of the machine gun reached them. Chase recognised the distinctive chugging booms immediately – a Browning M2, a weapon in service all over the world, practically unchanged for almost eighty years . . . because it was exceptionally good at ripping apart anything unlucky enough to appear in its sights.

'Shit!' he gasped as ragged holes burst open in the *Pianosa*'s superstructure. He clawed at the remaining clips on his suit – then looked round sharply at a sound from behind.

Another speedboat, rounding the ship's stern. More pirates aboard it.

They saw him.

Nina screamed as splintered metal and scabbed paint showered her. More bullets slammed overhead . . . then stopped. The machine gun's rattle paused, then resumed, now aimed at a different part of the ship.

She sat up, horrified by the sight before her. What was left of the dead man at the end of the corridor was mercifully obscured by smoke, but Lincoln was slumped against the wall at her feet. The white wall above him was stained with red, a lopsided hole at its centre where the bullet had continued on after inflicting its carnage. Nothing remained of his upper arm but a sickening stump of torn meat, streams of dark blood running down on to the deck.

'Oh, Jesus . . .' Ignoring the pain in her leg, she crouched beside him and checked his pulse. It was weak, irregular. 'Can you hear me?'

Lincoln's eyes fluttered open, struggling to focus. 'What happened?' he mumbled, trying to sit up.

Nina gently pushed him back. 'Keep still. You've been shot. Don't move.'

'My arm hurts . . .'

She choked back a sob. He hadn't yet realised what damage had been inflicted upon him. 'Oh, God,' she whispered, unsure what to do. There was a first aid kit in the lab, but she had no idea if it would be any use on a wound of this magnitude.

But it was his only chance of survival. 'Don't move,' she repeated. 'I'll be back as soon as I can.'

★

'Move!' Chase shouted. 'Get out of here!'

Bejo didn't need further prompting. Arms outstretched, he dived from the dock.

The driver turned the speedboat, swinging broadside-on to Chase so all four of its passengers could aim their AKs at him. Still trapped inside his bulky deep suit, a bright yellow target lying helplessly on the edge of the dock, there was nowhere he could go . . .

Except *down*.

With a yell, he rolled into the sea.

He hit the water on his side, facing the pontoon. The air tanks in the suit's back might give him some protection – unless the gunmen aimed at his head.

Water gushed in through the open collar, filling the casing. He started to sink.

Not fast enough.

The Kalashnikovs chattered. Bullets cracked off the dock above him, splashed into the sea behind. These pirates were as bad shots as their comrades in the other boats – but only one bullet needed to find its target.

He took a deep breath just before his head was pulled under the water. The suit was getting heavier by the moment, a weight dragging him down . . .

A bullet hit the back of the casing – and he was slammed against the float supporting the pontoon as the air tank ruptured, its pressurised contents spewing out in a churning rush. More bullets thwacked into the water around him.

He pushed himself away from the float. The escaping air forced him downwards, bubbles belching out of the collar past his face as he brought himself into a more upright position.

The pirates were still shooting, but now were just wasting ammo.

Even a small depth of water was enough to stop a bullet. Spent rounds spiralled slowly downwards around him.

He reached for the last catches on the suit's side. Once he got the body open, he could work the quick-releases for the sealing rings around his limbs. Then he could swim under the dock, get his breath back, and work out a plan of action.

The first catch clacked open. One more to go. He tried to hook his gloved finger under it.

He couldn't.

Chase tried again, clawing harder at the catch. It felt as though it was bent. But he could prise it open with his diving knife . . .

It wasn't there.

All his gear was still on the surface.

He forced back panic, pushing his fingertip harder against the catch. Still unable to get any purchase, he sank further into the depths.

4

Another fusillade of gunfire tore through the ship as Nina limped towards the lab. She shrieked, dropping flat beside a storeroom door as more holes exploded in the walls. Electrical sparks crackled angrily from a severed cable overhead.

The firing ceased. Nina held her breath, expecting it to resume at any moment, but nothing happened. The gunner had swept the length of each of the *Pianosa*'s decks. Either he thought he'd killed everybody aboard . . .

Or the next phase of the attack was about to begin.

Chase still couldn't get any purchase on the damaged clip. Caught unprepared, with no time to get any extra oxygen into his system, his body was rapidly burning through the limited amount of air in his lungs.

The punctured tank ran dry. He kicked, trying to slow his descent, but without air to provide buoyancy the deep suit was nothing but dead weight.

His leg muscles were cramping, lactic acid building up as the oxygen in his blood dwindled. He spasmed, the involuntary movement forcing air from his lungs.

He was about to drown—

Something thumped against him. He looked round – and saw

Bejo. His hand scrabbled against the side of the suit, fingernails pushing under the damaged metal . . .

The clip opened.

The deep suit's front unlatched, the last pockets of air inside it gushing upwards. Chase immediately tugged at the release for the seal on his left shoulder as Bejo did the same on the right. He desperately shrugged his arms free as the young Indonesian pulled at the rings round his thighs to unlock them. The deep suit was still hauling him down like an anchor.

One leg loose.

Fire searing his lungs, head pounding . . .

The other seal was released. Bejo grabbed him and kicked upwards as the suit dropped away, tearing off one of Chase's flippers.

He was clear – but he still had to reach the surface.

Where the pirates were waiting.

Holes had been blown through the lab's walls, the metal peeled back like the skin of a half-eaten orange. Some of Nina's equipment had been destroyed, the magnifying lens over the clay tablet shattered. But she ignored it, instead searching for the first aid kit – Lincoln's only hope of survival.

She found the green box in a cabinet. No time to check if it contained anything useful, and no point either. Either it did, or the maimed crewman would die. Clutching the box, she hurried back along the corridor.

She heard shouting.

Inside the ship.

The pounding of blood in Chase's head felt almost like physical blows, blackness roiling in from the edges of his vision as the shimmering waves on the surface drew tantalisingly closer, *closer* . . .

He breached the surface, taking in clean, fresh air in tremendous whooping gasps. Bejo burst from the water beside him. Chase's vision cleared – to reveal the speedboat bobbing less than twenty feet away. The men inside it spotted the gasping figures, expressions of surprise rapidly changing to anger.

'Not again!' Chase wheezed as he pulled Bejo back underwater, bullets churning the surface around them.

'Mr Lincoln!' Nina called. The smoke in the passageway had thickened, making her cough. 'Can you hear me?'

A faint moan reached her. She limped to where she had left him. The pool of blood had spread, little rivulets winding along the deck.

She put down the first aid kit and opened it. There were several rolls of bandages and a packet containing sterile gauze inside: at least she might be able to stop the bleeding. There didn't appear to be any painkillers, though.

'I'm going to put on a bandage,' she told Lincoln as she tore open the packet. 'I'll be as gentle as I can, but it might hurt.'

'Can't get . . . any worse . . .' he said in a strained whisper, eyes closed.

Hesitantly, Nina brought the piece of gauze to the wound. A nub of bone was visible amid the torn muscle, blood dripping from it. She fought past her fear and revulsion and pressed the pad against his arm. Lincoln let out a strangled screech.

'I'm sorry, I'm sorry,' she gasped. The gauze was already soaked, and she could feel blood on her palm. Keeping it in place, she groped with her other hand for one of the rolls of bandage. 'I'm going to—'

Someone cried out through the smoke, a panicked plea – which was cut off by a crackle of gunfire. Nina flinched. The shots were close by.

Lincoln forced his eyes open. 'Go.'

'But I can't leave—'

'Go!' He pushed her back. The blood-sodden gauze fell into the crimson pool.

Nina regarded him helplessly, then stood. More voices came through the smoke. Closer.

She gave him one final, fearful look, then turned and ran.

The firing had stopped, but Chase and Bejo stayed underwater, swimming some ten feet beneath the surface.

They passed under the pontoon dock. They could have surfaced between its floats for air, under the cover of the deck – but the pirates would expect them to do just that, and be watching. Instead, they kept swimming along the length of the survey ship. Debris floated above them, smashed pieces of—

The *Pianosa*'s boat.

The wrecked craft was inverted, smoke wafting from the edge of the hole where the RPG had blasted it. But its wood and fibreglass hull was still afloat, the curved keel above the water.

Chase surfaced inside the upturned boat. Bejo popped up next to him. 'You okay?' Chase asked. The young man nodded, panting for breath. 'Thanks.' He squeezed Bejo's shoulder in gratitude.

Engine noise. He looked through the hole to see that the first speedboat had already pulled up at the dock beside the gangway up to the main deck. Behind it, the RIB was coming to a standstill.

Its occupants jumped on to the dock. Chase assessed the pirates in a flash: dirty, scruffy, the wiry, slightly pot-bellied build of men used to intense bursts of adrenalin-fuelled physical exertion, followed by celebratory excess.

But there was one man who stood out: taller, harder-faced, conspicuously lacking the cheap gold chains the others wore. Not all the pirates were amateurs; Chase could tell simply from the way the man held his AK – sideways on its strap across his stomach, the barrel pointed down out of harm's way – that he had received proper military training in the past. The group's leader.

He barked an order, then quickly ascended the gangway, his entourage following.

Nina peered round the corner of the passageway, looking back towards Lincoln. She couldn't just turn her back and abandon him. Maybe their attackers would see he posed no threat and leave him alone, in which case she might be able to return and help . . .

She froze as a man emerged from the smoke, a red bandanna pulled up over his nose and mouth. He had a rifle in his hands, pointing it at Lincoln. He warily advanced, stopping a few feet from the injured crewman, and shouted back over his shoulder.

Nina remained still, terrified that he might spot her but unable to look away. The pirate shouted again. More men appeared through the smoke. One of them, clearly the leader, kicked Lincoln's leg, shouting in Indonesian. The wounded man looked painfully up at the new arrival, who shouted again.

Finally, Lincoln spoke.

'Fuck . . . you.'

The briefest flicker of anger crossing his face, the pirate leader shot Lincoln in the forehead with his AK. The back of his skull burst open, dark gore sluicing down the wall behind him.

Nina clapped a hand over her mouth to stop herself from crying out. *Move*, she told herself. *Run!* But her legs remained frozen, pinned to the spot by fear.

The pirate was about to step over the corpse when something caught his attention. He crouched, lifting something from the bloodied floor.

The piece of gauze.

He regarded it for a moment, then looked up, eyes filled with the realisation that someone else was still alive.

Now Nina ran.

The ravaged corridor blurred past her as she hunted for a hiding place. She reached the storeroom, the damaged cables still crackling on the wall outside it – then continued past it. She didn't know what was in the storeroom, but she *did* know that her lab contained somewhere she could hide.

Whether she would be safe there was another matter.

His breath recovered, Chase looked through the hole again. The only pirate he could see was standing beside the RIB's mooring behind the empty speedboat with his AK-47 slung casually over one shoulder. The rumble of the other speedboat's engine echoed off the ship's side, still searching for him and Bejo – but in the wrong place, on the far side of the dock's long arm.

'Wait here,' he said, then swam under the rear of the upturned boat. He surfaced slowly, only his eyes and nose exposed as he scanned the rest of the dock. The body of one of the Indonesian crewmen was sprawled halfway along it – but there were no more pirates in sight. He looked at the floatplane. The fire had mostly burned itself out, a few patches of spilled fuel still alight on the water below the wrecked wing. Its engine was still running.

He slipped back inside the boat. 'I'm going to get to the plane,' he told Bejo, 'see if the radio's still working. If I can contact the Coast Guard, they'll get someone out here to help us.'

'It could take hours for them to get here, Mr Eddie,' Bejo warned.

'I'm not sitting under this fucking thing until those arseholes leave. Not while Nina's still inside the ship.' He prepared to dive. 'You wait in here, though. No point both of us risking our lives.'

Bejo gave him a nervous look. 'Good luck, Mr Eddie. Try not to die, hey?'

'That's part of the plan. Actually, that's the *whole* plan.' Chase submerged once more.

He swam the short distance to the side of the dock. Surfacing between two of the pontoon sections, he checked on his enemies. The RIB driver's back was now to him as he looked up at the *Pianosa*, and the speedboat had moved away to lurk near the ship's stern.

Now or never.

Chase pulled himself out of the water, lying flat on the decking close to the dead crewman. Scattered all about him was the expedition's diving gear. He crawled along the dock. The boxes and crates would keep him hidden from the men in the speedboat for at least part of the way, meaning he only had to worry about the boatman. The pirate was still facing away, now swinging his Kalashnikov half-heartedly from its strap. *Amateur*, Chase thought with disdain, but it would only take one shout from him to raise the alarm . . .

He passed the plane's tail. No more cover, but he had barely ten feet to go to reach the cockpit. He looked round the last crate for the speedboat. It was moving slowly away from him, a couple of men standing and peering into the water to each side, guns ready.

If he moved quickly enough, he could make it before anyone saw him.

One last glance back at the boatman—

He was staring right at Chase. His expression was almost quizzical, as if he was wondering why there were now two bodies lying on the dock when there had only been one before . . . until his brain finally registered that one of them had just *moved*.

He fumbled with his AK.

Caught in the open, Chase was about to dive back into the water when he saw something lying nearby.

His speargun.

He snatched it up as the pirate brought his rifle to bear—

Chase fired first. The spear lanced down the length of the dock – and hit the pirate square in the chest, the Magnum round at its head blowing a fist-sized hole in his ribcage.

The dead man slumped backwards. But the pirates in the speedboat had heard the noise.

Chase dropped the empty speargun and dived back into the water as they started shooting.

The pirate leader kicked open the lab door, sweeping his gun from side to side before stepping inside.

Nina watched through the narrow slit of her hiding place. More men entered the lab behind him. For a moment, it was as if he was staring right at her. Then he moved out of sight, whispering something in his native language.

The only reason he would have to whisper was if he thought there was a danger of being overheard. He knew she was in here. She froze, not even daring to breathe.

The leader stepped slowly round the table, boots crunching on broken glass as he headed for the storage cabinet in one corner. Finger on his AK's trigger, he reached out, gripped the locker's handle . . . and yanked it open, aiming his gun inside—

A small wave of items clattered to the floor at his feet. The locker contained nothing but archaeological kit, tools used to examine and clean artefacts recovered from the sea. One of the pirates giggled.

The leader glared at him, immediately silencing the laugh, then gave an order. All but two of his men left the room to continue the hunt.

The leader, however, moved back to the table. He had found what he was looking for.

Nina's laptop, the expedition's cameras . . . and the clay tablet.

He brushed the broken pieces of the magnifying lens off the latter and picked it up, giving the strange text a cursory glance before shoving it into a large satchel. Then he turned his attention to the computer, unfolding a scrap of paper and reading the list on it.

Crunched up painfully inside the sonar array's case, the device itself now propped against one wall, Nina struggled to see what he was doing. He seemed to be looking for particular files. He tapped on the keyboard, performing a search, then smiled as it came up with a result. He slammed the laptop closed and picked it up, then pointed at the SLR camera. The pirate in the red bandanna took it. The third man asked a question, gesturing hopefully at something out of Nina's sight, but the leader just crumpled the paper in his fist and issued a command. His men turned and left the room. With a last look round the lab, the leader followed them, Nina's laptop under his arm.

Nina waited several seconds before opening the lid slightly. The pirates' footsteps had faded, but even so she held on a little longer before climbing stiffly out. She looked at the table.

That was why they had come here, why they had killed everyone? To steal the clay tablet?

She was about to go to the door when a sound from outside startled her.

One of the pirates was coming back.

Chase heard the speedboat getting closer, the thrum of its outboard a menacing animal growl behind him as he swam.

The pirates had stopped shooting, finally realising their bullets couldn't penetrate the water. But they were heading straight for him, picking out his shape through the shimmering waves.

The *Pianosa*'s keel was directly ahead, a dark, barnacle-crusted mass. If he went under it, he could surface for air – and if they followed him round the ship, he could double back and hopefully reach the dock before they caught up.

He swam deeper, passing beneath the survey ship.

Nina didn't have time to return to her hiding place. All she could do was dart into the locker, hunching down and pulling the door almost shut.

The pirate entered the lab. It was the third man, the one who had been rebuffed by his leader. Nina watched through the crack of the door as he glanced furtively round the room, then picked up the underwater camera.

'Thieving son of a bitch,' Nina whispered. She waited for him to leave. But now that he had one valuable piece of equipment, the thought had entered his head that there might be others. His gaze darted calculatingly over the room's contents.

He regarded the locker. Frowned. Nina knew why.

When he left the room, its door had been open.

Her hand groped through the cramped space, searching for anything among the loose items that she might be able to use as a weapon.

The pirate advanced on the locker. He gripped the handle, pulled it—

Nina blasted a spray of astringent powder into his eyes.

He shrieked and reeled back, clutching at his face with his free hand. His AK came up in the other. Nina leapt from the locker and slapped it aside. It fell from his hand – but the strap tangled round his arm. She couldn't wrest it from him.

Instead she raced for the door. Behind her, the pirate shouted as he fumbled for his rifle.

Back up the passageway, reaching the storeroom, sparks still popping from the damaged wiring—

Running footsteps ahead. Another pirate was coming back.

She barged open the storeroom door. A cramped chamber, packed with stacked wooden crates and maintenance gear and large paint cans. A porthole on the opposite wall, two .50-calibre bullet holes flanking it.

The porthole was too small for her to fit through.

Trapped.

She slammed the door shut behind her and yanked a crate down to the deck, jamming it against the entrance.

But it wouldn't hold them for long.

She looked back at the equipment. The twin cylindrical tanks of an oxy-acetylene torch were secured in a rack. But she didn't know how to use it, or even light it.

Come on, think, *something*—

A metal box about the same size as the sonar case turned out to contain a piece of gear she couldn't immediately identify, some sort of heavy-duty grinder or cutter. But simply hiding in the box wouldn't save her—

The door banged against the crate. The pirates were outside.

Chase surfaced on the *Pianosa*'s port side. Not far away was another boat, a sleek cabin cruiser. The machine gun he'd heard earlier was mounted on its bow, another pirate manning it.

Sudden noise to his right. The speedboat rounded the *Pianosa*'s bow, its occupants shouting warnings to the men aboard the cruiser. The machine gunner immediately swung his weapon round.

Looking for him.

Chase didn't wait to be seen, powering back under the surface, scraping against the barnacles.

He heard the chug of the .50-cal—

The huge bullets were even less effective at penetrating the water than the 7.62mm ammo of the AKs, smashing apart as they hit the surface. But the impacts alone slammed at Chase like miniature grenade explosions. Barely able to endure the assault on his eardrums, he swam back under the ship.

The two pirates didn't risk shooting through the metal door for fear of ricochets. Instead, they kicked at it until the crate finally broke.

A strange smell was the first thing they noticed as they burst in. The second was a loud hiss. Both came from the same source: a pair of metal cylinders propped against an angle grinder.

The valves on both tanks had been fully opened, the red and green hoses whipping about like enraged snakes as the gases escaped, filling the room, reaching the corridor outside . . .

The electrical cables sparked.

And the acetylene gas, mixed with pure oxygen for maximum combustibility, ignited.

The fireball rushed back into the confined storeroom, instantly engulfing both men in flames as the gas canisters hurtled across the room on a jet of scorching blue fire. One of the pirates was smashed against the door jamb with bone-cracking force. His companion hit the wall across the corridor, the blunt ends of the cylinders crushing his sternum before spinning away like a monstrous Catherine wheel.

The fireball dispersed. Nina flung open the box and jumped up, one arm covering her face to protect it from the dancing fires as she stumbled over the dead pirates. Looking right, she saw the flaming gas cylinders still whirling on the deck.

No way out that way. She went left, passing Lincoln's body before braving the smoke to find a way into the open.

Head ringing, Chase surfaced once more. He was back by the floating dock. The speedboat was still on the other side of the ship – but it wouldn't take long to reverse its course.

He pulled himself up, about to run to the nearby gangway – when he realised that there were men about to come down it. The pirates were leaving the ship.

All he could do was dive back into the sea and hope they hadn't seen him.

That hope barely lasted a second. AK fire kicked up the water above him. He swam deeper, already hearing the speedboat coming back.

5

Nina's eyes were watering from the smoke, but she finally saw daylight ahead.

But she could also hear gunfire, and shouting. She held in a cough as she cautiously looked outside.

Several men were on the starboard side of the main deck, some clomping down the gangway to the dock, others firing at the water. The pirate leader shouted a command. His men stopped shooting and hurried after their fellows. The leader was the last to go, casting a satisfied look at the smoking superstructure before following them to the dock.

Nina emerged, moving in a crouch towards the empty port-side boat hoist. When she was sure the pirates had gone, she stood.

Big mistake.

A shout came from her left. She whirled to see a motor yacht off the port bow, a man in its bridge pointing at her – and another pirate whipping round a huge machine gun.

'Shit!' She threw herself to the deck, scrambling towards the starboard side as the gun opened up—

The hammer-blow clangs of bullets pounding into the side of the hull and up through the decking were almost deafening. Debris showered her as machinery and deck fittings were torn apart. A hole the size of her fist exploded through the painted floor just a foot from her head, another bullet striking a thick metal cross-beam beneath the deck with a piercing bang. She screamed and moved faster towards the starboard hoist, the boat in it rocking and jolting as bullets peppered its hull.

The firing stopped. Maybe the gunner thought she was dead, or had run out of ammo. Nina didn't care, feeling only relief as she reached the starboard side of the deck.

It didn't last. From there, she had an elevated view of the dock. The floatplane at its far end had lost most of one wing; the *Pianosa*'s other boat had capsized, debris floating around it. Two bodies lay on the dock – one was a member of the ship's crew, but the other was unfamiliar; one of the pirates, a spear protruding from a bloody hole in his chest.

Eddie, she thought. He was the only member of the expedition who could have fired such a shot. Was he still alive – and if so, where was he?

The other pirates provided an answer. Some of the men on the dock started shooting into the water, quickly joined by more in a speedboat. Dozens of little waterspouts shot upwards where the bullets hit. The leader shouted again, sounding annoyed. The pirates stopped shooting – but there was no sign of anyone below the waves.

The pirate leader climbed into the larger of the two moored powerboats, the others splitting up to board the vessels. Engines started. They were leaving.

From her vantage point, Nina already knew they weren't simply going to sail away. The RIB had rocket launchers aboard, the bulbous dark green warheads already loaded.

They hadn't come just to rob the ship. They were going to sink it, remove all trace of the expedition.

One of the men in the smaller powerboat, almost directly below, looked up – and saw her. He shouted something, raising his gun—

Nina jerked back. The hoist controls were just a few feet away.

Above, the bullet-pocked boat was hanging out over the ship's side, still swaying . . .

She waited for the swinging boat to reach the furthest point of its arc – and kicked the hoist's emergency release lever.

The boat plunged downwards with a rattle of chains. The pirates barely had time to scream before over half a ton of steel and wood and fibreglass hit, crushing them flat inside their own boat. Blood spurted over the dock.

The men in the two remaining boats gaped at the sight. Only their leader, at the RIB's controls, was immediately able to overcome his shock, gunning the engine to curve his boat sharply away from the *Pianosa*.

Chase surfaced under the longer leg of the dock, seeing the RIB moving off. The other moored pirate craft, he saw with surprise, had become the bottom slice of a boat sandwich, its occupants reduced to a glutinous red jam.

'Nice work,' he muttered, looking up to see who had been responsible – and filling with relieved delight at the sight of a very familiar face peering over the deck.

His smile vanished as the RIB came about – and two men inside it raised Russian RPG-7 rocket launchers, aiming them at the *Pianosa*.

The first shot streaked across the water and hit one of the fuel barrels under the gangway. The explosion instantly consumed the others beside it, a huge ball of fire and filthy black smoke seething upwards. The heavy gangway broke loose, crashing aflame on to the burning dock and destroying several pontoon sections.

But the pirates weren't finished.

The second RPG hit the ship at its waterline, blasting a foot-wide hole through the steel. The sea instantly rushed in, greedily filling every space it found within. A third detonation, from the other side of the *Pianosa* – the cruiser had also fired a rocket.

Holed in two places, no crew left alive to contain the flooding, the survey ship was doomed.

And Nina was still aboard.

The pirate leader pointed away from the stricken ship, to the northwest. The surviving speedboat turned and surged off in that direction, the RIB following. The deeper rumble of the cruiser's engine rose as it joined the smaller boats in their escape.

Chase climbed on to what was left of the dock. It was now severed from the ship, slowly drifting away. 'Nina!' he shouted up at the *Pianosa*. 'Nina, are you okay?'

She crawled to the edge of the deck, dishevelled hair fluttering in the wind, and looked down at him. 'Eddie, God! Are you all right?'

'More or less. Is anyone else alive up there?'

'I don't think so,' Nina called back grimly. Toxic black smoke was belching from all the entrances to the superstructure.

Chase glanced at the waterline. The hole made by the RPG was now completely submerged, and dropping lower with increasing speed as the bow took on water. 'The ship's sinking – you've got to get off.'

'How? The gangplank's gone!'

'Find a life jacket, then jump.'

She looked dismayed. *'Jump?'*

'Might as well!' He turned his attention to the overturned boat. 'Bejo!'

Bejo surfaced beside the wreck. 'Mr Eddie! You okay?'

'Yeah,' Chase told him, pointing at Nina. 'Get ready to help her when she jumps in. Then bring her over here.'

'I don't want to jump in!' Nina protested, donning a life jacket. 'It's too high!'

'Well, if you wait a couple of minutes it'll be at water level and you'll just be able to *step* off, but I don't think waiting's a good idea!' He indicated the flickers of flame escaping from the ship's interior.

Nina reluctantly climbed over the railing. 'Oh . . . *craaaap!*' she shrieked as she closed her eyes and dropped into the sea. Bejo quickly reached her and raised her by the shoulders as she gasped and shook her head. He helped her to the dock.

Chase lifted his bedraggled fiancée from the water, then pulled Bejo out before starting for the other end of the dock. 'Where are you going?' Nina asked.

'If the plane's radio's still working, we can send a distress call.' He jogged to the battered Otter. There was an unpleasant moment when he had to push Ranauld's shrapnel-torn corpse aside to reach the instrument panel, but he saw from the lights on its fascia that the radio was still active.

He reached for the hand-held microphone under the panel and switched the radio to VHF channel 16 – the international distress frequency. 'Mayday, Mayday, Mayday. This is the research vessel *Pianosa* . . .'

The pirate leader looked down sharply as the speeding RIB's radio crackled. It had been set to receive on channel 16, listening for any distress calls from the survey ship. None had come – destroying the vessel's bridge and radio masts with the very first shot had seen to that.

But now a survivor was making a call – and worse, it was being answered. Someone aboard an Indonesian Coast Guard vessel was replying in halting English, asking for the ship's location.

The plane, he realised – it had only been damaged, not destroyed. Its radio was still intact.

No witnesses of the attack could be left alive. His employer had been very clear about that.

The speedboat was the fastest of their three remaining craft. He handed the RIB's controls to one of his men and beckoned the speedboat closer. 'There are still people alive!' he shouted across to its three occupants. 'Go back and kill them!'

The man at the speedboat's outboard tugged the red bandanna from his face and gave him an eager, malevolent smile, then swung the vessel about.

'Oh, bollocks,' Chase muttered as he concluded the distress call – and saw one of the retreating boats making a hard turn.

They had heard the message.

Stranded on what was left of the pontoon dock, he, Nina and Bejo had nowhere to run. Even if they dived underwater, the pirates could just wait them out, taking shots when they surfaced for air. And they had no weapons.

Except . . .

'What are you doing?' Nina called as Chase clambered into the cockpit.

'I'm going to meet them.'

'You're *what*?'

Chase didn't answer, instead pushing Ranauld's body out of the other side. 'Sorry, Hervé,' he said as the dead man splashed into the sea. He slid into the pilot's seat and examined the instrument panel. Most of the dials and gauges were a mystery, but it didn't matter. With half a wing missing, the Otter wouldn't be flying anywhere. The only controls he needed were the rudder pedals and the throttle.

The latter, he knew from having watched Ranauld the previous day, was a large lever on the central console. He pushed it experimentally from the marked 'Idle' position. The engine note rose sharply, the fuselage vibrating as the propeller increased speed. A good start. He stretched back across the cockpit, untying the mooring rope, then shoved the throttle forward.

A cutting wind whipped through the broken windscreen, the engine's roar driving into Chase's skull like a drill. He ignored it, pushing one of the pedals to turn the Otter away from the dock. The plane began to pick up speed – and also to lurch, every small wave on the surface magnified as the floats ploughed through them.

He opened the throttle further. The amount of rudder control increased as the Otter went faster, but the aircraft was worryingly unstable. The wrecked port wing meant it wanted to turn right, the weight of the other wing pulling that side down. But if he applied too much left rudder to straighten out, the plane would tip over.

Sawing at the pedals with both feet in a precarious balancing act, he looked ahead. Through the propeller's blur he saw the cruiser and the RIB retreating in the distance – and the speedboat coming at him.

More power. He couldn't let the pirates get into range of the dock. The Otter smashed through the waves. Spray gushed through the hole in the fuselage, soaking him. He was doing thirty knots, and increasing.

The speedboat was approaching fast. One of the pirates stood up, gun ready. The driver changed course, turning to pass along the Otter's port side.

The missing wing meant they had a closer approach. A better shot.

Chase turned straight at them. The plane began to tip over, a sickening slow-motion sensation as it approached the point of no return . . . then recovered as a wave impact pitched it back. The boat turned again, harder, the driver realising what he meant to do and trying to avoid the collision—

Chase ducked as the gunman fired. A burst of bullets clanked along the Otter's nose and through the cockpit. One of the remaining pieces of windscreen shattered, sharp fragments whipped back at him by the wind.

Then the boat was past him.

Chase pushed down hard on the rudder pedal.

The plane tipped – but this time he wanted it to. The starboard wingtip sliced into the water. The sudden drag swung the whole aircraft round, much faster than with the rudder alone. Then the centrifugal force of the tight turn pushed the Otter back upright . . . and Chase straightened out, aiming directly at the speedboat as he jammed the throttle fully forward.

The engine noise became a scream, the blast from the propeller almost blinding him. But he could still see just enough to make out the speedboat almost side-on to him as the driver desperately tried to turn out of his way, but too late—

The gunman's upper body instantly disappeared in a spray of red as the propeller hit him, his legs and abdomen remaining standing for a moment before the Otter's floats crashed into the speedboat's side and threw what was left of the body into the sea. Another man was clipped by the tips of the blades and flung over thirty feet into the air, an arc of blood tracing his path to a splashdown some distance away.

The driver barely managed to duck before the crash. The propeller scythed over him, missing by inches, but the force of the collision slammed his head against a seat.

Even braced for the impact, Chase was still thrown painfully against the control column. Clutching his bruised chest, he pulled back the throttle. The engine noise dropped to a low grumble.

He pushed himself up and looked outside. The speedboat was impaled on the Otter's floats. He climbed out, finding a foothold on the float and edging along it to the plane's nose. The propeller was still turning, so he jumped into the speedboat's bow, then hunched down to pass underneath it. The pirate was sprawled across the stern, starting to recover—

'Come in, number seven,' said Chase, grabbing him and banging

77

his head against the seat again. 'Your time is up!'

The pirate swiped an arm at Chase's face. He responded with a crunching headbutt, breaking the Indonesian's nose. The man screeched, spitting blood.

Chase pulled the pirate up by the bandanna round his neck. 'You speak English?' he demanded. He doubted the snarled reply was complimentary. 'Let's try that again,' he said, hauling him round so that his head was within inches of the propeller's buzzing tips. 'Do? You? Speak? *English?*'

'Yes!' shrieked the pirate, eyes wide with terror. He tried to twist away, but Chase forced him closer.

'Why did you attack us?'

'Don't know! Just a job!'

'Who hired you?'

Despite his fear, the pirate remained silent. Chase frowned and pushed him into the propeller. Most of the man's right ear disappeared with a meaty *thwat!* and a puff of blood. He screamed as Chase pulled him away.

'Who hired you?' Chase repeated, more forcefully. 'You've only got one more ear, then after that it's on to the softer bits.' He glanced down for emphasis.

'Don't know!' the pirate wailed. 'Only Latan knows!'

'Who's Latan?'

'Boss man, our boss!'

Chase remembered the ex-military man he'd seen leading the pirates. He looked for the retreating RIB. Like the cruiser, it was now just a dot in the distance, powering away at full speed. 'Where's he going?'

The pirate lashed out in an attempt to break free. Chase rammed a fist into the other man's stomach, then grabbed him again.

Thwat!

'Can you still 'ear me?' said Chase as his prisoner, blood now

78

running down both sides of his head, screamed again. 'Where's your base? Where's Latan going?'

'Mankun Island! *Mankun Island!*'

The name meant nothing to Chase, but he could tell from the desperation in the pirate's voice that he was telling the truth. He pulled him away from the propeller and threw him down in the stern. 'All right, Van Gogh,' he growled, 'stay there and shut up.' He sat down, one foot on the moaning man's chest as he tried to piece together what had happened. Whoever had hired this Latan to attack the expedition had been after something very specific, something so valuable – or such a threat – that everybody aboard the *Pianosa* had to be murdered to cover up the fact.

It had to be one of the artefacts Nina had found, but how could some old relic be worth so much carnage?

He saw the camera from Nina's lab under the rear seat. Whatever it was they'd been after, maybe there was still a picture on the memory card . . .

Movement caught his attention and he snapped his head round, seeing the menacing fin of a shark briefly break the surface before slipping back under the waves. The blood in the water must have attracted it—

The pirate twisted out from under his foot, clawing for something behind his back as he took advantage of Chase's momentary distraction. He sat up, clutching a pistol that had been hidden in his waistband.

Chase rolled backwards, sweeping a savage kick at the pirate. His heel smashed into his chin with tooth-snapping force. The pirate was thrown back, firing a shot wildly into the air as he toppled over the stern to splash into the sea.

Heart racing, Chase pulled himself upright to see the pirate surfacing. Blood streaming down his face, he flicked up the gun—

And was dragged under the water, so shockingly fast that the gun was already submerged again before he could pull the trigger. A plume of bloody froth belched up as the tiger shark which had just clamped its ferocious jaws round the pirate's chest pulled its meal down into the depths.

Chase let out a startled half-laugh as he watched predator and prey disappear. He regained his breath, then hummed a few bars from the *Jaws* theme, looking back towards the half-sunken *Pianosa* and wondering how long it would take to get back to Nina with a smashed boat stuck to his plane.

After all, swimming was definitely an unsafe option.

6

'Attacked by pirates in the morning,' said Nina, 'and a twenty-eight-hour flight in the afternoon. I don't know which is worse.'

The humour was forced; she was still horribly shaken. But in dealing first with the Coast Guard, then with officials from the Indonesian government after being airlifted to Jakarta, she had concealed her true feelings beneath a mask of officialdom. She was still the leader of the expedition, and she had a responsibility to give the authorities as clear and dispassionate an account of events as possible.

Now, the United Nations wanted to hear that account as well. In person. A flight had been hastily arranged to return her to New York. Gruelling though the long trip would be, Nina was certain it would pale compared to the interrogation she would endure at the UN.

'Yeah,' said Chase. 'Private flight with no other passengers? Horrible. Still, at least you won't have to worry about getting stuck next to a screaming baby.'

'No, just you looting the minibar.' Chase's expression suddenly became evasive. 'What?'

'Well, the thing is,' he began, not quite meeting her gaze, 'I, er . . . won't be going with you.'

'You *what*?'

'I'll come back to New York as soon as I can, I promise! But there's something I need to do here first.' He lowered his voice. They were waiting in the United Nations' offices in Jakarta, and as well as UN staff there were also officials from the Indonesian government and its law enforcement agencies buzzing around. 'There was something I didn't tell the cops. I know where the pirates were going: some place called Mankun Island. So I'm going to head over there and have words.'

'Why the hell didn't you tell them?' Nina said. 'If they know where the pirates are, they'll be able to catch them!'

'No, they won't – it'll take too long. Even if they decide to go after the pirates tomorrow, it'll be too late. They'll be gone – and we'll never find out who hired them. But Bejo knows where this island is, and he knows people in the area. We'll fly up there, get a boat and check the place out tonight. Before those bastards have a chance to fuck off with their money.'

'Or maybe you'll get yourself *killed*. And Bejo too.'

'He wants to do it,' said Chase. 'The guys on the ship were his friends.'

She shook her head. 'Eddie, this is a terrible idea. If anything goes wrong . . .'

'It won't,' he assured her.

'I don't suppose it would make any difference if I told you that I really, *really* need you with me in New York, and as your boss *ordered* you to come?' One look at his expression gave Nina her answer. 'Yeah, thought not.'

'I'll be fine,' he promised. 'And I'll keep Bejo out of trouble. Enough people've died today. Enough *good* people,' he added with chilling emphasis.

Resigned, Nina rested her head on his shoulder. 'Just don't do anything stupid, okay.'

'Hey, you know me, love.'

'That's why I said it.' She kissed his cheek, then stood. 'I'd better get to the airport. Don't want to keep the UN waiting, huh?'

'Who knows, maybe by the time you get back to New York, I'll have found out what all this is about.'

'Maybe,' she echoed glumly. They regarded each other for a long moment, then embraced and kissed.

'See you soon,' said Chase as they reluctantly moved apart.

'I'd better.'

'We're close,' Bejo warned.

It was now night, a clinging, muggy humidity sticking Chase's dark shirt to his skin. But he ignored the discomfort as he turned off the little boat's outboard. 'You sure it's the right place?' he asked. In the distance, he saw a handful of lights.

'Nobody lives on Mankun, not usually,' Bejo told him. 'Pirates use it sometimes. Not often, though – too far from shipping lanes.'

'They came a fair old way to get to us, though.' They were almost eighty miles from where the *Pianosa* had been attacked: a long run for the pirates to reach their base. But it meant less chance of anyone looking for them here.

He picked up a pair of battered binoculars for a closer look. The lights resolved themselves into bulbs hung on a cluster of tumbledown wooden shacks on the shore of a small inlet. Beyond them rose damp, dark rainforest. The biggest of the structures extended out into the water, apparently a covered dock. There was a large boat inside. The motor cruiser? It was an expensive vessel – maybe the pirates planned to sell it.

'Mr Eddie,' Bejo said, voice tense. 'Look left.'

Chase panned the binoculars to find what had caught the young man's eye. Almost invisible against the black water was a boat, a very faint light at its bow. The dim yellow glow picked out the outline of a seated man – and the glint of metal in his hand. A rifle.

'They pretend to be fishing,' said Bejo. 'But they're lookouts. They warn the other pirates if the police or the Coast Guard come – anyone else, they just kill.'

Scanning left and right, Chase saw two more 'fishermen' lurking in the distance. Nobody could get within half a mile of the inlet without being spotted.

Nobody in a boat, at least.

He gave the binoculars to Bejo. 'Okay,' he said, picking up a sheathed knife, 'wait here. I'll signal you when it's clear to row in.'

'Good luck, Mr Eddie,' Bejo whispered as Chase climbed into the water, barely making a splash.

The pirate keeping watch from the small boat was not only bored, but frustrated. Every so often, he heard noises from the shore, whooping and cheering as his comrades celebrated the success of their mission. Sure, not everyone had come back from it, but it wasn't as though the men were close friends. He barely knew the names of most of them, the entire operation having been put together literally overnight, its members hurriedly recruited from seemingly every desperate dive on the Sumatran islands. What he resented was being stuck out here on guard duty while the others drank and gorged and gambled. Latan had even rounded up some whores from somewhere. And here he was, bobbing half a kilometre away with nothing but a lamp and a Kalashnikov for company . . .

A small sound brought his thoughts back to his job. It sounded like bubbles breaking the surface. A fish?

Seeing no sign of any approaching boats, he leaned over to find the source. A couple of bubbles popped a handspan from the boat's side. The pirate looked more closely, seeing a pale shape below the surface. A *big* fish. No need for a net; he could just reach in and grab it—

It reached out and grabbed *him*.

Chase's hand locked round the man's neck and dragged his face underwater to silence him as his other hand drove the knife deep into his neck with a *chut*. He kept hold as the pirate thrashed and wriggled . . . then went limp. The AK-47 splashed into the water, bumping against him as it sank. He waited a few seconds until he was sure the man was dead, then surfaced and climbed aboard.

'Don't rock the boat,' he told the corpse. He looked out to sea, holding his hand in front of the lamp to signal Bejo.

Ten minutes later, they were ashore.

After rowing to meet Chase, Bejo had silently guided the little boat to make landfall a short distance from the rotting buildings, waiting in the water until they were certain there were no patrols on shore. There weren't. That the pirates only had three men on watch in the boats showed they weren't expecting trouble.

They were wrong.

Bejo pulled the boat ashore as Chase squeezed as much water as he could from his clothes. 'What's the plan, Mr Eddie?'

'The plan is for you to stay here and wait for me,' Chase told him. He could see the young Indonesian's disappointment even in the dark.

'But I want to come.' He started towards the shacks.

Chase held him back. 'When I said "stay here and wait for me", I was being polite. What I meant was "stay here so you don't get your fucking head blown off!" Wait here.'

'But—'

'Stay!'

'I'm not a dog, Mr Eddie!' Bejo protested in an irritated whisper as Chase cautiously made his way along the waterline.

He reached the first building, the large covered dock. As he'd thought, the cruiser was inside, the .50-cal still mounted on its bow.

It hadn't even been unloaded, a belt of ammo dangling from it. He shook his head. Amateurs.

He moved on. The other shacks were lit inside and out by bulbs strung from their roof beams, a generator puttering away somewhere to power them. He crept to the nearest shack and peeped through a gap in the wood. A strong smell of hot grease and searing meat hit him, something sizzling in a large wok atop a camping gas hob. The skinned carcass of a goat hung from the ceiling, chunks of flesh having been crudely carved from it. A man was drunkenly whacking away with a large cleaver.

It wasn't Latan. Chase moved on, slipping round the shack to the waterline. A rickety walkway ran along it, connecting the huts to a jetty. The RIB was moored to the latter, along with a couple of small rowing boats.

It struck him that the RIB was the only boat capable of a fast getaway; the cruiser would have to be untied, started up and reversed out of the dock. Once trouble started – and it would – the inflatable powerboat would be the first place the pirate leader would run.

He had to make sure Latan didn't get away. Sabotage the engine, maybe? Or . . .

A noise behind him, a creak of rotten wood. Chase spun, fists ready to pummel the pirate—

'Mr Eddie!' squeaked Bejo, throwing up his hands in fright as Chase arrested a blow inches from his face.

He hauled Bejo into the shadows between two of the shacks. 'I told you to stay put!' he hissed.

'They killed my friends!' the teenager insisted. 'I want to help – I *can* help. I just heard some of the pirates talking about Latan. They say he's waiting for a man to come here with money.'

'They haven't been paid yet?' That explained why they were still here, then – and if he could identify Latan's employer . . . 'Okay,' he said reluctantly, 'stick with me. But do *exactly* what I tell you, all right?'

'Okay, Mr Eddie,' Bejo replied, smiling. 'So what do we do?'

Junk was scattered round a tree stump between the shacks. Chase picked up a coil of rusted steel cable. 'Keep watch here, warn me if anyone's coming.' He started to creep along the jetty.

'Where are you going?'

Now it was Chase's turn to smile. 'To make sure that boat's tied up properly.'

It took a couple of minutes to complete his work. Job done, Chase moved back ashore, and accompanied by Bejo continued his search for the pirate leader. The largest and noisiest shack contained about a dozen men, most of them engrossed in a fast-paced dice game that involved a lot of aggressive shouting as the others looked on and drank.

Still no sign of Latan. They passed through the shadows to sneak up to a small hut. Sounds of activity came from within, but this definitely wasn't gambling, except with the possibility of contracting a sexually transmitted disease.

Feeling uncomfortably like a voyeur, Chase looked through a hole to see a bored-looking woman lying on a ratty mattress as a drunken, sweaty man pounded away at her. The bearded Casanova wasn't Latan, however, so Chase withdrew. He was about to carry on to the next shack when he realised Bejo wasn't following. He glanced back to see the young Indonesian gawping at the scene inside the hut, mesmerised. In equal parts impatient and amused, he moved back to pull him away—

A large man with a crooked scar running from his temple to his cheek threw open the gambling den's door and strode towards the hut, shouting angrily. Chase pushed Bejo down, then froze. He was in shadow, his clothes dark, but the pirate was only a few feet away as he banged on the door. If he looked to the side, even for a moment, his eyes would adjust enough to make out the shapes hiding there.

But he didn't, instead continuing to hammer at the door. The man inside said something that was unmistakably the equivalent of 'Give me another minute!' This didn't satisfy the scarred pirate, who kicked the door open and stomped inside. A yelp, some thumping, and then the interrupted lover was flung out into the open, trousers round his ankles. The door slammed shut. The bearded man yelled a half-hearted insult at the hut, then gathered up his dignity and his pants before trudging back to join the men in the gambling den.

Chase and Bejo remained still until he was inside, then crept round the back of the love shack. The next shack contained only a man sprawled across a bunk, snoring and drooling, with an overturned bottle of whisky beside him. Not Latan. Then a dark, empty shell of a hut, its ceiling half collapsed. They were running out of places to search . . .

A new noise. Not from the pirates – from the sky. A helicopter.

Chase and Bejo dropped flat behind some rusting fuel drums as several men emerged from the largest shack. A fierce wind whirled round the camp as the chopper appeared over the trees. The men were armed, but not on alert. They were obviously expecting the new arrival.

Chase finally spotted Latan, emerging from a small hut at the edge of the derelict settlement. Carrying a canvas bag in one hand, the pirate leader was tugging a shirt over his bare shoulders with the other. He joined his men, and they moved to an open area near the treeline as the helicopter switched on its spotlight and descended.

'Wait here,' Chase told Bejo. 'Seriously, don't move.' He checked that nobody else was coming from the buildings, then quickly crawled on his stomach to another pile of abandoned junk closer to the landing site. He wanted to get a good look at whoever Latan was meeting.

The helicopter touched down, two men in dark jungle camouflage fatigues and bearing SIG assault rifles jumping out from either side, clearly unimpressed by the pirates facing them. As the rotor blades wound down, a third man emerged and surveyed the scene before striding towards Latan. About Chase's age, mid to late thirties, he guessed; tall, blond, eyes commanding. A professional soldier.

'Are you . . . Mr Vogler?' Latan called over the falling noise of the helicopter.

The blond man stopped a few feet from him. 'I am.'

'Where is our money?'

'Where are the items?' Vogler countered. His English was crisp and precise. Chase knew the accent: Swiss.

Latan opened the bag, showing him Nina's laptop and the clay tablet. 'Here. But . . .' His momentarily hesitant expression suggested that he knew he was about to chance his luck, but was greedy enough to try anyway. 'We want more money. None of my men were supposed to die.'

'Ironic,' said Vogler, unconcerned. 'I was actually thinking about *cutting* your payment. I heard a rumour from Jakarta that there were survivors – and our deal was that you eliminate every-one aboard.'

'We kill everyone,' Latan insisted.

'Then you completed the deal as agreed – and you will accept the agreed payment.' Vogler gave him a cold look. 'I'm sure your friend in Singapore explained that. Trying to deceive the Covenant of Genesis would be very dangerous.' Chase made a mental note of the odd name – the pirates' paymasters? 'We would usually have done a job like this ourselves, but time was a factor. So be grateful for the work . . . and the money.'

He gestured to one of his men. The soldier reached into the helicopter, taking out a briefcase and bringing it to him.

'Your payment,' said Vogler, opening the case and showing its contents to Latan. Chase couldn't see how much was inside, but Latan's eager expression suggested it was plenty. 'Now, give me the artefact.'

Latan dumped the canvas bag at his feet. Vogler crouched and examined the items inside, then looked up sharply. 'What about the cameras?'

'We saw no cameras,' said Latan. 'They must have sunk with the ship.'

Vogler regarded him unblinkingly. 'Are you sure?'

'We saw no cameras,' Latan repeated. Vogler didn't appear convinced, but after a moment he zipped up the bag and handed over the briefcase.

'Then our business is concluded,' he said, lifting the bag and turning for the helicopter. He paused, looking back. 'I hope I have no reason to see you again, Mr Latan. If there is anything you wish to say, now is the time.'

Latan had already opened the case and was flicking through the banknotes inside, but Vogler's words wiped the avaricious smile from his face. 'No, nothing,' he managed to say.

'Good.' Vogler and the two soldiers climbed back aboard the chopper, which brought its rotors to full power and took off in a whirlwind of leaves, disappearing over the dark jungle.

Chase kept his eyes fixed on Latan. Some of the other men eagerly tried to grab their shares out of the case, but Latan snapped it shut. Disappointed, they headed back to the large shack, while their leader returned to the smaller building from which he had come. Chase waited until everyone was back inside, then rejoined Bejo.

'Okay, I'm going to have words with Latan. You keep hiding here until I come back. Unless everything goes pear-shaped – then you run like buggery!'

'Pear-shaped?' Bejo asked, puzzled.

'You'll know. Don't take any chances – just run. Okay, see you soon.' Leaving Bejo hiding amongst the barrels, he crept across the camp to Latan's hut.

'Got you, you bugger,' he muttered as he looked under a half-closed shutter to see Latan's hard features in the dimly lit room beyond. The pirate leader had claimed the best – or least worst – shack for his own private use, and done the same regarding its other occupant. He sat shirtless on a bed, an attractive young woman in a tight red minidress stroking his back as she whispered in his ear. Soft music was playing from an iPod connected to a small pair of speakers.

Chase also saw the briefcase – and an AK propped up in a corner. It was within reach of the bed, but if Latan was preoccupied with the woman . . .

He went to the door and peered through a crack. The woman unzipped her dress and shrugged it off her shoulders, Latan's hands groping her bare breasts. It was a good job he'd made Bejo stay behind; the clunk of his jaw dropping would have alerted the entire village.

The pirate was still within an arm's length of the Kalashnikov. Chase frowned. *Come on, you horny bastard, move away . . .*

The pair finally changed position, the woman lying prone on the bed with the now-naked Latan on top of her. She let out a little grunt of discomfort as he thrust into her.

Chase opened the door, and advanced carefully across the wooden floor with the knife in one hand. The couple faced away from him, the AK just out of Latan's reach. All Chase had to do was get to the gun before the pirate realised he was there—

The floor creaked beneath his foot.

Latan was preoccupied, but the woman turned her head – and squealed at the sight of the knife.

Training kicking in, Latan lunged for the rifle.

If he fired even a single shot, the other pirates would be alerted—

Too far away to make a grab for the gun, Chase grabbed something else instead.

Latan gasped like a choking cat as Chase's free hand clamped round his genitals. The pirate's twitching fingers stopped just short of the AK-47. Chase pulled. The fingers hurriedly withdrew.

'This isn't my usual sort of thing, by the way,' said Chase. 'Just so you know.' He nodded at the woman, who was pinned beneath Latan and watching fearfully. 'Sorry to interrupt, love. Don't mind me.'

'I fucking kill you!' the pirate rasped.

'Takes a lot of balls for someone in your position to make threats,' Chase told him amiably, 'but you don't have 'em.' He tightened his grip, and Latan gave a strangled groan. 'So this guy who hired you, Vogler – who is he and where do I find him?'

'Fuck you – *gnngh!*'

'You won't have anything to fuck *with* if you don't tell me,' said Chase, jabbing the point of his knife against the pirate's testicles, drawing blood. 'Last chance. Or I'll fucking feed them to you.'

'Never met him before tonight!' Latan moaned. 'He talked to me through a middleman in Singapore last night.' He glanced at the briefcase. 'Hired us to get the computer and the tile with writing on it, then sink ship.'

'*Why* did he hire you? What's so important about that tablet?'

'Don't know, he didn't say!'

Chase frowned. Latan was probably telling the truth. 'What about this . . . this Covenant of Genesis?' he asked instead. 'What is it?'

He felt Latan tense. 'I – I can't tell you!'

'Oh, you can,' Chase said. 'Get up.' The woman turned over,

arms clutched protectively over her chest, as the pirate leader crawled backwards off her. Chase did a double take as he saw there was more to Latan's companion than met the eye. 'Whoa,' he said, amused. 'You're no lady – you're a man, baby, a man!' He withdrew the knife so the pirate could sit up. 'So you're into ladyboys, eh? And I thought pirates preferred Roger the cabin boy—'

The 'woman' suddenly sprang to life, whipping up both feet flat against Latan's chest and shoving him backwards with surprising force. Latan slammed into Chase, whose grip on the pirate's jewels was jolted loose as he staggered back. With a roar, the naked man whirled to face his attacker.

Chase brought up the knife to defend himself – but instantly changed his plans as he saw the transsexual reach for the gun. Her hand closed round it—

The knife thunked deeply into the battered old weapon's wooden grip, transfixing the ladyboy's hand. She screamed – and her finger clenched convulsively on the trigger. The AK-47 blasted a spray of bullets into the ceiling. Shouts rose outside as the other pirates heard the gunfire.

Chase punched Latan in the face, knocking him down, and ran.

7

Chase sprinted through the little settlement. He passed the rusting fuel drums – Bejo was gone. The kid had done the right thing and got the hell out; now it was his turn.

Yelling from the large shack. He snatched up the handle of a broken oar and smacked it into the face of the first pirate to emerge, ducking round the shack's side as more pirates jumped over the fallen man and came after him. He saw the sea ahead, the jetty extending out into the darkness. Maybe rigging the RIB hadn't been such a good idea – he could have used it to escape—

A man ran out on to the walkway in front of him. He saw Chase and raised his gun.

Chase hurled himself through an open window into the neighbouring hut: the pirates' makeshift kitchen. He landed on a table, which collapsed in a shower of rice and clanging metal bowls. He jumped up, finding himself beside the sizzling wok as the pirate appeared at the window and brought his AK to bear.

Chase snatched up the wok and whipped it round, its contents sluicing out. Boiling fat splashed across the walls – and the pirate's face. The man screamed as his skin instantly blistered.

A door across the room crashed open. Still holding the wok, Chase spun to see two more men rush in. Neither had a gun – but one saw the meat cleaver on a bench near the hanging goat and ran to pick it up.

The other man, a thick-necked, heavily tattooed thug in a string vest, charged at Chase, knotted hands outstretched—

Chase let him close in – then slammed the wok against the side of his head. The sturdy metal bowl rang like a gong, but that was nothing compared to the sizzling hiss as the hot metal burned the pirate's cheek like a branding iron. He collapsed, overcome by pain.

The second man approached more warily, the cleaver in his hand. Chase heard shouting outside. It wouldn't take the others long to realise where he was . . . and surround him.

A frying pan against Kalashnikovs. Not good. He had to get out into the open.

The pirate wasn't going to let him. He came closer, swinging the hefty blade. Chase jumped back, bringing the wok up like a shield. Another swipe, aiming for Chase's hand. Metal clashed against metal – and the wok's bowl broke off the handle to hit the floor with a hollow bong.

He retreated, throwing the handle at the pirate's face. The man swatted it away, then gripped the cleaver with both hands as they circled each other. Chase bumped against a bench, knocking over a plastic bottle of cooking oil. The glutinous liquid blurped out, spattering on the floor.

The pirate swung.

Chase threw himself backwards, the tip of the blade ripping his shirt across his left pectoral before it struck a metal pole supporting the roof, hacking clean through it at a steep angle. The top half of the pole clanged to the floor, the roof creaking.

Men rushed through the open door—

Chase flipped the plastic bottle at the naked flame of the gas hob.

The oil ignited, the bottle bursting open and showering liquid fire across the kitchen. The pirates who had just entered were engulfed, hideous screams filling the room as they staggered blindly in a futile attempt to escape the searing fat.

But the sudden inferno reached Chase too as it spread to the spilled oil on the floor. His dark jeans were still wet from his swim, but the fire leapt up to light the drops of splattered grease on his clothes. 'Oh, shit!' he gasped, jumping back and swatting at his burning leg. He bumped against the hanging carcass, setting it swinging.

The pirate with the cleaver took another swipe, forcing him back towards the blaze. Chase was now cut off from the door, and his opponent was between him and the nearest window. The dead goat caught fire. He flinched away as it swung back and forth, looking for an opening, a weapon. Nothing. The pirate advanced, flames reflecting dully from the cleaver's blade as he pulled it back for another strike—

Chase plunged his hand into the carcass and spun it round, a shield of meat and bone. The cleaver hacked deep into the dead animal with a crack of breaking ribs. He felt intense heat on the back of his head as his hair started to burn, but held firm as he slammed the flaming goat into the other man's face and knocked him backwards, jolting the cleaver from his grip.

A *crack*. The ceiling beam from which the carcass was suspended broke. Chase threw himself sideways as it fell, landing perilously close to the rapidly spreading fire.

He jumped up. The pirate also recovered, looking much less confident without his weapon. Seeing a chance, Chase ran at him.

The other man grabbed the severed length of metal pole and whipped it up like a baseball bat. Chase raised an arm just in time to protect his head from the blow, but still took a jarring hit to the elbow.

The pirate swung again. The pole whacked against Chase's kneecap. He stumbled and fell. Before he could recover, another fierce strike smashed painfully down across his back. Powerful hands seized him by the throat.

Thumbs dug into his neck, choking him. The pirate hauled him round to look him in the eye, triumph clear in his expression as he tried to crush Chase's windpipe—

Chase clapped both his cupped hands hard against the pirate's ears, rupturing his eardrums. The pressure on his throat disappeared as the pirate screamed – but Chase didn't let go, gripping the other man's head and yanking it sharply downwards.

On to the broken end of the support pole.

The sharp spike of metal pipe stabbed straight through the pirate's eye socket and punched into his skull.

'You'll need more than an eyepatch to cover that,' Chase told the dead man as he stood. The fire had spread to the walls and ceiling, the shack being consumed around him.

The only exit was one of the windows. He jumped through it, landing on the waterfront walkway.

Two men on the jetty saw him. Opened fire.

Chase ran past the burning shack as bullets ripped into it, blazing splinters spraying out in his wake. Ahead was the covered dock at the edge of the settlement. If he ran into the darkened jungle, an environment in which he had plenty of survival and combat experience, he should be able to escape the pirates – but that would give Latan a chance to escape and warn his paymaster . . .

The option was removed as someone fired at him from the treeline. The surviving pirates had spread out to form a perimeter, trapping him inside. Latan, thinking tactically. The pirate leader wasn't fleeing, but had organised his forces to catch the man who had attacked and humiliated him.

More shots, more shouts. They were closing, hounds after the fox.

Foxes. Bejo ran to him, frightened eyes wide. 'Mr Eddie!'

'When I said run, I meant *away*, not *towards*!'

'They found the boat!' Bejo gasped. More bullets seared past. The only place they could go was into the dock. Chase crashed through the double doors, slamming them shut behind himself and Bejo. The planks would provide no protection against bullets, but at least they would be out of sight for a few seconds.

Bejo turned in a rapid, panicked circle. 'Oh, very bad, very very bad! What do we do?'

The cruiser was tied up in front of them. Chase looked to its bow. The .50-cal—

He grabbed the handrail and jumped up. The ammo belt was still hanging from the machine gun, but it was almost spent, maybe twenty rounds remaining.

He heard movement outside, Latan bellowing instructions as the pirates ran to the doors.

Chase looked frantically round. There was a toolbox on the deck, a ball of twine amongst its contents. He snatched it up and tied the end to the Browning's trigger, then looped it round the rear grip before running to the side of the boat. 'Bejo! Get in the water!'

A splash from below – then the doors crashed open. Pirates rushed in, AKs at the ready . . . as Chase plunged into the water, pulling the twine as he fell.

The Browning swung towards the door and roared, eating through the remaining bullets in less than four seconds.

It was more than enough. The storm of lead swept across the dock, the force of the .50-cal at point-blank range literally explosive. The men were practically vaporised, limbs flying, heads exploding like watermelons stuffed with dynamite.

The machine gun ran dry, the last links of the spent ammo belt tinkling to the deck. The sound of chunks of the pirates hitting the ground was considerably wetter.

Chase surfaced, peering over the dock as a headless body slumped to its knees and keeled over in front of him. Bejo popped out of the water, gasping. He was surprised by the sudden lack of a threat. 'What happened to the pirates, Mr Eddie?'

'They're in pieces of eight.' Bejo was about to climb on to the dock when Chase stopped him. 'You don't want to look up there.' He pointed at the dock's open end. 'Swim out that way and wait for me.'

Climbing out, he took in the rest of the scattered, splattered bodies, feeling absolutely no sympathy or remorse – not after what the pirates had done to the people aboard the *Pianosa*. 'Amateurs.'

Someone was still alive, though, a quavering voice calling out. Latan. But his anger and arrogance was gone, replaced by shock. When Chase picked up a fallen AK-47, the pirate leader turned and fled.

Chase pursued. Latan was heading for the RIB. Chase went round the other side of the flaming kitchen on to the walkway, running to intercept him at the jetty—

A thick arm lashed out from round the corner of a shack, clotheslining Chase to the floor. The big, scar-faced man scowled down at him.

Chase raised the AK, but the pirate kicked it from his hand, then drove his heel down into the Englishman's stomach. Chase groaned. The man lifted his foot, about to stamp on his head, but Chase grabbed it and twisted hard to throw him off balance. The pirate staggered back into the shadowed, overgrown gap between the shacks, almost tripping over the tree stump.

Chase heard the whine of a starter motor. Latan had reached the RIB. Clutching his aching stomach, he got up, seeing the dull line of the steel cable he had earlier secured round the stump.

Scarface saw it too, and immediately realised what Chase had done. He shouted a warning, but the RIB's engine drowned him out. The cable was still slack: he tried to pull the looped end off the stump.

'No you fucking don't!' Chase wheezed, shoulder-barging him. The pirate fell over the stump and landed in the junk behind it. Chase moved to kick him in the head—

The man slashed at his leg with a jagged spike of rusty metal. The tip ripped through his jeans. Chase lurched away as the pirate stabbed again, barely escaping having the six-inch shard plunged into his thigh . . . but catching his heel on a root and falling backwards.

Still clutching the makeshift dagger, the pirate leapt up. The RIB surged away from the jetty. The cable flicked back and forth on the ground beside Chase, hissing metallically.

The pirate dived at him, the spike plunging down at his chest. Chase whipped up both hands to catch the man's wrist, stopping the bloodied point an inch above his heart. Face contorting, yellowed teeth bared, the pirate pushed harder, his weight forcing the trembling blade lower, lower . . .

Pressing into the skin, piercing it—

Whack!

'Get off him!' yelled Bejo, hitting the pirate across his back with a length of rotten wood, knocking him off Chase. The plank snapped in half, the blow only distracting rather than hurting the muscular pirate, but it was enough.

Chase grabbed the whipping cable and looped it round his neck.

Too late, Scarface realised what was about to happen—

The other end of the cable had been firmly fastened to the RIB's outboard. The retreating boat reached the limit of its length – and jerked to an abrupt stop as the line snapped taut. The loop round the pirate's neck closed to nothing in an instant, neatly snipping off his head. It thumped off the tree stump, expression frozen in shocked horror. The look on Bejo's face was almost identical.

'You okay?' Chase asked as he kicked the decapitated corpse away and stood. Bejo nodded wordlessly, mouth hanging open as Chase retrieved his AK and looked out to sea. The RIB's engine was still running, but the boat was drifting at the end of the cable, the propeller shaft broken. In the light of the burning hut, he could see that the sudden stop had caused Latan to slam head first into the boat's steering wheel . . . then bounce back into his seat, leaving most of his face behind. He wouldn't be giving warnings to anybody.

'Mr Eddie,' said Bejo in a strained voice. Chase turned – to find a gun pointing at his chest. The transsexual prostitute stood before him, shakily clutching a revolver in her uninjured hand. From the anguished rage on her face, her relationship with Latan had been more than merely that of hooker and client.

'Oh, bugger,' muttered Chase. Being gunned down by a ladyboy wasn't even remotely how he'd pictured himself going out. 'Okay, sorry about your boyfriend,' he said, stalling, 'but he *was* kind of a bad guy. Nice, er, lass like you could do a lot better . . .'

She spat something in Malay, thrusting the gun at his face. 'Pretty lady is very angry with you,' said Bejo, raising his hands.

'Yeah, I got the gist.' She thumbed back the hammer. 'All right, so you're a bit upset,' Chase continued, getting worried, 'but shooting me won't make you feel any better. Trust me, I've shot plenty of people, and—' His eyes flicked to something behind her, and he raised his eyebrows in surprise. 'Bloody hell, it's *Latan*! Latan's alive!'

It was a feeble gambit that would never have worked on anyone with training – but the young transsexual half turned to look, hope clear in her eyes. Chase could have simply whipped up his AK and shot her, but instead chose the less fatal option of kicking her in the groin. She crumpled to the ground and curled into a foetal position, moaning. Bejo winced. 'Not very nice thing to do, even to angry lady.'

Chase pulled the revolver from her hand and tossed it into the sea. 'If she really was a lady, that wouldn't have hurt so much.'

As Bejo worked out what he meant and regarded the fallen figure with surprise, Chase surveyed the village. The blaze had spread to the other shacks, including Latan's – which meant that not only had the money gone up in smoke, but so too had any clues there might have been amongst the pirate's belongings. There was nothing more to be found here.

He made sure there was a boat the two prostitutes could use to get off the island, and then he and Bejo returned to their craft. As he'd hoped, the two remaining lookouts had decided that *not* investigating the gunfire and burning buildings on the shore would be their best bet for a long and healthy life, leaving the way clear.

As Bejo guided the boat back out to sea, Chase wondered once more why the tablet Nina had found had caused so much death. With Latan gone, he had lost one lead – but at least now he knew the identity of his paymaster, Vogler, and the organisation for which he worked.

But what *was* the Covenant of Genesis?

8

New York City

Despite having slept as much as she could during the long flight, Nina's internal clock was still twelve hours out of synch when the UN jet landed, her body telling her it was evening while her native city was only just getting started for the day.

And it promised to be a long one.

Picked up by a driver and taken to the United Nations headquarters, she wondered what was in store. The expedition to the Java Sea had received the full backing of the IHA, and therefore the UN itself, and there was no possible way the pirate attack could have been predicted . . . but the fact remained that she had been in charge of an operation on which numerous people had died. Somebody would be held accountable, and in all probability it would be Nina herself.

What would happen next? She wasn't sure. Despite having been a part of the IHA since its founding almost three years earlier, this would be her first time at the focal point of an investigation. She had faced senior officials before, but they had been debriefings following operations with a successful conclusion: not the least of which was saving New York, and the UN itself, from nuclear destruction.

This time, though, the conclusion had been anything but successful.

She took an elevator up through the glass and steel slab of the Secretariat Building to the IHA's offices, her gloom weighing more heavily upon her with each passing floor. The moment she stepped out of the lift, it became clear the feeling was justified.

'What's going on?' she asked as she hurried through the security doors into the IHA's reception area, seeing the staff milling about in mixed states of confusion or anger.

'Dr Wilde!' said Lola Gianetti, leaving the reception desk to meet her. 'Oh, thank God you're back. I heard what happened – we all did. It's terrible!'

'I know, I know. But what's all this?' People were congregating outside the secure server room, one man repeatedly banging on the door.

'The server's gone down,' Lola told her. 'People have lost everything.'

'So why don't they use the backups?'

'No, I mean, they've lost *everything*,' Lola clarified ominously, leading Nina through the throng. 'Jerry and Al are in there trying to fix it.'

'Wait, they're both in?' That definitely meant something bad had happened; the IHA's lead computer technicians normally worked different shifts.

'Yeah, Al's been there all night, and he called Jerry in at about five a.m. Come on, coming through, move it!'

People peppered Nina with questions as she reached the door. 'Whoa, okay, hold it!' she said, raising her hands. 'I only just got here, and I probably know less about what's going on than you do. Everybody go back to your offices, have a coffee or whatever, and as soon as I know what's happening I'll let you know. Whatever it is, it's not going to be solved by standing in reception re-enacting the storming of the Bastille.'

'Nina, I've lost the entire Egyptian database!' protested the door-banger, a historian called Logan Berkeley. 'That's over half a terabyte of material, and they're saying it's completely gone!'

'It's *not* completely gone,' Nina insisted. 'Even if we lose the servers, and even if we lose the *backup* servers, we've still got the off-site backups.'

'Yes, but I've still lost—'

'A day's work, at most. It's a pain in the ass, I know, but it's not the end of the world, okay?' She swiped her ID card over the door's electronic lock.

Berkeley tried to follow her in. 'I still need to ask them how long—'

Nina stopped in the doorway. 'Hey, hey!' she snapped. 'This is a secure area – authorised personnel only. Go on, get your ass back outside. Shoo, shoo!' Berkeley reluctantly retreated.

She closed the door and slumped against it, taking a deep breath. 'Okay, guys. What's the bad news?'

The server room was a windowless space lined with rack-mounted computers and hard drives, forming a miniature maze round the central workstations. Jerry Wojciechowski, an over-weight middle-aged bearded man resembling a geek Santa, and Al Little, younger, thin almost to the point of emaciation and fuelled entirely by energy drinks, were working furiously at their computers. Al, even darker bags under his eyes than usual, looked up at her. 'We got burned, Nina. Some fucker hit us with a virus.'

She knew from the mere fact that he'd sworn in front of her that the situation was dire; normally, he only blurted out the first half-syllable before gulping it back and apologising. 'What've we lost?'

'Everything,' said Jerry. 'Literally. It was a worm – it scrubbed all the drives down to the bare metal.'

'And it nuked the backup RAIDs as well,' Al added. 'Even some of the desktops in the office.'

'How the hell did it do that?' asked Nina. 'I thought all this was impossible to hack!'

'So did we,' Jerry told her mournfully. 'We upgraded everything after that breach two years ago to beyond military grade. We're running the same operating system as the NSA. It's totally secure. In theory.'

'Except,' said Al, 'that this fucking thing came straight in without tripping a single warning. The only way it could do that is if whoever sent it had access codes for the entire system.' He let out an angry snort. 'We've lost absolutely everything since the last tape backup for off-site storage. And that was two days ago.'

'So, when you say *everything* . . . that includes emails and files uploaded to the shared server?'

Jerry nodded at her, and a sickening realisation struck Nina. The IHA's very existence was built on secrets: her discovery of Atlantis three years before had, to her horror, given a madman the key to creating a genetically engineered plague . . . which he had very nearly unleashed upon the world. To a certain extent, the IHA's mandate of finding and protecting other ancient wonders was a cover for a darker mission: to ensure that they didn't fall into the wrong hands.

But as the events leading to the death of Hector Amoros had proved, the wrong hands could at first appear to be the right ones. The IHA's search for Excalibur, the sword of King Arthur, had supposedly been undertaken so that Jack Mitchell, an agent of the US government's defence research agency DARPA, could stop the blade's unique properties from being used to create a new weapon that drew on the power of the very earth – but Mitchell had gone rogue, wanting that power for himself. He had been in charge of a black project so secret that neither DARPA nor the Pentagon knew of its existence, even as it threatened to plunge the world into war.

But if whoever sent the virus to wipe her pictures of the mysterious artefacts – and she was certain that that was the true objective, all the other destruction of data merely to cover the fact – was able to bypass the IHA's security . . . that meant they knew the IHA's true purpose. Knowledge supposed to be restricted to the highest levels of power.

Whatever was going on was bigger than she had thought. Bigger than she had *feared*.

She rushed out into reception—

To find herself face to face with an old enemy.

Not one who had ever tried to kill her, admittedly. But Nina still felt the brief, involuntary chill of unexpectedly encountering an adversary, long-forgotten loathing rushing back full-force. 'Professor Rothschild,' she began, before remembering that outside academia the hard-faced old woman no longer had any power over her. 'Maureen,' she said instead, informality used as a weapon to deny her status. 'What are you doing here?'

'Nina,' said Rothschild coldly, doing the same. The dislike was mutual. 'May I speak with you?'

Nina saw Lola hovering behind Rothschild's shoulder, worriedly mouthing something, but she couldn't tell what. 'I'm kinda busy right now, Maureen,' she said, wanting to get rid of her as quickly, and dismissively, as possible. 'Whatever it is, it'll have to wait. Lola can book you an appointment, but I wouldn't expect anything earlier than next week. I've got a lot of IHA business to take care of.' She turned and strode away to her office.

'Handling IHA business is no longer your concern, Nina,' Rothschild said.

There was a note almost of gloating in her voice that brought Nina to a stop. 'Excuse me?'

'Ah, Dr Wilde,' Lola said apologetically, hurriedly rounding Rothschild and presenting a sheet of paper to Nina. 'I meant to tell you when you got here, but there was so much else going on. Sorry.'

Nina quickly read the text, an official UN statement. *'What?'* she barked. Sensing an impending explosion, Lola retreated to her desk.

'As you see,' said Rothschild, now with nothing *but* gloating in her voice, 'the UN has just confirmed my appointment as the new Director of the IHA. I won't officially be taking up the post until the day after tomorrow, but I wanted to get things moving in the right direction. Which I've already seen is something that is badly needed. The agency has lacked a clearly defined vision and strong leadership since the death of Admiral Amoros – I'm here to put it back on the proper course.'

'Oh, you are, huh?' said Nina, angrily crunching the paper into a ball. 'I'm sure all your years of attacking any theory that's even slightly outside the historical orthodoxy makes you the *perfect* choice to run the IHA.'

Rothschild glanced at the entrance to one of the conference rooms. 'Perhaps we should continue this discussion in private?' she suggested condescendingly.

'I'm fine right here,' Nina snapped. 'And how did you get appointed in the first place? You weren't on the shortlist. You weren't even on the longlist – and if you had been, I would have crossed you off it!'

'Making decisions based on petty personal vendettas is precisely the kind of negative quality the IHA can do without in its senior staff,' Rothschild replied. 'And since you ask, I was quite surprised to be approached. But when the Senate recommends you to the UN, it would be foolish not to take the opportunity.'

'The *Senate*?' said Nina, stunned. 'But that's insane! Why would they do that?'

Rothschild's lips tightened. 'Perhaps because they were as tired as everyone else of the appointment process being deliberately dragged out so that the Interim Director could pursue her pet projects with the minimum of oversight?' Nina was so outraged by the accusation that she couldn't even form a response before the older woman spoke again. 'One of my first priorities will be a full review of all IHA projects that are not directly related to the agency's global security mandate. Anything that fails to meet strict cost-effectiveness criteria, or is based on shoddy mythological theory, will be terminated immediately.'

'Shoddy mythological theory like Atlantis, you mean?'

'My *other* immediate priority,' said Rothschild coldly, 'will be to begin a full inquiry into the utter disaster that was your Indonesian expedition. The loss of life is of course a tragedy, but there is also your arbitrary abandonment of the original excavation site, the financial irregularities—'

'What financial irregularities?' Nina demanded, furious.

'I mean the money you promised to the ship's captain for what I believe you described as "additional expenses". Just because part of the budget is labelled as discretionary doesn't mean it's your personal slush fund.'

'That's not what happened at all, and—'

'You'll be able to present your version of events to the inquiry,' said Rothschild. 'This catastrophe reflects extremely badly on both the IHA and the UN. The facts need to be determined, responsibility decided . . .'

'Blame apportioned?'

A faint smile curled Rothschild's thin lips. 'Indeed. If I were you, I would put all my efforts into as complete an account as possible of what happened in Indonesia. And I'd recommend that your . . . *friend* Mr Chase does the same. Where *is* Mr Chase, by the way?'

'Still over there,' said Nina, being purposefully vague to deny Rothschild any more ammunition.

'I see. After the UN organised a private flight for the specific purpose of bringing you both back to New York. I hope you're not going to add the cost of his scheduled ticket to the discretionary budget as well?'

'I wouldn't dream of it,' she growled. 'But if you'll excuse me, *Maureen*, I still have work to do.' She held up the crumpled ball of paper. 'This says you aren't officially the IHA's Director for two more days, which means I'm still in charge – and you've wasted enough of my time. Lola, I'll be in my office. Don't put any calls through unless they're urgent. Or Eddie.' She turned her back on Rothschild and entered her office, slamming the door behind her.

9

Nina arrived at the United Nations building having spent the night worrying about Chase. After her confrontation with Rothschild the previous day, she had checked her voicemail to find a message from him. Her relief at hearing his gruff Yorkshire tones was muted by the terseness of the message, which told her little other than that he was on his way back to New York – and that he was 'knackered'. She could tell he had been through a tense, dangerous time, but not knowing what had happened made her worried and frustrated.

Since then: nothing.

The first thing she did on arriving at the IHA was check if he had left any messages. He hadn't. She stared blankly out across Manhattan from her office window before sharply turning away. She knew she ought to continue working on her report, in preparation for the inquiry, but her concerns about Chase were too distracting. She needed something else to focus her mind.

Like the pictures on the memory card recovered from her stolen camera.

She copied the files to her new laptop, putting the card in her jacket pocket before opening all the high-resolution images. One in particular dominated her attention, a close-up of the clay tablet, showing the strange text in great detail. She steepled her fingers against her lips as she tried to make sense of it.

Nothing. A few characters – a triangle with what might be a tree or a flower above it; three horizontal lines one above the other, the topmost curling back round on itself – appeared more symbolic than others, reminding her of the stylised pictograms forming the basis of the ancient Chinese and Japanese writing systems, but what they actually represented remained a mystery. Others stood out from the elegant, curved characters making up the bulk of the script by their stark and angular nature, a number of V-shapes pointing in different directions, small dots between the lines, followed by blocks of tightly packed little marks . . .

What did they mean? What was the secret someone was willing to kill to protect?

She had no idea.

Keeping the picture open in the background, Nina reluctantly returned to her report, forcing herself to the recall the unpleasant details of the events aboard the *Pianosa*. But the image kept drawing her attention over the course of the morning. She almost closed it to remove the distraction, but something about it was sounding a bell in the back of her mind. Something familiar.

What, though? The text resembled no alphabet she knew.

So, if it wasn't an alphabet, then—

Nina jolted upright. The meaning of one particular type of symbol had just leapt out at her as if illuminated in neon. 'Why the hell didn't I see it before?' she cried. 'Dumbass!'

The blocks of closely spaced markings weren't letters. They were *numbers*. Atlantean numbers. They weren't quite the same as those she had seen on various Atlantean artefacts, but were close enough to be recognisable as from the same family: considering the apparent age of the tablet, an earlier version.

She grabbed a pen and paper and scribbled them down, converting them to the more familiar Atlantean equivalents, then rapidly performing the complex mental arithmetic to transform the unique numerical system into base ten. Each set turned out to be quite large, getting more so after each of the V-shapes to which they seemed linked. A record of something, then, a count. But what? It could be anything: numbers of people, distances, even the amount of fish caught by the boat in which it had been found.

But she had discovered *something*. The fact that it appeared to use a form of the Atlanteans' numerical system meant that whoever made the tablet was in some way connected to them, however far separated by geography and time. And if the Atlantean language could be deciphered, so could this.

Maybe it already *had* been deciphered. While Nina was necessarily well versed in ancient languages, it wasn't her specialty – she was an archaeologist, not a linguist. There were experts whose specialised knowledge far eclipsed her own. Her former mentor, Professor Jonathan Philby, had been one such expert, but he was no longer alive.

He'd had peers, though – well, more like rivals, she remembered. Even at the pinnacles of academia, one-upmanship was still a driving force. The names escaped her, but a few minutes' trawling through online archives for some of Philby's papers gave her one: Professor Gabriel Ribbsley of Cambridge. She vaguely recalled Philby once naming him as one of the world's top palaeo-linguists . . . after himself, of course. Judging from Ribbsley's own extensive list of published papers, that still appeared to be the case.

She got Lola to obtain his contact details, then sent a brief email of introduction, accompanied by the barest details of her reason for contacting him – considering recent events, it seemed prudent to keep the recovery of her pictures of the clay tablet as quiet as possible. That done, she forced herself to go back to work on the report. Her experience with tenured professors had taught her they would respond to external enquiries in their own time, and the more prestigious the university, the greater that time would be – all the way up to the heat-death of the entire universe.

So it came as a surprise when Ribbsley phoned less than twenty minutes later.

'This is, uh, quite an honour, Professor,' she said after introductions had been made.

'Oh, the honour is all mine, Dr Wilde,' Ribbsley replied. Nina couldn't quite place his accent; there was an undertone that made her think his upper-class English manner was a hard-won affectation. Southern African, perhaps? 'After all, it's not every day one gets a request for assistance from the discoverer of Atlantis, and so many other great treasures. I visited the tomb of Arthur at Glastonbury just a month or so ago, in fact. They needed help with the Latin inscriptions – makes one wonder what on earth they teach these days, if something that simple poses a problem! But the tomb itself was quite impressive, so well done, well done.'

'Thank you,' said Nina, picking up a less subtle undertone, this one decidedly patronising. 'But yes, I hope you'll be able to help me. If you can spare the time.'

'That depends what it is. I hope for the sake of your reputation it's not Latin!' He chuckled at his own joke.

'No, it's not,' Nina told him, not feeling obliged to join in. 'It's related to some Atlantean text that was recently discovered. I see from your list of papers in the *IJA* that you've done a considerable amount of work on the subject.'

'Well, I'd hardly be able to call myself the world's top palaeolinguist with a straight face if I hadn't!' He laughed self-congratulatingly again. 'Mind you, I had a head start over the likes of Frome and Tsen-Hu and that imbecile Lopez. Hector Amoros asked me to do some preliminary work before the discovery of Atlantis was even officially announced. Benefits of having friends in high places.'

'You knew Hector?'

'In passing, poor chap. He was only an amateur, of course, but a moderately capable one.'

Nina held back a sharp comment that Amoros had actually held a Master's degree in the subject. 'This text . . . while we've found some Atlantean characters in it, there are others we haven't been able to identify. I was hoping you might be able to look at it.'

'I'd be delighted. Just email me what you've got, and I'll cast an eye – or maybe even two! – over it as soon as I can.'

'That'd be a huge help, Professor. Thank you.'

'No problem at all, Dr Wilde. As I said, it's an honour. Not everybody gets to change how we look at human history, after all.'

Was there a hint of jealousy under his bonhomie? But still, she'd managed to get his help. Someone of Ribbsley's experience might spot in an instant something that had escaped her.

She certainly wasn't going to send him everything she had, though, or even any of the photographs. Instead, she called up the picture of the tablet and carefully copied a single section of text including one of the V-shapes and the Atlantean numerals on to a sheet of paper, which she scanned and emailed to Ribbsley.

Thinking it would take some time for him to work on the text, she returned to her report. Again, she was surprised to get a call in short order.

He was less ebullient, more focused. 'Dr Wilde. This text you sent me, it doesn't appear to be an accurate transcript. I don't see any Atlantean characters in it.'

Nina smiled; it was her turn to congratulate herself. 'Really, Professor? It only took me a few minutes to find them, and I didn't even know they were there.' An exaggeration, but it had at least taken his smugness down a notch. 'I could send you another scan, mark them for you . . .'

Ribbsley didn't sound amused. 'Or you could just show me. I assume you have a webcam.'

'Er . . . yeah.' It took a minute to set it up, but Nina was soon able to see him in a window. The overblown self-confidence in his voice was reflected in his face; he was looking down his nose at her, and she doubted it was solely because of the camera's position. A smirk seemed permanently etched round his mouth; his hair, though greying and thinning, had been carefully styled to conceal both facts. In the background, she could see several framed photographs of him, always white-suited, shaking hands with international dignitaries.

'There you are, Dr Wilde,' said Ribbsley. 'Now, if you'd care to point out what I've apparently been too blind to see?'

'Of course, Professor.' Nina held up the drawing. 'These characters here, the ones arranged in blocks?'

'What about them?'

'They're numbers. The forms are slightly different, but they're definitely related to the Atlantean numerical system.'

Whatever reaction she'd expected from Ribbsley, it hadn't been the stunned look he gave her, his confidence shaken – however briefly. 'Numbers?' he said, before repeating it more strongly. 'Numbers! Of course!' He examined his screen closely.

'You see? The symbols definitely correspond to each successive power of the Atlanteans' modified base eight system. They're arranged differently, but the actual symbols are close enough—'

'They are, they're very close,' Ribbsley interrupted. 'Numbers! I should have seen it at once . .' He seemed lost in thought for a moment before turning back to the camera. 'Unfortunately, Dr Wilde, apart from the numbers, you know exactly as much as I do about this text. The other characters are completely unfamiliar.' His gaze intensified. 'Where did you say it was obtained?'

'I didn't,' Nina told him pointedly. 'That's classified information, I'm afraid.'

He wasn't pleased at being denied, but quickly covered it. 'I understand. But without some hint of a point of origin, there's really nothing more I can do to help. Would that I had the time to scour through records of every extinct language in my library in search of similarities, but alas . . .'

'Alas, indeed,' said Nina, wishing she could reach through the screen to slap the smugness off his face. 'Still, thank you for your help anyway, Professor.'

'Not at all. Again, an honour to speak to you. We really must meet in person sometime – I'm sure we'd have much to discuss. Goodbye.'

'Good—' Nina said, but Ribbsley had already terminated the link. 'Bye, jerk,' she added quietly.

She glanced at her laptop's clock. Lunchtime. She'd been so occupied with work that she hadn't realised she was hungry, but now she couldn't deny it. Time to go and find something to eat.

Before she did, though, she called Chase's cell phone again. Nothing. Still unobtainable.

Where the hell was he?

Chase trudged blearily through the airport gate. Unable to get a direct flight back to New York at short notice, he had been forced to cobble together an ad hoc itinerary, from Jakarta to Singapore, then on to Delhi, and – after a long wait for a connecting flight – to his current location, Dubai. He had another lengthy stopover before he could fly on to Paris, but at least from there it would be the last leg of his journey to New York.

He checked his watch. Midnight in Dubai, four p.m. in New York. He needed to talk to Nina; he had left a brief message on her office voicemail before he left Singapore to assure her that he was all right, but was looking forward to a longer conversation. First things first, though. Make his way to the departure area, check in, then find a way to kill time until the Paris flight boarded . . .

If he reached it. His tiredness vanished instantly, replaced by wariness, as he realised he was being watched. An Arab man in the uniform of the airport police stood nearby, accompanied by three large white guys in dark suits and mirrored sunglasses . . . and the mirrorshades were all pointing his way. One of the trio held up a sheet of paper as if comparing the picture on it to Chase's face, then nodded.

That didn't look good.

They approached him, the officer holding up a hand. 'Mr . . . Chase?'

'That's right.' The three men stepped forward, moving to surround him.

'These men would like to talk to you.'

Chase eyed them, seeing himself reflected sixfold in the lenses. 'You're not going to make me miss my flight, are you, lads? It cost me a bloody fortune.'

'You'll be taking a different flight, Mr Chase,' said one of the men. His accent was American.

'Yeah? Where to?'

The man's mouth was a cold, hard line. 'Guantánamo Bay.'

'Any word from Eddie?'

Nina looked up from her work to see Lola in the office doorway, a cup of coffee in her hand. 'No, not yet,' she said gloomily. She glanced at the windows to see with surprise that it was dark. 'Whoa! What happened to the afternoon?'

The big-haired blonde smiled and came to her desk. 'You were zoned out again. I wish I could do that – it must be great to be able to concentrate totally on one thing. I guess that explains why I'm the receptionist and you're the boss!'

'Until tomorrow.'

Lola handed her the coffee; Nina nodded in thanks. 'That's why I'm still here so late – Professor Rothschild sent me a big long list of admin stuff she wants to see tomorrow, so I've been collating it all. Do I still call her "Professor" if she's not actually teaching, by the way?'

'I have a feeling she'll insist on it,' Nina told her, sipping the coffee.

'Yeah, I kinda got that impression. To be honest, I'm . . .' She lowered her voice. 'I'm not looking forward to her taking over.'

Nina laughed sarcastically. 'Tell me about it.'

'Yeah. But I don't care what she says, you did just as good a job at running the IHA as Admiral Amoros.'

That went some small way towards improving Nina's mood. 'Thanks,' she said with a smile.

'Well, you looked like you needed it. And it's my job to make sure you get what you need, after all!' They shared an appreciative moment, then Lola regarded the printouts and documents on Nina's desk. 'Do you know how much longer you'll be working?'

'I'll be a while. You go home, I'll lock up. Or is Al still here?'

'No, he went home. I *made* him go home. He was here all last night fixing the servers – he would have slept in the computer room if I hadn't stood in the doorway and not let him back in.'

'That sounds like Al all right,' Nina said. 'But don't wait around for me.'

'Okay.' Lola returned to the door, then looked back. 'Dr Wilde . . . don't worry about tomorrow. I'm sure everything'll be fine. And I'm sure Eddie'll be fine too.'

'I hope so. Thanks, Lola.'

'No problem.' She left, heading back to reception.

Nina took another sip of coffee, then switched on her desk lamp. Lola was right – she really *had* zoned out, fixated on the task at hand. Probably, she mused ruefully, so that she wouldn't have to think about the two things currently worrying her: the future of her career once Rothschild took charge of the IHA, and, more important, what had happened to Chase.

She needed a break. Of course, she thought with amused self-awareness, her idea of a break wasn't the same as other people's. Forget going for a walk or having a snack; switching to a different kind of work was just as good as a rest.

She brought the picture of the clay tablet back up, absently toying with the pendant hanging from her neck, a scrap of an ancient Atlantean artefact turned good-luck charm, as she scrutinised different sections of the text for several minutes before finally leaning back. Maybe she was going about this in the wrong way. Rather than trying to translate the text, she might have more luck at figuring out the tablet's *purpose*.

She closed her eyes, posing questions to herself. Why had it been made in the first place? To convey information, obviously. What kind of information? Something complex enough to need a permanent written record. Where was it found? In a boat.

Okay, so what kind of complex written information would you normally find in a boat?

Nina suddenly clutched her pendant, eyes wide. She knew what the tablet was.

She grabbed a pen, drawing each of the V-shapes from the photograph. Even though they faced in different directions, each formed a forty-five degree angle.

Like the shapes formed by the eight main points of a compass. The symbols were *directions*. Her pendant had been the subconscious clue, the orichalcum fragment once a part of an ancient Atlantean navigational instrument: a sextant. And the faint

120

markings upon it were subdivisions, more accurate measurements.

Like the dots within the V-shapes. The lines gave the general heading, the dots a more precise bearing. The tablet was a *chart*: a navigational map for the mysterious sailors of over a hundred millennia earlier . . .

'Damn,' Nina whispered. If the start point was the Java Sea excavation site, then the end could be another settlement. If she could locate that . . .

Her enthusiasm rapidly faded. For one thing, she still had no idea of the meaning of the rest of the text. For another, it was unlikely the IHA would be willing to let her embark upon another expedition – even more so with Rothschild in charge.

But at least she'd discovered *something* . . .

A faint sound outside the office caught her attention. She looked up at the doorway. 'Lola?' No answer, though she heard a door closing. Lola must have just left. She shrugged and turned her attention back to the image on the monitor.

If it was a navigational chart, the symbolic characters could represent landmarks. Set sail in the indicated direction until you reached a particular landmark, then change course and head to the next. Assuming the excavation site was the start, then a traveller following the chart would first go roughly southwest, southwest again on a slightly different bearing to the triangle/tree/whatever symbol, another short stint in a similar direction, then an abrupt change to head southeast for a long distance. She needed a map . . .

Movement at her door. She glanced up, expecting to see Lola.

Instead, she saw a man with a knife.

A *bloodied* knife.

Nina jumped from her chair and snatched up her phone to call for security. But the swarthy, black-haired intruder reached her desk before she punched in the first digit, his glistening blade slashing through the cord. The phone went dead.

She threw the receiver at him. The man easily batted it aside and rounded the desk, coming for her. She ran the other way and raced for the door – but he was faster, tackling her before she reached it.

'Help!' she screamed at the corridor beyond the doorway. No answer but silence. 'Help me!'

He slammed her face first against the floor. Dazed, nose bleeding, Nina was unable to resist as he seized her by her ponytail and hauled her upright. He gripped her tightly round the waist from behind; a moment later, the black blade was at her throat.

He dragged her back across the room. She tried to pull the knife away, hacking at his shins with one heel. He twisted and smashed her head and shoulder against the window. The glass cracked. As Nina cried out, he kicked the chair aside and shoved her against the desk. 'The computer,' he hissed. She couldn't place the accent. 'Wipe the drive. Use a secure delete, blank it.'

'Who are you?' Nina whispered.

In response, the blade's edge pushed deeper. 'Wipe the computer! Trash everything!'

Terrified, she obeyed, then moved the cursor to the 'Secure Empty Trash' menu option. She hesitated; he jerked the knife to one side. A trickle of hot blood ran down her neck. 'Do it!'

She did. A warning message popped up: was she sure? The knife slid back, a lethal prompt. Hand shaking, she tapped the return key. A progress bar slowly filled up as the files were overwritten. Gone for ever.

The pressure on her neck didn't slacken. 'The photos weren't on the IHA servers,' her attacker said. 'How did you put them on your computer?'

Nina didn't answer immediately, as much out of fear as reluctance. He shoved her harder against the desk, making the lamp shake. 'Memory card,' she told him.

'Where?'

'In my jacket.' She gestured at the chair. Her jacket was hung over its back.

The man turned his head to look, the blade lifting slightly—

Nina snatched up the lamp and smashed the bulb in his face.

He lurched backwards, one elbow hitting the window and widening the cracks. Nina spun and struck again, trying to bash the lamp's heavy base against his skull, but his other arm came up to deflect it. She jumped back as he slashed at her with the knife – and hacked straight through the power cord, its severed end sparking as it hit the floor. The black blade was carbon fibre, non-conductive. Invisible to the UN's metal detectors.

Nina dropped the lamp and threw herself across her desk. Papers scattered, the laptop's hinge cracking under her. Her sleeve ripped as the tip of the blade whistled past, cutting a shallow gash in her bicep before stabbing into the wooden desktop.

She lashed out with one foot, catching him hard in the chest and sending him staggering backwards. Rolling off the desk, she ran for the door. 'Help! Anyone!'

Nobody in the corridor. She rushed down it, heading for reception and the elevators beyond. But the security doors between reception and the elevators, installed to safeguard the IHA's classified materials, were closed. Locked, a red LED confirming that she was trapped.

And her keys were in her jacket.

Nina changed direction, going to Lola's desk. She could call security, raise the alarm—

She recoiled as she saw Lola slumped behind the desk, arms clenched to her stomach.

Blood was pooled beneath her.

Nina fought down nausea to pick up the phone – only to find that the coiled cord had been cut, bloody fingerprints smeared over the plastic. Lola must have tried to call for help . . . and paid the price.

The man barrelled from her office and charged down the corridor towards her.

No way out, except—

Clutching her ID badge, Nina ran to the server room. She swiped the badge at the reader as she grabbed the handle. The door rattled against the frame.

Too fast. The lock hadn't had time to disengage before she tried to open it. The killer was sprinting straight at her. Another swipe. Come *on*—

A click. The handle moved. Nina shoved the door open and threw herself inside, spinning round to slam it shut. Without an ID card, the man wouldn't be able to get into the server room – if she could close the door in time . . .

The door banged. But not against its frame.

Nina shoved it again. It flexed, but still wouldn't close. 'Shit!' She looked down. The toe of a combat boot was wedged in the gap.

She threw herself against the door, trying to force it shut. But she knew it was futile. He was much bigger than her, sheer weight and brute force in his favour—

A *whump* as he threw himself against the other side, knocking her backwards. She tried to push back, but the nearest server rack was slightly too far away for her to brace her feet against it. Another blow. Nina's soles squeaked over the linoleum floor as she fought for grip, but she couldn't hold her position. One more attack, and he would be through . . .

She jumped away just as he lunged again. The door flew open, the intruder stumbling as he burst into the room – but Nina tripped too, the swinging door catching her and sending her tumbling into the server racks. She tried to pull herself up, her fingers finding purchase on the recessed handle of one of the drawer-like server blades above her.

The man was quicker to recover. He saw Nina on the floor and plunged the knife at her chest—

She yanked the server out of the rack. There was a splintering crack as the carbon fibre knife stabbed through the circuit board just above her head. The man tried to pull it out, but it was stuck, the server rattling in its frame.

Nina kicked at his knees, rolled to her feet and ran down the length of the server room. There was only one exit, the door through which she had entered. Even if she rounded the central island of workstations, her attacker would still reach it before her.

Unless he couldn't see her.

There was a red fire alarm box on the back wall. She yanked its plastic handle, taking a deep breath. A whooping klaxon sounded, which would summon help – but it was the fire suppression system itself that could give her a chance to escape.

In a closed, windowless room inside a skyscraper, filled with banks of computers holding vital classified data, water was not an option as an extinguisher – it could potentially cause even more damage than a fire. Instead, valve heads in the ceiling spewed out powerful jets of halotron gas, a swirling white cloud rapidly filling the space.

And hiding Nina.

One hand over her nose and mouth, eyes half shut as the dense mist enveloped her, she ducked and moved as quickly as she could round the central workstations. The man coughed violently, caught unawares by the cold, choking vapours. He was still by the open server rack, trying to retrieve his knife. If she reached the door quickly enough, she could get out before he recovered.

If she could *find* the door. The fog was already so thick that she couldn't even see an arm's length ahead, the overhead lights just a faint, diffuse glow – and the red-lit exit sign above the door completely obscured. She groped blindly through the haze. The room wasn't that big – surely it couldn't be much further—

She bumped into a chair, which knocked against one of the desks. Something fell over, plastic clattering.

The coughing stopped. He knew where she was.

Nina sprang upright, no longer caring about stealth as she ploughed forward. One shin barked against something hard-edged; she ignored the pain, staggering on until her hand closed round the corner of a desk. The door could only be a few feet away. She looked up and saw a faint red glow. The exit sign. She rushed to it, outstretched hands finding the door.

Where was the handle, the *handle*—

There!

She rushed through into suddenly clear air. The security doors were still sealed; the fire marshals hadn't had enough time to respond. She slammed the door, muffling the hiss of the gas jets, and ran for her office. Her attacker would hopefully lose several precious seconds trying to reach the exit. If she could find her keys and get back to the security doors before he emerged, she could take the stairs until she met the first responders coming up them—

She heard the hiss of gas over the fire alarm as she reached her office. He had opened the door – and would be coming after her.

Could she barricade herself in her office's private bathroom? Maybe, but the door had only a simple bolt – a couple of good kicks would break it, and then she would be trapped in an even more confined space.

Phone—

Not her desk phone, its cable severed, but her cell. It had been on her desk before the fight – where was it now? She searched for it amongst the scattered papers. *There* – below the windows. If she could hold him off in the bathroom even briefly, the knowledge that she had called for help might force him to retreat before the building's exits were secured . . .

She grabbed the phone and turned to run for the bathroom—

He was in the office.

No way she could reach the door. She backed up as he advanced. He no longer had the knife, but his fists were raised, ready to beat her, grab her, choke her.

Nina pulled her chair between them in a last-ditch attempt to block him. The man kicked it forcefully back into her. She thumped against the desk – and he grabbed her by the throat, thumbs gouging hard into her windpipe as he forced her to the floor.

She tried to scratch at his eyes, but his arms were longer than hers, her nails falling just short. His grip tightened. She clawed at his arms, his chest, but to no avail. The pain rose as she struggled to breathe, hands flailing over the carpet, the spilled papers—

Electrical flex—

With the last of her strength, Nina jammed the severed power cord into his eye.

There was a harsh electrical spark *inside* his eye socket – and the man sprang upright, reeling back against the window. The cracked glass broke, wind gusting through the jagged hole. He clutched his face, smoke coiling out from beneath his hands.

Nina had felt some of the electric shock, but only a fraction of what the assassin had experienced. Still choking, she dragged herself up on the desk and looked round. He stared back – with only one eye, the other an oozing burnt hole. Agony was overcome by pure fury as he saw her—

With a yell of equal rage, Nina snatched up her battered laptop and swung it at his head.

Keys scattered as the machine smashed in his face, knocking him into the window . . .

Which gave way.

He toppled backwards over the sill and plunged screaming for over twenty storeys in a shower of glass – and hit the pointed top of a flagpole in the plaza below. The gilded wooden spike punched straight through his ribcage, his body slowly slithering down the pole on a trail of blood.

Bruised and bleeding, Nina staggered back to reception, where she held Lola until the fire marshals finally arrived.

10

Cuba

The American naval base at Guantánamo Bay, Cuba, was a freak of international diplomacy. The land on which it stood granted in perpetual lease to the United States by a treaty with the then US-friendly republic in 1903, the base became a huge thorn in the side of the Castro regime following the revolution of 1959. But Cuba lacked the firepower to retake it by force or the legal authority to evict the occupants under international treaty law, so eventually settled for surrounding the base with cacti and landmines and trying to ignore its very existence. This suited the United States just fine, so for decades the name 'Guantánamo Bay' remained nothing more than a curious footnote for military and political historians.

Until 2002, when it became infamous around the entire world.

Chase had been to Cuba before, albeit undercover, during his military career, and had even very briefly passed through the US naval base between legs of a long flight. But following the tedious journey from Dubai, it wasn't to the base proper that he was taken by the grim, taciturn men who had intercepted him.

It was to the notorious military prison.

An escort of armed Marines met their unmarked plane when it

landed. Chase and the three men were put aboard a bus and driven round the ragged-edged bay, passing through ring after ring of high fences and security checkpoints to an isolated group of buildings near the island's southern coast.

It was the most secure, most secretive, and most feared part of the entire facility, remaining active even when the rest of the detention centre had been closed down. Its only official name was nondescript, uninformative, yet somehow chilling. *Camp* 7.

The bus stopped outside a windowless single-storey structure. More Marines were waiting, and Chase and the suited trio were again surrounded by armed men before being taken into the building. It seemed to be the camp's administrative centre, the small reception area dominated by warning notices and security cameras. A soldier sat in a booth behind a sheet of armoured glass, a metal door beside it. One of the men with Chase held up an ID badge; the soldier nodded and pushed a button. The door slid open.

Chase was led through and marched down a corridor to a door. 'Room 101, is it?' he asked. None of the mirror-shaded agents got the joke. 'Oh well. You want me to go in?'

He took it from the lack of an answer that they did; unsure what to expect, he turned the handle and stepped through.

The room beyond was a small office, as grimly bland as the rest of the building. There was another door in the back wall, but Chase was for now only interested in the man behind the desk beside it. Black, in his fifties, close-cropped hair greying at the temples. Like the Marines he wore a tan utility uniform with a digital camouflage pattern, but his rank insignia revealed him to be an officer: a colonel. The nametape on his chest read 'Morris'.

The colonel didn't bother glancing up from the document he was reading as Chase entered, which annoyed him. 'Ay up,' he said loudly. 'Well, I'm here. You going to bother telling me why?'

Morris finally looked at him. 'Mr Chase?'

'Yes?'

'Mr Edward Chase?'

Chase gave him a toothy grin. 'You'd look a bit of a tit if I said "No, *Edgar* Chase", wouldn't you?'

'Are you Edward J. Chase?' Morris impatiently asked.

'Yeah, you got me. So now what? Fitting for an orange jumpsuit?'

'I'm afraid I have some bad news, Mr Chase.' Chase felt a jab of fear and worry. Had something happened to Nina? But that didn't make sense – why would they bring him to Cuba?

But there *was* someone else he knew in Cuba – more specifically, in Guantánamo Bay . . .

Morris stood. 'It's about your ex-wife,' he said, confirming Chase's thought.

'Sophia?'

'Yes. I regret to inform you that Sophia Blackwood is dead.'

It took Chase a moment to respond, his feelings very mixed. 'Can't say I'm going to break down in floods of tears,' he said, sarcastic callousness covering his other emotions. 'She *did* try to kill me. And nuke New York.'

'Which is why she was here. As the country's biggest terror suspect since 9/11, she couldn't be kept in the regular prison system. The other inmates would have killed her before the trial.'

'So what happened?'

'See for yourself.' Morris went through the door at the office's rear. Following him, Chase found himself in a small white-tiled morgue, stainless steel fixtures gleaming dully under the bright overhead lights.

On a table lay a body, covered by a sheet.

'She tried to grab the sidearm from one of the Marine guards,' said Morris, standing beside the head of the supine figure. 'He was forced to fire to protect himself and others. The bullet hit her in the face at point-blank range.' He took hold of one end of the sheet. 'I should warn you that the damage was considerable.'

'I've seen headshots before,' Chase told him. But even he was caught off guard as Morris gently pulled back the sheet from her face – not so much at the carnage that was revealed, but by the knowledge that it had been inflicted upon someone he had once been very close to. Had *loved*.

Jaw tightening, he stepped closer. The entry wound was an inch below the outer corner of her right eye, the skin around the blood-encrusted hole discoloured and burned by muzzle flame at extremely close range. The right eye was missing, the eyelids sunken deep into the socket. The eyeball had probably been torn apart by splinters from the shattered cheekbone.

As for the other side of her face . . . most of it was gone.

He had seen similarly horrific wounds before. The bullet would have flattened and tumbled after the initial impact, breaking apart as it tore through the cheekbone and exploding outwards from the other side of her skull. Half the upper jaw was gone, the remains of the top lip hanging limply into a gaping dark space beneath. The left eye socket was nothing but a shredded mess.

He also knew from the bullet's path, through her face rather than into her brain, that she had probably remained alive for several minutes afterwards.

'Cover her,' he said, voice flat. Morris lowered the sheet over the dark-haired figure. Chase regarded the slim shape for a long moment, then turned to the officer. 'Why'd you bring me all the way here to see that? In fact, why'd you bring me here at all? We got divorced five years ago – I'm not her next of kin.'

'Actually, you are.' On Chase's confused look, Morris led him back into the office. 'Since she had no immediate family, she listed you as her sole beneficiary.'

'Wait, she named me in her *will*?' Chase said in disbelief. 'Why the hell would she do that?'

'I have no idea. All I know is that she did, which is why you were brought here – to take possession of her belongings and the relevant paperwork.' He handed Chase a folder.

He opened it. The first item was indeed a will – he recognised Sophia's signature immediately. And it did name him as both executor and sole beneficiary. 'Hang on a minute,' he said, puzzled, leafing through the rest of the documents, 'does this mean I'm suddenly a billionaire? 'Cause Sophia was married to two really rich blokes, and after they died – I mean, after she killed them – she inherited all their money . . .'

Morris revealed a small hint of emotion, a faint smile. 'Unfortunately not. As a terror suspect, all her financial assets were frozen when she was charged. Whether they're ever freed or not is up to the Supreme Court. But I wouldn't hold your breath.'

'Yeah, I thought so.' The majority of the other papers detailed the various frozen bank accounts around the globe. 'Liechtenstein, the Caymans, Hong Kong . . . it's like an offshore banking world tour.' He spotted a Zürich bank address on one sheet with the number of a deposit box. 'Didn't know the Swiss gave out people's bank details, though. Thought secrecy was their big selling point.'

'They do when terrorists are involved. Like your ex-wife.'

Chase closed the folder. 'You know, you could have told me what this was about in Dubai, instead of the whole bloody cloak and dagger business.'

'Not my decision,' Morris said. 'But they wanted you to see the body and collect her belongings personally. As well as this.' He gave another document to Chase.

'What's that?'

'Death certificate. You'll need it to make any claims concerning frozen assets.'

Chase looked at the certificate, then placed it in the folder. 'Somehow, I don't think it'd be worth the effort.' He glanced back at the morgue. 'What're you going to do with . . .' he almost said 'the body', but instead finished, 'her?'

'That's up to you.'

'Cremate her,' Chase decided.

Morris nodded. 'And the remains?'

'I'm not taking them with me. What would I do, stick the urn on a shelf as a conversation piece? Just . . .' He shook his head, already ashamed of the tasteless remark. 'Just scatter them in the sea.'

'And a service?'

'She wasn't religious. Just say that . . .' He hesitated, trying to find the right words. 'That whatever it was that went wrong, that made her do all those things, it's over now. And that I'll remember her as the person she was when we first met, not the one she turned into.'

'I'll make sure of it,' said Morris quietly.

'Okay, so what now?' Chase asked after signing a release form. 'How do I get back to New York?'

'I assume the plane that brought you here will fly you on.'

'It'd bloody well better,' he growled. 'I'm not paying for *another* flight . . .'

11

New York City

Nina took a deep breath as she paused at the door. As Rothschild had promised – or threatened – one of the first items on her agenda as the newly appointed Director of the IHA was to hold a formal inquiry into the events in Indonesia. But it had already expanded to cover what had happened the previous evening in the United Nations' own headquarters. And Nina suspected that no matter what she said, Rothschild would find a way to make it reflect badly upon her.

At least she had heard from Chase, however briefly. But she hadn't understood what had happened to him – all he'd said was that he was flying back to New York from Cuba. *Cuba?* But the important thing was that he was coming home.

Not in time to attend the inquiry, though. Another black mark against her in Rothschild's book.

Steeling herself, adjusting her jacket, she entered the room.

The members of the inquiry were already present: three senior UN officials, a representative from the US State Department, and Rothschild. Once the proceedings got under way, it didn't take long before Nina started to feel that she was on trial . . . with

Rothschild as both prosecutor and judge.

'So you say you have absolutely no idea of the identity of the man who attacked you last night?' the elderly professor asked, eyes narrowing.

Nina held in her exasperation. She had already given a statement to the FBI, which in cases of serious crimes was granted jurisdiction within United Nations territory, and she knew full well that Rothschild had a copy. 'As I'm sure you read in my statement,' she answered, 'no, I did *not* know his identity. Just as I did *not* know the identity of the pirates who attacked the *Pianosa*, or who hired them. I only know *why* they attacked, which was to steal the artefact the expedition discovered.'

'But why would they do that?' one of the UN officials asked. 'What was so special about it?'

'I don't know. All I know is that it had writing on it in an unknown language. Unknown to me, I mean. Somebody obviously recognised it.'

The State Department representative flicked through his papers. 'Dr Wilde, how could these, ah, conspirators have seen the artefact? You say that only a few of the expedition members saw it after it was brought to the ship.'

'I uploaded digital photos of the artefact to the IHA via satellite link. By the time I got back to New York, all the data on the server had been erased by a virus – including the photos. I don't believe for one moment that the timing was a coincidence. Someone knew the images were there, and planted the virus to destroy them – and used top-level access codes to do so.'

Rothschild's already thin lips tightened still further. 'Are you accusing someone within the IHA of planting the virus?'

'No, because there isn't anybody specific I *can* accuse. But the only way anybody outside the *Pianosa* could have known about the artefact is if they saw the photos I uploaded to the server. Once they realised what we'd found, they arranged for the pirates to steal the artefact itself, and at the same time wiped the IHA's servers with the virus. If Eddie and I hadn't survived, nobody at the IHA would even have known the artefact existed, because all evidence of its discovery would have been destroyed. But once they found out I had another copy of the photos, the *conspirators*,' she said with a slightly mocking nod towards the man from the State Department, 'sent a man to kill me and erase the copies. The same guy who ended up as a new flag in United Nations Plaza.'

'These copies,' the other UN official said, 'where did you get them? I thought the pirates destroyed all your records of the expedition.'

'Eddie – Mr Chase – recovered a camera's memory card from the pirates. I brought it back to the UN so I could continue analysing the artefact.'

Rothschild leaned forward with the coldly pleased air of someone who had just successfully lured an animal into a trap. 'And as a result, a man was killed right here in the Secretariat Building and a United Nations employee was severely injured.'

'And I was attacked in my own office!' Nina angrily reminded her, pointing at the cuts and grazes on her face. 'Let's not forget that part, huh? Has there been any news on Lola's condition, by the way?'

'Ms Gianetti is in a critical but stable condition,' said Rothschild.

Nina sighed in relief. 'Oh, thank God. I really thought she was going to die.'

'That does seem to happen to people around you rather a lot, doesn't it?' Rothschild's tone grew harder. 'I've been reviewing your official reports on your IHA operations. The *Pianosa* expedition, Bill Raynes's excavation team at Atlantis, Dr Lamb in England, two of the IHA's own non-executive directors, Jack Mitchell, Hector Amoros himself . . . all dead. To say nothing of the shocking number of people who seem to have died as,' her mouth twisted in distaste, 'collateral damage.'

'Jack Mitchell was a criminal and a traitor.'

'And that entitles you to appoint yourself judge, jury and executioner?'

'He was trying to kill us! Just like the guy last night. If I hadn't stopped him, Lola would be dead by now, and so would I.' She gave Rothschild a nasty look. 'Which would make things a lot easier for you, wouldn't it?'

'I'm not sure I like your tone, Ms Wilde,' said Rothschild.

'I don't really care, *Mrs* Rothschild,' Nina replied, throwing the subtle insult back at her. 'If I'd died, your job here would be much simpler, because you wouldn't have to ask the obvious question about what happened last night.'

'Which is?' said the first UN official.

'Which is, how did the man who attacked me know I had the photos? Only Eddie and I knew about the memory card. And I didn't put the pictures on the server – I copied them straight to my laptop, so again there was no way for anyone to know about them. Only one other person in the entire world knew they existed . . . Gabriel Ribbsley.'

Rothschild sat ramrod-straight. 'Dr Wilde,' she said, voice clipped, 'are you accusing *Professor Gabriel Ribbsley* of being involved in this conspiracy?'

'I guess I am,' Nina shot back. 'Personal friend of yours, is he?'

'As a matter of fact, he is. But that's hardly relevant.' She banged a hand on the desk. 'You cannot sit here and accuse one of the world's leading academics of being an accessory to attempted murder! The idea . . . it's absolutely outrageous!'

'Well, why don't we give him a call, see if he's got a good explanation for why a man tried to kill me just hours after I spoke to him?'

'Absolutely not.' Her hand banged down again. 'Dr Wilde, this inquiry is not a criminal investigation – if you have any wild accusations to make, you should make them to the FBI.'

'Oh, I already have, don't worry,' said Nina coldly.

'But this inquiry *is* here to investigate the catastrophe of the Indonesian expedition, and, in my view, your entire career at the IHA. Regardless of the eventual outcomes, your previous operations establish a clear pattern of behaviour – one of reckless irresponsibility, a callous disregard for the lives of others and an utterly cavalier attitude towards the exploration of priceless historical sites.'

Nina was outraged. *'What?* Now wait a minute—'

'No, *you* wait, Dr Wilde,' Rothschild said, raising her voice as she held up a sheaf of papers. 'These are your own accounts of your previous expeditions, and they make for alarming reading. You claim to be a scientist, but there's precious little scientific investigation – just brute force and destruction. It's archaeology by bulldozer – no, worse than that, archaeology by *explosive*. For everything you've discovered, much more has been lost for ever because of the violence you seem to attract.'

'Well,' Nina said through her teeth, 'maybe the next time some asshole shoots at me, I should let him hit me so the bullets don't chip anything!'

'Which is exactly my point. There shouldn't *be* people shooting at you. You are not an archaeologist, Dr Wilde. You are a glory hunter, a grave robber, using – no, *abusing* – your position at the IHA to embark on your own personal quests, without caring about the consequences. Wherever you go, chaos follows . . . and people die. Well, no more. This is something the IHA is no longer willing to tolerate.'

'Meaning what?'

'Meaning that, until a determination of your degree of culpability in the deaths of the expedition members can be made, as the Director of the International Heritage Agency I am suspending you from your post, without pay, effective immediately. The same goes for Mr Chase.'

Nina gaped silently at her for a moment before rage finally pushed the words from her mouth. 'This is bullshit!' she cried. 'You don't have that authority! Not without a review by the UN . . .' She realised that both the UN officials now looked uncomfortable. 'Son of a bitch,' she muttered under her breath, before raising her voice again. 'You'd already decided how this was going to end before I even walked in the room!'

'The damage to the IHA, and to the United Nations, needed to be addressed as quickly as possible,' one of the officials said feebly.

She glared at him. 'Oh, so I get sacrificed on the altar of public relations, do I?'

The other official spoke up. 'When the investigation clears you, you'll be reinstated, of course.'

'*If* the investigation clears you,' Rothschild countered.

'I'm sure it'll be completely impartial and unbiased,' said Nina bitterly. She stood. 'Well, if I'm suspended, there's no point my hanging around here, is there?'

'There is one more thing, Dr Wilde,' Rothschild said. 'The memory card, the one with the pictures of the artefact . . . what happened to it?'

'It got wiped,' Nina answered.

'So there are no more pictures of the artefact?'

'No.'

'I see.' Rothschild pursed her lips. 'Let us hope that means an end to the violence, then.'

'Yeah,' said Nina. 'Let us hope.'

She turned away and left the room, closing the door behind her . . . then reached up to feel the memory card, still in her jacket pocket.

★

Still filled with anger, Nina gathered her possessions from her office, slamming books and journals and mementos of her past adventures into a cardboard box.

She paused as she picked up one particular souvenir – a framed photograph of herself at the White House, receiving the Presidential Medal of Freedom from President Victor Dalton for her part in saving New York from nuclear annihilation.

Dalton . . .

Following the FBI's examination of the room, the telephone had been replaced along with the broken window. Nina hesitated, then: 'What the hell.' She called Lola's replacement and asked to be put through to the President.

'Of . . . the United States?' came the uncertain reply.

'That's the one.'

It was a long shot; Nina had no idea if Dalton were even currently in Washington, and was sure he had an infinite number of other concerns. But she figured that she was owed a favour – at the very least, he could return her call.

The response was not immediate, giving her time to finish collecting her belongings. But eventually, the phone rang. 'Hello?'

'Dr Wilde?' said a woman. 'Please hold for the President.'

Another pause, then a click of connection. 'Dr Wilde,' said an instantly recognisable voice.

'Mr President,' she replied. 'Thank you for taking my call.'

'No problem at all. I could hardly keep a true American hero waiting, could I?' He chuckled. 'What can I do for you?'

Nina wondered for a moment how best to address the subject, deciding to get straight to the point. 'Mr President, it's about the appointment of Maureen Rothschild as the new Director of the International Heritage Agency. I don't believe she is the right person for the job, and I think that her suspension of myself and Eddie Chase is completely unwarranted.'

'Your suspension.' For some reason, Dalton seemed unsurprised at the news. Surely he couldn't already know about it?

'Yes, sir. In my opinion, she made the decision based solely on her personal dislike of me, without any consideration of the damage it would cause to the IHA's operations and its global security mission.' Nina had a more forceful – and ruder – version of her argument circling in her head, but thought the diplomatic edit should do the trick.

Or not. 'Dr Wilde,' said Dalton, disapproval evident in his tone, 'are you aware that Professor Rothschild was appointed as IHA Director on my personal recommendation to the Senate committee and the UN?'

'Uh, no sir, I was not,' Nina answered, startled.

'She has my total confidence and support, as well as that of the United Nations. Are you saying that support is misplaced?'

'I, er . . . Yes, quite frankly, Mr President,' she said, a shudder running through her as she realised she had just challenged the most powerful man on the planet.

'Then,' said Dalton, tone even harder, 'we'll have to disagree, Dr Wilde. Professor Rothschild has my full backing. If her decision inconveniences you—'

'*Inconveniences?*'

'— then that's unfortunate. But as Director, she has full authority. If you have a problem with that, you should take it up through proper UN channels, rather than trying to take advantage of your past service to this country for personal gain.'

'That – that's not why I—' Nina began, but Dalton cut her off.

'We both know that's *exactly* why you called me, Dr Wilde. Now, I appreciate everything you've done in the past for the United States – I would hardly have awarded you the Medal of Freedom otherwise – but that does *not* grant you a hotline to the Oval Office to solve your personal problems. Do I make myself clear?' When

Nina couldn't find an answer immediately, he sternly added, 'Dr Wilde? Am I clear?'

'Yes, Mr President,' Nina mumbled, chastised.

'Good. Now, I have business to attend to. Goodbye, Dr Wilde.'

The phone clicked, leaving Nina trembling in anger and humiliation, feeling as though she'd just been punched in the gut.

Dalton put down the phone, then turned his chair towards the windows looking out over the White House's rose garden, a small but satisfied smile on his lips.

Nina Wilde and her fiancé had made themselves his enemies four months earlier, without even knowing it, by destroying a secret weapon controlled by his black-ops agent Jack Mitchell. In the overall scheme of things they were very *minor* enemies, with no power to harm him in any way, but Dalton had still taken a certain pleasure in arranging for the vast apparatus of the United States government to bedevil their lives. Tax audits and overzealous immigration checks had been petty compared to depriving the couple of their jobs, however. The moment he'd learned about Nina's enmity with Rothschild, he'd seen an opportunity for something more hard-hitting.

Now it was done, he could focus on more pressing matters – in which, like the proverbial bad penny, Nina Wilde and Eddie Chase had turned up. With them out of the way, that left the Covenant of Genesis.

His smile vanished at the mere thought of the organisation. Now *there* was a dangerous enemy – and one that even with his vast resources he couldn't yet deal with, not without being destroyed himself. How they had obtained such politically – and personally – damaging knowledge he had no idea. But they had, and as their representative, an Israeli, had calmly explained, they would use it without hesitation if he did not agree to their . . . *request*.

And what a request. If the public ever learned what he had done to appease the Covenant, it would end his career more quickly than the release of any of the organisation's other information about his dealings.

Fortunately, he had at least been able to persuade the Covenant to let one of his operatives join them. One of his *best* operatives. A man who would find any possible opportunity to eliminate any threats to him . . . and maybe even shift the balance of power to where it belonged.

In his favour.

He turned back to his desk and picked up one particular phone. 'Get me Michael Callum.'

The tall, granite-faced man, hair a bristling pure white, pushed a button on his secure cell phone to end the call. 'That was the President,' Callum told the other occupant of the luxurious Washington, DC hotel suite.

'So I gathered,' said Uziel Hammerstein, unimpressed, as he lit a cigar. Callum looked pointedly at the 'no smoking' sign by the door. The Israeli made a vaguely amused noise. 'What, are you going to have me sent to Guantánamo for smoking?'

'So what did your esteemed leader have to say?' came an English-accented voice from the phone on the glass coffee table between the two men.

Callum frowned at the voice's undisguised sarcasm. 'You'll be glad to know, Professor Ribbsley, that Nina Wilde is no longer a problem. She's been fired, and the digital images of the tablet have been erased.'

'Good,' said Ribbsley. 'I doubt she would have been able to translate any of the text, but once I knew I was looking at a navigational chart, it didn't take long to work out where it led. She might have been able to do the same. Of course,' he went on, his cutting tone returning, 'if Hammerstein's goon had done his job rather than letting her throw him out of a window . . .'

Hammerstein bared his teeth, the cigar clenched between them. 'Careful, Professor. Just because we've agreed to your demands doesn't mean I have to put up with any of your crap. Goldman wasn't just a colleague, he was a friend.'

'My condolences on your loss,' said Ribbsley, in a deliberate monotone.

Callum regarded the Israeli coldly. 'Your man shouldn't even have been operating on our turf.'

Hammerstein leaned back in the leather armchair, blowing a smoke ring across the table at him. 'The Covenant works wherever it has to, Callum. Our mission is more important than your politics.' The white-haired man narrowed his eyes.

'Speaking of your mission,' said Ribbsley, 'have the preparations started yet?'

'Vogler is in Australia already,' Hammerstein told him. 'Zamal is on his way. Your flight is being arranged right now.'

'First class, of course.' Not a question: an expectation.

'Yes, first class,' said Hammerstein, sharing a contemptuous look with Callum.

'Excellent. In that case, I'd better finish packing. See you down under, gentlemen.'

'You shouldn't have caved in to his demands,' snapped Callum the moment the call ended.

'We had no choice. We needed him to translate the tablet Vogler recovered from Indonesia – and we'll need him to translate any new finds at the site.'

'Even so, if it'd just been money he wanted, it wouldn't have been a problem. Not even Ribbsley could be that greedy. But this . . .'

'Ribbsley's a man of very particular tastes. Unfortunately. Which is why we're allowing you to act as . . . caretaker.' A faint smile. 'I

145

assume Dalton has already authorised you to *take care* of things when the mission is completed.' The Covenant leader stood. 'I have to go. There's a lot of work to do, and Australia is a very long flight away.' He left the suite without any pleasantries of departure.

Callum stared at the door after it closed. Dalton had indeed granted him licence to take care of the problem of Ribbsley's demands . . . and more besides. The Covenant had gone too far. This was a direct threat to the authority of the President of the United States, and had to be dealt with.

But subtly. The Covenant had enormous power behind it. He had to wait for the right opportunity, pick his moment, or the consequences could be ruinous.

When that moment came, though . . . he would be ready.

12

Chase entered the apartment and flopped down on the couch. 'Hi, honey, I'm home. Don't I get a kiss hello?'

'Thank God,' said Nina, hurrying in from the kitchen and kissing him. 'I think we've both got a lot of catching up to do.'

'Yeah,' Chase said, taking in her cuts and bruises with a concerned expression. 'You want to go first?'

'No, you,' she said, sitting beside him. 'Why the hell were you in *Cuba*?'

'Don't worry, I wasn't getting another of those.' He nodded at the Fidel Castro figurine on a shelf, a ceramic cigar-box holder now used to store loose change. 'No, I had words with those pirates – Bejo's fine, by the way – and saw some bloke paying them off.'

'What about the tablet?'

'He took it. And your laptop.'

'Damn. So this guy, was he Cuban? Did you follow him there?'

'No, I was taken – by a bunch of your guys.'

'My guys?'

'Yanks. Three goons dressed like Agent Smith. They stuck me on a plane to Guantánamo Bay.'

'What?' Nina gasped. 'Why would they take you there?'

'Because I know someone there. So do you. Sophia. She's . . . she's dead.'

'Oh,' was Nina's only immediate response. She had absolutely no

147

love for Chase's ex-wife, but could tell that however stoic he seemed outwardly he was affected within. 'What happened?'

'She tried to escape and got shot. They wanted me to see the body. It was a mess.'

She put her arm round him. 'Oh, Eddie, I'm sorry . . . Are you okay?'

He didn't answer for a moment. 'I'm . . . I don't know,' he admitted, shaking his head. 'It's weird. I couldn't stop thinking about her on the flight back.'

Nina's face twitched in disapproval, but she managed to keep it from Chase, barely. 'In what way?'

'I'm going to miss her, in some weird way. I didn't think I would after everything she did, but . . .' He sighed, to his surprise feeling a weight growing on his heart the more he spoke. 'She didn't use to be like that. Not when I first met her – hell, I wouldn't have married her if she had been. And I know that she blamed me for some of how she turned out.'

'That's crazy,' Nina told him firmly. 'You don't believe that, do you?'

'No, but . . .' Another sigh, and he stared down at the floor. 'I'm pretty sure *she* did.'

'Oh, Eddie . . .' She hugged him sympathetically. 'You can't blame yourself for what happened to her. Any of it.'

Another moment of silence, then he looked at her. 'So what about you?' he asked, glad to change the subject.

Now it was Nina's turn to recount recent events. 'Wait, I got *fired*?' asked Chase when she finished.

'You weren't fired, you were suspended,' Nina corrected. 'Although I kinda get the feeling Rothschild wants to make it the same thing. Miserable old bitch.'

'Sod her – what about this bloke who tried to kill you and Lola? Have they found out who he was?'

'No, nobody's identified him yet. I'm not even sure what part of the world he was from; I didn't recognise his accent.'

'I recognised mine,' said Chase. 'The guy who paid off the pirates was Swiss.'

'Swiss?'

'Yeah. His name was Vogler. And he's part of something called the Covenant of Genesis.' He noticed Nina's reaction. 'You know what it is?'

'Only in a biblical context,' she said, sitting up thoughtfully. 'In the Book of Genesis, God made a pact – a covenant – with Abraham. In return for acknowledging God – Yahweh, or Jehovah, depending how you translate the original Hebrew Tetragrammaton – as the one true and supreme deity, Abraham's descendants would be granted everlasting ownership and rule of the land on which they lived.'

'This Abraham's not the one who sang about the Smurfs, I take it.'

'Hardly. Didn't you ever go to Sunday school when you were a kid?'

'My nan tried to make me a few times. I'd just hang about until she'd gone, then bugger off to play with my mates.'

'Y'know, that explains a lot . . . Anyway, Abraham's a key figure in all three major religions that came out of the Holy Land: Judaism, Christianity and Islam. In fact, they're collectively called the Abrahamic religions, after him.'

'That's what I like about you,' said Chase. 'It's always an education.'

'I do my best. Even if it's an uphill struggle.'

'Tchah!'

Nina grinned, then continued. 'The three Abrahamic religions actually share a lot of common elements. The Jewish Torah is essentially the same as the first five books of the Old Testament, and the Koran regards the Torah and the Bible as holy books. As far as Genesis goes, the Koran has quite a lot of differences in the specifics, but the fundamental story's the same – Adam and Eve, the expulsion from paradise, the Great Flood, Abraham . . . they're all there, just interpreted differently by the three religions.'

'Yeah, and hasn't that caused trouble over the years.'

'My fiancé, master of understatement. But as for what the Abrahamic covenant's got to do with an artefact we found on the other side of the world, I've got absolutely no idea.' She glanced at the memory card, which sat in the Castro cigar-box holder, half hidden by coins. 'The language on the tablet wasn't related to any used by the three religions, even the most ancient forms of Hebrew. And besides, the depth we found it at shows that it predates any of them by a long way. So why the Covenant of Genesis?'

'Maybe they were big fans of Phil Collins,' Chase suggested.

Nina managed a small laugh, then shook her head in puzzlement. 'I don't get it. What did the tablet say that was so dangerous to them that they'd try to kill us over it?'

'You said it was some sort of chart,' Chase reminded her. 'Maybe we can figure out where it goes.'

'But I don't know how they measured distances. The numbers could be feet, miles, stadia, moon units . . . anything!'

'Won't know unless we try, will we?' He stood, took Nina's hand and led her to the small room she used as a study, picking up the memory card along the way.

Once Nina's iMac was booted up, she copied the photos to it. 'Maybe we should put that in a safety deposit box or something,' she said of the card, not entirely joking.

'Why'd you tell Rothschild that it got blanked?'

'Because I don't trust her. And not just because I don't like her, either. She's a friend of Ribbsley's, and she did everything she could to play down the idea that he told someone I had the text. I wouldn't put it past her to let him know that I still do. Oh, oh, and get this,' she added excitedly, 'I tried calling Ribbsley myself. And guess what? He's suddenly become "unavailable". Not even his college knows when he's coming back. Kind of a coincidence, huh?'

'He's probably scared you might go to Cambridge and deck him.'

'I was tempted, believe me. Okay, let's see . . .' She opened the close-up of the tablet, pointing out the different elements she had noticed. 'These are the Atlantean numbers, with the compass bearings in front of them, and then I think these sections of text describe each successive destination. Only problem is, I've got no clue how to translate them.'

Chase examined the image. 'Have you got that sea level program on here?'

'GLUG? Yeah.'

'Bring it up, put in the sea level from a hundred and thirty-five thousand years back. If it's directions, it'll help if we're looking at the right map.'

Nina gave him an admiring glance. 'Smart man.'

'I'll remember you said that, next time you tell me off for watching action movies.'

She ran the program and entered the figures, the sea level round Indonesia dropping by a hundred feet and causing islands to rise and swell, then placed a marker at the co-ordinates where the tablet was discovered. 'All right,' she said, flicking back to the digital photo, 'if we assume for now that the dig site is the start point, then the first direction is between south and southwest.' A look at the other bearings on the tablet narrowed things down. 'These dots, they appear in groups of a maximum of eight, just like the Atlantean system. So if there are eight sub-bearings in each compass octant, that makes eight sets of eight, plus the eight cardinal bearings . . .'

'Seventy-two,' said Chase. 'Just in case you needed any help.'

'I *think* I can manage. So their navigational system worked to an accuracy of seventy-two "degrees" to a circle, meaning each dot equals five degrees. In which case,' she said, going back to the map, 'the first number takes you on a bearing of two hundred and ten degrees, which takes you . . .'

'Here.' Chase indicated a point. 'That's the first place where you'd reach land.' He took a large atlas from a shelf and found the pages covering Indonesia. 'Nearest town today would be this place, Merak.' It was west of Jakarta, a headland marking the boundary between the Java Sea and the Sunda Strait, which separated the Indonesian islands of Sumatra and Java. He compared the paper map to the one on the computer. 'The strait was a lot narrower back then.'

'A hell of a lot,' Nina agreed. 'There's only really one place where you'd be able to sail through, this channel here.' She compared the two maps. 'And it's right on a bearing of two hundred and ten degrees from where we found the tablet!'

'That's a good start. So where next?'

Nina worked out the next bearing. 'This direction, to the triangle-thing.'

'What triangle-thing?' Chase asked.

Nina moved the mouse cursor to it. 'This triangle-thing. With the flower or the tree or whatever on top of it.'

'You mean the volcano?'

She looked at him, surprised. 'What?'

'Well, it's obviously a volcano, isn't it? It's a drawing of a mountain with smoke coming out – what else could it be?'

Nina slapped herself on the forehead. 'I am such an *idiot*! How did I not see it?' She zoomed in on the image. 'I was so fixated on the idea of its being a symbolic character that I didn't even think it might just be a simple pictogram.' Another comparison of the two maps. 'So, a volcano, which volcano . . .'

'The really famous one?' Chase suggested with a smile. 'Krakatoa.' He pointed it out in the atlas. What remained of the obliterated volcanic island lay at the centre of the southern half of the Sunda Strait.

'That works for me.' Nina quickly found another book and leafed through it to show Chase a nineteenth-century woodcut illustration: an almost cartoon-perfect volcanic cone, smoke rising in a plume from the summit. 'The largest volcano on Krakatoa used to be huge. It'd make an unmissable landmark if you were travelling by sea.'

'Well, if it really *is* using Krakatoa as a landmark,' said Chase, 'then you can work out all the distances, can't you? If it says Krakatoa's three hundred zogs or whatever from where we started, it should be a piece of piss to convert that into miles. Seeing as you've already got the directions, you'll be able to work out exactly where it takes you.'

'Again, smart man. I knew there was a reason why I wanted to marry you.'

'I thought it was the screaming orgasms?'

'Very funny. But let's figure this out . . .'

Several minutes of work with pen, paper and protractor yielded a result, the course laid out by the ancient tablet travelling through the Sunda Strait and round the headland at the westernmost tip of Java, before crossing the expanse of the eastern Indian Ocean to . . .

'Australia,' Nina said, tapping the country's North West Cape just above the Tropic of Capricorn. 'That's where the chart takes you. Whoever these people were, they reached as far as Australia. A *long* time before anyone else. The earliest known signs of human occupation only date back fifty thousand years. These people were there over eighty thousand years before that.'

Chase looked at the computer map. 'They took a big risk, going straight across the sea like that. They could've just kept going along the Indonesian coast.' The lower sea level meant that the eastern islands of Indonesia reached practically all the way to Australia, which itself had merged with New Guinea to extend the continent northwards to the equator.

'They didn't need to,' Nina realised. 'Why would they? They had the sailing skills and navigational abilities to cross the sea directly. It'd save them days, maybe even weeks. And they kept going.' There were still more bearings on the tablet. A few more minutes, and the rest of the course was revealed, travelling down the western coast of Australia and using Shark Bay's vast dogtooths and the Houtman Islands as landmarks before finally terminating at a point over a hundred miles north of the city of Perth. On the modern map, there was nothing of note about the spot, even the nearest small town a good twenty miles away.

'That's it?' said Chase, unimpressed. 'There's not a lot there.'

'There must have been *something* there,' Nina said, more excited. 'A settlement, maybe, or a port – something worth travelling all that way for.' She zoomed in on the sea level map, bringing up the present-day position of the coast as a yellow outline. 'It must have been in this bay – it'd give them shelter from the sea, and there'd be fresh water from this river.' A closer zoom revealed individual contour lines. 'Look how steep the sides of the bay are. They couldn't have built a settlement right on the shoreline, they'd need somewhere flatter . . .'

She scrolled further inland. 'Somewhere like *that*.' Above the eastern end of the small bay was a gently sloping plain. 'If you were building a settlement, it's got everything you need – water, farmable land, sheltered access to the sea . . .' Enthusiasm rose in her voice. 'It was above sea level back then, and it's still above sea level now . . . so if there *was* a settlement there, we might still be able to find it!'

'You think it's buried there?'

'Yes! Absolutely! If we go there, we might be able to excavate it!' She leaned back, already compiling a mental list of everything she might need.

'Not wanting to piss on your chips,' said Chase, 'but I don't think the IHA's going to go for that right now.'

Nina snorted. 'Who needs the IHA? This'd be *proper* archaeology, just a map and a shovel and a brush, no need for computers or submersibles or millions of dollars of hardware. I'll show that shrivelled old bitch what being an archaeologist is really all about,' she added, more to herself than to Chase.

'Calm down, Lara,' he said. 'So you want to jet off to Australia to find the lost city of . . . of whoever the hell these people were?'

'Why not? It's not as though we've got anything else to do right now. We're both suspended, remember?'

'Yeah, but there was one thing the IHA was handy for – paying for everything!'

'That's what credit cards are for,' said Nina. Chase decided not to tell her how much his flights had cost. 'Come on, we can do this! We fly to Australia, check out the site, do some digging – the worst that can happen is that we don't find anything, and even then at least we had a vacation to take our minds off everything.' She stood, hands pressed together eagerly. 'Whaddya say?'

He could tell from the almost manic glint in her eyes that she was not going to take no for an answer. 'You do remember that there's someone else trying to find it as well, right?'

'The Covenant of Genesis? Maybe, if they're even capable of figuring out where to look.'

'We just did it in half an hour,' he pointed out. 'They've got the original tablet to work from, and you even told that Ribbsley guy about the numbers on it. What if that was the only thing they were missing?'

'All the more reason to find it before them. Come on, Eddie! A few days, that's all I'll need. If there's nothing there, then fair enough, that's the end of the line. But if there *is* something there . . .'

'Great. More flying,' Chase complained. But she had a point; if there really was anything at the new site and the Covenant found it first, they would presumably destroy it, making all the deaths aboard the *Pianosa* even more meaningless. 'Oh, all right. Let's go to a land down under.'

Nina kissed him. 'Thanks, Eddie.'

'Just one thing, though – I'm not doing all the bloody digging!'

13

Australia

Shielding his eyes from the sun's glare, Chase stepped out of the Land Rover Defender and surveyed the landscape. 'As the Aussies say . . . crikey.'

Nina joined him, tugging down the brim of her baseball cap until it almost touched her sunglasses in order to shade her pale face. 'I can see why.'

It was three days since their decision to make the long trip across the Pacific to Australia; three days of intensive preparation and expensive travel arrangements. But now they were finally there, having driven north from Perth, turning westwards off the main highway on to a rough track . . . and into a spectacular desert land-scape. The rolling sands were a vivid yellow, almost like a child's crayon drawing, and protruding from the dunes were dozens of angular limestone pillars, ranging from knee-height to some that towered over Chase. 'They look like film props,' he said, touching one to check that it wasn't made of polystyrene and plaster.

Nina consulted her guidebook. 'We're fairly close to the Pinnacles Desert. It says it's full of these formations – some of them are four metres tall. Must be a hell of a sight.'

'We could take a detour and have a look,' Chase suggested.

She regarded the strange rocks for a moment before shaking her head. 'Let's find the place we're looking for first. Besides, it's a national park – they might not want us carving it up in a jeep.'

'Oh, so when *you* want to look at bits of old rock it's a national emergency, but when *I* do . . .' He grinned at her as they climbed back in. 'Okay, so how much further to this place?'

'The map says about . . . seven kilometres. Just over four miles.'

Chase looked at the track, which though winding and bumpy had so far been relatively easy for their 4x4 to negotiate. 'Shouldn't take us too long. What was the name of the place again?'

'Trouble Cove,' she said, with another look at the map. 'Australia has such great place names! Hangover Bay, Useless Loop, Billabong Roadhouse . . .' A cheeky glance at Chase. 'Bald Head . . .'

'Oi,' he warned, swatting at her with one hand as he started driving. She giggled. 'So what do you want to do when we get there?'

'We should have plenty of time before sunset to look around before putting up the tent.' Nina examined her notes, serious again. 'If we concentrate on the area near the edge of the bay, that's the most likely site.'

They continued along the track, desert sand gradually giving way to patches of vegetation as they drew closer to the coast, heathland speckled with bright flowers and low, wind-sculpted trees. Wildlife also appeared, a small group of kangaroos pausing in their leaping travels to watch the passing vehicle, and an emu popped its head up suspiciously from behind a bush before scurrying away. Though hot, it was certainly one of the most picturesque wildernesses they had travelled through.

Finally, they crested a rise, and saw the shimmering turquoise ocean. 'Wow, look at that,' said Nina, taking off her sunglasses for a better look. 'That's really— Aah!' She jolted forward in her seat as

Chase stamped on the brake, bringing the Defender to a sudden crunching halt. 'Eddie! What the hell?'

He hurriedly reversed over the rise and pulled to a sharp stop. 'Remember how I said the Covenant would be trying to find this place too?'

'Yeah?'

'I think they already have.' He jumped out and hurried to the rear door, opening it to take a pair of powerful binoculars from their gear. 'Come on. But keep low.'

Nina nervously followed him back up the track. Near the top, he dropped to his stomach and crawled under a scrubby bush. She did the same. One hand shading the lenses to prevent the sun from reflecting off them, Chase took a closer look at Trouble Cove.

'What is it?' Nina asked. 'What do you see?'

'That I won't need to do any digging.' He handed her the binoculars.

Nina scanned the area ahead. To her shock, it was bustling with activity. Grubby yellow excavators were digging out large trenches, men moving in behind them to clear away more sand and dirt with shovels. Parked nearby were several 4x4s and heavier flatbed trucks, presumably used to transport the earthmovers across the desert, as well as a rather incongruous Winnebago recreational vehicle. She also spotted several large tents on one edge of the dig. 'Jesus.'

'That's a pretty serious operation,' said Chase.

'You're not kidding.'

'We need to get closer.'

'We need to do *what* now?'

'I want to get a better look at them,' he clarified. 'See if that guy Vogler's there, if they really are these Covenant people.'

'I don't think they're there to build vacation condos,' Nina muttered. It was hard to tell from this angle, but there seemed to be something in the trenches.

'Come on.' Chase took back the binoculars and crawled down the other face of the slope, Nina behind him. They carefully made their way closer, staying low behind the patches of vegetation. The ground became rockier, the track entering a winding gulch marking the path of a long-dry river. Nina expected Chase to enter it to take advantage of the cover, but instead he crawled between the boulders along the top, following a ragged line of small bushes.

He stopped suddenly and flattened himself on the ground, gesturing for Nina to do the same. She heard the raucous sound of an engine.

'Quad bike,' said Chase, warily raising his head. Nina peered through the bushes. About a hundred yards ahead, she saw a man in desert camouflage bounding through the dunes on a fat-tyred little Kawasaki 4x4. A rifle was slung over his back. 'He's running a patrol – there're more tracks on the ground. That must be their perimeter.'

Nina looked past him to the dig site. They were now about half a mile from its centre, close enough to make out the rattle and roar of the machines. 'Eddie, give me the binoculars.'

She focused first on the trenches, seeing the remains of buildings at the bottom. Even through the encrustation of sand and soil, the similarity to the underwater ruin in the Java Sea was clear: the same curved walls, the same large, carefully placed bricks.

But her thrill of recognition was immediately blown away by her horror at what was being done to the ruins. The excavators weren't merely clearing the dirt around them – they were ripping them apart. Even as she watched, another toothed steel bucket smashed one of the walls. As the machine pulled back, men came in to continue the destruction by hand.

'Jesus,' she hissed. 'They're just wrecking everything. They must be looking for something specific . . . and they don't care what they destroy to find it.' Panning across the site, she suddenly stopped when she saw an unmistakable figure standing at the edge of a trench. 'Son of a *bitch*!'

'What?' Chase asked.

'It's Ribbsley!' Dressed in a white suit and a Panama hat, the Cambridge professor was sipping from a plastic water bottle as he gazed at the devastation below. 'The guy in white – that bastard's overseeing the whole thing! And I led him right to it by telling him about the Atlantean numbers on the tablet.' She let out a frustrated growl.

'It's not your fault,' Chase assured her. 'You didn't know he was working for these arseholes.'

'But I shouldn't have trusted *anyone*, not after what happened. Shit!' She returned the binoculars to him. '*That's* archaeology by bulldozer, not anything I've ever done.'

'Ay up,' said Chase, finding the figure in white, then examining the men standing with him. 'Vogler's there too. Take a gander.' Nina peered through the lenses once more. 'The blond guy, right of your mate the Man from Del Monte. That's him.'

She saw a man in desert camouflage, wearing sunglasses. He seemed to be about Chase's age, mid-thirties. Two other men, similarly dressed, also stood nearby. They were both older than Vogler, one olive-skinned with cropped black wavy hair and a cigar in his mouth, the other goateed and apparently Middle Eastern, wearing a black military beret. 'Who are the other guys?'

'Dunno, but I'm guessing they're in charge. They're not getting their hands dirty.'

'What are we going to do?' Nina asked. 'They beat us to the site. And the way they're working, there won't be anything left by the time they leave.'

'Then we'll have to get in there before they finish.'

'Y'know, I think the guys with guns might have something to say about that.'

'If they catch us. I think I can get us in there without being seen.'

'And then what?'

He grinned. 'What do you think? We're going to find whatever it is they're after. Before they do.'

Nina had expected the digging to stop at sunset. But it continued, glaring floodlights on poles casting a stark light over the excavators as they continued tearing open the ground. From the amount of earth that had been cleared since she and Chase arrived, she estimated that the dig had been going for at least a couple of days. Ribbsley and the Covenant had assembled their operation even more quickly than they had – and put vastly more resources behind it.

Lurking in the bushes, Nina and Chase observed the Covenant's pattern of activities. There were always two men on quad bikes circling the perimeter, coming close to their position at one extreme and going right up to the edge of the cliffs at the other. It took slightly under two minutes for each man to complete half an orbit; two minutes to find a way into the site without being seen.

The sound of digging suddenly stopped. Nina saw some of the excavators pulling back. She took the binoculars. Another structure had been partly exposed at the end of the trench; one of the scoops had knocked a hole in the curved wall. A man shone a torch into it, then clambered through. 'They've found something,' she said.

'Must be important,' said Chase, seeing the other machinery stop. 'Everyone's downed tools.'

Nina kept watching. After a minute, the man emerged and climbed a ladder out of the trench, hurrying across the site to be met by Vogler and the two other leaders of the group. Some animated discussion followed, and then the trio went to the Winnebago. She had seen Ribbsley retreat to it earlier; he emerged again . . . but not alone. 'Looks like Ribbsley's got a girlfriend.'

A woman with short, spiky blond hair had also emerged from the RV, standing beside the professor with her back to Nina. A moment later, someone else entered her field of vision – a hard-faced, white-haired man. Unlike the other members of the Covenant, who all wore desert camouflage, he was dressed in nondescript civilian khakis. 'And there's someone else, some guy with white hair.' There was something vaguely familiar about him, but she couldn't place what.

'Let me see.' Chase took a closer look through the binoculars. 'She's got a nice arse, whoever she is.'

'Eddie!'

'What? She does. Huh, Whitey doesn't think so, though. He's pretty pissed off, telling her to get back inside.'

Nina looked at Chase, surprised. 'You can lip-read?'

'A little bit. It's handy when someone's trying to tell you something while you're being shot at.' He tried to make out Ribbsley's reply, but the brim of the Panama hat covered most of his face. 'Looks like Ribbsley's arguing with him.' He looked briefly over at Vogler and his two companions. 'Vogler's saying . . . something about not wasting time, they need to . . . I think he said "translate the find".'

Nina's heart jumped. 'They've found another artefact.' She glared at the white-suited figure. 'That son of a bitch lied to me. He *knew* what the language on the tablet was – he was probably already translating it when I spoke to him. All he needed to find this place was the numerical system.'

Chase watched as the white-haired man took out a pair of handcuffs. The woman raised her hands in protest. His expression darkened – then he lunged forward and punched her hard in the stomach. She dropped to her knees. Before she could recover, the man roughly yanked up her arms to cuff them behind her back.

Chase's hands tightened on the binoculars. 'The bastard just hit her,' he growled as the blonde was dragged upright. Ribbsley was also angry – but not enough to intervene. Chase looked back at the trio. Vogler had an expression of mild distaste, while the cigar-smoking man's face was carefully neutral. The bearded Arab, on the other hand, wasn't bothering to conceal a cruel smirk. 'And none of the others are trying to stop him. Fuckers.' Half dragging the struggling woman back to the Winnebago, the white-haired man slammed her against the side of the vehicle before entering it and pulling her after him.

Ribbsley said something to Vogler, obviously complaining about his companion's treatment. He received no sympathy, the Swiss man gesturing towards the newly uncovered structure. Trying to salvage some degree of authority, Ribbsley strode past Vogler, waving arrogantly for the others to follow.

Nina saw the white-haired man emerge from the Winnebago and go after the others. The blonde woman remained inside. 'I've got to see what they've found. Once Ribbsley's translated it, I don't think they'll leave it intact.'

Chase searched for the quad bike riders, seeing one of them coming into view off to the right. 'Soon as this guy goes past, follow me down to that rock. Keep as low as you can.' They waited as the rider continued his circuit. 'Okay, *go!*'

He slithered quickly out from the bush. Nina followed more awkwardly, crawling in his wake as fast as she could. They dropped into a shallow, dusty ditch where Chase rose to a crouch, scurrying along until he reached another tangle of bushes. He popped his head up to check the way was clear, then shoved through them, snapping off a large branch to make Nina's passage easier.

'Okay, keep crawling,' he said as he dropped and headed for the boulder, Nina following. 'If I go "Hssst!" then drop flat and *don't move* until I say – or someone starts shooting at us.'

Nina didn't like the sound of that – but she liked the rising noise of the second quad bike even less. The rock loomed ahead, a ragged crescent lit from one side by spill from the floodlights.

She looked to the right. The quad bike's headlight came into view, jolting over the sandy ground. Getting closer.

Chase was almost at the rock. Nina scrambled after him. Plants scratched her face as she brushed past them. The headlight grew brighter.

He would see them at any moment—

'Hssst!'

Nina dropped flat. The headlight was coming straight at her. It got closer, *closer*, the engine a strident roar . . .

The Kawasaki veered away to pass on the other side of the boulder.

'Roll!' Chase ordered.

She did, plants crunching under her. Chase did the same, rolling round the rock after her. The quad bike's rear lights cast an unreal glow over the ground; he stopped inside the boulder's shadow, waiting until the red light faded before moving.

'Okay, go!' he hissed, pointing across the tracks to a ditch. Stooping, Nina hurried to it. Chase followed more slowly, backing over the tracks and sweeping the branch to cover their footprints. Even though he was trying to match the marks as closely as possible, if the riders slowed to look they would immediately notice the lack of any tread patterns, an erased line pointing at the intruders.

He just had to hope they didn't slow down.

Another headlight, the other bike coming round the circuit.

'Eddie, come on!' Nina called. He was almost across, only the last few footsteps to remove.

Engine noise getting louder—

'*Come on!*'

Done. He dropped the branch and leapt backwards to land beside

Nina. The quad bike was almost on them. Its headlight swept across the path of their footprints, the hastily scrubbed patches standing out clearly . . .

The quad rasped past in a spray of sand, wiping out the evidence of their passage with a new set of tracks from its fat, knobbly tyres.

Nina blew dust from her face. 'Jesus! Could you *possibly* have cut it any closer?'

'I dunno. Want me to try again? Just run back across . . .'

She huffed. 'Come on.'

They moved down the shadowed side of the ditch, heading for the thrum of a diesel generator ahead. Signalling for Nina to stay still, Chase crept up the stony slope for a look, then slid back down to her. 'Looks like they're taking a break – most of the men are over by the tents. There's still a few hanging around, though, so we'll need to be careful.'

'You know which way to go?'

'Yeah. There's a trench – if we drop into it, we can go almost all the way round.'

They crawled up and took shelter behind the generator, checking there was nobody nearby before moving along behind a loose line of parked vehicles. One of them was Ribbsley's Winnebago, a top-of-the-range model the size of a small bus. Chase hesitated as they reached it. 'What?' Nina asked.

'We should help that woman. Even if she's Ribbsley's girlfriend, the rest of them weren't big fans.'

'Eddie, I know you always want to be the white knight and help damsels in distress,' said Nina, 'but you can't right now. If we help her escape, what happens when they find out she's missing? We can't do anything – not yet, anyway. Maybe after we've found what we're looking for.'

'You're all heart,' Chase said, unimpressed. Nina gave him a dirty look, then continued onwards.

They reached the trench. Chase took another look at the surrounding area. A couple of men were working on an excavator's engine, but their backs were to them. He looked past the machine at the tents. The rest of the men were eating, which would hopefully keep them occupied for a while. He also noticed that they appeared to be divided into three groups, seemingly on ethnic lines, and that each group favoured a different type of assault rifle – Belgian FN SCARs, Israeli TAR-21s and Swiss SIG SG-551s – although all shared the same 5.56mm ammo.

Before he could think about that any further, Nina nudged him. 'Is it safe?'

'Yeah, looks like it's teatime. Think they'd mind if I blagged a sandwich?'

'Let's not find out.' She climbed into the trench. Chase checked that the mechanics were still occupied, then followed.

·Staying close to the wall, they advanced. The broken remains of buildings protruded from the trench floor, tracks from the excavators' caterpillar treads running right through them. 'I can't believe this,' Nina said, anger rising as they passed another smashed wall. 'This isn't archaeology, this is just *vandalism*. If it's not what you're looking for, destroy it.'

They reached the end of the trench. Chase climbed up first, then pulled Nina after him. They were close to the spot where the discovery had been made. Hiding behind a pile of sand, they crawled to the edge of the next trench and peered down.

A man stood outside the curved wall marking the trench's end. Another two men were carrying a wooden reel of electrical cable, laying the line behind them as they reached the broken hole in the wall. They climbed through, unreeling more cable as they disappeared from view. Other lights were visible inside the buried structure: torch beams.

Nina could make out voices, but not clearly enough to hear what was being said. She was sure one of them was Ribbsley's, though; the arrogant, affected English accent was quite distinctive. 'Sounds like Ribbsley's giving a lecture,' she whispered to Chase.

'About what?'

'The translation, I guess. God, I hope he hasn't figured it all out already.'

They moved back as the two men emerged from the hole and retreated up the trench. A short time later they returned, one carrying a pair of metal stands, the other two heavy-duty electric lamps. After another minute, the flitting torchlight was replaced by a constant, even glow. The men re-emerged and went back up the trench, the third man going with them.

Nina and Chase exchanged looks. If the occupants of the ruin left it as well, the way would be clear for them to climb down and go inside . . .

Ribbsley's muffled voice kept talking, pausing occasionally as the others asked questions. After several minutes, there was movement. Vogler climbed out of the hole, followed by the two other Covenant leaders, then Ribbsley. He made a show of brushing dust off his suit as the white-haired man emerged behind him. 'So you *can* translate the full thing, right?' he asked Ribbsley. His accent was American.

'Of course I can,' Ribbsley replied sniffily, adjusting his hat. 'I recognised most of the symbols on sight, and once I check my notes on my laptop I'll be able to identify the others quickly enough. The numbers will be a nuisance, but now that I know they follow the Atlantean system it's just a matter of converting them to base ten.'

'Could this lead us to the origin of the Veteres?' asked Vogler. Nina frowned at the odd word.

'Possibly. But it won't be as straightforward as finding this place. There are no bearings, no directions – it's not a chart, like the object you obtained in Indonesia. It seems to be more of a record, a historical account left by the Veteres.' Now dust-free, Ribbsley tugged imperiously at his lapels. 'But I'll crack it, I assure you. Now, I suggest a recess for supper; then I'll get my laptop from the camper and return to work.'

'Why waste time?' demanded the bearded Arab. 'Get it now.'

Ribbsley looked down his nose at him – an expression Nina remembered. She wasn't the only person to whom he considered himself superior. 'You may be willing to work all night on an empty stomach, Mr Zamal, but I'm certainly not.' He set off along the trench, Vogler and the second of the Covenant members flanking him. Zamal and the white-haired man exchanged looks that made it clear they shared the same low opinion of the professor, then followed.

'The bloke with white hair,' said Chase once they were out of earshot, 'I know him from somewhere.'

'You too?' Nina asked. 'Any idea where?'

'No. But I definitely recognise him.' He shook his head. 'Doesn't matter for now. Soon as they're out of sight, we'll climb down.'

'How long do you think we'll have?'

'Could be half an hour, could be five minutes. Depends how fast they eat.'

'Somehow, I don't think Ribbsley's the kind of man who rushes his food,' said Nina. She looked after the retreating men, puzzled. '*Veteres* . . . why would they use that as a name?'

'You know what it means?'

'Yes, it's Latin – "Ancients" would probably be the closest translation. But the context it's used in usually relates to family, like distant ancestors. I've never heard it in an archaeological sense.'

The group passed from view along the trench. Chase stood. 'Maybe you'll be able to figure it out once we're inside. Come on.'

He lowered her down, then jumped to the bottom of the trench.

Nina moved to the hole in the wall and glanced warily into it. It seemed empty – of life, at least.

But the answers to many questions waited within. She stepped inside.

14

The buried structure's interior was dome-shaped, the design and construction practically identical to the ruin at the bottom of the Java Sea. But this was intact; apart from the section broken open by the excavator, the only damage was at the far side of the room, where a tall doorway was blocked by rubble.

The contents of the room had fared less well, though. From the dust covering everything, Nina knew it hadn't been the result of the Covenant's work. Whatever had caused everything to tumble and scatter across the floor had happened centuries ago, even millennia. It appeared more like the result of an earthquake than deliberate destruction.

The chamber seemed to have been a storage area, shelves of brick and long-corroded wood toppled and broken, contents smashed on the ground. Stark shadows radiated outwards from the two lamps at the chamber's centre, bringing the debris into sharp relief. As Chase kept watch on the trench, Nina knelt to examine the dusty artefacts. 'This is like the one we found underwater,' she said, holding up a broken clay cylinder. This too had a closely wound groove spiralling up its length. There were others nearby, most also damaged, but she spotted one that was intact and picked it up. One end had a hole at its centre, while the other had a short inscription in the unknown language running around it.

'What is it?' Chase asked.

'No idea.' A perusal of other cylinders showed that each inscription was different. She put down the object, then moved to the lamps . . . and saw what they had been brought to illuminate. 'Oh, my God. Eddie, look at this.'

Chase crossed the room, debris crunching under his boots. 'Okay, so now we know what that lot were looking for.'

A section of the wall had been covered with a layer of plaster, creating a smooth surface. Parts were cracked, and some sections had broken off . . . but most of it was still intact, revealing line after line of ancient writing.

Nina recognised numbers within the text, and a handful of symbolic characters, but the rest of it was as impenetrable as the words on the clay tablet. Excited, she took out her camera.

'Careful with the flash,' Chase warned. 'We don't want anyone to see it.'

She switched off the flash, then started taking pictures. 'This is amazing,' she said. 'A record of an unknown race . . .'

'If there's a little picture of a UFO in there,' said Chase, stepping past her to look more closely, 'then I'm right, and they're aliens.'

'They're *not* aliens.' She used the zoom to capture images in more detail. 'Eddie, your shadow's in the shot.'

'Sorry.' He backed away, the rubble filling the doorway catching his attention. 'Hey, check this out. This didn't collapse. Somebody blocked it off.'

Chase was right, Nina saw; the large bricks in the opening were too regularly aligned to have been tumbled there by any natural means. She turned in place, examining the rest of the chamber. 'There's no sign of any bodies. It must have been sealed from outside.' A thought occurred, and she went to the inscription on the wall. 'This might be a final record, a sort of time capsule. Something they left for others to find after they moved on.'

'Question is, does it say where they went?' Something caught

Chase's eye, a glint of metal across the room, and he went to pick it up. 'Oh, 'ello. This look familiar?'

'It does.' It was a cone of copper sheet, scratched and dented, but unlike the flattened one they had found in Indonesia this one still had its shape. 'Any sign of what it might have been used for?'

He prodded at the shattered objects on the floor. 'No. Everything's wrecked.'

'See if there's any more of them.' Nina ran a fingertip along the ancient plaster, surprised at its even application and smoothness. Like the building itself, it had been made with a precision and care that was rare in early civilisations – and unknown in the era of pre-history from which it seemed to have come. Who had built it? Who were these people . . . and why was the mysterious Covenant of Genesis so determined to conceal them?

'I don't see anything,' Chase said from the other side of the room. 'There's more of those cylinders, and some clay tablets, but they're all broken.' He picked his way back to the hole, glancing out at the trench – then retreated sharply. 'Shit! They're coming back! Hide, hide!'

'*Where?*' Nina gasped, looking round in panic as Chase vaulted a pile of bricks and hunched down in the deep shadows behind it. Pinned in the light from both lamps, there was no way she could cross the chamber to join him without being seen by the approaching men, and none of the fallen shelf stacks appeared to offer enough cover to hide behind.

No choice—

She hopped over the closest and flattened herself along the length of its shadowed side – and clapped both hands over her mouth to hold in a yelp of pain as something stabbed into her left buttock.

Vogler entered the chamber first, Ribbsley following – and complaining. 'This is ridiculous. For the supposed guardians of civilisation, you're remarkably lacking in it. How's a man supposed to work without getting a decent meal?'

The others came in behind him. 'The Triumvirate voted to continue with the work as quickly as possible,' said Zamal.

'Two out of three,' Ribbsley said irritably. 'At least Vogler here showed some courtesy. Not like you and Hammerstein. And you wouldn't even have voted at all if *he* hadn't opened his mouth.' He glared at the white-haired American. 'He's not even a member of the Covenant, so why he gets any say I have no idea. There's no reason even for him to be here.'

'You know that was part of the deal, Professor,' said Vogler. 'But please, the sooner we start, the sooner we will be finished.'

'Oh, very well.' Still annoyed, Ribbsley crossed the room, pausing to pick up a couple of the clay cylinders – including the one Nina had examined earlier. '"Wind sea" – no, "sea of wind, seasons, wind,"' he read from the inscription on the first. '"Winds of the seasons of the sea of wind", I suppose.' He checked the other. 'And "fish of the sea of wind". The usual gibberish. Why did they make so many of these things just to hold one line of meaningless text?' He put them back down and continued across the chamber to stand before the text on the wall – barely four feet from Nina. Another step, and he would see her . . .

Instead, he opened up his laptop computer, cradling it in one arm as he peered at the text on the wall, then brought up a list of words written in the ancient language. 'Let's see . . . ah, I was right – the first line is a title of sorts. I was only missing a couple of words. Something along the lines of "The account of the final days of the people of the one great tree", although the syntactic structure is different. It's a very logically constructed language, actually – reminds me of Esperanto—'

'Is that what the Veteres called themselves?' Zamal interrupted. He moved forward for a closer look. Nina held her breath, tears in her eyes from the stabbing pain, hearing his footsteps getting nearer—

'Don't block the light,' Ribbsley snapped, waving him back. Zamal scowled, but obeyed. 'They seem to have a great deal of reverence for trees – it's a word that's appeared a lot in the texts you've brought me over the years. Perhaps they worshipped them.'

'Pagans,' Zamal sneered.

'Maybe, but their beliefs certainly lasted for much longer than Islam's been around, hmm?' Smirking at the frowning Arab, he returned to the translation. 'Ah! Now *this* is interesting. It says they left here a long time before to . . . to "escape the beasts".'

'Beasts?' asked Hammerstein, glancing round the room and fingering his holstered gun as if expecting some animal to jump out. Chase, watching through a small gap in the pile of rubble, tensed.

'That's the closest translation. Although I can't imagine what kind of beasts would be terrorising them in Australia. Giant wombats, perhaps!' He laughed, then looked back at the wall. 'But these beasts, whatever they were, were dangerous enough to drive them out of this settlement. They sailed for many days, probably weeks, to . . . to "the land of wind and sand".' They all exchanged puzzled looks.

'Are you sure that's what it says?' the white-haired man demanded.

'Yes, I'm positive,' said Ribbsley testily. He jabbed a finger at the inscription, Nina just able to see him indicate particular symbols from her awkward position. 'Wind, sand, land. Absolutely unmistakable.'

Zamal scratched his beard thoughtfully. 'Wind and sand. A desert.'

'But that could be anywhere,' Vogler said. 'A journey of weeks by sea could have taken them to Asia, Arabia, even Africa.'

'Let's hope the rest of the text is more enlightening.' Ribbsley read on. 'They built a new home, a "great city" in a valley near the sea with "tiny mountains of fire" – well, that's the symbol for a volcano, although I don't know how one could be tiny.' He scanned through several more lines. 'I think you will definitely find this part fascinating. It says they lived in peace in their city for many years – until their god drove them out.'

'Their god?' asked Hammerstein.

'It's actually a concatenation of several words and symbols – literally, it reads "the one great tree". I misunderstood the context in the title, but there's nothing else it can mean here. A supreme being, one that punished them for . . . "giving the gift of God to the beasts".'

As Ribbsley had expected, that aroused considerable interest in the other men. 'What gift?' said Zamal.

Ribbsley gave him a patronising sigh. 'Perhaps if you'd let me finish, I might be able to tell you. Now, it says their god punished them by "taking the sea", which I assume means a fall in sea level, so we should be able to match the date to the onset of an ice age, and sending wind and sand to kill the trees . . . and they had to leave the city before the wind and sand killed them too.' A pause as he checked his laptop. 'They tried to . . . "preserve", I suppose, to preserve the city by closing . . . no, "sealing" the valley so the river would grow and be covered by . . . oh, what a surprise. Wind and sand. I must say, they did have the most banal and repetitive prose style.'

'It sounds like they flooded their city,' Hammerstein suggested. 'Blocking a valley to make the river grow – they built a dam. What else does it say?'

'It seems,' said Ribbsley, 'that after they left their city, they came back here. But not everyone made it – they lost a lot of people, and also . . . oh, Mr Zamal, I think you'll appreciate this part. It says that during the voyage, they lost many of "the voices of the prophets".'

The Arab looked stung. 'Prophets?'

'That's what it says. Well, well. They have something in common with Islam after all!'

'Blasphemy,' growled Zamal. 'They may have *called* them prophets, but they were not the servants of Allah.'

'Perhaps,' said Ribbsley, clearly amused at having found a way to rile him. 'But it's still an intriguing thought, isn't it?' He turned back to the text. 'Once they made it back here, the beasts soon attacked. They tried to, ah . . . something about a "safe wall" – oh, of course. They tried to fortify the settlement. But there were too many of the beasts, so they . . . hmm. Interesting.'

'What happened to them?' Vogler asked. 'Does it say where they went next?'

'Wherever they meant to go, I don't think they got very far.' He raised his free hand, turning and sweeping it theatrically around the chamber. Nina squashed herself harder against the rubble, the pain increasing. 'This seems to be where they made their last stand. The chamber is associated with something called "the tree of the gift" – apparently they couldn't take it with them, so they buried it and left a message in the hope that their people might find it again in the future.'

Hammerstein pointed at the text. 'Is that the message?'

'So it seems. But there's certainly no tree in here. As for what happened to the Veteres . . . well, that's where the story ends. They never came back, so either they settled elsewhere – or were all killed trying to escape these beasts.'

'But we know there definitely *is* another settlement,' said Vogler. 'Their city. If we can locate it, we can destroy it.'

'*After* I've the chance to explore it,' Ribbsley said, closing his laptop. 'That was our deal. I may not be able to share it with the world, but at least I'll have discovered something nobody else has ever seen. Not even Nina Wilde.'

Nina's heart almost stopped at the unexpected mention of her name. She was terrified that Ribbsley had spotted her, but then he continued: 'Of course, we have to find it first, which means working out exactly where this "land of wind and sand" is.' A pause, then a camera flash lit the room, followed by another as Ribbsley photographed sections of the inscription. Behind him, Vogler and Hammerstein traded suggestions as to the location.

Chase, meanwhile, overheard another conversation as Zamal and the American, standing near the hole in the wall, conversed in low voices. 'Once he learns where the city is,' said Zamal, 'his job will be done. And then . . . you can kill his woman.'

'That'll make my boss very happy,' the white-haired man replied. 'And you too?'

'I wouldn't say happy. But there'll be some . . . job satisfaction.'

Zamal smirked, then looked round as Ribbsley finished taking his photographs. 'That should be enough to work from for now,' the professor announced. 'But now, gentlemen, perhaps I could *finally* be allowed to have some supper?'

'I have no objections,' said Vogler. 'And I don't think the Triumvirate needs to call a vote.' Hammerstein shook his head, while Zamal merely shrugged.

'Excellent. Then if you don't mind, I'll go and find out what Fortnum & Mason have in store for me tonight.' The laptop under his arm, Ribbsley crossed the chamber and climbed out through the hole. The others followed him.

Nina waited as long as she could bear, then jumped up, flapping at the object embedded in her backside. 'My ass, my ass!' she hissed through gritted teeth as she hopped about in pain. 'There's something stuck in my ass!'

'Ah, you never want to try new things,' Chase whispered jovially as he glanced through the hole to make sure the men had left, then came over.

'Get it out, get the damn thing out!' She let out a keening moan. 'What *is* it?'

'It's a needle.' He reached for it. 'Hold still, let me just . . .'

She stifled a shriek as he tugged it out, her eyes flooding with tears. 'Oh, ow, son of a *fuck*, oww!'

'It's a big one,' said Chase, holding up the bloodied needle, a good four inches long, to show her.

'And it's been in here for thousands of years! I've probably caught some extinct disease off it.'

He patted her arm. 'I'll give you a jab when we get back to the Landie. But we need to go – I heard them say that as soon as Del Monte finds this city, they're going to kill his girlfriend. We've got to rescue her.'

'How? He'll be with her by now!'

'I'll come up with something.' He moved back to the hole. Nina started to follow, then picked up the two clay cylinders that Ribbsley had examined. 'What're you doing?' Chase asked impatiently.

'Ribbsley translated the text on them.'

'So?'

'So, it'll give me something to work from – I've got to try to translate the rest of the inscription before he does!' She dropped both cylinders into a pocket and joined him. Nobody was outside, the way clear.

They retraced their path through the camp. The two mechanics had joined the other men in their evening meal – and so, Chase saw as they climbed cautiously from the trench, had the three Covenant leaders, the white-haired man . . . and Ribbsley. 'Come on, hurry up,' he said as they reached the parked vehicles. 'We can grab his girlfriend and make a run for it before he gets back.'

Nina still wasn't convinced of the wisdom of the rescue mission, but said nothing. They reached the Winnebago, which had lights

179

on inside it. Chase tried to peek through a window, but the curtains were drawn. 'Okay, wait here,' he told Nina. 'I'll go in and get her. If anyone looks like they're coming this way, knock on the door.'

'And then what?'

'One step at a time. Back in a tick.' He opened the side door and darted inside.

The Winnebago's interior was large enough to be divided into individual rooms. Chase found himself in a well-appointed lounge, an expensive hamper open on a table. There was a wine-bottle-sized space amongst the contents, so he guessed Ribbsley had gone to get a corkscrew, or ice.

Which meant he would be back very soon.

Nobody was in the front of the RV, and he could see that the bathroom was unoccupied, which left another door at the rear of the lounge – the bedroom. He went to it, turned the handle, stepped inside—

And froze in shock.

The blonde woman on the bed stared back at him in equal surprise, but recovered more quickly. 'Hello, Eddie,' said Sophia Blackwood.

15

'Sophia,' said Chase, 'what the *fuck* are you doing here?'

'I might ask you the same,' she replied, her near-flawless face – its only imperfection a scar across one cheek, courtesy of Nina – and aristocratic voice exactly as he remembered them, despite the very different hairstyle. 'Although rather less coarsely.'

'No, I mean what are you doing here, still *breathing*?'

'It's a long story.' She changed position, revealing that her hands were still cuffed behind her back – and attached to a short chain fixed to the bed. 'I'd tell it to you, but I'm not exactly sitting comfortably.'

'Didn't know you were into bondage.'

Sophia gave him a once very familiar look of annoyance. 'It's hardly by choice. My, ah, associates have this funny idea that given half a chance, I'd try to escape.'

'Or kill them.'

'That would be the other half of the chance.' She rattled the chain. 'I assume you came in here looking for someone to rescue. Don't stop on my account.'

Chase laughed mockingly to cover the whirling confusion of his feelings. 'Yeah, right. Last time I saw you, you shot me with a poison dart!'

'Yes, I thought you might bring that up. Would it help if I said I was really very sorry?'

A noise – Nina rapping on the door. 'Shit! Someone's coming.'

Sophia rattled the chain again, now with a calculating smile. 'It'd be terrible if I shouted to the entire camp that you were here.'

'I could just kill you.'

'Cold-blooded murder of a defenceless woman? Not really your style.'

Now it was his turn to smile, icily. 'I've got a piece of paper that says you're already dead. I'd just be making it official.'

Another knock, more frantic, then the Winnebago's door opened and Nina rushed inside. 'Eddie, what're you doing?' she said, seeing him in the bedroom and hurrying over. 'Ribbsley's— Gah!'

'Nina as well?' said Sophia, arching an eyebrow. 'Quite the reunion we've got going on.'

'You told me she was dead!' Nina spluttered to Chase.

'Yeah, looks like they were a bit quick with the death certificate. Where's Ribbsley?'

'On his way back!' She tugged at his arm. 'Come on, we've got to go!'

Sophia shook the chain once more. 'A-*hem*.'

Nina stared at her. 'Are you *kidding* me?'

'If you don't, I'll raise the alarm.'

'Too late now anyway,' said Chase, hearing movement outside. He pulled Nina into the bedroom and shut the door. A moment later, they felt the Winnebago shift on its suspension as someone entered the lounge.

'Oh, Sophia,' called Ribbsley in a sing-song voice, 'I'm ba-ack! Sorry about the wait, but I needed to get some more ice. Still, pleasures are greatest in the anticipation, as the saying goes.' He opened the bedroom door—

Chase yanked him inside. The ice bucket he was carrying fell to the floor, ice cubes scattering as the champagne bottle in it bounced across the room. Chase drew back his other fist to punch him.

'Don't hurt him!' Sophia ordered, concern in her voice. Chase gave her a surprised look, but lowered his hand.

Ribbsley stared at Chase in fear, then saw Nina behind him. His eyes widened. 'Dr Wilde?'

Nina stepped round Chase – and punched Ribbsley square in the face. '*That* was for telling the Covenant about the photos of the tablet, you son of a bitch! A friend of mine almost died because of you.' She moved back, eyeing Sophia. 'Okay, now will somebody tell me what the hell is going on here? Starting with why you're still alive?'

'I have Gabriel to thank for that,' Sophia said, looking at Ribbsley as he clutched his nose. 'The Covenant needed him to translate the text and lead the expedition to find this place. He had a condition – for me to be freed from Guantánamo. Since the Covenant have influence over certain people in high places, they were able to arrange it.' She glanced at Chase. 'How exactly did they do it?'

'They showed me a body with half its face missing and said it was you,' he said grimly. 'They must have found someone who looked a lot like you – then killed her to take your place.'

'Really? She must have been a very good likeness if she was able to fool you.' Sophia's expression revealed nothing more than mild interest at the revelation.

Nina was more emotional. 'You don't care that some innocent woman was *murdered* to get you out of jail? No, of course you don't. You don't care about anyone but yourself.'

'Except him, apparently,' Chase said, pushing Ribbsley into a corner. 'Why's he so special, Sophia?'

'Why do you think, Eddie?' Sophia asked. 'He loves me. He has done for years, ever since I was his student at Cambridge.'

'Eddie?' said Ribbsley, regarding Chase with a look now less of fear than of distaste. 'Eddie *Chase*?'

Chase grinned at him and nodded. ''Ow do?'

'This?' Ribbsley cried, his Rhodesian accent growing stronger as he became more agitated. '*This* is the man you left me to marry? This, this . . . *thug*?'

'Prefer "yob" myself,' said Chase mildly.

Ribbsley ignored him. 'I cannot believe this, Sophia! What on earth could you possibly have seen in him? He's just some crude, uneducated, loutish . . . *Neanderthal*!'

'Hey!' Nina snapped. 'You're talking about my fiancé, asshole!'

He sneered at her. 'Ah, that famous New York charm. That explains what *you* see in him, I suppose. You're about on a par in terms of class.'

'Oh, *do* be quiet, Gabriel,' Sophia chided. He looked stung. 'Nina, I assume you're here looking for the same thing as Gabriel and the Covenant – the lost civilisation of the Veteres.' She sighed. '*Such* a pretentious name. But the thing is, Gabriel has a rather considerable advantage. He knows their language, and you don't. But if you free me . . . I can give you a way to negate that advantage instantly. Because I know it too.'

'Sophia!' said Ribbsley, horrified. 'What are you doing?'

'Sorry, darling, but I need to put my best interests first.' She looked back at Nina and Chase. 'There's another reason why I'd prefer you to find it before the Covenant. The moment Gabriel's job is done . . . they'll kill me.'

'She's right,' said Chase. 'I heard that white-haired bloke talking about it.'

'Wouldn't that be a shame,' Nina muttered.

'They won't,' said Ribbsley, pushing out his chest. 'I won't let them.'

Sophia sighed. 'For God's sake, Gabriel. Are you really that full of yourself? If it ever got out that I'd been spirited from Guantánamo and was still alive, it would spark the biggest witch-hunt in American history. And you know where it would end.' She gave him a meaningful look. 'So once you find what the Covenant are looking for, Callum will kill me.'

'Callum!' Nina exclaimed, the memory finally coming to her. 'I *knew* I'd seen him before. Eddie, don't you remember? At the US embassy in London – he was one of the guys working with Jack Mitchell!'

The name and face connected for Chase too. 'But I thought he worked for DARPA?'

'Jack lied about working for them, so maybe this guy did too.'

'You already know him? My my, such a small world,' said Sophia sarcastically. 'But no, he doesn't work for DARPA. His name's Michael Callum, and he handles very, *very* black operations for certain parts of the American government. But now you see why I'm extremely motivated to help you. I'm already officially dead – I'd prefer not to be that way for real.'

Nina almost laughed. 'Do you seriously think that I want to help *you*? You tried to kill us and nuke New York!'

'Oh, you're not still holding a grudge about that, are you?' Sophia sighed. 'Besides, you need me. Do you want to spend fifteen years puzzling out the Veteres language, like Gabriel did, or would you like a head start?'

'Sophia, don't do this,' Ribbsley warned. Chase shoved him back against the wall. 'I can protect you!'

'Sorry, Gabriel, but Eddie can do a much better job.' She addressed Nina again. 'I can also tell you everything I know about the Covenant. I can help you . . . if you help me.'

'Bollocks to that,' said Chase. 'We can't trust you. Besides, Nina'll be able to figure all this out without any help.' He glanced over his shoulder at her. 'Nina?'

She stood in silence, regarding Sophia with a calculating expression. 'Nina!' Chase repeated. 'Hang on, you're not seriously thinking about saying yes, are you?'

'She . . . has a point,' Nina admitted reluctantly. 'I can't translate the language.'

'You worked out enough to find this place.'

'Those were numbers, Eddie. All I did was follow a map. But the inscription in that chamber is a whole lot more – and I won't be able to work it out without help.'

'Yeah, but *her* help?' Chase objected. 'First chance she gets, she'll stab us in the back!'

'Then we don't give her the chance.'

'*What?*'

'We *need* her, Eddie.' Nina moved closer to the bed, looking Sophia in the eye. 'Okay. We'll take you with us. But let me make this perfectly clear – you do exactly what we tell you, and if you try to screw us over in even the tiniest way, we'll dump you on the doorstep of the US embassy so you can go straight back to Guantánamo Bay . . . or I might even kill you myself.'

Sophia raised an eyebrow. '*You'd* kill me?'

'You'd be surprised what I can do when people piss me off.'

'Ah, yes. That redhead temper again.'

Nina gave her a smile devoid of all humour. 'You better believe it. Do we have an understanding?'

'We do indeed,' said Sophia, nodding. 'I'd shake hands, but . . .' She jingled the chain holding her cuffed hands.

'Well, Professor Ribbsley,' said Nina, turning to him, 'I take it you've got a key. Unless this is some sort of personal kink I'd rather not know about.'

'You don't know what you're doing,' Ribbsley said. 'You have no idea just how powerful the Covenant really is.'

'But I soon will, won't I? The key? Unless you want Eddie to find it for me.'

Ribbsley hurriedly delved into his trouser pocket, producing a key ring. Nina took it and went to the bed, Sophia turning to let her reach the chain. The first lock came away, the chain clinking on to the pillow; after another moment, one of the ratchets was opened, allowing Sophia to bring her arms out from behind her back.

'Oh, that's such a relief,' she said, massaging her newly freed wrist. 'Now, if you wouldn't mind opening the other one . . .' She held up her arms.

Nina had other ideas. 'Actually . . .'

'Wait, what are— Hey!' Sophia protested as the open bracelet rasped shut around her wrist once more.

'You seriously think I'm going to let you run around loose?' She moved back to the door. 'While we're at it, it'll slow the Covenant down if Ribbsley doesn't have his notes. Where's his laptop?'

'We can't waste time, we need to get out of here,' said Sophia. 'The Covenant takes a very military approach to things – they won't be eating for much longer.'

'What about loverboy here?' Chase asked, indicating Ribbsley. 'We can't drag him along as well.'

'Knock him out,' Sophia suggested. Ribbsley's eyes bulged wide in fright.

'Not kill him?' asked Nina mockingly. 'Very generous of you.'

'He *did* get me out of Guantánamo, so I owe him that. As I said, I don't want to see him get hurt.' A look at Chase. 'I'm sure you can do something relatively painless.'

'No!' Ribbsley cried, close to panic. 'Sophia, please, don't do this!'

Chase shoved him back against the wall, hand gripping his throat. Ribbsley gagged. 'Keep your bloody voice down!'

'The laptop,' Nina insisted. 'Where is it?'

'Oh, very well,' Sophia said. 'It's—'

A noise from outside, boots crunching on sand and stone. Right at the door.

'Professor Ribbsley?' said a voice. Zamal. A long silent moment, tension rising . . .

Ribbsley suddenly kicked at the fallen bucket. It flew up to clang noisily against the wall in a shower of flying ice, spilling a bottle of Bulgari aftershave from the bedside cabinet. Chase punched him hard across the jaw, dropping him limply on to the bed – but the damage had been done.

'Ribbsley!' Zamal shouted. 'What's going on?'

Chase ran into the lounge, heading for the door. Before he could reach it, it opened and Zamal rushed inside – only to take a blow to the head that sent him reeling back against a counter.

But he recovered fast, grabbing for his holstered gun. Chase charged, gripping his wrist just as he drew the gun and bashing his hand against the edge of the counter. Zamal snarled and jabbed a knee up at Chase's groin, but the Englishman twisted sideways just in time to avoid a fight-ending blow.

Zamal used the shift in Chase's balance to thrust away from the counter. Both men lurched across the room, still grappling for the gun as they crashed into the RV's kitchen area. Zamal's gun hand came up, the weapon shaking as he strained to break free. Chase fought back, pushing him round . . . and inadvertently pointing the gun at the two women as they entered the lounge. Nina yelped and dropped to the carpet below the line of fire, Sophia hastily retreating behind an armchair.

Chase shoved Zamal back. The gun swung back and forth as they struggled. Nina scrambled forward on her hands and knees as the barrel waved towards her.

Zamal punched Chase in the side. He flinched, giving the Arab the chance to turn and force him down on the kitchen counter, left hand clamping round his throat. A cutlery rack toppled over, its contents clashing across the stainless steel. Zamal twisted his wrist, trying to point the gun at Chase's head . . .

Chase punched him again, but Zamal blocked the blow with his upper arm as he pushed Chase down harder. Spilled cutlery jabbed at the side of his head. He threw another punch, with no more success, then clawed at the counter, searching desperately for a knife as Zamal's grip tightened.

His fingers closed round a cold metal handle. He snatched it up, striking at Zamal's face—

It wasn't a knife.

It wasn't even a fork. It was only a spoon, the back of the rounded head striking Zamal's brow with an almost comical *smack!* that brought a mocking look from Chase's opponent.

The look changed instantly to one of enraged pain as Chase rolled the spoon over in his hand and jabbed it at the bearded man's eye as if trying to scoop it out of his head. Zamal roared and jumped back. Chase leapt up, both men spinning round – and pointing the gun at Nina again. She shrieked and dived out of the way, landing behind the RV's driving seat.

Ribbsley appeared in the bedroom door, wielding the champagne bottle. He saw Chase and Zamal battling for the gun and ran at them, raising the bottle like a club.

Sophia jumped out from behind the chair, grabbing a black leather briefcase with her cuffed hands. 'Gabriel!' He froze, the bottle held high, and looked round at her in surprise. 'Take *this*!' She swung the briefcase and hit him in the chest. Ribbsley stumbled, dropping the bottle, and fell through the open door to land on his back in the sand outside. The case thumped down beside him. 'Nina! You've got the keys! *Drive!*'

Nina realised that she still had Ribbsley's key ring – and on it was one key with the fat black plastic head of a remote locking system. With a worried look at the struggling men, she dropped into the driving seat and shoved the key in the ignition.

Chase kicked back with one foot to give himself leverage on the refrigerator, throwing Zamal against the wall. He smashed the other man on the cheek with the point of his right elbow, then managed to get a grip on the gun. Zamal responded by punching him in the ribs. Chase grunted in pain. He elbowed Zamal in the head again, trying to wrench the gun away—

Zamal realised he was in danger of losing his weapon – and squeezed the trigger.

The shot punched through the Winnebago's roof. Chase yelled as his hand was burned – the heel of his palm had been partly covering the automatic's ejection port. He let go, and Zamal twisted his wrist around to point the gun at his head, pulling the trigger again—

Clink.

No shot. Chase's grip on the gun's slide had stopped it from cycling properly, needing a manual operation to complete the reloading action.

Chase took immediate advantage of the misfire to slam a sledgehammer punch into the Arab's stomach. Zamal bent at the waist as the wind was knocked out of him, and took a follow-up blow to the face.

The engine started. 'Go!' Sophia yelled. Nina released the hand-brake, put the Winnebago into drive, stamped on the accelerator . . .

And the seventeen-ton vehicle wallowed as its wheels spun in the sand.

The movement sent Chase and Zamal reeling across the lounge. Sophia snatched up the champagne bottle, waiting for a chance to strike.

Nina tried again, pushing down the pedal more gently. The Winnebago rocked, then gained traction and jolted forward. She swung the steering wheel to bring the enormous RV towards the dirt track away from the coast.

The gunshot had attracted attention. Through the windscreen, she saw men running towards them. Grimacing, she shoved the accelerator down harder.

Zamal and Chase traded more blows, neither willing to relinquish their grip on the other as they staggered back and forth across the room. Sophia was still waiting for a clear strike. 'Eddie!' she said impatiently, holding up the bottle. 'Turn him round!'

Chase saw what she had in mind, and with a furious burst of strength forced Zamal's back towards her. The bottle flashed down, smashing over the Arab's head and showering Chase with frothing champagne. Zamal's knees buckled.

'Waste of a Cuvée Winston,' said Sophia, almost sadly, before moving to the door and holding it open. 'Throw him out!'

Chase half dragged the groaning Zamal across the room. 'Okay, mate,' Chase grunted. 'Holiday's over.'

The track ahead curved, low limestone embankments rising on both sides. Nina threw the RV into the bend without slowing, the front bumper clipping the outer bank.

Chase lurched, Zamal grabbed him – and both men toppled out through the open door.

16

Chase landed on top of Zamal, knocking the breath from both of them as they rolled to a stop in the Winnebago's dusty wake.

Chase recovered first, coughing. The Arab was lying prone a few feet away.

He still had the gun.

Zamal realised this at the same moment as Chase. He tugged the slide to unjam it and brought the weapon round—

Chase punched him so hard that his beret flew off. This time, Zamal stayed down. 'Guess the champagne went to your head,' Chase said. He looked round to see the Winnebago retreating into the desert – and one of the quad bikes swerving off its patrol route after it.

It wasn't the only vehicle in pursuit. He could hear the second quad bike cutting through the excavations behind him – and the rasp of a third Kawasaki starting up. All that, plus shouting from the camp as the rest of the Covenant forces mobilised, told him that he really needed to be somewhere else.

He pulled the gun from Zamal's limp hand and staggered painfully after the Winnebago.

Nina found the switch for the headlights. The bumpy desert landscape lit up before her.

A noise to one side, an engine. In the mirror she saw one of the

192

quad bikes bounding towards her. And something picked out by the headlight's glare above the handlebars, a line of dark metal in the rider's hand—

'Shit!' Nina gasped, ducking as flame spat from the rifle's barrel. Bullets punctured the Winnebago's slab-like side. 'Eddie, keep down!' No answer. 'Eddie?'

Sophia took cover behind Nina. 'He fell out!'

'He *what*?' She was about to stamp on the brake when another burst of gunfire deterred her. Instead, she increased speed, the RV pitching over each bump like a ship in heavy seas. 'Why didn't you tell me?'

'Eddie can look after himself.'

'Well, I hope *we* can!' Another turn was coming up fast, a bank channelling the Winnebago to the right. Sophia grabbed the fat leather seat for support as Nina turned hard, feeling the big, top-heavy vehicle begin to tip over. 'Whoa!' She had to ease off . . .

'If you could keep all the wheels on the ground, it'd be helpful,' Sophia said dryly as the RV dropped heavily back down, loose objects clattering round the cabin behind them.

'It'd be even more helpful if you'd shut your goddamn yap!' The track curved back to the left, rising out of a little gully. She swung the wheel back, the Winnebago rolling even harder.

Where was the quad bike? Nina checked the mirrors, seeing no sign of it behind them.

Engine noise, very close, *too* close—

It wasn't behind them. It had drawn level, zooming over the rise in a straight line to catch up while she had been forced to weave through the gully. She looked sideways to see it just yards away, the rider swinging the rifle round in one hand, aiming at her . . .

Nina ducked, hauling on the wheel to slew the Winnebago off the track at the quad bike. The rider fired a burst before he was forced to swerve away, shattering the side window and ripping a pair of bullet holes in the panoramic windscreen, a web of silver cracks obscuring Nina's view.

'Sophia!' she yelled, the RV ripping through bushes before she swung it back on to the track. 'I can't see ahead! I need you to—'

A red cylinder flew past her head and smashed through the damaged windscreen; one of the Winnebago's fire extinguishers. 'Is that better?' Sophia asked, dropping into the passenger seat.

'Oh, just fine,' Nina growled as a gritty wind blew through the new hole. But at least she could see again. She looked for the quad bike. Its headlight was now in the mirror – it had been forced to drop in behind them to avoid a stand of trees.

The sound of bullet impacts echoed up the cabin from the Winnebago's rear. 'What the hell's he shooting at?'

'The tyres, maybe?' Sophia suggested with considerable sarcasm. 'Or the gas cylinders? Or the hundred gallons of fuel?'

Another burst of gunfire – then a low *whoomph* reached them from the bedroom as something ignited. 'Or your boyfriend's napalm aftershave,' said Nina frostily. They turned to see flickers of flame through the bedroom door.

'Maybe it *is* a little overpowering,' Sophia quickly agreed.

'That'd better not have been the only fire extinguisher you just threw out the window.'

'I think there's another one.' Sophia made her way unsteadily back down the length of the bucking vehicle.

Nina checked the mirror again. The quad bike was still tucked in behind them – and further back, she spotted other lights racing through the desert. 'Oh, God, Eddie, where are you?'

Chase was having quad bike problems of his own. The nearest bike was closing fast, the cyclops glare of its headlight casting his long running shadow into the night ahead. Still running, he twisted and fired off a shot. It hit the bike's front with a metallic crack.

But it caused no damage. The bike kept coming. He turned to shoot again—

Too slow. The Kawasaki swept past – and the rider kicked him square in the back, hurling him face first to the ground. The gun spun from his hand. Spine on fire, he rose to his hands and knees as the quad bike made a skidding turn to come back round for another attack.

Where was the gun? It couldn't have landed more than a few feet away . . .

The bike charged straight for him. He crawled forward, hands sweeping back and forth through the sand, finding nothing but stones.

The light was blinding, from his low viewpoint looking like a locomotive about to crush him.

Sand, stones—

Metal!

Chase snapped up the gun and fired just above the headlight. There was a startled scream, and the rider fell backwards – then the quad bike veered sharply, hitting a rock and flipping over to barrel across the sand—

Straight at Chase.

He threw himself sideways, rolling over and over as the tumbling bike slammed down beside him, showering him with grit and broken bodywork. It bounced a couple more times before finally coming to rest on its side.

Pain rippled up Chase's back, but he fought through it and stood, looking towards the camp. The other quad bike was still coming, and he could see more headlights moving along the track.

He limped to the battered bike and pulled it back on to all four wheels. The engine had stalled; he mounted the saddle and tried the starter. It whined in protest, the engine reluctantly turning over on the third attempt.

He could see the Winnebago's rear lights in the distance – and something else, a flickering glow through its rear window that looked suspiciously like a fire. 'Oh, Christ,' he moaned as he twisted the throttle, the engine revving raggedly. 'What's she done now?'

'Have you found the fire extinguisher?' Nina shouted down the Winnebago's cabin.

'Yes!' came the answer from the bedroom.

'And?'

'It's on fire!'

'Oh, that's, that's . . .' Nina struggled for words. '*So* not good,' was all she could come up with. She looked back, seeing Sophia making a hasty exit from the bedroom as a curtain caught light behind her. 'You've got a kitchen and a bathroom back there – throw some water on it!'

'In what?' Sophia snapped, holding up a teacup.

'How about *pans*? Don't you cook?'

'Of course I don't cook! What am I, a peasant?'

Nina's scathing reply was cut off when she saw the quad bike trying to overtake again. She turned to force the rider off the track. He dropped back slightly, but had no trouble riding up the low embankment flanking the trail – unlike the Winnebago, which shook violently.

And in the other mirror, she could see two more quad bikes charging across the desert . . .

Chase was gaining rapidly on the lumbering RV, cutting straight across the sand to intercept it. The first quad bike had gone wide, trying to overtake – he guessed that the rider planned to get far enough ahead to stop and take a head-on shot at the driver.

He wasn't going to let that happen.

The third quad was about fifty metres behind, following him. Even though he knew its rider was armed with a rifle, Chase doubted he would take a shot . . . yet. At speed over rough terrain, firing one-handed, he would have only slightly more chance of hitting than if he fired up into the air hoping the bullet would come down on his head.

But the odds would improve dramatically at closer range.

A boulder leapt into his headlight beam; he dodged it, then angled back at the Winnebago. It was definitely on fire, burning curtains whipping from the bullet-smashed rear window.

Chase leaned into the dusty wind and forced the throttle to its limit.

Nina was thrown against the wheel as the Winnebago hit a large hump, rocking sickeningly. Sophia fell on to the lounge's leather couch, clinging to its padded arm.

The RV hadn't taken the landing well: something was grinding under the floor. The wheel felt heavier in Nina's hands. Either the power assistance was failing, or the steering had been damaged.

'How's the fire?' she called.

Sophia glanced back. The flames had now spread into the main cabin. 'Getting bigger! Where's the bike?'

'Getting closer!' The quad bike had drawn level again. Then it surged past, sweeping across the sand to cut in just ahead of the RV. Nina yelped, swerving to avoid it – realising a moment too late that she would have been better off trying to *hit* it. By the time she straightened, the Kawasaki was clear and pulling away. The rider's rifle stood out in the headlights, slung over his back. 'Dammit!'

The trail ahead dipped, dropping into another gully. The quad held its speed as it slithered round a corner, but Nina was forced to brake to prevent the Winnebago from running wide and hitting the wall. The grinding grew louder as she pulled the wheel, but mechanical concerns paled against the knowledge that the rider ahead was gaining ground to set up an ambush – while the two other bikes were catching up from behind.

Chase saw the Winnebago ahead, picked out by little running lights along its length – and the trail of smoke behind it, glowing red in the RV's tail lights. He was almost on it – but he realised he didn't have a plan for what to do when he caught up. If Nina and Sophia stopped to escape the burning vehicle, the rider behind him would shoot them – and there was no way the compact quad bike could carry three people.

The man behind cut his options still further as gunfire cracked across the desert. He looked back. The undamaged Kawasaki had gained ground, its rider close enough to attempt a shot. He was resting the rifle's barrel on the handlebars, shooting from the hip. Not very accurate – but if he got any closer, he wouldn't need to be.

The Winnebago was just ahead, its roof almost level with the top of the gully. He steered parallel to it.

A second shot tore past, closer.

He was alongside—

Chase squeezed the last ounce of power out of the quad – and turned sharply, leaping off the edge of the gully.

The bike cleared the gap, landing on the Winnebago's roof—

And fell through it, steel and aluminium instantly buckling under the weight.

The RV's back end collapsed, side panels bowing outwards as the entire rear wall broke loose and crashed aflame on to the trail. The quad bike fell on to the bed, pitching Chase over the handlebars. He smashed through the scorched partition wall in a shower of sparks to land on his back in the lounge.

Sophia regarded him in surprise. 'Ay up,' Chase said with a dazed wave.

'What the hell was *that*?' Nina shrieked.

'Just my ex-husband making a typically overblown entrance,' Sophia told her.

Nina looked back. 'Eddie!'

'Hi, love. With you in a minute,' he said, brushing away stinging embers before going to the bedroom door.

Behind him, Sophia saw the gun lying amongst the splinters. She hurried across the room to pick it up, glancing calculatingly after Chase.

Chase entered the devastated bedroom, looking through the gaping hole where the rear wall had been to see the pursuing rider swinging on to the trail behind them as the RV climbed out of the gully. He reached for the gun – to find nothing there. 'Buggeration and fu—'

The rider lined up the rifle—

Chase threw himself down amongst the debris, taking cover behind the quad bike on the bed as a three-round burst ripped into the Winnebago's mangled tail-end. A few seconds later came another crackle of gunfire, the bullet impacts lower down.

Chase knew why. He was aiming at the tyres.

He poked his head up, seeing the rider steering towards the Winnebago's side for a better firing angle – and realised with alarm that his own battered Kawasaki was now on fire. Worse still, a broken metal spar had punctured its fuel tank, a dribble of petrol seeping into the mattress . . . which was burning in several places. 'Fuckery!' he concluded.

No way to put out the flames. He had to get rid of the quad-bike before the fuel tank ignited.

The engine was still burbling. Chase jumped up and grabbed the handlebars, pulling the bike around as he blipped the throttle. The rider saw him and swung back, switching targets from the rear wheels to the Englishman—

Chase twisted the throttle.

The quad bike surged from the bed as he dropped flat, flying out of the flame-licked back of the RV straight at the other bike. The trail of leaking fuel spattered through the flames – and ignited, an arc of fire rushing after the quad bike as it tumbled at the screaming rider . . .

The bikes collided, the fiery streak catching up an instant later. Chase's bike blew to pieces in a fireball that lit up the surrounding desert, the explosion of the second quad following almost simultaneously.

Burning fragments rained down on Chase. He weathered the pain, waiting until the heat of the fireball had faded before opening his eyes . . . to see a fat tyre bounding along the trail after him, engulfed in flames.

'Shit!' he gasped, rolling aside just as the blazing wheel careered past and bounced off the partition wall, spinning back at him. He yelped and hurled himself on to the burning mattress as it flew over his head into the desert night.

Rubbing frantically at his arms where hairs had caught light, Chase leapt through the hole in the wall, running past Sophia to the kitchen area. 'Ow, ow, fuck! Water, I need water!' He reached the sink and turned on the taps, splashing water over himself.

Nina looked back. 'Eddie, are you okay? What happened?'

'Wheel,' he gasped. 'On fire.'

'Was it rolling down the road?' Sophia asked.

Chase gave her a less-than-amused glare, shaking off the water. His forearms were covered with mottled red blotches, but none of the burns seemed serious. 'Got the guy behind you.'

'There's another one in front,' Nina told him.

'Yeah, I know.' He turned, gaze darting over the strewn debris on the floor. 'I had a gun . . .'

'This gun?' asked Sophia. Chase froze as he saw the automatic in her cuffed hands, aimed at his chest. She looked him in the eye, smiled slightly . . . then flipped it round and held it out to him.

He snatched it from her. 'You're welcome,' she said sarcastically. 'I just wanted to prove that you can trust me.'

'I wouldn't trust you any more than I could cough up a dog.'

She sniffed. 'Charming as ever, I see.'

He ignored her, quickly checking how many bullets remained in the magazine before joining Nina. 'How far ahead is he?'

She pointed down the track. The last quad bike had now gained a lead of over a hundred yards, a dust trail glowing like a nebula in its rear lights.

Chase checked the speedometer. For all the noise coming from the RV's transmission, it was barely managing thirty miles an hour over the rough terrain. The rider would have just enough time to slam his quad bike to a stop, take aim at the driver and fire before the Winnebago reached him . . .

'Keep driving,' he said to Nina, hunching down in the passenger-side footwell. 'The moment he stops, tell me.'

'What're you going to do?'

He waggled the gun. 'What do you think? Just don't slow down.'

Sophia returned to the couch, bracing herself. 'Can I remind you both that we're still on fire?'

'Feel free to bail out whenever you like,' Nina shot back. The quad bike was still pulling away, but now drifting over to one side of the trail . . .

Brake lights flared.

'He's stopping, he's stopping!' she yelled.

'Drive straight at him!' Chase ordered.

Nina pushed the accelerator down harder, each bump pounding the wallowing RV. The quad bike slewed to a stop, its rider swinging his rifle from his back. 'Eddie, he's got a gun—'

'I know! Keep going!'

The rifle rose . . .

Chase sprang up and fired as fast as he could pull the trigger, shattering the windscreen. Bullets kicked up dirt around the Kawasaki, the Winnebago juddering too much for him to get a proper fix – but that wasn't why he was shooting.

It was to distract the other man, forcing him to switch to a more dangerous target.

Chase.

Click. Empty magazine.

The rider changed his aim—

Chase dived to the floor as a burst of rifle fire ripped through the remains of the windscreen. '*Hit him!*' he roared.

The gunman saw that he'd missed, switched back to his original target – and realised that she was driving the massive RV right at him.

Nina cringed in her seat, shutting her eyes—

The gunman hurled himself aside as the Winnebago's flat nose slammed into the quad bike like an express train, smashing it apart. There was a jolt as the front wheel ran over something, followed a moment later by another as the rear wheel did the same.

'Oh God, oh my God!' Nina shrieked, flapping her hands in near-panic. 'I ran him over!'

'No, he got out of the way,' said Sophia, looking back. 'Although I don't know why you care. He *was* trying to kill you.'

'Maybe because I'm not a psycho?' She took the wheel again and checked the mirrors. More lights, some distance behind – but closing. Full-size 4x4s racing after them. 'Eddie! How much further to our jeep?'

Chase looked ahead. 'Not far.' He jumped up. 'Nina, let me drive!'

'What're you doing?' she asked as they traded places.

'I'm gonna find out if you can drift a Winnebago!' The ground ahead was littered with large rocks, the track dropping into the gully. 'Hang on!' Nina looked dismayed, but grabbed the bullet-ripped passenger seat.

Chase kept his foot down hard on the accelerator as the Winnebago reached the gulch – then sharply raised it. The RV's front end dipped heavily with the sudden loss of power . . . as he turned hard and yanked on the handbrake.

With a shuddering crunch of gravel and sand beneath the tyres, the Winnebago skidded round in a handbrake turn, moving practically sideways as he dropped into the gully. The burning RV's rear end clipped the steep wall. It stopped abruptly, almost throwing Chase and Nina from their seats. Chase looked up to see the other wall of the gulch barely a foot beyond the windscreen. 'All right!' he crowed. 'Thank you, action movies!'

He kicked open the driver's door, waving for Nina and Sophia to follow. 'Okay, so you're fast *and* furious,' said Nina, confused, as they ran through the gulch. 'But how does that help us?'

''Cause that thing's going to blow up—'

There was a bright orange flash and a loud *whump* of igniting fuel, followed a second later by a much more violent explosion as the Winnebago's propane tanks detonated, knocking them to the ground.

'Any second,' Chase finished. Behind them, the huge RV was engulfed in flames, completely blocking the gully. 'They'll have a job getting through that – and they'll have to go a long way round to get past those rocks.'

'Where's your truck?' Sophia asked.

'Just up here.' The Land Rover was parked off one side of the track. They ran to it and piled in, Chase quickly swinging the 4x4 round to race back towards the distant highway. He checked the mirror. The pursuing vehicles had indeed been stymied by the blazing hulk of the Winnebago, and it would take several minutes for them to skirt the field of boulders. 'Don't think they'll catch up.'

Sophia held up her cuffed hands. 'In that case, perhaps you could take these off?'

Nina toyed with the key. 'Once we're out of here. And once we find out what the hell's going on.'

'I'll tell you everything I know. When we're safe.'

'How often does *that* happen?' said Chase, driving the Land Rover off into the night.

Zamal's seething rage came to a boil as he limped back to the camp, his jaw aching from Chase's punch. He had been opposed to bringing Sophia Blackwood along from the very beginning, but to his disgust Vogler and Hammerstein had caved in to Ribbsley's lust-driven demand, arguing that without him they would be unable to take advantage of the chart Nina Wilde had discovered.

Pathetic! Considering how much money Ribbsley had taken from the Covenant over the years he had been translating Veteres texts for them, he should have been grateful not to have been dragged from his Cambridge home and forced to do the work at gunpoint.

And now the decision had backfired horribly: Blackwood had escaped. With Nina Wilde!

Zamal blamed Vogler; he might not have always agreed with his predecessor, Lorenzo di Bonaventura, but he respected him – and knew he would not have given in to Ribbsley. The protégé did not match up to his mentor.

He reached the encampment and found the others waiting for him. 'I don't care what deals you made,' he snarled at Ribbsley. 'When I catch your woman, I'll *kill* her.'

'She's got to be found,' said Callum. 'If anyone realises she's still alive—'

'Blackwood is your problem,' said Vogler dismissively. 'Not ours. Dr Wilde is our biggest threat. We can assume she saw the inscription.'

'Then we have to eliminate her before she translates it.' Hammerstein shot Vogler a cold look. 'If those pirates you hired had actually done their job and killed everyone on the *Pianosa*—'

'Blaming each other isn't helping us find them,' said Callum, stepping into the centre of the group. 'We need to get organised, right now—'

Zamal grabbed him by the collar. 'Do not tell us what to do, *American*,' he snarled, before pushing him back. 'You are only here because we allow you to be. Do not forget who is in charge.' Callum said nothing, regarding him with an expressionless, basilisk gaze.

'He's right, though,' said Vogler. 'We have to find them. And we'll have to destroy this site, tonight. Professor, have you got all the information you need from the chamber?' Ribbsley nodded. 'Good. Then keep working on it. And Professor . . .' An almost apologetic look. 'I'm afraid that Ms Blackwood is now a threat to the Covenant. She can't be trusted.'

'I'm glad we agree on something,' Zamal hissed. The three Covenant leaders walked away, Callum following.

Ribbsley remained still, however, looking down at the object in his hands – the briefcase. 'Oh, I wouldn't say she can't be trusted,' he said to himself with a hint of a smile, opening it. Inside was his laptop.

Containing all his research.

Sophia had known full well what was in the case – and deliberately kept it from Nina and Chase. The smile became a full one. 'I wouldn't say that at all . . .'

17

'So,' said Nina to Sophia, 'what's your story?'

'Yeah,' Chase added. 'And what the hell did you do to your hair?'

After reaching the highway, they had driven towards Perth for some distance before turning off the main road and back towards the coast. It was a slower, less direct route south, but also one with – they hoped – less chance of anyone looking for them.

Now, not long after sunrise, they were the morning's first patrons of a small truck-stop diner. The only other person in the ramshackle building was the middle-aged waitress, who after serving coffee to the new arrivals retreated behind the counter to read a romance novel to the scratchy accompaniment of an old jukebox in one corner.

'Not my idea, I can assure you,' Sophia said, running her hands through her spiky hair. Both handcuff bracelets were now fastened round one wrist so as not to attract attention. 'Blonde really isn't my colour. Though it could have been worse.' She glanced at Nina's red hair. 'But Callum insisted, on the off-chance that some random outback passer-by might see my real hair and go, "Wait a minute, that's the sheila who tried to blow up New York! I thought she was dead!"'

'But, unfortunately, you're not,' said Nina.

'Ooh, your repartee cuts like paper,' Sophia sneered, giving Nina a disdainful look – then spotting her engagement ring. For a moment she seemed both shocked and angry before her contemptuous mask came back down. 'Please don't tell me you're getting married.'

'We're getting married,' Nina told her with an icy smile.

'We did think about inviting you,' Chase added, 'but then you died.'

'Speaking of which,' said Nina, 'how about you tell us why the Covenant arranged for you to be snuck out of Guantánamo.'

Sophia sat back. 'Part of that comes down to why I was put in there in the first place.'

'Because you'd've been killed before you ever got to trial in a regular prison,' said Chase.

She sniffed. 'Hardly. Do you really think anybody would have cared if Large Marge had shanked me in the shower? That way, they would have avoided an incredibly long, costly and complex trial that would have exposed America's border security as a hopeless pork-barrel shambles. After all, despite all the billions of dollars they've spent on Homeland Security, the only thing that stopped a nuclear explosion was a balding Yorkshireman sticking his hand in the mechanism.' She glanced at Chase's left forearm and the long X-shaped scar running along it.

'And it still hurts,' Chase rumbled.

Nina made a disgusted sound. 'I can't believe this. You tried to be the biggest mass murderer in history, but you're talking about it like . . . like it was *nothing.*'

Sophia shrugged. 'What do you want me to do, cackle maniacally and proclaim that the world has not seen the last of Sophia Blackwood? I had a plan. It failed. I was caught. By you. Obviously I was . . . rather angry about that at the time.' She gave them a dark look that made it clear embers of resentment still burned within her. 'But that was then – and there are other people

I've had more reason to be angry at since. Specifically . . . Victor Dalton.'

'The President?' asked Nina, puzzled. 'Why him?'

'He put me in Guantánamo – even though I'd already been kept in a regular high-security prison for months. Hardly the nicest surroundings . . . but it was like a stay at the Dorchester compared to Camp 7. And it was practically the first thing he did after his inauguration. Do you know why?'

'He thought you needed to work on your tan?' Chase suggested.

'Ah, that rapier wit. So there *is* something you and Nina have in common,' said Sophia. 'No, Eddie. The reason he sent me to Guantánamo is that I was a threat to him. I could destroy his presidency, just like that.'

Nina eyed her dubiously. 'Oh, yeah? How?'

'Do you remember the night we first met?'

'Sure. René Corvus's yacht.'

'Yes. I was with Richard Yuen. And Victor – Senator Dalton, as he was at the time – was there as well.'

Nina nodded, remembering the evening. 'Yeah. And?'

'And later that evening, he and I had a . . . private meeting in one of the cabins.'

Chase coughed on his coffee. 'You shagged the *President*?' he blurted. The waitress glanced up from her book.

'Eddie!' Nina cried, batting his arm.

'Eloquently put, as ever,' Sophia said. 'But yes, I did.'

Chase shook his head. 'Bloody hell. And you did it with your ex-husband, current husband and future husband all on the boat at the same time. Just can't get enough, can you?'

'Oh, Richard knew about it. And so did René. They just didn't know about each other knowing.'

Nina's head was spinning. '*Why?* Why did you do it?'

'Business, of course. He hadn't won the party's nomination yet, but he was by far the leader in the polls. So both Richard and René thought – once I put the idea into their heads – that having a little, ah, *influence* over the next President of the United States would be very useful.'

'You recorded it,' Chase realised. 'You hid a camera somewhere and taped the whole thing.' He made a face. 'That's really, really . . . gross. I mean, I've met the man. He's not exactly George Clooney.'

Sophia smirked. 'It's funny, Eddie – a lot of my friends said exactly the same thing when I married you.'

Nina shook her head. 'No, this is insane. There is no way that you enticed Victor Dalton into bed and recorded the whole thing. He had the Secret Service with him, for God's sake!'

'The Secret Service doesn't just protect the presidential candidates,' said Sophia. 'It protects their *secrets*. Why do you think it's called that? All men of power have their lusts, their addictions, their perversions – they come with the kind of personality that craves power in the first place.'

'Perfect match for you, then,' said Chase.

'Can we stop talking about – about lusty addicted perverts?' Nina demanded. 'So you made a recording. Then what?'

'Then, I kept it very close to me,' Sophia continued. 'Do you remember in Shanghai, Eddie, that I took us to Richard's office to open his safe?'

'He had your passport in there,' Chase recalled.

'Yes, but I could have got it at any time. I really went to pick up a memory stick with a list of all Richard's less-than-legal campaign contributions, not just to Dalton but to several other politicians as well – and also the digital recording. I had it with me in New York and Botswana, and then when I went to Switzerland with Richard I put it in a bank deposit box.'

'And it's still there, I bet,' said Nina.

'Yes. Which is why Dalton wanted me as far out of sight as

possible. If I were in the normal system, I'd have visitation rights, access to counsel, lawyers – people I could conceivably tell about the recording and use to arrange its release to the media.'

'Which would kill Dalton's career stone dead. The President, having an affair with the terrorist who tried to nuke New York . . .'

'Exactly. But since Dalton declared me an enemy combatant as soon as he took office, he could ship me off to Cuba where I was denied all those things. Which was why when Gabriel got the Covenant to demand my release, Callum came as well – as my executioner. I have knowledge that can bring down the President, so I can't be allowed to live.' She smiled, a broad, mocking grin. 'Oh, by the way, now that you know about the recording, the same applies to you. You've just become enemies of the most powerful man in the world. Congratulations!' She took in their stunned expressions with smug satisfaction. 'Although from what I picked up from Callum, I gather that you already were.'

'*What?*' Nina gasped.

'I don't know the details – he didn't exactly confide in me. Something to do with you sabotaging a black operation.'

Nina and Chase exchanged worried looks, thinking back to the events of four months earlier. 'Dalton *knew* about it?' Chase asked.

'Of course he knew,' said Sophia with a hint of impatience. 'Presidents always know, otherwise why bother having them? The man at the top gives the orders.'

'Except when the Covenant do,' Nina said, fixing Sophia with a questioning stare. 'You said you'd tell us about them. So, who are the Covenant? And how do they have the power to tell the President what to do?'

Sophia took a long sip of coffee, the silence in the room broken by the crackle of the jukebox changing records. 'Obviously, I don't know everything,' she said at last. 'They don't exactly regard me as a confidante. Even Gabriel was reluctant to tell me too much. But,' she went on, leaning closer, 'I have my ways.'

'Yeah, we know,' Nina muttered. 'Just the facts, okay?'

'Very well,' said Sophia sourly. 'The Covenant of Genesis is a black operations unit – but one that doesn't belong to any country. It was established to protect the mutual interests of three very old, very powerful and very wealthy . . . well, *organisations* isn't quite the right word.'

'Do you mean, like the mafia or something?' Chase asked.

Sophia laughed. 'I suppose there are some people who'd say that. But no, the right word is actually . . . *faiths*.'

It took Nina a moment to take in Sophia's full meaning. 'Wait, what? You mean, faiths as in religions?'

Sophia nodded. 'Three religions – all different, but with a common origin. Three leaders, one from each religion, sharing control. Vogler represents Christianity, specifically the Roman Catholic Church. Hammerstein is an Israeli, representing Judaism. And Zamal, a Saudi, comes from the fount of Islam. Between them, they have one mission – to suppress all knowledge of something that threatens everything they believe in.'

Chase leaned closer, intrigued. 'Which is?'

'I, ah . . .' Sophia hesitated. 'I don't actually know.'

'You don't *know*?' Nina snapped.

'Gabriel wouldn't tell me,' said Sophia, folding her arms huffily. 'That was something I couldn't get out of him. I was only helping him with the translations. All I know is that it's very old, it involves people he calls the Veteres, and that the Covenant is using him to locate all traces of them – so they can be destroyed.'

'How long's he been working for them?'

'A long time; longer than I've known him. At least fifteen years. But the Covenant's been around for a lot longer, more like fifty years.'

'That means that whatever it is they're trying to hide, they've been very good at it,' Nina realised.

'Very good – and very ruthless. They kill anyone who finds any evidence of the Veteres. I was with Gabriel at a site in Oman about eight years ago; I didn't know what was going on at the time, but now I've realised that the Covenant must have destroyed it, and killed the people who discovered it.'

'Doesn't sound very religious,' said Chase. 'What happened to the whole "Thou shalt not kill" thing?'

'I imagine they pay it about as much attention as we do.'

'Hey!' Nina protested. 'I haven't killed anyone!' Chase and Sophia looked at her. 'Well, not deliberately . . . And they were all trying to kill *me*!'

'I'm sure Saint Peter will accept that as an excuse,' said Sophia.

Chase put a reassuring hand on Nina's back. 'So now what do we do? If three really powerful religions want us dead, and now the President of the United bloody States wants us dead too, then we've got a big problem!'

'The way to stop Dalton is simple enough,' said Sophia. 'Go to Switzerland, get the recording, and release it to the media. He'll be out of the White House within a week.'

'There's an easier way,' Chase said. 'You just walk into the nearest TV studio and say, "Hey, guys, I'm still alive! You'll never guess who let me out of Guantánamo . . ."'

She frowned. 'Just one slight problem with that plan, Eddie. I'd be arrested. And then I'd be killed. Getting rid of Dalton doesn't help me if I'm dead.'

'I dunno,' said Nina, 'I don't see any downsides.'

Sophia glared poisonously at her as Chase chuckled. 'Even if we get the recording,' he said, 'and get rid of Dalton, that still leaves the Covenant. How do we get them off our backs?'

'The same way as Dalton,' said Nina decisively, sitting upright.

'We find what they're afraid of before they do, and expose it to the world.'

'That simple, hmm?' Sophia said, raising an eyebrow.

'That simple,' Nina repeated. 'We've got the photos I took of the inscription; we've got your knowledge of the language; we've got . . . whatever the hell this is,' she added, taking out one of the grooved clay cylinders and holding it up to the light. 'That's just as much as the Covenant.'

'Gabriel will still be able to translate the text,' said Sophia. 'I was only assisting him – he knows much more than me.'

'You mean you're actually admitting to an inadequacy?' Nina scoffed, leaning back in her seat – only to jump in pain. 'Ow!'

'What?' Chase asked.

'Son of a . . . I just sat on where that needle jabbed me in the ass!'

'So it wasn't a bite from a funnel-web spider?' asked Sophia. 'What a shame.'

There was another crackle from the jukebox as the record changed again. 'A funnel-web?' Nina growled, rubbing her aching backside. 'I'd have thought your kind of spider was a black . . . widow . . .' She tailed off, holding up the cylinder – then whirling to look at the jukebox. 'Jesus!'

Chase followed her gaze as the next song started. 'Is that "The Safety Dance"? Bloody hell, I haven't heard that in years.'

'Not the record!' Nina exclaimed, staring with growing excitement at the cylinder. 'I know what this is!'

'You do?' Sophia asked.

'Yes! But I need somewhere I can work – we've got to find a motel, get a room.'

'Three in a bed, eh?' said Chase suggestively.

'Eddie! And we need something else.' She called across the room to the waitress. 'Excuse me – can you tell me how to get to the nearest hardware store?'

★

Travelling south towards Perth, they reached a small town that was home to a motel – and a hardware store.

Nina worked at their motel room's small desk, which soon resembled a cross between a craft fair disaster and a mad scientist's lab. The trip to the store had resulted in the purchase of several sheets of card, duct tape, a length of wooden dowel, a lamp stand, an electric screwdriver . . . and a set of large needles of the kind used to repair canvas and other heavy fabrics.

'You think it'll work?' asked Chase.

'Soon find out. I'm almost finished.' She tore off a piece of tape and used it to fix the screwdriver to the side of the desk with its empty chuck pointing upwards, then pushed a short piece of dowel on to one of the screwdriver's bits, having previously drilled a hole into one end. When it was on as far as it would go, she used another piece of tape to secure it, then inserted the bit into the chuck. Switching the screwdriver to its lowest setting, she experimentally pulled the trigger. The dowel spun with a low whirr.

'Okay,' she said, 'that part works. Now, let's see about the rest . . .'

She picked up a cone made from a sheet of card, taping it to the metal stem of the lamp stand by its narrow end. Once it was in place, she took one of the needles and carefully inserted it eye-first into the point of the cone before using more tape to hold it there. Then she slid the lamp stand across the desk, poising the needle above the piece of dowel . . .

'All we need's a dog,' said Chase, with some pride at what Nina had managed to assemble, 'and we've got His Master's Voice.'

Sophia regarded the construction incredulously. 'You've built a *gramophone*?'

'That's right,' Nina replied, picking up the cylinder. 'That's what this is – it's an audio recording! The groove's like the one on a record, or more like an old wax cylinder, I suppose. There have

214

been examples of pottery accidentally recording ambient sounds while they were being inscribed with a stylus on the potter's wheel – I think the people who made this developed the technique into something with practical applications.' She indicated the cone. 'They used copper rather than cardboard, but the principle's the same – the cone's used to pick up the vibrations of sounds and transmit them through the needle on to the soft clay when the recording's being made, and then amplify them like a loudspeaker when the fired, hardened cylinder is played back. And I know the size of the needle they used because, well, I got one stuck in my butt.'

Chase peered at the second cylinder on the desk. 'So what did they record on them?'

'Voices, presumably. Religious sermons, speeches by their leaders . . . maybe even songs.' Nina carefully lowered the cylinder on to the makeshift turntable, sliding the dowel into the hole at its base. 'Soon find out.'

For once, Sophia actually seemed unsettled. 'So you're saying that if this works, we might hear a hundred-thousand-year-old *voice*?'

'A hundred and thirty thousand, if my dates are right. That's well over half as long as humans have even *existed*.'

Chase grinned. 'Who says it's human? Maybe it's aliens talking.'

'It's *not* aliens,' said Nina in professional exasperation. She moved the lamp stand until the needle's tip lightly touched the start of the groove near the cylinder's top. 'Okay. Here we go . . .'

Holding her breath, she switched it on.

The cylinder rotated, the screwdriver's motor whining and grumbling at the extra weight . . . but even over the noise, they clearly heard something emerge from the improvised loudspeaker.

A voice. But like nothing they had ever heard before.

'Fuck me,' said Chase, suppressing an unexpected shiver. 'Are you sure that's not an alien?'

Nina had a similar response to the unnatural sound, a low, almost sinister moaning – but the sensation running up her spine was as much a tingle of excitement as it was the shock of the unknown. 'It's not at the right speed,' she realised, stopping the motor and adjusting the settings before moving the needle back to the starting point. 'Let's try again.'

This time, the voice sounded more like the product of a human larynx, though still slurred. It formed four distinct sounds – words, Nina assumed – before pausing, then speaking again.

'It's still not at the right speed,' said Sophia, now fascinated. 'It needs to go faster.'

Nina increased the screwdriver's speed and restarted the motor. The voice spoke again, now revealed as male – though with a strange sonorous reverberation to it. She strained to listen, picking out another sound beneath the speech, a faint, almost mechanical squeaking or groaning.

The speech lasted for a minute before the needle finally reached the end of the groove and scraped across the cylinder's base. Nina hurriedly switched off the screwdriver.

'What was he was saying?' Chase wondered.

'Hopefully I'll be able to figure that out – and that it'll be something useful,' Nina told him as she delicately lifted the cylinder from its makeshift spindle. 'Give me the other one.'

The recording on the second cylinder lasted slightly longer, recorded by a different man with a faster pattern of speech – though still with the same odd, throaty echo to his words. It began with three words rather than four, followed by a pause before the speaker continued.

Nina played the beginning back, then regarded the cylinder thoughtfully. Inscribed around its top were three words in the ancient language. 'What if . . . what if the first words on each recording are like a title?' she thought out loud, removing it from the screwdriver and laying it beside the first. 'So that whoever's listening knows they've got the right cylinder?' She thought back to the chamber. 'Ribbsley knew what these symbols were; he translated them. What did he say?'

Chase tried to remember. 'Something about the sea. And wind.'

'Sea of wind,' said Nina, Ribbsley's words coming back to her. She examined the first cylinder more closely. 'Wind! Damn it, I should have figured that out already. Look!' She pointed. 'This symbol, the three horizontal lines with the top one curling back on itself – it's a representation of the wind!'

Sophia was dubious. 'In a cartoon, perhaps.'

'Maybe, but that visual shorthand came from real life originally – it's how dust or sand look if they're being blown along a plain. Or a beach, and we know these people lived along the sea. Which means that this wavy line is, well . . . wavy! It's their symbol for the sea. Wind and sea, together – sea of wind.' She examined the remaining characters. 'The last one is also wind, and the third one's not symbolic, it's a word.' She tried to recall what Ribbsley had said. 'Seasons! "Sea of wind, seasons, wind." Whatever that means.'

'Maybe it's a weather report,' Chase suggested. 'The prevailing winds'll be different depending on the time of year. Useful thing to know if you're planning on sailing across the Indian Ocean.' Both women looked at him, impressed. 'Yeah, that's right. I'm not just an awesome sex machine.' Now they exchanged knowing looks. 'Oi!'

'What does the other cylinder say?' Sophia asked.

'Something similar – "fish of the sea of wind", I think. Although the sentence structure's reversed from English. It's literally "wind sea, fish". Like the way the first cylinder uses a hierarchical structure almost like database cataloguing. The main subject is "sea of wind", category "seasons", subcategory "wind". For an ancient language it's actually very efficient.'

'They're not the same,' Chase remarked.

'What?'

'The words for "wind". They weren't the same. Not the way Captain Caveman pronounced them.'

Nina replayed the start of the recording. Chase was right. Though the first and last words were written identically, the intonation of each was different. She played the second recording again. The pronunciation of the word matching the symbol for 'wind' was the same as its first use on the other cylinder.

'Is it significant?' Sophia wondered.

'It could be,' said Nina. 'Some languages like Mandarin put a lot of emphasis on intonation.' She turned the first cylinder in her hands, comparing the first and last inscribed symbols. 'They look exactly the same, but have different pronunciations . . .' Her face lit up. 'Of course! They're heterophones!'

Chase lifted a questioning eyebrow. 'Ways for straight men to talk to each other?'

'*No*, Eddie. It's from Greek, it literally means "different sound". Like "wind" as in blowing air, and "wind" as in winding up a watch – the written words look the same, but the meaning changes in speech depending on pronunciation. So one of the symbols here *does* mean "wind" in the weather sense, but the other's something else.' Nina held the two cylinders next to each other, the wind symbols almost touching. 'Maybe the word that appears with "sea" is a modifier. It's not literally "the sea of wind", but something the Veteres would know from the context.'

'Stormy sea?' Sophia suggested.

Nina considered it, then shook her head. 'It's too transitory. I dunno, it seems more like a name, something descriptive, like the Yellow Sea.'

'It must be something connected to wind, though,' Chase pointed out. 'Otherwise why would they use the same symbol?'

She nodded. 'So what else would the wind have meant to an

ancient civilisation? Apart from allowing them to sail, what does the wind do to them?'

'Same thing it does to us,' said Chase. 'Makes you cold.'

'Cold,' said Nina, mulling it over. 'The Sea of Cold, a cold sea.'

'But all seas are cold if you're in open water and the wind's blowing, even in the tropics,' said Sophia. 'There must be more to it than that.'

'There is.' Nina sat upright as the answer struck her. 'They lived in the tropics. It never gets cold – even during an ice age, the temperature at the equator would still be in the mid-sixties. But when the Veteres left Indonesia, they headed south, to Australia – and according to the inscription, they went on to somewhere else to build their city. "The land of wind and sand", Ribbsley said. But since he didn't know about the heterophones, he got it wrong. If the alternative pronunciation does mean "cold", then they went to a land of *cold* and sand. A cold land.' She smiled. 'We're in the southern hemisphere – what's the coldest land you can think of ?'

'Antarctica,' Chase and Sophia said simultaneously.

'Right! And if you go back a hundred and thirty thousand years, temperatures were several degrees higher than today. Antarctica would still have been cold – but habitable along the coasts. It'd be like living in Alaska, or Siberia. Tough – but survivable.'

'Where does the sand come into it, though?' Chase asked. 'I mean, Antarctica's not exactly famous for its beaches.'

'It's another mistranslation,' said Sophia. 'Or rather, a misinterpretation – not by us, but by the Veteres.'

'What do you mean?' Nina asked.

'Think about it. If you've lived your entire life in a hot, coastal climate, and then you move to Antarctica, you're going to experience a certain amount of culture shock. Everything is different. And one thing you will certainly never have seen before is *snow*. It's made of fine grains, it covers the ground, the wind picks it up and blows it . . . so you're going to compare it to something with which you're familiar.'

'Sand!' said Chase. 'The land of cold sand . . . that's what they called snow. Cold sand!'

'So they did go to Antarctica,' Nina said excitedly. 'They left Australia and headed south, across what they called the Cold Sea . . . and built a new city there, away from the "beasts".'

Sophia looked surprised. 'What beasts?'

'Dunno,' said Chase. 'And your boyfriend didn't know either. But they sounded pretty nasty.'

'Some sort of predators,' Nina added. 'Ribbsley thought they wiped out the Veteres who returned to Australia after leaving their city . . . which would definitely fit with Antarctica's being its location,' she realised. 'The higher temperatures a hundred and thirty thousand years ago were a blip, relatively speaking, only lasting a couple of thousand years; they were followed by an ice age. And if the temperature fell at the equator, you can imagine how much colder it got at the poles. They *had* to leave, or freeze to death.'

'And then they got eaten by killer kangaroos,' said Chase ruefully.

Nina put down the cylinders. 'But we can find where they lived. Ribbsley's translation said they built the city in a valley near the sea, and when they left they dammed up the valley and flooded it. So it'll still be there – in a frozen lake under the ice.'

'And how are we supposed to find that?' Sophia said sceptically.

Nina grinned. 'I know just the man to ask . . .'

18

Sydney

'Hey, Nina!' cried Matt Trulli. 'How's it going?'
'Kinda weirdly, to be honest,' Nina replied. They embraced, Nina kissing his cheek. 'Great to see you again, Matt.'

'Well, you timed it right,' said the pudgy, spike-haired Australian. 'Another day and you'd have missed me – I'm off to Antarctica for three weeks! Flying out to the survey ship tomorrow. This your first time in Oz?'

'Yeah. Seems a nice place, though.' She looked up at the Victorian Classical architecture of Sydney Hospital.

'Nice place?' Trulli hooted in mock offence. 'That the best you've got to say?'

'Hey, c'mon,' Nina said, grinning, 'I'm a New Yorker. Nothing compares!' She tipped her head towards the nearby statue: a large boar, dark all over its body except for the snout, which was the sculpture's natural bronze. 'I do like this, though.'

'Oh, Il Porcellino?' he said with some pride. 'Great little fella, everyone loves him. Rub his nose – it'll bring you good luck.'

'I could certainly use some.' Nina rubbed the pig's snout, then touched her pendant for added fortune. 'Il Porcellino, though? Doesn't sound very Australian.'

'Nah, the original's from Italy – just like my grandad!' Trulli stroked the statue's snout as well, then turned back to Nina. 'So, what brings you down under?'

'Long story.'

'I've got time. Come on, we'll take a stroll. The Opera House is just up the road – we'll grab a coffee.'

They started northwards, heading towards the harbour. As they walked, Nina gave him a potted account of her recent discoveries and exploits – minus, for the moment, any mention of Sophia or Dalton. 'Crikey,' Trulli muttered when she finished. 'Sounds like these Covenant blokes are bad news.' He suddenly looked worried. 'They won't be coming after me now, will they?'

'They won't know we've met you,' Nina assured him. 'Hopefully they don't even know that we're in Sydney. We were watching for people following us while we drove across the country. Didn't see anyone suspicious.'

Trulli glanced nervously over his shoulder, as if expecting to see assassins springing out from every corner. 'Hope you're right. The way you attract trouble, you really do need all the luck you can get.'

'Luck, and the help of good friends,' she corrected. 'Oh, by the way, how was the champagne?'

'Oh, ripper, thanks! You said you'd send me a thank-you gift, and you weren't kidding. Two cases of proper vintage bubbly shipped to my door? Hell of a nice surprise.'

'Well, you did save our lives.'

'By phone, too!' said Trulli. 'Didn't even have to get my feet wet, for a change.'

'Hopefully you won't have to this time, either,' said Nina as they reached the harbour front. Ahead, over the sparkling water, rose the impressive arch of Sydney Harbour Bridge. She took in the sight. 'Okay,' she admitted, 'maybe, just maybe, that's *almost* as good as the Brooklyn Bridge.'

'Ah, give it a rest, Nina. We've got you beat and you know it. And you haven't even seen the Opera House yet.'

'Funny how you stop worrying about bad guys when your Aussie pride's at stake,' Nina remarked with amusement.

'Well, a man's got to have his priorities!' Trulli smiled, then became more serious as they continued along the harbour. 'So these Covenant guys, they're looking for some lost city, but you think you can beat them to it. What do you need from me?'

'Maps, to start with,' she told him. 'UNARA did a complete radar survey of Antarctica not long ago, didn't they?' The United Nations Antarctic Research Agency was a sister organisation to the IHA, and Trulli's current employer.

'Sure did – it's what I used to pick a test site for the project. The ice is over four kilometres thick in some places, but the satellite scans were still able to reach the bedrock. Any underground lakes should be on the map.'

'Do you have a copy of GLUG on your computer?' He nodded. 'Great. That should narrow things down.' She tried to visualise the frozen continent. 'Is there any land down there that's above the Antarctic Circle?'

'Yeah. Actually, the test site's above it – the Wilkes Coast. I picked it because it's about as warm as the place gets, *and* it's in Australian territory.'

'All the comforts of home, huh?'

They rounded a large apartment building, and for the first time the instantly recognisable stacked-seashell shape of the Sydney Opera House on its low headland was revealed to Nina. She had seen it many times in photographs and on TV, but viewed in person it was still a startling piece of design.

'See? Now tell me you've got anything like *that* in New York,' Trulli said gloatingly, seeing her expression.

'The Guggenheim?' Nina suggested. He made a dismissive noise. 'Oh, all right, I'll give you a point. Just one, mind.' They shared a smile.

'Glad to hear it. But yeah, I should be able to help you find this lake, no problem. Then what?'

'Right now, just finding the thing's my first concern. Then Eddie and I can start worrying about what to do next.'

'Where is Eddie, by the way?' Trulli asked.

'He's gone to visit an old friend . . .'

Chase stared at the twin sawn-off shotgun barrels pointing at his chest. 'Is that any way to say hello to an old friend?' he asked, hands raised.

A figure emerged from the darkness behind the gun, regarding him suspiciously. 'Eddie?' said the shaven-headed, thick-necked man. 'Eddie Chase?'

'Yeah, it's me.'

The shotgun was lowered, the man's frown replaced by a sunny smile. 'Why didn't you say so, you stupid pommie bastard? Come in, mate! Eddie Chase, fuck me!'

'No thanks, you're not my type,' said Chase, returning the grin and lowering his hands. 'I've got someone with me – okay if she comes in?'

'Sure, mate, sure!' The man stepped forward, revealing multiple tattoos. He squinted at the bright daylight, then raised a bushy eyebrow as the Englishman unlocked the handcuff bracelet that he'd used to secure the annoyed Sophia to the run-down bungalow's porch. 'Public bondage, mate? Save that for the mardi gras.'

'I didn't want her doing a runner,' Chase explained.

Sophia pulled her arm away from him, the empty bracelet dangling from her wrist. 'Yes, because this charming neighbour-hood is exactly the kind of place where I want to start a new life.'

The man looked her up and down, impressed. 'Christ, Eddie. Is she a crimo or a supermodel?'

'Definitely the first one,' Chase told him, leading her inside. 'Sophia, this is an old mate of mine from the Australian SAS, Bob "Bluey" Jackson. Bluey, this is . . . my ex-wife. Sophia.'

'*Ex*-wife?' Bluey said. 'You must have had termites in that fucking wooden blockhead of yours to let a cracker like her slip out of your hands!'

'Oh, *Bluey* Jackson,' said Sophia icily. 'You know, I think Eddie might have mentioned you.'

'Oh, really?' Bluey puffed out his chest. 'What'd he say?'

'Nothing terribly memorable.' His face fell. 'Though I do seem to recall something about, what was it, Eddie? Oh, yes. Appalling flatulence.'

Bluey gave Chase a hurt look. 'You told her about my Afghan squirts? Christ, mate, that was supposed to be something to keep between blokes!'

Chase smirked. 'Just be glad I didn't tell her about the—'

'All right, all right! Christ.' Bluey ushered them inside, surveyed the untidy garden and the street beyond with a wary eye, then shut the door, plunging the interior into near-darkness.

'Why's it so dark?' Chase asked.

'We need to keep the windows covered. So we don't get any stickybeaks seeing what we're up to.'

'And what *are* you up to these days?'

'Still in the same line of work,' Bluey said as he led them through a door. 'Just being a lot more high-tech about it.'

'You're not kidding,' said Chase as he took in the room's contents. Several computers were lined up on a row of tables along one wall, connected to numerous scanners and colour laser printers. A large laminating machine was whirring away in one corner, and there were several other pieces of equipment he couldn't even identify.

Perched on a stool by the laminator was a petite Asian woman. From her features, Chase guessed she was Vietnamese, in her early thirties. Although she was pretty, her pinched, sour expression detracted from her looks. She glared at the new arrivals. 'Bluey! Who are they?'

Bluey put the shotgun down on a table and went to her. Sophia eyed the weapon, edging almost imperceptibly closer; Chase firmly interposed himself. 'It's all right, he's an old mate,' Bluey said, tone conciliatory. 'Eddie Chase.'

'Eddie Chase?' The woman perked up. 'Oh, Eddie Chase! The one who helped you?'

'That's the one. If it hadn't been for him, we'd never have met. Eddie, this is my wife, Hien.'

'Nice to meet you,' said Chase. Hien hopped off the stool and shook his hand vigorously.

'Nice to meet you too!' she said. 'Bluey talks about you. Says you're . . .' She screwed up her face again, trying to remember. 'Ah! "Not a bad bloke for a smelly pom."'

Chase gave Bluey a look. 'Cheers, mate.'

'Don't you just love her?' Bluey said through a sheepish grin.

'Although I have to say, Eddie,' Sophia piped up, 'there certainly were occasions when you could have spent more time in the shower.'

'I should've got a gag to go with those handcuffs,' Chase muttered.

Bluey chuckled. 'Now I see why she's your ex, mate. So . . . what can I do you for? I'm guessing this isn't just a social visit.'

''Fraid not. Someone's after us, and we need help.'

Bluey's eyes narrowed, and he moved back towards the shotgun. 'What kind of someone? Police?'

'No, more like mercs. But mercs with some very high-up connections.'

He put a hand on the gun, eyeing the door. 'You weren't followed, were you?'

Chase shook his head. 'No, I checked. But they're not going to give up.'

'So you need new IDs, right?' He looked back at Hien, who now had an odd expression as she regarded Sophia. 'What's up?'

Hien didn't answer. Instead, she raised one hand to block out Sophia's blonde hair . . . and her eyes widened in shock. She yelled in Vietnamese, prompting the confused Bluey to pick up the shotgun, then ran to a computer. A few seconds of typing, and Google brought up a page full of pictures of Sophia with long dark hair, taken at the time of her arrest in New York. 'Terrorist! She's that terrorist! With a nuclear bomb!'

'Jesus!' said Bluey, recognition crossing his face. He pointed the shotgun at Sophia, who sighed and raised her hands. 'She bloody is, too! Eddie, what the fuck are you doing bringing her here? We'd be up shit creek far enough if we got caught making new IDs for refugees – but fucking *terrorists*?'

'Hey, I'm not exactly happy about it either,' Chase told him. 'If it'd been up to me, I would've left her with the bad guys.'

'Oh, thank you, Eddie,' Sophia said coldly. 'Good to know where we all stand.'

'But we need her, which means we need to get her an ID so she can travel. And we'll probably need new passports and stuff ourselves to be on the safe side.'

'Who's "we"?' Hien demanded.

'Me and Nina, my fiancée. Nina Wilde.' Chase saw them both react to the name. 'Yeah, *that* Nina Wilde. Discoverer of Atlantis? Found the tomb of King Arthur? You know the one.'

'Jesus,' Bluey said with a half-disbelieving, half-admiring whistle.

'And she's your fiancée? Y'know, mate, for an ugly bugger you don't half pick up some cracking sheilas.' Hien scowled. 'But they're nothing compared to you, darlin'!' he hurriedly added with a big smile.

'Why do you need help from a terrorist?' demanded Hien, not mollified.

'The bad guys needed her – we're trying to stop them,' said Chase, deciding to simplify the explanation. 'They're looking for something, and we need to find it before they do. If we don't . . . well, we're dead, pretty much. And that's why we need your help.'

'And what happens after? To *her*?' Hien jabbed an angry finger at Sophia.

'I hadn't really thought that far ahead,' Chase admitted.

'Then you should!' She indicated the handcuffs. 'You think she's going to try to escape – what happens if she does? We'll have helped! I'm not going to be part of that. Helping people start a new life is one thing, but this? No!'

'I wouldn't have come if there was any other choice. But you're the only people who can help us.' Chase gave Bluey a pointed look. 'As a favour.'

'Aw, Christ, mate, that's not fair,' said Bluey plaintively. 'If it was just you, then no problem. But . . .'

'You *owe* me, Bluey,' Chase insisted. 'Like you said, you wouldn't have met Hien if it hadn't been for me.'

Bluey chewed his bottom lip, then turned to his wife. 'Hien . . .'

'No!' She turned on her heel and stalked out.

'Back in a minute,' he told Chase and Sophia, before following Hien and closing the door behind him. Shrill shouting came through the wood.

'Well, this takes me back,' said Sophia, listening. 'You know, I rather miss married life.'

'Yeah, but your arguments ended with a gunshot,' Chase reminded her.

'Oh, only twice. I must say, she's got an awfully big voice for such a little woman. No wonder he carries a shotgun in his own house. What exactly did you do to help him, by the way?'

'Got him out of some legal trouble,' he said evasively.

'What kind?'

'The putting a bullet into someone he shouldn't have kind.'

'Really?' Sophia seemed almost impressed. 'And I thought I knew all your dark secrets. So you helped cover up a murder, did you?'

'It wasn't like that,' said Chase, uncomfortable at the memory. 'The guy was a total scumbag – he deserved it. He was an Afghan warlord who was robbing every refugee who came through his territory, and raping and killing anyone who didn't pay up. Problem was, he could get away with it because he was one of *our* Afghan warlords, who was supposed to be helping us fight the Taliban.'

'But your friend Bluey took matters into his own hands, I take it.'

'Yeah. We were coming back from an op when we ran into this arsehole and his men beating up some refugees. Bluey told him to stop, he told us to fuck off and let him get on with it . . . so Bluey shot him. Then his men tried to kill us, so we shot them as well.'

'And then you lied about what happened on the official report, I take it.'

'I said that the guy pulled a gun on Bluey, so it was self-defence. The politicos weren't happy about their "trusted ally",' the words dripped with sarcasm, 'getting killed by one of our guys, but the refugees backed us up, seeing as we'd just saved their lives, so that was the end of that. If I hadn't, Bluey'd still be in some shithole Afghan prison right now.'

'How very noble of you,' said Sophia, equally sarcastic.

'What the fuck would you know about being noble?' Chase snapped. 'Kill a bad guy to protect an innocent, I'd do it again in a second. Remember that.' The last was delivered with a clear undertone of threat. Sophia took the hint and remained silent.

The shouting stopped and the door opened again. Bluey entered, red-faced. Behind him, Hien's expression was black with anger, her arms folded tightly across her chest. 'All right, mate,' said Bluey with exaggerated heartiness, 'we've, ah, reached an agreement. We'll help you out.' Hien muttered something through clenched lips. 'So long as this means we're all square. Sorry, Eddie, but, well . . .'

'That's okay. I understand.' Chase extended his hand, and Bluey shook it. Hien's scowl deepened, but she said nothing more.

'So, what do you need?' asked Bluey. He indicated the machines around him. 'You name it, we can do it.'

'Passports?'

'Just tell us the country! Got Australian, American, British, Canadian, Russian . . . even rustle you up a North Korean one if you fancy.'

'British'll do us,' Chase said. 'What about the biometrics?'

Hien snorted derisively, pride in her work momentarily overcoming her displeasure. 'Biometrics? Hah! Cracked them before they even came into use.'

'Wonders of the Internet, mate,' said Bluey. 'We've got friends all over the world who share this stuff around. Takes governments ages to change anything, but every time they do, somebody'll bust it open in less than twenty-four hours.'

'And how long'll it take to make new passports?'

'Less than twenty-four hours,' Bluey told him with a half-hearted grin. 'Just need to take some pictures, pick a name, get your biometrics, all that. Anything else?'

'Credit cards'd be useful.'

'No worries.' He reached into a drawer and took out a stack of different ones, fanning them out like a pack of colourful playing cards.

'That'll do nicely.' This time, it was Chase's turn to grin. 'They're not stolen, are they? Don't want to be racking up a fortune on some little old lady's card.'

'Nah. Got a load of dummy accounts set up, so you just pick a name you like. Don't use it too often, though. First unpaid bill, and alarms go off.'

'Won't need to, hopefully. Either we find what we're looking for, or . . .' He let the unsaid alternative hang in the air.

'Got you, mate,' said Bluey, briefly downcast. 'Hey, what about your fiancée? Will she need a passport as well?'

'Probably, but she's got something else to sort out first.'

'No probs. Just bring her in. All right, then – time to take some snaps!'

19

'O kay,' said Trulli, 'where do you want to start?'

'Good question,' Nina replied. Now at the engineer's apartment, she was using his computer to run the GLUG program, cycling between it and UNARA's survey of Antarctica, the rocky landmass hidden beneath the desolate ice cap laid bare by the probing radar beams. 'It must be somewhere in eastern Antarctica – it's the nearest place to make landfall from their settlement in Australia.'

Trulli zoomed in on the appropriate section of the radar map, the edge of the Ross Sea on the left side of the screen, the Shackleton Ice Shelf on the right. 'Still a bloody big area to cover. The coastline's two thousand kilometres long!'

'Let's see if we can narrow it down, huh? You got the sea level data from a hundred and thirty thousand years ago?'

'Give me a sec,' said Trulli, calling it up. A few clicks, and a yellow line was overlaid on the map, inland of the current icy coastline. 'There.'

'Okay, so we need to find any underground lakes within . . . the inscription translated as just "near" the sea, so let's say five miles. Eight kilometres.'

Trulli zoomed in further, adjusting the program's settings so that underground lakes showed up in a vivid false-colour magenta, impossible to miss against the dull grey shades of the buried rock.

'You do realise that the lake might not even be there any more?' he asked as he scrolled along the coast. 'If a glacier moved over it, it'd erase anything that was underneath.'

'If it has, then I'm wasting my time and the Covenant's already won,' said Nina. 'But if it's still there, we've got to find it.'

'And if you do, then what? It'll be buried under God knows how many metres of ice.'

'We'll have to drill down to it somehow. Maybe we could borrow your equipment once you're finished.'

Trulli chuckled. 'Yeah, I'm sure Bandra'd be happy to do that.'

'Bandra?'

'Dr Bandra. The expedition leader.'

'I thought you were the expedition leader?'

'I'm the technical leader,' he explained. 'Bandra's the scientific leader. As long as the project's still officially in a test phase, I'm in charge. Soon as Cambot's good to go, he takes over.'

'Cambot?'

He smiled. 'My latest gizmo. Combination ice borer, mini-sub and semi-autonomous robot. Just what you need for poking about under kilometres of ice – and he's environmentally friendly, too. No need to fill the drill shaft with thousands of litres of freon and avgas to stop it from freezing up. Really cool, if you'll pardon the pun.' His attention snapped back to the screen. 'Oh, hey. Got a lake here, about four clicks from the old coastline.' He switched from an overhead view to a three-dimensional topographic map, the magenta blob of the lake now seeming to hang some distance above the bedrock.

'That's not it,' said Nina as he rotated the map to view it from other angles. 'The city was in a valley, which they flooded – so the lake has to be on rock rather than ice. We're looking for something that's surrounded on at least three sides by the terrain.'

'That's not the fella, then.' Trulli returned the image to an overhead view and continued searching. 'But yeah, Cambot still needs a final test before we can let him loose on a proper scientific survey, so we're going to drill into a lake that's not of any scientific interest. So if anything goes wrong we don't accidentally screw up a million-year-old ecosystem. If everything works, then we move on to Lake Vostok. Four kilometres of ice to drill through – should give Cambot a real workout!'

'The only downside is that you have to live in Antarctica for weeks to do it.'

'Well, it'll be an experience, won't it? And at least there I won't be snacking all the time.' He patted his stomach. 'I could stand to lose a few kilos, don't you think?'

She smiled. 'Not my place to say. Oh, is that another lake?'

Trulli switched back to the 3-D view. 'Yep. Less than half a kilometre from the old coastline, and on the rock to boot. Fits your bill so far.' He rotated the image. 'Definitely in a valley . . . and the seaward end looks a bit crook, if you ask me.'

'Could it be a dam?'

'Maybe, but I can't say for sure, not at this resolution.'

'How deep is the lake?'

Trulli checked. 'Not very. Maybe twenty metres at the deep end.' He adjusted another setting, revealing the shape of the ice above it in translucent, glass-like form. 'Some weird shapes, though. The ice on top of the lake's mostly flat, but there're these indentations in the ceiling. Wonder what . . . ah, I know!' He clicked his fingers. 'Volcanic vents, that's it. They warm the water and it rises up and melts the ice above them. Not enough to reach the surface, though – the lake's about forty metres down.'

'Volcanic vents?' Nina echoed, remembering something. She quickly went back to her notes on the inscription. '"Tiny mountains of fire", of course! Can you get in any closer?'

'Yeah, but the resolution's not high enough to show any details.'

He moved the virtual camera closer to the lake, then changed the colour of the water so it too was translucent, revealing the shape of the terrain in more detail.

'There's something in the lake,' Nina realised, almost elbowing Trulli aside to get a better look. 'See, there – something on the ground. It could be a building.'

'Or it could be a rock,' Trulli pointed out. 'The resolution's only about five metres per polygon; anything smaller just gets averaged out. And there's still a hell of a lot of coastline to go; there could be plenty of other lakes. You ought to check everything else out before you get too excited about this one.'

Nina had to concede his point. 'Okay, okay. But mark this site so we can come back. I've got a feeling about it.'

He gave her a sidelong look. 'The kind of feeling you get when you're about to find something amazing?'

She smiled. 'That kind, yeah.'

'The kind of feeling that usually means somebody's going to try to kill you?'

Now she pouted. 'All right, smart guy. Just mark it, will you?'

There were indeed other underground lakes along the Antarctic coastline. But none of them matched Nina's deductions so closely.

She zoomed in on the image. If it really was the location of the lost city, then it was well positioned. The coastline of that era had a large bay that would give boats shelter from the fierce conditions in the open ocean, and the valley in which the lake had formed would have provided further protection from the harsh winds sweeping the continent. Given its latitude, outside the Antarctic Circle at sixty-six degrees south, it was even possible that the considerably warmer climate of a hundred and thirty millennia earlier would have allowed vegetation to grow. The inscription had certainly made reference to trees.

It *was* the right location. Somehow, she was sure of it. And without knowledge of the recordings contained on the cylinders, there was no way the Covenant could find it. It was her discovery, hers alone.

The problem was, how could she possibly get to it? She was still suspended from the IHA, so its resources were unavailable – and besides, telling the IHA about her findings would, she was sure, result in their being passed on to the Covenant in short order. And Antarctica was hardly a place that could be visited on a whim. Expeditions took time and planning – and money – to organise.

So the only way to get there would be—

Her cell phone rang. 'Hello?'

'Hi, love.' Chase.

'Where are you? Did you meet your friend?'

'Yeah, we just finished. Got everything sorted, for the moment. Are you still at Matt's?'

'Yeah. Eddie, listen, I know where the city is. I've found the site in the Antarctic, I'm certain of it. We need to get there and check it out.'

A sarcastic snort came from the other end of the line. 'Right. I'll just pop into the travel agent and get some tickets to the South Pole.'

'I'll take care of it. Just get over here. You've got the address?'

'Yeah. What do you mean, you'll take care of it?'

'I think I've got a way. Or I will have, in about five minutes.' She glanced over her shoulder at the sound of Trulli re-entering the apartment. 'See you soon. Bye!'

'Nina, wait—'

She disconnected and went into the next room as Trulli took a couple of bags of groceries into the kitchen. From the brightly coloured packaging inside them, she guessed he hadn't been stocking up on fruits and vegetables. 'I thought you were giving up on snacks while you were in the Antarctic?'

'Well, I'm not there yet,' he said with a grin. 'Might as well get a few home comforts for the trip.'

'Speaking of the trip,' she began, wondering how he would respond, 'can you show me your test site on the map?'

'Sure, no worries.' He followed Nina back to the computer. The screen still showed the lake she had been examining; he switched to the overhead view and zoomed out, scrolling further inland. 'There we go.'

She glanced at the scale. The test site was about seventy kilometres from 'her' lake; just over forty miles. In the vastness of the frozen continent, that was practically nothing. 'What were the criteria you used to pick that particular lake? You said it was of no scientific interest.'

'That's right,' said Trulli, nodding. 'Lake Vostok's huge, and it's over half a million years old, so if there's any life down there it might have evolved completely differently, which is what the expedition's going to try to find out. But the test site needed to be a lot newer and smaller, somewhere that couldn't support its own ecosystem, so if anything went screwy we wouldn't damage it.'

'How much younger?'

'Dr Bandra reckoned a hundred and fifty thousand years old was the cut-off point. So we found a bunch of lakes that fit the bill, and I picked one that looked like a good test for Cambot.'

'You picked the lake?'

'Yep.'

Nina put an arm round his shoulders. 'Matt . . . what would you say to trying a *different* test site?'

'What, at this short notice? It'd—' He suddenly realised where Nina was heading. 'Aw, what? You must be joking!'

'I wish I were. But really, is one underground lake that much different from another?' She scrolled the map back to the other lake. 'I mean, this one's less than a hundred and fifty thousand years old, it's small, it's not even that far from where you were going to go . . . and there might just be something absolutely incredible at the bottom of it. You can kill two penguins with one stone.'

'I don't want to kill *any* penguins!' Trulli protested. 'For Christ's sake, Nina, I'm flying out there with a five-million-dollar robot *tomorrow* – I can't just say, "Oh, by the way, fellas, I've decided to change the test site"!'

'Why not? You're in charge. And the expedition isn't actually on site yet, is it?'

'No, they're still at sea. But—'

'So it doesn't make much difference, does it? Just say that you reviewed the map data and found a better site.'

'Dr Bandra'd go absolutely mental,' he said unhappily. 'And what if something goes wrong? If Cambot carks it because the conditions aren't what he was designed for, then that's five million dollars down the Swannee, and probably my balls on the block for it!'

Nina pressed on. 'But if I'm right, then not only do you get to test out your robot, but you also find the most amazing archaeological discovery since Atlantis. And how would you rather test your cameras – looking at bits of rock and ice, or the ruins of an unknown civilisation?'

'Yeah,' he snorted, 'one that'll get me killed if I tell anyone about it.'

'Which is why we'd need to keep it quiet until it can be revealed to the world in one go – we make it too big for the Covenant to silence. Once it's exposed, then the genie's out of the bottle, and there's nothing they can do about it. Matt,' she said, moving round so they were face to face, 'this could be the most incredible find *ever*. Bigger than Atlantis, even. But if we don't find it before the Covenant, it'll be lost for ever, because they want to destroy it. We *have* to find it.'

'But what if you're wrong and there's nothing there?'

'Then you've annoyed this Dr Bandra by changing the test site. But your robot'll still get its workout, so you're no worse off. And,' she went on, conviction lighting her eyes, 'I don't think I *am* wrong. And, y'know, I've got a pretty good track record with this sort of thing.'

Trulli tipped back his head to stare up at the ceiling in resignation. 'Oh, Christ. All right. I'll think about it.'

'Think fast, Malkovich. You're flying out tomorrow. Oh, and we'll be coming as well. Me, Eddie and . . . someone else.'

'What?' Trulli demanded, sitting up sharply. 'Oh, come on! I can't do *that*!'

She fixed him with an intense, determined gaze. 'If you're worried about supplies, we'll bring everything we need. Hell, I'll pay for any extra fuel myself if I have to. But I've *got* to be there. I *have* to see it for myself. You know I do.'

He pressed a hand to his forehead. 'Okay. I'll see what I can do. The ship does have some free space – there're fewer people involved in the test stage than there will be at Vostok. But you can deal with Bandra when he starts complaining. And he *will* start complaining.'

'I can handle him,' she assured him, before kissing his cheek. 'Thanks, Matt. I knew I could rely on you.'

'I'm just a sucker for redheads, aren't I?' he said, sighing.

Chase and Sophia arrived at Trulli's apartment half an hour later. Trulli greeted Chase warmly, before regarding his companion with interest . . . and a hint of puzzled recognition. 'I'm Matt,' he said. 'Matt Trulli.'

'Yes,' Sophia replied, somewhat dismissively. 'I know who you are.'

'You do?'

'Of course. You used to work for my husband. My *late* husband, I mean.'

Nina shot her an exasperated glare as the gears turned in Trulli's head, making him step back in shock. 'You remember that part where we said about keeping your mouth shut?'

Trulli turned to her, jabbing a finger nervously over his shoulder at Sophia. 'That's – that's Sophia Blackwood!'

'Yeah, I know,' Nina answered.

'She tried to kill you!'

'I *know*!'

'The news said she was dead!'

'The reports were premature,' Sophia told him, with a wolfish smile. Trulli backed away still further.

'*Sadly* premature,' said Nina. 'Still, it doesn't matter. We'll be moving on tomorrow.'

'Where to?' Chase asked.

'Antarctica.'

He was surprised. 'And how'd you arrange that?'

'Matt agreed to help us. He's flying out tomorrow, and we're going with him.'

'Just like that?'

She grinned. 'You're not the only one who can be charming and persuasive.'

'Right,' he said, sounding distinctly dubious.

Nina wasn't keen on his tone. 'What?'

Chase turned to Trulli. 'Matt, can you keep an eye on Sophia while I have a word with Nina in private? Just don't let her get hold of anything sharp and pointy.'

'Uh . . . sure,' Trulli said uncertainly, leading Sophia into the next room.

'So Matt's taking us to Antarctica, is he?' asked Chase when they had left.

'Yeah. Look.' Nina pointed out the lake on Trulli's computer. 'I think that's where the lost city is – it matches everything I've worked out from the inscription.'

'And he's okay with changing his plans so you can take a look?'

'Apparently so, seeing as he said yes.' Nina folded her arms. 'What's up with you?'

'I'm just a bit worried.'

'About what?'

'About you.'

'Me?' Nina said, surprised. 'Why?'

'Don't you think you're pushing things too hard?'

'What do you mean?'

'I mean, twisting Matt's arm to get him to take us to Antarctica at five minutes' notice. What about everybody else there? They're not going to be quite as happy to help when three new people turn up and start pissing around with their expedition – especially when one of them's a bloody terrorist!'

'Matt's in charge, and he says it won't be a problem,' Nina insisted. 'And I didn't twist his arm. I just asked, and he agreed to help. Like he always does.'

'And what happens when the other people on the expedition complain? He'll get fired.'

'Matt's a smart guy. He'll be able to find other work with no trouble.'

Chase made a disbelieving noise. 'That's not the bloody point! Have you heard yourself? You're so determined to find this place, you're not even thinking what might happen to anyone else. Yeah, Matt could get fired – or a fuck of a lot worse. Did that even occur to you?'

'Of course it did,' said Nina, offended – and, for a moment, uncertain whether or not it had. It *must* have done, she quickly rationalised. If it hadn't, that would make her as bad as Sophia . . .

'And what about you working with Sophia?' Chase continued, as if picking up her thoughts. 'For fuck's sake, you want each other dead.'

'I don't like it either. But we need her, and I gave her my word.'

'You think she cares about that?'

'Probably not. But *I* do. We've got more chance of figuring out what the Covenant are doing with her help – and if we do that, it gives us the advantage. We can expose them to the world and get our lives back.'

'From what Sophia said, these people are basically religious fundamentalists,' Chase said grimly. 'I've been in a war against one lot of 'em, and they're not exactly good losers. So three of them, working together? Even if we do beat them to this lost city, I don't think they'll leave it at that.'

'And what would you rather do?' Nina countered, growing angry. 'Nothing? We can't hide from them for the rest of our lives. And I wouldn't want to even if we could.'

'I'm not saying we should. I'm just saying that maybe you're running into this so fast, you're not thinking about the consequences. For other people, as well as us.'

Her expression softened slightly. 'You're thinking about Mitzi, aren't you?'

'Yeah,' said Chase, jaw clenching at the memory of a dead friend. 'She got killed because I rushed her into a situation without thinking it through. I don't want that to happen again. And I don't want you having to learn the same way I did.'

She took his hand. 'Eddie, you know I don't want anyone to get hurt. Not Matt, not anybody. Hell, I don't even *actively* want anything bad to happen to Sophia.' The small joke prompted the very slightest upward twitch of Chase's mouth. 'But if we don't do something about the Covenant, then there're only three things we'll ever be able to do – we run, we hide . . . or we die. And I don't like any of those options. Especially the third one. That really sucks.'

Again, his mouth curled into a near-smile. 'You've got a point.' He gently squeezed her fingers. 'But I want to make sure you know what kind of risk you're taking. We don't have any backup this time; no IHA, no rich guys. If anything goes wrong, we're on our own.' He looked at the Antarctic map on the computer. 'And in about the worst possible place to get in trouble on the entire bloody planet.'

'Then we'll just have to make sure that nothing *does* happen.'

'Right, like that's ever worked for us.'

'There's a first time for everything,' said Nina. She smiled, then took his other hand. 'We can do this, Eddie. The city's there, I'm certain of it.'

'Hope you're right.'

'I am. I promise.'

'Can I get that in writing?' The threatened smile finally broke through. 'All right. If you think freezing our arses off with Pingu is the only way we can beat these wankers, then we'll have to do it. But you just be really careful.'

'I will. Good job you'll be there to pull me out of any crevasses.'

'I meant of Sophia.' Chase's expression became serious again. 'If she gets the chance, she'll try to escape. Or kill us.'

'So let's not give her any chances.'

Chase nodded, then looked down at his black leather jacket. 'Think I'll need something a bit thicker than this, then.'

20

Antarctica

The sea rushing below the Bell BA609 tilt-rotor was a serene, perfect blue under the stark sunlight. But the day's brightness was deceptive; even at the height of the Antarctic summer, the temperature was barely above freezing.

Huddled inside a thick parka, Nina peered over the pilot's shoulder to watch the approaching coastline with awe. The land ahead was dazzling, a wall of ice rising practically vertically out of the sparkling ocean. Ice floes whipped past, tiny dots huddled on one. 'Oh, wow, Eddie!' she said. 'I just saw my first penguins!'

Chase grinned. 'Maybe we can p-p-p-pick one up on the way back.'

'This is not a sightseeing tour,' growled the man beside the pilot. Dr Rohit Bandra, Nina had quickly discovered after landing on the RV *Southern Sun* following the long flight in the tilt-rotor from Tasmania the previous day, was not someone who responded well to the unexpected. He had immediately launched into a huge argument with Trulli about the unscheduled arrival of his 'assistants', and it had taken all Nina's persuasive powers – and fame – to mollify him even slightly. Apparently, news of her suspension hadn't reached the South Pole.

He was still fuming, however, and had made it clear that the moment Trulli's tests were successfully completed – and the expedition switched from a technical to a scientific exercise – the unwelcome guests would be sent packing, accompanied by a sternly worded complaint to the IHA. Although Trulli had downplayed it with his usual casualness, Nina could tell he was actually very worried about what it would mean to his career, and now felt horribly guilty for having involved him.

But her concerns faded as they approached the coastline. The sea was full of drifting ice; the *Southern Sun* was anchored over eighty miles offshore to keep clear of the floes calving off the ice cap that stretched away to the horizon, a slice of blinding white sandwiched between the deep blues of the ocean and the sky. More ice floes below, densely packed like crazy paving, then the cliff rolled past to reveal nothing but solid whiteness ahead.

They had arrived in Antarctica.

'Feet dry at oh-eight seventeen,' said the pilot, a Norwegian called Larsson. 'Rough air ahead. We're in for some chop.'

'You're not joking,' Chase said as the Bell lurched, hit by the winds sweeping across the endless plains. He tightened his seatbelt. The other occupants of the cabin – Nina, Sophia, Trulli, Bandra and a pair of Trulli's engineering assistants, David Baker and Rachel Tamm – quickly did the same.

Larsson checked the GPS, adjusting course. The newly selected test site was seven miles from the coast, the ice sheet having expanded hugely over the millennia. The terrain became more rugged, the flat plain rising up into mountains of pure ice, jagged chasms splitting the surface between them. The walls of the ravines changed colour as they got deeper, turning from white to startling, almost unreal shades of cyan and turquoise. 'That's beautiful,' said Nina, amazed. 'Why's it that colour?'

'Compression, Dr Wilde,' said Bandra, voice filled with don't-you-know-anything condescension. 'The weight of the snow and ice above it squeezes out all the trapped air and turns it solid, so it absorbs red wavelengths of light. Hence, blue ice.'

'Yeah?' said Chase. 'And I thought blue ice was the stuff that falls out of the bogs on planes. Cheers, doc, you learn something every day.' Bandra looked more annoyed than ever, though Nina and Trulli both smiled at his deflation.

Something else below caught Nina's attention: a column of what looked like smoke rising in the wind. She found its source, a strangely elongated and angular cone of ice protruding from the surface like a stalagmite. 'Volcanic vents – we must be in the right place,' she said, seeing more of the formations in the distance.

'How far to the site?' Trulli asked.

Larsson checked the GPS again. 'About two kilometres.' He pointed ahead. 'Past that crevasse.'

Nina craned forward for a better look. It was a blank expanse of snow, not even broken by a volcanic vent, a deep ravine angling away towards the coast before it. The lack of landmarks made it difficult to judge scale, but the plain seemed at least a couple of miles across. The lake hidden beneath it, according to the radar survey, was considerably smaller.

'I still want to make it perfectly clear that I object in the strongest possible terms to changing the test site,' said Bandra as the tilt-rotor began to descend. 'I will be complaining to the UN about the IHA's appropriation of UNARA's resources.'

'Yeah, we got that, Dr Bandra,' said Nina wearily.

'But surely, Dr Bandra,' said Sophia with mischievous innocence, 'it doesn't matter where the test takes place? After all, ice is ice.'

'Ice is most certainly *not* ice!' Bandra huffed. 'Do you have *any* kind of scientific background at all, Miss Fox, or are you just another freeloading tourist like Mr Chase?'

She smiled. 'Actually, I have some experience in the nuclear field.'

Trulli coughed at that, and Nina and Chase both gave 'Miss Fox' – the name on her fake passport – warning looks. Fortunately, none of the others picked up on her black joke.

The tilt-rotor dropped towards the centre of the ice plain, Larsson zeroing in on the precise GPS co-ordinates Trulli had provided and transitioning the aircraft from flight to hover mode, the engine nacelles on the wingtips pivoting to turn the oversized propellers into rotors. The Bell hung hesitantly above the centre of the vortex of blowing snow and ice crystals before landing with a bump.

Larsson peered out, leaving the engines running at just under takeoff speed. 'Okay, the ice seems stable. But take a thickness reading before you unload any of the gear. I'd want at least ten metres under us to be safe.'

'On it,' said Trulli. He and Baker climbed out with a radar measuring device and circled the aircraft, hunched in their parkas as they took readings. Finally, Trulli gave Larsson a thumbs-up. He returned it and powered down the engines.

'We're over the lake,' Trulli told Nina as he re-entered the cabin. 'The ice is about forty metres thick, like we thought.'

'How long will it take to drill through?'

'Don't jump the gun! We've got to get Cambot set up first; that'll take a couple of hours. But forty metres . . .' He stroked his chin, thinking. 'I don't want to push too hard, not on a first test run, so maybe half an hour. Unless you want to find one of the thinner patches of ice above the volcanic vents and drill through there.'

'How thick were they?'

'Twenty, twenty-five metres.'

'So it halves the amount of time we have to stand around in the Antarctic. Sounds good to me.'

Bandra frowned at them. 'And do you really think that is a proper test of the drill? It has to get through four *kilometres* of ice, not twenty metres!'

'Cambot's got to crawl before he can walk, eh?' said Trulli, picking up more equipment. 'All right, everybody, let's kick some ice!' Even Chase groaned at the pun.

Nina climbed out, immediately glad of her layers of clothing as she stepped on to the plain, the spiked crampons on her boots biting into the frozen surface. She put on a pair of mirrored sunglasses to shield her eyes from the glare of the sunlit snow. Apart from the tilt-rotor, there was no shelter from the constant, cutting wind. The landscape seemed completely flat, not so much as a rock breaking up the hard-packed surface snow. Despite having visited several barren deserts, she had never seen anywhere so utterly empty and lifeless.

Trulli and Baker took about twenty minutes with their radar device to find an area of thinner ice, only twenty-one metres thick. After marking the position with a red flag on a pole, the preparations for the test began.

Cambot, Trulli's robot submarine, was a segmented metal cylinder some nine feet long and three feet in diameter, one end capped with a menacing array of interlocking drill heads and the other with pump-jet nozzles and folded fins surrounding a complex spool mechanism. Assisted by Rachel, Trulli and Baker carefully lowered it on to a sled. Chase, Nina and Larsson joined in to help them slide the heavy machine to the flag. Sophia elected to watch from the cabin, while Bandra made a show of 'supervising' without actually applying any physical effort.

Leaving Cambot at the flag, the engineers returned to the helicopter to bring over a generator, then set about erecting a winch system to lift Cambot by its tail, suspending the drill heads just above the ice. This took a while, the others returning to the BA609 for hot coffee. Disconcertingly for Nina, the sun barely moved in the sky for the whole time: at this point of summer, so close to the Antarctic Circle, daylight lasted almost twenty-three hours.

Once the submarine was hanging like some huge cybernetic fish on display as a catch, everyone examined it, even Sophia's interest piqued. 'So how does it work?' Chase asked.

Trulli was on a ladder, connecting one end of what looked like a long length of rubber hose to the robot's stern. 'Most of it's pretty straightforward. We lower it, it drills down into the ice – but it's heated as well so it'll go through faster. The drills get up to sixty or seventy Celsius once they're at full speed, and the body's at about thirty degrees, so the meltwater keeps it lubricated while it's going down.'

'So where does the truly Trulli stuff come in?' Nina asked.

He grinned. ' "Truly Trulli," ' never heard that before. Nah, the clever business is all here at the back.' He patted the spool. 'See, usually when people do deep ice drilling, they fill the drill shaft with antifreeze, otherwise it ices over in no time. But that's not really an option here, 'cause as soon as we broke through into the lake, it'd pollute the ecosystem and kill what Dr Bandra's trying to find.' He held up the hose. 'This is the clever bit. It's basically a length of flexible pipe, but folded back on itself – like when you turn a pair of trousers inside out by reaching down the leg. Only here, the trousers can be however long we want – kilometres, even.'

'Bloody big trousers,' said Chase.

'We run all the control and power cables down inside both layers of the hose – they've got a non-stick coating so they slide over the inside of the umbilicus. This way, it doesn't matter if the top of the drill shaft ices up. But as Cambot goes down, he unrolls more and more of the hose out behind him from this drum here.' Trulli nodded at it. 'Once he breaks through into the lake, we disconnect him from the umbilicus so he can swim free. But because we're still feeding the power cable through to him, he can explore for as long as we want, then recover him by drilling back up through the ice. In theory.'

'Let's hope it works,' said Bandra, as cold as the surrounding landscape. 'It would be a horrible waste of everyone's time and money if something went wrong.'

'Only one way to find out,' Nina said. 'How much longer to get ready, Matt?'

'Not long. Just got to finish the hook-ups, run all the system checks, then we're set.'

It took him another twenty minutes, using a laptop inside a battery-heated bag to carry out the final checks. 'All right!' the Australian finally announced, sitting on a folding canvas chair. 'Let's give it a whirl.'

As well as the laptop, the bag contained a control unit bearing twin joysticks and several dials. 'Stand back,' he warned as he turned one of the latter. The drill heads rotated reluctantly at first before warming up and spinning more smoothly. He increased the revolutions, checking figures on the laptop's screen before looking up in satisfaction. 'Everything looks good. Nina? You want to give the word?'

'I think it'd be better if Dr Bandra had that honour,' she said. 'Dr Bandra?'

He accepted with poor grace. 'Go on then, Trulli, get on with it.'

Trulli shrugged and operated the controls. The winch lowered the submarine until the whirling drill heads touched the ice. There was a loud rasp, the sub's nose instantly obscured by spray as it dug into the hardened surface. Nina looked up at the winch frame. The outer layer of the umbilicus was indeed staying still, the slick, shiny inner layer slowly slithering into its open end. The sight was vaguely unsettling, reminding her for some reason of guts.

Cambot was in no particular rush to descend; it took over two minutes before the robot's cylindrical body completely disappeared from view. Churning water spewed up behind it. But the shaft was already freezing, the exposed surface taking on a glutinous quality with surprising speed.

'All right,' said Trulli, checking the readings. 'Cambot's cutting through the ice at a hundred and twenty centimetres per minute. So he'll take, uh . . .'

'Fifteen minutes to reach the lake,' Nina told him. 'Since he's already covered the depth of his own length.'

'Thanks. Wish I could do sums in my head like that – it'd save me a fortune in calculator batteries!'

Another round of coffees in the tilt-rotor followed, Trulli waving everyone back to the shaft almost fifteen minutes later. 'Okay, he's getting close,' he announced. 'The ice is a bit thinner than I thought – must be irregular. Oh, and I wouldn't stand there, mate,' he told Chase, who was investigating the now-frozen opening. 'All the weight of the ice on top of it means the lake water'll be under pressure. Soon as Cambot breaks through, it'll come fizzing up like a can of Four-X on a bumpy ride!'

Chase retreated, Trulli also moving back. Everyone stood in a line, anticipation rising. Even Bandra seemed excited. 'Less than a metre,' Trulli said, watching the screen intently. 'But the ice could break any time, so watch out. Half a metre – whoa, there it goes!'

The expedition members tensed, but nothing happened for a few seconds – then the cap of ice over the shaft suddenly exploded upwards as a geyser burst through the surface. It reached over thirty feet in the air, dropping back down in a cloud of spray. The fountain continued to gush for several seconds before finally dying down.

'And . . . he's through!' Trulli said triumphantly. He checked some more readings. 'Okay, time for stage two. Capping off the umbilicus, deploying fins and releasing Cambot for free operation . . . now.'

He operated more controls, seemed satisfied. 'Okay, let's see what's down there.'

Nina watched the screen as the Australian worked the controls. Trulli had configured one window to show a live video feed, which at the moment showed little but a cyan fog, but the display next to it was more revealing. It was a LIDAR display, similar to the scanning system used on some of his previous submarines, sweeping back and forth a blue-green laser beam of a wavelength that could easily penetrate water. The resulting image was only monochrome, but she could clearly make out the 'roof' of ice covering the ancient lake.

Trulli turned the submarine to view the bottom of the drill shaft. The end of the umbilicus dangled from it, swaying languidly as the robot's movements pulled the other cables through it. The ice surrounding the hole seemed almost to be glowing in shades of blue and turquoise, daylight from the surface penetrating the translucent mass. 'Okay,' he said, turning to Nina. 'Where d'you want to start?'

'Where did the sub come out?'

Trulli checked the co-ordinates. 'Near the seaward end of the valley.'

'By the dam?'

'If that's what it is.'

'Check it out first,' Nina said. Trulli nodded and guided the sub downwards. As he had thought, there was a large indentation in the ice ceiling, a rough dome formed by rising heated water from a volcanic vent below. It took a couple of minutes for Cambot to emerge into a larger open space.

The blue glow was still present even through the greater thickness of ice, but Nina was focused on the LIDAR image as Trulli steered the sub to the end of the valley. Off to the side, the terrain was steep and rocky . . . but ahead, the slope leading up to the roof of ice was much more shallow and smooth.

'*Is* it a dam?' Sophia asked.

Bandra made a sarcastic noise. 'How could it be a dam? Antarctic beavers, perhaps?'

Nina switched her attention to the video feed as the sub moved closer. Under the spotlights, the slope's surface could be seen as loosely packed earth. 'How wide is it?'

'Let me get a sonar reading . . . It's a smidge over three hundred metres across,' said Trulli. 'Maybe twenty-one metres at the highest point. Goes right across the valley.'

'Completely blocking it,' Nina realised. 'It *is* a dam. They built it to flood the valley and hide everything under the ice, just like the inscription said.'

Bandra was getting increasingly irate. 'What inscription? Who are "they"? Dr Wilde, what is going on?' He stood face to face with Nina. 'I demand an answer, right now!'

Chase put a hand on his shoulder. Bandra tried to shrug it off, concern crossing his face as the Englishman's grip tightened. 'All right, doc, keep calm,' Chase told him. 'You don't want to get overexcited in a dangerous place like this, do you? That's how accidents happen.'

'This – this is outrageous!' Bandra screeched. 'Let go of me!'

'Eddie,' said Nina. Chase shrugged, then lifted his hand. Rapid puffs of angry breath steamed from the Indian's nostrils. 'Dr Bandra, I promise I'll give you a full explanation soon. But for now, it would be enormously helpful if you could just please be patient. And quiet.'

'This is *my* expedition!' Bandra hissed in impotent frustration. He stalked off towards the tilt-rotor.

Trulli grimaced. 'Well, dinner conversation's going to be awkward tonight.'

'Don't worry about it, Matt,' said Nina. She looked back at the screen. 'Turn the sub around, let's see the valley floor.'

Trulli obeyed, Cambot swinging round and descending. Objects appeared at the limit of the scanning laser's range. Large blocks, possibly boulders . . . but suspiciously regular in shape. She looked back at the video display as the sub drew closer. It was hard to judge scale, but the blocks seemed large, at least as tall as a person.

But whatever their size, one thing was immediately clear.

They were rectangular. Flat sided. Hard-edged.

Man-made.

'Keep going,' Nina gasped. The others reacted with equal astonishment as Cambot continued past the blocks and headed for a new contact on the LIDAR. A wall, curving round, rising upwards to form a dome-shaped building of carefully carved stone . . .

'It's the city,' whispered Nina. 'The lost city of the Veteres. We've found it.'

21

'You knew it was there all along,' Bandra said angrily, stabbing an accusing finger at the images on Trulli's laptop as Cambot continued its exploration. 'You knew, but you hijacked my expedition to find it! Why?'

'I didn't have a choice,' said Nina. 'There'd been . . . a security breach at the IHA. Lives were lost.'

'What?' Bandra's expression changed to one of horror. 'So you decided to put the lives of a UNARA mission at risk instead?'

'No, because as far as we know, UNARA's security hasn't been compromised. Nobody knows we're here,' she explained, exasperated. 'And I didn't know for sure that the city was here, only that there was a strong possibility.'

'But now that you do, now what? You can't get to it! We don't have the equipment to carry out an exploratory dive.' Bandra scowled. 'You may have made an archaeological find, Dr Wilde, but you've done so at the expense of another scientific mission – *my* mission. As soon as we return to the *Southern Sun*, I'll be making a formal complaint to the UN about your actions.'

'You're entitled to do that, of course,' Nina said, forcing back her own rising anger. 'But I'll ask you to wait until after we've explored the city. However we do that.'

'I most certainly will *not* wait,' he told her, seething. 'You think that a few interesting finds and some TV appearances give you the right to dictate to the rest of us?'

'No, I don't,' she said, voice cold. 'But I *do* think that my position as Director of the IHA gives me that right.'

'What!'

'The IHA is as much about global security as archaeological preservation. This is now a security issue.' She put her hands on her hips, regarding him stonily. 'I'm sorry, Dr Bandra, but you leave me no choice but to invoke my authority and place this site, and this entire expedition, under IHA jurisdiction.'

Bandra's rage rose to such a level that he seemed about to melt his own hole through the ice. 'You – you can't do that!'

'I just did. And you know damn well that I have the authority, so I'm giving you an order – you are not to contact the IHA, or anyone else, until I authorise it. Am I perfectly clear?'

For a moment, she thought he was going to hit her. Chase took a small but pointed step closer. Lips twisted, Bandra whirled, almost slipping on the ice as he stomped back to the tilt-rotor.

'Christ, Nina,' said Trulli quietly, 'I know he's a bit of a dick, but that was harsh.'

Sophia, on the other hand, smirked. 'Nina, I have to admit, I'm almost impressed. I never thought you had it in you. Of course, it would have been much better if you actually *had* the auth—'

'Don't,' Nina said, stepping almost nose to nose with her. After a long moment under her hard, unblinking gaze, Sophia turned and walked away, though not without a dismissive sniff.

Chase moved up behind his fiancée. 'Hey,' he said softly. 'You okay?'

She faced him, trembling with a mixture of anger and adrenalin from the confrontations. 'N-no, not really.'

'C'mere.' Chase hugged her. 'You know what? Fuck Sophia, *I* was impressed. You should have been in the army, you'd have made a decent drill sergeant with an attitude like that. It'd scare the shit out of the new recruits.'

She let a half-hearted laugh escape into the cold air. 'He was right, though. What *are* we going to do about the city? We can't get down there, and the only way we can get the gear and resources we'd need is by contacting UNARA or the IHA – and as soon as we do that, the game's up.'

'Worried about the Covenant?'

'Them, and Bandra. I think that when he finds out I've pulled a snow job on him, *he'll* try to kill me.'

'I'll watch out for you. Against Bandra *or* the Covenant.'

'Thanks.' She managed a small smile. 'But it doesn't change the fact that we can't actually get to the city. All we can do is look at it on a screen – and that's not going to be enough. We need to get inside it.'

Trulli looked up from the laptop. 'I, er . . . I've got an idea.' He glanced towards the plane, which Bandra was circling, kicking up snow. 'Only I don't think he's going to like it. But, well, in for a penny, right?'

'What are you thinking, Matt?' Nina asked.

'Well, that dam blocking the valley – it's just made of soil and maybe some stones, you think?'

'Probably. If they put it together in a hurry, they'd do it in the simplest way possible – just pile up as much earth as they could.'

'So it's probably not going to be all that dense, right? Even if it's tightly packed, soil isn't as hard as solid ice . . .'

Nina realised where he was going. 'Matt! Oh my God, you're a genius!'

'Yeah, I know.'

'Wait, why's he a genius?' Chase asked.

'Because he can use the sub to drill through the dam and drain the lake!' she proclaimed. 'Will it work, though?'

Trulli gestured in the direction of the coast. 'We saw a crevasse back there, so if I can get Cambot to it the water'll drain out, but I want to make sure that it's big enough for us to get the plane into so we can pick him up afterwards. It *is* a five-million-dollar sub we're talking about, after all!'

'If it works, how long will it take to drain the lake?'

'No idea. I mean, we don't even know the exact dimensions. But based on the size of the lake from the radar map, it'll be . . .' He called up a calculator on the laptop and took off a glove to tap in figures. 'I'd say at least twenty-four hours. But it could easily be more.'

'What about the ice?' asked Chase. He banged a heel on the frozen surface. 'If you drain the lake out from under it, the whole roof might cave in.'

Trulli looked pensive. 'There's a chance . . . but it's a minimum of twenty metres thick, so it should be okay. A metre of ice'll support a big truck. There might be some local falls, though. Especially if those volcanic vents are still active. If there's steam rising, it might melt parts of the ice.'

'But you definitely think you can get your robot through the dam?' Nina asked.

'In theory, yeah. The cable's easily long enough, and we've got plenty of power.' He looked worried. 'It's just that if the dam isn't just earth, if it's filled with rocks, then Cambot won't be able to drill through – and we won't be able to get him back out.'

Nina put a hand on his arm. 'You've already done a hell of a lot for us, Matt. If you don't want to risk it . . .'

He pointed at the structures on the screen, entombed below them. 'Nah, I think it'll be worth it. Hell, this is easily as big as Atlantis, maybe even bigger. And maybe I'll get on the cover of *Time* with you this time – or at least *Popular Mechanics*!'

'So you'll do it?'

Trulli grinned. 'Get me a coffee, and I'll see what I can do!'

★

As Trulli had thought, the piled soil of the earth dam was indeed easier to drill through than the hardened ice above the lake, Cambot progressing at over a metre and a half per minute. Even so, it still took the better part of two hours before the robot cut all the way through the base of the dam and reached the ice beyond. By this time, Bandra had found out what was going on and become even more livid, but also resigned to the fact that it was an all-or-nothing operation: the only way to retrieve the expensive submarine now was for it to reach the crevasse.

Trulli, Baker and Rachel took turns to monitor Cambot's progress, the others going back and forth to the tilt-rotor to find respite from the chill wind in its cabin. Nina was idly wondering how much longer the expedition's supply of coffee would hold out when Rachel, at the controls, waved frantically. Everyone hurried over, Trulli taking back the laptop to check the readings.

'We're almost through!' he said excitedly. Nina watched the screen. With nothing to see while the robot was drilling, Trulli had switched off the cameras, but now he reactivated them. Although the image was obscured as icy slush swept along Cambot's cylindrical body, the glow of daylight through the ice was clear.

And it was not the blue of deep, thick ice. This was a pure white, coming through only a few metres, if that . . .

A sound like a muffled gunshot rolled across the plain from the direction of the crevasse. The image suddenly flared as Cambot was flung out into the light of day. A blue-white cliff face blurred across the screen before being obscured by churning water. Another crack of ice came from the edge of the plain, almost drowned out by a hissing roar.

The winch shuddered, cables zipping rapidly into the umbilicus as Baker hurriedly pulled a lever to let it run freely. Rachel watched the spinning reel nervously, hand poised over a control on the generator to detach the power line if needed, but then it stopped with surprising abruptness. The view from the video camera jolted violently.

Chase winced. 'Bloody hell. Even though it's a robot, I still felt that.'

Warning signals flashed red on the laptop's screen. 'I think he hit something,' Trulli said, dismayed. 'How wide was that crevasse?'

'Eighty, ninety feet.'

Now it was Trulli's turn to wince. 'There you go, then. He just got blown into the wall on the other side. Christ, that waterspout must be bloody powerful.' He turned to look. A cloud of spray rose above the edge of the plain, sunlight glinting off billions of ice crystals as the water began to freeze in mid-air.

'How badly is it damaged?' Bandra demanded.

'The hull's still intact, and the internals survived well enough to give us telemetry,' Trulli told him, flicking through different screens for more information. 'Looks like we lost the LIDAR turret and some of the fins, though.'

Bandra glowered at Nina. 'I hold you personally responsible for the damage, Dr Wilde.'

'Bill the IHA,' she told him curtly. The noise of escaping water was a constant thunder, thousands of gallons being blasted out of the shaft every second. But how long would it take to drain the entire lake?

There was no way to know. All they could do was wait for nature to take its course. 'I think,' she announced, 'that pretty much wraps it up for the day.'

Chase entered the small cabin aboard the *Southern Sun*, finding Nina and Sophia examining photo printouts of the inscription within the buried chamber in Australia. 'Ay up.'

'Where've you been?' Nina asked.

'Listening to Bandra shout at Matt. Surprised you didn't hear him down here, he was pretty pissed off.' He picked up a page of Nina's notes. 'What're you up to?'

'Trying to translate the inscription,' Sophia told him.

'Any luck?'

'Some,' said Nina. 'We've been concentrating on the parts about the city, to see if we can get an idea of what's down there. For a start, the "tree of the gift" that Ribbsley mentioned? Whatever it was, it's not unique. The city has one too.'

'And it's not the only tree they made a big song and dance about. Here.' Sophia indicated one particular section of the ancient text.

Nina looked more closely. 'Something about . . . "lowering" themselves to their god to reach the tree of the gift? Kneeling in supplication, maybe?' Sophia nodded. 'Then some stuff about prophets, and a gate to the tree of . . .' She pointed at the word. 'I don't know what that means.'

'It's "life",' Sophia told her. 'The tree of life.'

'The tree of life?' Nina repeated, startled. 'As mentioned in the Book of Genesis? No wonder the Covenant want to find it.'

'It was certainly very important to the Veteres – some kind of link to their god.' Sophia pursed her lips. 'Interesting that they were monotheistic. Primitive cultures were usually polytheist.'

'Not necessarily. Zoroastrianism dates back to at least the ninth century BC.'

'They worshipped Zorro?' Chase said, miming the swipes of a sword in a Z-shape. 'That's my kind of religion!'

Nina and Sophia gave each other tired looks. 'And you want to marry him,' Sophia said.

'You *did* marry him.'

'Life is a series of right and wrong paths.'

'Oi!' Chase protested. 'Anyway, this lot aren't exactly primitive. I mean, look what they built.' He indicated a LIDAR printout of several dome-shaped buildings, then added with a cough, 'Helpedbyaliens.'

'Will you shut up about goddamn aliens?' snapped Nina. She turned back to Sophia. 'Does it say anything more about what this tree of life actually is?'

'Not that I can see – or at least that I can translate.'

'You're doing okay at the translation,' Chase said to Nina.

'I'm a quick study,' she replied.

'Yeah, I know. Keep this up and you won't even need Sophia.'

Nina arched an eyebrow. 'Wouldn't that be a shame?' Her expression became more suspicious as she regarded the Englishwoman. 'You wouldn't be holding back on anything to keep yourself useful, would you?'

Sophia sighed, somewhat sarcastically. 'What would that gain me? My interests are best served by helping you and Eddie.'

'And *our* interests would have been better served if you'd given me Ribbsley's notes when I asked,' said Nina. 'At least he doesn't have them either. Unless that Winnebago had a fireproof safe.'

'That Ribbsley bloke,' Chase asked Sophia, 'what do you see in him, anyway? He's not rich, he's not a sexy hunk like me.'

Sophia appeared irritated. 'He's an intellectual equal. Which of course you could never appreciate.'

'He's more on your moral level as well,' said Nina. She looked back at the photos. 'If there's nothing more about the tree of life, what about the tree of the gift? Or the gift itself? Ribbsley said their god punished them for giving it to the beasts, but what was it?'

Sophia's irritation faded as she concentrated on the text. 'I'm not sure. It had something to do with making use of "tiny mountains of fire"—'

'The volcanic vents. We got that.'

'Literal, if not very poetic. There's also what looks like "earth sky fire", whatever that means.'

'Sky fire – lightning?' Chase suggested. 'Or an aurora. You get them at the South Pole, right?'

'Yeah,' said Nina. 'But "earth" seems like a modifier. How would you get an aurora in the earth?'

'I have no idea.' Sophia tapped the picture. 'But there's more here about these mysterious "beasts". Apparently, the Veteres brought them with them to Antarctica.'

Chase snorted. 'Well, that scores a ten on the stupidometer.'

Nina's response was more thoughtful. 'These beasts were a threat they were trying to escape . . . but they brought them along anyway? And then gave them God's gift?'

'Thought that was me,' Chase said, grinning. Both women ignored him.

'It doesn't make a huge amount of sense,' admitted Sophia. 'What sort of gift could you give an animal that would arouse God's wrath?'

Nina shook her head. 'Unless it was a Jesus chew-toy, I can't think of anything either.' She picked up the LIDAR image. 'I just hope that whatever it is, we'll find out down there tomorrow.'

'Feet dry at oh-seven seventeen,' Larsson announced.

The BA609 was retracing its journey from the previous day – and, somewhat to Nina's annoyance, with the same passengers. Baker and Rachel were going with Trulli to locate and recover Cambot, but why Bandra had insisted on coming along, other than to add to his ever-growing list of grievances, she had no idea.

Still, so long as he didn't do anything to interfere, she could tolerate his presence. And the fact that he had let her take the front seat was a small sign of his acceptance of her authority, however grudging.

She donned her sunglasses and looked ahead. The location of the ice field and the crevasse was immediately obvious; a cloud of spray was still rising up from the latter, drifting westwards in a long plume.

'Okay, first thing,' said Trulli from behind her, 'we need to see if Cambot's still in the same place. Pehr, swing over the ravine and take a look.'

Larsson transitioned to hover mode, descending into the ravine. The hole through which the water was still gushing was somewhat larger than it had been the previous day, a section of the ice cliff above having sheared off as the escaping jet ate away at it. Through the spray, Nina could see fallen chunks of ice strewn everywhere, water flowing past them towards another, lower plain in the distance.

'All right!' Trulli exclaimed. 'Cambot's still where he was yesterday.' He pointed; Nina spotted the robot wedged against the other side of the canyon, encrusted in ice and frost.

'Looks like it's frozen in,' said Chase. 'Bring any pickaxes?'

'Better than that, mate. Got some gas!' He patted a red metal cylinder in one of the cargo racks. 'We can just melt the ice right off him, no worries.'

Larsson ascended and circled the previous day's landing site to look for signs of the ice's having been weakened by the draining lake. There were no new cracks evident, but he still landed cautiously, leaving the rotors running until he was sure the plain wasn't going to drop out from under them.

The team made their way back to the drill site. Trulli and his assistants had detached the cables from the submarine by remote control and reeled them back in the previous day, so the manhole-sized opening had completely frozen over. However, it was plain that the water level had lowered beneath it; the ice covering the shaft was semi-translucent, revealing a circle of darkness below. 'Shouldn't take long to break through,' Chase decided.

'How are we going to see how low the water is?' Nina asked.

'I don't suppose you brought another robot with you, Matt?'

Trulli put down a heavy insulated pack on the ice and unzipped it. 'Afraid not, but I've got something that'll do the job. Bit crude, but it'll work.' He took out a small digital camcorder in a plastic housing designed to protect it from the cold and wet. 'We'll just lower this on a string! If I set the gain for low-light conditions, it'll give us an idea of how big the cavern is as well.'

'Quite the *bricoleur*, aren't you?' said Sophia.

Trulli gave Nina an uncertain look. 'Is that good?'

'Surprisingly, yes,' she told him, raising an eyebrow. 'She actually complimented someone. I don't know if you should feel honoured or worried.'

'I wouldn't let her pat you on the back, put it that way,' Chase added.

Baker used one of the gas cylinders to melt through the ice capping the shaft. Frozen lumps dropped into the darkness below. Splashes followed, but only after a few seconds, and quite faintly.

Trulli rigged up his improvised probe, setting it to record before lowering it down the shaft on a length of line marked with a red stripe at one-metre intervals. Nina counted them off; the camera passed twenty metres with no trouble, clearing the bottom of the shaft. Thirty metres, forty, now below the roof of the chamber proper. Trulli paid the line out more slowly. The camera housing would float; as soon as it reached the surface, the line would go slack. Forty-five metres. Forty-six, forty-seven . . .

'How deep was the lake?' Chase asked. 'Must be near the bottom by now.'

'About twenty metres,' said Nina. 'So sixty metres below us, more or less.' She checked the line again. Fifty-one metres, fifty-two—

'Whoa,' Trulli said. He hesitantly lowered his hands, then raised them again until the line became taut. 'That's it, we've reached water. Just under fifty-three metres.'

'So only about seven metres still to drain?' Nina asked. 'It'll be empty sooner than we thought.'

'The drainage tunnel must have got wider.' He raised his hands further. 'Okay, hopefully if I swing it a little bit, the camera'll turn enough to get a three-sixty of the cavern. Then I'll pull it back up and we'll have a look.' He slowly twisted the line in his hands, then began the laborious process of returning the camera to the surface.

Once it was recovered, he removed it from the housing and opened its LCD screen, then rewound the recording to the point when the camera cleared the bottom of the ice dome. With the water gone, the amount of light coming through the ice was quite surprising. At the bottom of the screen, Nina could see the lake's surface, the current clearly visible as the water surged towards the hole drilled in the base of the dam. Knowing the depth of the remaining water gave her a sense of scale that the sub's cameras had failed to provide. The dam was indeed a quite impressive structure, making up in sheer size for what it lacked in complexity.

So what about the city?

The camera continued to descend, still swinging, but to her growing irritation the image only panned over the dam and the valley sides. She wanted to look *up* the valley to see what lay at the other end. 'Okay, fast forward, fast forward,' she said impatiently. The lake's surface rushed closer, then the camera suddenly tipped over at an angle. 'Okay, hold it! The camera's reached the water. Play it.'

The image bobbed for several seconds before levelling out as Trulli pulled the line taut. Nina held her breath as it swung round. Even though it was barely above the water level, it should still reveal *something* . . .

The movement slowed. She almost groaned. The camera was going to swing away again before she saw anything—

'Stop!' she gasped. Trulli froze the picture.

The camera *had* caught something. Just barely, at the side of the picture as it reached the end of its lazy sideways swing, a grainy shape lit by the ice-blue glow from above.

It was a building, so tall that its top disappeared into the overhanging ice, towering over everything around it.

A temple.

She stood, eyes wide with amazement as she faced the others. 'We have to get down there. As soon as we can.'

22

To Nina's immense frustration, *soon* wasn't soon enough. It took the remaining water several more hours to drain away, hours in which she was reduced to pacing impotently across the ice under the disapproving eyes of Dr Bandra. Trulli and his team could at least accomplish something in the meantime; Cambot had finally been left high and dry, allowing Larsson to fly them into the crevasse to free the dented robot from the ice. The most she could do was get Chase to lower the camera down the shaft again in the hope of getting a better look at the buried city. But even though subsequent recordings revealed more detail, they were still too grainy and unsteady to do more than hint at what lay below.

She needed to see it with her own eyes.

As Trulli and Baker worked on the winch, Chase assembled equipment of his own, strapping gear to the sled used to transport the submarine. 'No idea what's down there, so we need to be prepared for anything,' he told Nina and Sophia as he secured some smaller items with duct tape.

'A tent?' Sophia asked. 'Planning a long stay, are you?'

'Hope not, but if something goes wrong we might need it. Got sleeping bags, food, a camping stove, climbing gear, first aid kit – useful stuff. Just in case.'

'At least we won't run out of gas for the stove,' said Nina, tapping a foot against one of the gas cylinders.

'Nah, that's just in case we find something valuable stuck in the ice and need to get it out without whacking it with a pickaxe. See? I'm getting the hang of this archaeology business.' He smiled. 'And if you're wondering why I'm putting it all on a sledge, it's because I'm not carting this bloody lot about on my back!'

Bandra came over. 'All this equipment belongs to UNARA, you know,' he said, pointing at a laser rangefinder Nina intended to use to measure the cavern. 'If there's any loss or damage, you'll be responsible for it.'

Nina let out an irritated breath. 'Let me get this straight, Dr Bandra. You've seen the video, you know there's something incredible down there . . . and the biggest thing on your mind is nickel-and-diming me over a couple of boxes of Band-Aids?'

'You've hijacked my expedition and treated me with nothing but contempt, Dr Wilde,' he said. 'I consider it a professional and personal insult. So you'll forgive me if I refuse to go along with your cavalier attitude to the work.'

'Fair enough.' She cocked her head to one side. 'So I'm sure you'll forgive *me* if when I reveal this amazing discovery to the world I omit all mention of you? After all, you clearly don't want to be associated with me.'

Bandra looked concerned. 'Actually, that wasn't quite what I meant . . .'

'No, no, I completely understand,' Nina went on, 'and I respect your position. Nobody will know you had anything to do with it.'

'It shows admirable integrity,' Sophia added.

'Your name won't even be mentioned.'

Bandra glanced at the hole in the ice. 'We'll . . . discuss this further once we actually know what's down there,' he said, turning back to the tilt-rotor.

'You enjoyed that,' Chase said to Nina once he was out of earshot.

'Yup,' she replied smugly, before walking to the hole. The shaft dropped away to a circle of darkness sixty feet below.

Where something incredible was waiting for her. A feeling of anticipation was already rising in her stomach. She was so close to finding out the truth . . .

By the time Trulli and Baker had readied the winch, Chase had pulled the sled over to them. 'All set,' he announced, giving Trulli a walkie-talkie.

'So who's going down first?' asked Trulli.

Chase looked at Nina. 'I ought to, to make sure it's safe, but . . .'

'I'm going first,' Nina insisted.

'Yeah, I thought so.'

'I have to, Eddie.' She pointed at the safety harness that Baker was securing to the winch line. 'Fix me up.'

Chase gave her the other walkie-talkie. The harness was fastened round her, and she moved to the edge of the shaft as Trulli prepared to operate the winch controls. 'See you down there,' she said to Chase.

'Be careful,' he replied.

'Don't plunge to your horrible screaming death!' Sophia said cheerily. Nina huffed, then eased herself down until the harness took her weight. 'Let's go,' she told Trulli.

The winch whined, and she dropped down the shaft.

At three feet wide, the tunnel was claustrophobic, all the more so with her bulky cold-weather clothing. The ice changed in consistency and colour as she descended, the milky whiteness near the surface turning to a glassy translucent blue. Below, she saw the opening getting closer, still nothing but darkness beyond. The temperature was already noticeably lower, prickling at her cheeks.

The walkie-talkie crackled. 'You okay?' asked Chase.

'Fine, thanks. How deep am I?'

'Fifteen metres. You should be coming out into the open soon. If you start swinging, let us know and we'll slow down.'

'Will do.' But eagerness had already overcome any discomfort. The bottom of the shaft drew closer, closer . . .

She was through.

The cavern opened up around her, her eyes adjusting to the strange lighting conditions. The dome-like ice ceiling was glossy, lumps and bumps smoothed out where rising warm water from the volcanic vents below had gnawed away at it. Looking down, she spotted drifting steam. For one worrying moment she thought she was dropping right into the vent, before she saw it was off to one side.

Her excitement rose as she made out structures below in the half-light. The lake had mostly drained. There were still some areas of water that had pooled below the level of the shaft cut through the dam, already freezing over, but most of the cavern was clear.

Which meant, she realised as her descent brought her below the icy ceiling, that she would be able to see what lay at the other end of the chamber.

She twisted on the line, turning round . . .

The sight took her breath away.

Illuminated by the soft, impossibly pure cyan light coming through the ice above, the city looked unreal. Almost below her was some kind of multi-level construction, small buildings and bridges spanning a maze of catacombs dug out of the ground. A paved road led past it, heading uphill from the dam into the heart of the settlement. Smaller roads split off from it on either side, themselves dividing to form an almost tree-like pattern. The 'branches' were surrounded by clusters of igloo-shaped stone buildings – just like the ones she'd seen in Indonesia and Australia.

Except these were intact.

They weren't the only structures that had survived their long entombment. Following the line of the main road, which seemed to be lined with statues, her gaze fell on the temple she had glimpsed on video. In real life it was even more spectacular. Like the other buildings it was circular, but much taller, requiring elegantly curved buttresses to support the walls. Its roof was so high that it actually disappeared into the cavern's icy ceiling, making it at least sixty feet tall, possibly more – all she could make out through the ice was a vague shadow.

High, thin windows were spaced out on two levels around its circumference, and the main door was equally elongated, close to twenty feet tall. Darkness waited beyond it, ominous – and tantalising. The heart of the city, the secret of the Veteres, was somewhere within.

There was something else about the temple, which she dismissed as mere decoration before realising how complex and extensive it was. What appeared to be long lines of copper plate ran up the temple walls from the upper windows, like the road expanding into a tree-like pattern – not only flat along the wall, but also outwards from it. The strange arrangement also disappeared into the overhanging ice. What its purpose might be, she had no idea.

But something she could determine was that there was something else *behind* the temple. Parts of the building appeared to have been cut out of a cliff face, its summit just below the ice. She looked over her shoulder at the dam. Had it been built to a particular height specifically to cover whatever lay behind the temple?

She put the thought on hold; she was almost at the ground. 'Okay, nearly there,' she said into the walkie-talkie. 'Slow it . . . okay, I'm down.' Her boots bumped on the ground, which crackled under her crampons. Everything was covered with a layer of glinting ice and frost, surface water having rapidly frozen as the lake drained away. She unfastened the harness. Breath steamed from her nostrils; it was much colder than on the surface. 'All right, I'm down and safe.'

'What's it like down there?' Chase asked.

'It's . . . it's kinda *wow*.'

He laughed sarcastically. 'Right, that helps. If you have to get a new job after all this, don't bother trying to be a tour guide.'

Sophia was lowered down, almost as awed by the sight of the lost city as Nina. The sled came next, followed by Chase. 'So, you absolutely sure this wasn't built by aliens?' he asked Nina, indicating the glittering, blue-lit buildings. ''Cause that's usually what stuff buried in the Antarctic ice turns out to be. Just ask Kurt Russell.'

'I don't know,' Sophia said. 'It has a certain Lovecraftian air, if you ask me. Perhaps we'll meet a Shoggoth.' A beat. 'Lead the way, Nina.'

Chase chuckled, though Nina was unamused. 'No aliens, no Elder Things, no . . . no flying spaghetti monsters,' she said impatiently, going to the sled. 'This was built by people just like us. They just happen to have been around a lot earlier than anyone thought. And if we can get on with it, please, that's what we're going to prove.' She unfastened the straps and began taking equipment from the sledge.

Chase picked up the heavy-duty, spike-tipped tripod she had just unloaded. 'We're not going to cart this around with us, are we? That's why I brought the sledge in the first place – so we wouldn't have to!'

'Oh, yeah. Duh,' Nina said, replacing the rangefinder that the tripod had been designed to support. 'We can do a proper laser survey when we come back. I don't think we need to know the cavern's exact dimensions right now. "Damn huge" is near enough.'

'You're *right*!' Chase shouted as he returned the tripod to the sled. Faint echoes came back to them from the depths of the space. 'So, where are we kicking off?'

'Over there.' Nina pointed towards the plume of steam rising from the nearby labyrinthine area. 'We'll start with what's closest and work our way up to the temple.' She switched on a powerful flashlight to test it. The brilliant beam sliced through the sapphire-blue glow of the cavern like a laser. Satisfied, she clicked it off again; now that her eyes had adjusted to it, the light permeating the ice above was more than bright enough to see by.

'Okay, Matt,' Chase said into the radio, 'we're setting off.'

'Got you,' came the reply. 'So what's it like down there?'

Chase took in the sight of the frost-crusted temple dominating the city. 'Nina got it right. It's kind of . . . *wow*.'

Trulli snorted. 'Fat lot of use you are. You better bring me some awesome photos, okay?'

'Will do. Talk to you soon.'

They crossed the short distance to the walled edge of the maze, Chase towing the sledge. Nina looked towards the dam, picking out the dark spot of the drainage shaft drilled through it. Even though it had been less than an hour since the water level had finally dropped below its bottom edge, the surface was already frozen, shimmering glassily. Given another hour in the frigid cavern, it would be thick enough to walk on.

The steam rising from behind the wall told her there were warmer conditions ahead, however. Finding an opening, they went through. 'What the hell's this?' Chase asked. The outer wall enclosed an excavated area, inside which had been built a grid-like series of walls, a marked contrast to the curves found elsewhere. The pit had remained full of water as the lake drained, now frozen over . . . but it was obvious from the metal bars covering each chamber that whatever had once been inside them was meant to stay there. 'A prison?'

'I don't know,' Sophia said thoughtfully. 'It looks more like the hypogeum at the Colosseum in Rome. Remember? The area under the arena where the gladiators and animals were kept before contests.' Chase nodded.

'You've been to Rome?' Nina asked him. 'With her? You never mentioned that before.'

'I've been to loads of places I haven't told you about, and can we not get into this again? But yeah, it does look like it.' The underground area at the centre of the Colosseum was made up of small, high-walled chambers connected by narrow corridors, and the structure before them followed a similarly functional pattern. 'So what did they keep in here? Gladiators?'

'Or animals,' Sophia said. 'Beasts.'

Nina shone the light into the nearest chamber, but could make nothing out through the milky ice. Instead, she directed the beam across the pit. Walkways and stone bridges criss-crossed it, intersecting at what she took to be guardhouses. Steam rose beyond them. 'That must be where the volcanic vent is. Let's take a look, then head into the city.'

They crossed a bridge into one of the squat guardhouses, the first fully intact construct of the Veteres Nina had entered. Disappointingly, it was empty except for what appeared to be a coiled whip hanging frozen on one wall, though its design still told her something; the slit-like windows round the room would have given the guards a view of the chambers below while keeping them hidden from the occupants, a primitive panopticon.

But who, or what, had they been watching?

Chase went to the little building's other entrance, ice crunching with each step. 'If they used the volcanic vent to get hot water, they've still got plenty.'

Nina and Sophia joined him, looking out across the pit. The layout of the walls changed, the cell-like chambers becoming larger. Some were even roofed rather than being open to the elements. But what Chase had called their attention to was natural rather than man-made. Somewhere beneath the pit, the heat of the vent was still warming the water . . . and it had kept flowing from its source even as the rest of the trapped lake froze around it, carving weaving gullies through the new ice.

'It's like a maze,' Chase remarked. One section of the pit was more open than the others, and the hot streams had gradually melted their way to it, eating twisting, steaming gouges out of the ice.

Nina was more interested in the walls surrounding it. 'If this was a hypogeum, that space might have been an arena.' She crossed a bridge over a passage, peering into the cramped cells below in the hope of spotting some revelatory detail, but seeing only ice and stone. 'Maybe there's a way down where the hot water's melted the ice.'

'Is that really necessary?' sighed Sophia. 'Hypogeum, prison, slave pens, zoo – whatever it is, it's not going to hold anything more important than the temple. And time's become an issue.' She pointed at the cavern's ceiling. 'Haven't you noticed?'

'Noticed what?' Nina began, before it struck her. Literally. A fat drop of falling water burst on her shoulder. Others plopped down around them, the frequency slowly increasing.

'Shit!' Chase said, realising what was happening. He raised the walkie-talkie. 'Matt, we might have a problem. The steam from the volcanic vent's starting to melt the ice. I don't know how long it'll take before there's any danger, but it might be worth moving the plane away from the hole. And I wouldn't sit around it, either.'

'That could screw up the radio,' replied Trulli, his voice already distorted.

'Have to chance it.'

'Could it really collapse?' Nina asked nervously.

'I dunno. The ice is pretty thick. But some bits might fall off, and ten pounds of falling ice'll fuck you up as much as ten tons from that height. Sophia's right – we ought to get moving.'

Nina reluctantly accepted his advice, crossing another bridge to bring them through the outer wall near the rest of the city. Away from the rising steam, the dripping stopped. They tromped across a patch of open ground, where she noticed the remains of vegetation under the ice. 'God punished them by sending the cold to kill the trees . . .' she said, remembering the inscription in Australia.

'Know what it reminds me of, Eddie?' asked Sophia, smiling. 'The Yorkshire Moors.'

'Tchah,' said Chase, jokily dismissive. 'At least Yorkshiremen don't run off to a different continent when it gets a bit nippy. This lot were wimps!'

They reached the first structure. Nina estimated the 'igloo' to be roughly eleven feet tall, and around twenty feet in diameter. The neighbouring buildings, abutting it at the base, appeared identical. 'No windows . . . no doors, either. How do you get in?'

They moved round the group of structures, finding that they were arranged in a circle. Other domes nearby were clustered in the same way, between seven and ten to each group. Eventually they came to a paved road, one of the small branches Nina had seen coming off the main route running through the centre of the city; a gap between two of the buildings led into a kind of courtyard. Smaller domes, presumably for storage, filled the gaps between the clustered groups, the entrances of which were finally revealed: tall, thin archways facing the centre of the courtyard.

It was Chase who realised the logic behind the design. 'It's for shelter,' he said. 'Valley like this, near the coast, you'd get a lot of wind blowing through it. Put 'em all together in a circle and you get some protection.'

'They're houses,' said Nina. 'Maybe each cluster was for one particular family group.' She went to one of the archways and switched on her flashlight, moving cautiously inside. The entrance was over seven feet high, but somehow it still felt cramped.

'Anything inside?' Chase called to her.

'Nothing.' The interior, like the guardhouse, was empty, puddles frozen on the stone floor. The Veteres had apparently taken everything with them when they made the long voyage back to Australia. 'Doesn't look like we're going to find anything here,' she had to admit, turning back. 'Let's try that main road.'

They moved along the side road, passing more groups of domes before emerging on the central route bisecting the city. The first things that caught their attention were the statues along its sides. The larger than life figures were oddly stylised, tall and thin with high foreheads, long necks and small mouths. 'They look like African tribal art,' said Nina.

Chase nodded. 'Like that ugly bugger you used to have.'

'It was a lot nicer than your stupid Fidel Castro thing,' she said defensively, aiming her torch at another statue across the road. The first had been male; this was female, a woman holding what looked like one of the clay cylinders they had found in Australia. It stood on a small plinth – with writing on it. 'Now, what does this say?' she wondered, crossing the road for a closer look.

Sophia came with her. 'That's the word for "prophets",' she said, pointing it out. 'The other word is "keeper", or "holder".'

'Keeper of the prophets? A priest?' Nina turned. Uphill, the temple rose imposingly, the cold light glinting off the copper strips at its summit.

They continued, passing more statues. Men and women, some holding objects that apparently denoted their role in the ancient society while others simply stood in poses of authority, but all clearly figures of great importance. The line came to an end at a high, free-standing archway; some sort of ceremonial gate, Nina guessed. Beyond it, they followed the road to the temple. More statues lined it, apparently representing the same people as the ones further downhill – but this time, they were not in poses of authority. Quite the opposite.

'What's wrong with this lot?' Chase asked, leaving the sledge to regard the bowed, kneeling figures with curiosity. 'Lost their contact lenses?'

'They're praying,' Nina said. She looked to each side of the road, seeing only open land. 'No more houses. This whole section of the city's devoted to their religion. The statues are people the Veteres considered important in their society . . . but even they bow to their god.'

She tipped her head back to take in the full height of the temple. Even with the torch beam, she still couldn't tell how much of the building was buried within the overhanging ice. She brought the circle of light down to the massive open doors. It disappeared, swallowed by the darkness within.

'Maybe he's still inside,' said Chase. 'You know, their god. Frozen.'

'I hardly think these people would take every last chair, plate and spoon with them but leave their god behind,' Sophia said.

Nina walked to the entrance. 'Only one way to find out.'

Chase and Sophia switched on their own torches as they followed her. The sound of ice crunching beneath their boots changed as they moved inside, echoing from the inner walls of a large, high space.

Nina suddenly stopped, flashlight aiming upwards. 'Eddie?'

'Yeah?'

'You know you said their god might still be in here?'

'Yeah?'

'You were right.'

23

The other two torch beams moved upwards to join Nina's. 'Christ on a bike,' said Chase, amazed. 'That's a *big* fucking statue.'

The stone figure before them was at least sixty feet tall, a giant standing against the back of the high circular chamber, reaching almost to the domed ceiling. It was male, carved in the same elongated, blocky style as the statues outside, but on a much greater scale. Its right arm hung down by its side, holding what looked like a sickle; the left was extended across the chamber, palm upturned as if scattering seeds. It wore a necklace of copper, or possibly gold, the style reminding Nina of an ancient Egyptian *menat* necklace of the kind worn by the pharaohs, though with several long metal counterpoises extending down over its chest. A similarly ornate belt ran round the statue's waist, a long copper loincloth descending from it.

And between its feet, at floor level between the statue's heels, was a low opening, less than three feet high, leading to another chamber behind it. The rest of the room before the mighty figure was empty, an open space in which the faithful could worship.

Nina directed her light at the statue's head. It had the same high forehead and narrow jaw as the smaller statues outside. She was about to look at the necklace when something else caught her attention – not on the statue, but just behind it. 'That remind you of anything?' she asked.

'It's a stained-glass window,' said Sophia unenthusiastically, more interested in the gold adorning the statue's accessories.

'No, I don't mean the window itself – I mean its shape.'

Chase saw what she meant. 'Lofty's got a halo.' The window was circular, lines of coloured glass radiating outwards. It was unmistakably a representation of a light or fire surrounding the figure's head.

'Yeah. Now that *is* interesting.'

'What, so the sixty-foot-tall bloke inside a temple buried in Antarctica isn't?'

'You know what I mean. Haloes are an almost universal piece of religious iconography – they appear in ancient Egyptian, Roman and Greek art, as well as Buddhist. But they're most closely associated with the Abrahamic faiths, even Islam. Modern Muslims don't portray Muhammad in artwork, but ancient Muslims did, and he was almost always shown with a halo or heavenly fire around his head.'

'But this predates any of them,' Sophia pointed out. 'By a long time.'

'I know. That's why it's so interesting.' She crossed to the hole between the statue's feet. 'The way to the tree of the gift . . . Let's take a look.' Small icicles hung from the top of the low opening. She swatted them with one hand, sending them tinkling to the ground, then crawled through the gap. 'It *is* a form of supplication,' she said. 'If you want to follow the path, you've got to grovel at your god's feet.'

The passage was short, emerging in a circular room about fifteen feet across. She stood, finding that the room was actually a shaft, extending upwards. Unlike the enclosed temple, the open shaft was blocked by a roof of ice. She could make out the other side of the stained glass window, but of more immediate interest was a set of steps, blocks of stone protruding from the wall at roughly two foot intervals, spiralling upwards. Icicles hung from them, thicker and heavier than the little ones she had dislodged.

'Come on through,' she called. Chase and Sophia soon appeared. 'I think I know what this is for – apart from being a stairwell, obviously. It was open at the top, so if you were inside the temple, daylight would come in and light up the halo behind the statue's head.'

'Fascinating,' said Sophia in a bored tone. She examined one of the stone blocks. 'Are we supposed to climb up these? They look rather slippery. Maybe we should go back to the sledge and get the climbing gear.'

'I thought you were the one in a hurry,' Nina countered.

'That was when we were on solid ground. I'm more than happy to slow things down if it means not plummeting to my death.'

'Eddie? What do you think?'

'We could get the ropes,' Chase said, 'but it'd mean a lot of buggering around, and it'd definitely slow us down.' He climbed the first few steps, the crampons' spikes making a grating rasp. 'If you're worried, then yeah, I'll rig something up, but if you think you can keep your footing . . .'

'I'll be fine,' Nina proclaimed. 'Don't think you can manage, Sophia? English rose wilting?' Sophia looked annoyed, but took the first step.

Chase leading the way, Nina at the rear, they picked their way upwards, backs pressed against the wall. Ten feet, twenty. Nina paused to cast a light towards the top of the shaft, seeing a darkened passageway opposite the giant window. 'Well, at least we'll be able to get out.'

'Would've been a good idea if you'd found that out before we started climbing,' Chase said. He put his foot on the next step and climbed up. Ice crackled – then with a sharp snap a piece on the outer face of the block broke loose, an icicle on the underside dropping with it. Both shattered into millions of fragments on the stone floor below. Chase grunted, double-checking his footing.

'Good thing it didn't fall from above us,' said Nina. The ice sheathing the blocks overhead was thicker, the icicles longer – and sharper.

They kept ascending, passing thirty feet – the halfway mark to the icy ceiling. At around forty feet up, Chase stopped. A large chunk of ice had become frozen against the wall, sticking out enough to make getting past it a tricky proposition. He looked up. The coating of ice got thicker higher up. He guessed that lumps had broken loose from the ceiling as the water level dropped, bobbing on the surface, only to stick to the wall as it froze.

'Hold still,' he said, taking a small pickaxe from his belt. 'I'll have to chip this thing off the wall.' The clink of metal on ice echoed round the shaft as he hacked away at it.

Nina used the wait to take a better look at the window above. The metal used to hold the pieces of coloured glass together was not lead, but gold. 'Wow, look at that,' she said, amazed. 'I think we just found one of the world's most expensive windows.'

'They certainly weren't short of gold,' Sophia remarked. 'Did they bring it with them, or did they find another source here?'

'Antarctica's got plenty of mineral deposits – it's just getting to them that's the problem. For us, anyway. Not having to dig through hundreds of feet of ice would have made it a lot easier.' She looked past the other woman to Chase. 'How's it going, Eddie?'

'Not bad,' he said, still chipping away. The ice creaked, its weight pulling it loose. A final strike of the pick, and the misshapen block of ice broke away with a gunshot crack, plunging downwards to explode against one of the steps below. Smashed shards rained over the bottom of the shaft.

'Anyone need ice?' Chase said with a grin. 'Okay, we'll—'

Another crackle, this one deeper, more menacing. The layer of ice coating the wall above them fractured, a jagged line leaping over their heads towards a much larger hunk of precariously hanging debris.

A smaller crack shot straight up to the icicles hanging from a higher step—

With a sound like breaking bones, the frozen spikes fell.

Chase tried to dodge, but had nowhere to go. One spear of ice hit his arm, slashing through his coat. Another hit the step, shaking it.

He toppled forward—

Sophia slammed an arm against his chest. He wavered, back arched, arms whirling . . .

She pushed harder, one spiked boot slipping with a shrill of metal on stone. Chase hung at the point of no return . . . then tipped backwards against the wall with a relieved gasp.

But the danger wasn't over.

More ice showered over the trio as the crack above them widened. The large lump higher up ripped free, scattering shards in all directions. Nina yelled as it whooshed past, barely missing her – but hitting the previous step.

This time, it wasn't the ice that broke, but the stone, the weight of the plummeting mass wrenching it out of the wall. The preceding step almost followed, left hanging by one corner as the rest of the debris smashed on to more steps below before hitting the floor with a hideous echoing crash.

'Shit,' Chase gasped, looking past Nina at the damaged wall. 'Think we're going to have to find another way down.' With one step missing and another on the brink of giving way, the next secure footing was six feet away and nearly three lower – a dangerous leap given the treacherous ice.

Sophia's arm was still across his chest. 'Thanks,' he said to her.

She nodded. 'You're welcome.'

'Although . . . I'm a bit surprised.'

'What, that I didn't let you fall?'

'Yeah. Realised that you couldn't live without me after all?'

She smiled. 'Not quite. It's just that, for the moment, my chances of survival are far higher with you around. Saving you was simple self-interest.'

'And if it'd been me who was about to fall?' Nina asked, regarding her coldly. The smile vanished; the loathing in Sophia's dark eyes gave her a crystal-clear answer.

'So now what do we do?' Chase asked, recovering his composure.

'We go on,' Nina told him. 'I mean, we don't really have much choice. Are you okay?'

He pulled at his torn sleeve to check the wound beneath, wincing at a jab of pain. 'Arm's cut. Doesn't look too deep, but I'll need to bandage it. It can wait till we get to the top, though.' Pushing himself against the wall, he stepped across the gap to the next step.

More carefully than before, they continued upwards, ascending the spiral until they reached the level of the window. A narrow ledge led round the shaft to it. The glazing was almost fifteen feet in diameter, the shape of the statue's head vaguely discernible beyond.

But it was the passageway opposite the window that dominated their attention. The entrance was arched, a vaulted ceiling retreating into the dark. The floor was thick with pooled ice. Pillars with ancient writing scribed upon them lined each side . . .

Glinting with gold.

Sophia stepped eagerly forward, but Nina put out an arm to stop her. 'At least let Eddie get fixed up first, huh?'

'There's no need to wait,' Sophia said impatiently. 'Whatever it is the Covenant want, we've beaten them to it. And it's just down there.'

'And it'll still be there in five minutes. Eddie, do you need any help?'

Chase had shrugged off his coat and retrieved a first aid kit from his pack. 'Nah, I'll just sit here and stitch myself up while you two keep arguing.'

'Oh, don't you start. It's bad enough having her sniping away in one ear without you doing the same in the other.'

He snorted. 'You're the one who brought her along. I would've left her in Ribbsley's camper van if it'd been up to me.'

'That hasn't stopped you getting all pally with her again, has it?' she snapped.

Chase gave her a disbelieving look. 'Where the fuck did *that* come from? We swap a couple of jokes and suddenly you think we're nipping off behind the icebergs for a quick shag?'

Nina's look of disgust was matched by Sophia's. 'I can assure you, Nina, that absolutely did not and will not happen.'

'It better not,' Nina muttered.

Chase glared at her. 'You going to help me, or what?'

She huffed. 'What can I do?'

'Just pull my sleeve back a bit so I can get at it,' he told her, peeling the torn material from the cut.

Nina held the fabric open as he ran an antiseptic swab over the cut. 'Does it hurt?'

'Take a guess,' Chase said, grunting as he pinched the edges of the cut together and applied a Steri-Strip dressing across it, then wrapped a bandage over it. 'That should hold it – unless we have to do any climbing or anything else that'll rip it.'

'Let's hope there's an easier way back down.' Nina looked round as he put his coat back on, and saw Sophia crouching by one of the pillars. 'Hey! I said to wait.'

'Yes, you did,' was the dismissive reply. 'I can read some of this text – it's talking about the tree of life.' She stood, anticipation clear on her face. 'Whatever it is, it's here.' Sophia's flashlight illuminated the passage, revealing a chamber at the far end. 'Come on.'

She hurried down the corridor. Exasperated, Nina caught up, Chase following.

The three torch beams swept across the chamber's entrance to reveal what lay inside. Beneath the omnipresent ice, Nina made out stone shelves, much like those she had seen inside the ruined chamber in Australia . . . but these were intact.

And still held their contents.

'Oh . . .' she said in wonder as she entered the room, moving the light along the length of one of the shelves. It was filled with clay tablets, a long rack containing dozen upon dozen of the flat rectangles, standing on edge like books. She continued to pan the beam, revealing more tablets . . . and more . . . and more.

And beyond them, more shelves. And more. The chamber stretched away as far as her light could reach, a vast warren of ancient knowledge. Chase and Sophia also probed the room, finding yet more stacks of tablets receding into the distance.

'We – we need more light,' she gasped, pulling off her backpack and fumbling in it for a packet of glowsticks. Almost dropping them in her haste, she bent them to crack the inner glass tubes, chemicals mixing and fluorescing to give out an orange light, the first warm colour she had seen since entering the frozen cavern. 'Look at this! Look!' she cried, almost skipping into the nearest aisle in her excitement as she placed glowsticks on the shelves. 'It's a *library*! It's the entire knowledge of the Veteres!'

Chase rummaged in his own pack for a lamp and switched it on, noticing a large gap on a shelf. 'It's not *that* entire. Somebody's taken a bunch of stuff off this shelf. Hate to think what the overdue fines are after this long.'

'There are more missing over here,' Sophia added, peering down another aisle. 'And here, too.' Whole sections were empty, entire shelves gaping.

Nina took off her gloves, lifting a tablet at random. The ice crackled before finally giving up its prize. She recognised a handful of the words upon it; there was mention of wind, cold and storms. A record of the weather?

Another snap of ice from a few aisles away. 'This one seems to be about some sort of dispute between families,' said Sophia after a few moments.

Nina retrieved a couple of glowsticks and moved deeper into the maze, stopping at an empty shelf. Examining it, she made out words carved into the stone slab itself. 'Sophia, look at this,' she called. Sophia and Chase joined her. 'I think it's an index – it'll tell us what's missing, rather than what's been left behind.'

Sophia brushed away the frost. 'I think it says "grain". Some sort of crop, anyway. And that's "water" – not the sea, but fresh.'

'Something about farming?' Chase suggested. 'Like how to grow grain?'

'How to *irrigate* grain,' Nina realised. The reason why some sections of the library were empty while others had been left completely intact was becoming clear. 'That's something that'd be useful if you had to pack up and start from scratch. But historical records, accounts of legal disputes . . . not so much.'

'You think they took the missing tablets with them?' asked Sophia.

'They cleaned out the rest of the place when they left, so there's no reason why they wouldn't take valuable knowledge with them – the kind of knowledge that would help them survive. But this . . .' She pulled another tablet free. 'This is still an incredible find – it'll give us an amazing amount of information about how the Veteres lived. But when they went back to Australia to escape the changing climate, they left it all behind, because it would just be dead weight. And when you're sailing thousands of miles in primitive boats, the last thing you want aboard is dead weight.'

Sophia sounded almost offended. 'So all this is worthless? They took all the most important tablets with them and left the junk behind?'

'It's *not* worthless,' Nina said irritably, professional pride insulted. 'I just said—'

'It's of absolutely no use to us right now. And it doesn't help us deal with the Covenant. We already knew the Veteres left here and went back to Australia – we're no better off than we were before. Just a lot colder.'

'There's still plenty more to look at,' Chase said, standing beside Nina. 'This tree they kept going on about might be just round the next corner.'

Sophia swung her torch back and forth, finding only more shelves. 'Somehow I doubt that, Eddie,' she said with a sneer.

'I don't mean *literally* the next corner, for fuck's sake. Christ, this is just like when we—'

'It's *not* literal,' Nina interrupted. Chase and Sophia looked at her. 'The tree, I mean,' she continued, mind racing as a new idea took form. 'It's not literal – the translation doesn't literally mean tree! Ribbsley got it wrong, just like he did about wind and sand – it's symbolic, something with multiple meanings depending on the context.' She paced rapidly back and forth along the aisle. 'What else can a tree represent? What's the symbolism behind it?'

Sophia quickly overcame her anger to focus on the problem. 'Growth and change,' she said. 'Or cycles, cycles of nature.'

Chase's thoughts were more practical. 'You get wood from trees. Or fruit.'

'The tree of the gift,' said Nina, 'the tree of life. If it's not a literal tree, then what is it? The *something* of life, the *something* of the gift.'

'It'd help if we knew what the gift was,' Chase said.

Nina tried to remember the Australian inscription. 'The Veteres thought their god was punishing them. And their term for "god" included "tree" – "the one great tree", wasn't it?' Sophia nodded.

'So to them god and tree were interlinked. What were they thinking? How did their minds work?' Words clicked through her own mind, alternative meanings flashing past like possible solutions to a crossword clue. 'So what is God? God's the creator, the provider, the giver of life . . . the *source*,' she concluded. 'The source of life, the source of the gift, the one great source. And a tree is a source, of lots of things – it gives you shelter, food, wood . . .'

'It fits,' Sophia realised. 'They used the word tree as a symbolic representation for source – of anything.'

'Which means,' Nina said, looking at the shelves, 'that we're in "the source of the gift". The library is the source of the gift.'

'So what *is* this gift?' Chase demanded.

'It's knowledge!' Nina said, laughing. 'The gift from their god was *knowledge*! The ability to record and pass on everything they'd ever learned to their descendants, who passed it on to *their* descendants, and so on. And all of this at a time when we thought humans hadn't even developed cave paintings. My God, this is amazing!'

'Their god wasn't quite so impressed,' said Sophia. 'He tried to destroy them, remember? For "giving the gift of God to the beasts".'

Chase looked dubious. 'How do you give knowledge to animals?'

The answer came to Nina. 'You train them. That's what the hypogeum must have been – a training area. Start them out in harsh, cramped conditions under constant supervision to break them, then move them to easier surroundings once you've got control. First the stick, then the carrot. I doubt PETA would approve, but it'd work.'

'So their god decided to freeze them to death for teaching their dogs to fetch? Bit steep.'

'That's primitive religion for you. If things go bad, the only conceivable explanation is that you've somehow angered your god.'

'So if "the tree of the gift" is actually the source of knowledge,' said Sophia, 'what about "the tree of life"? The source of life?'

'I don't know,' Nina replied, 'but that sounds like something the Covenant would be interested in, don'cha think?' She gathered up the glowsticks. 'Let's find it.'

The library extended for some distance. Nina judged that roughly a fifth of the storage space was empty – which meant that in their flight to warmer climes, the Veteres had been forced to abandon four-fifths of their entire recorded knowledge: an incredible loss to any society. Had they simply sacrificed too much of the knowledge they needed to survive?

They made their way through the maze, eventually reaching the far wall – and discovering the entrance to another room. 'It's not a library,' said Chase, stepping inside. 'Don't know what it is, actually.'

Ally-ally-ally . . . his voice echoed back. Exchanging puzzled looks with the others, he raised his torch, and saw that the new chamber's roof was domed. Nina moved her light across the room. It was circular, with what looked like pieces of machinery spaced around its edge. There was another, larger machine at the centre, a conical copper tube extending upwards from it almost to the ceiling.

'Curiouser and curiouser,' said Sophia, moving to the nearest machine. 'It looks like a potter's wheel.'

'They must have made some bloody weird pots,' Chase opined as he approached an identical device on the opposite side of the entrance. There was indeed a large wooden wheel at about waist height, a metal rod rising from its centre, but mounted behind it on a hinge was a large copper cone, a thick needle protruding from the narrow end . . . 'They're gramophones!' he exclaimed. 'Like the one you made in Australia, Nina.'

'This must be where they played the recordings on the cylinders,' Sophia said.

Nina went to the chamber's centre, holding out a glowstick to illuminate the machine there. 'No,' she realised, looking up at the copper tube. 'It's not where they played them. It's where they *made* them. This room . . . it's a *recording studio*. Look.' She followed the tube up to the ceiling, where the interior surface of the dome was marked with odd indentations radiating out towards each gramophone. Even through the ice, it was easy to tell they had been carefully carved into a very specific pattern. 'The sound of the original goes up the tube to the roof – and then goes outwards to each of the cones around the room. It's a whispering gallery!'

'Like the dome of St Paul's Cathedral?' asked Sophia.

'Yes, only this one's designed to send the sound out in multiple directions rather than just to the point diametrically opposite. Pretty sophisticated, even today. The Veteres just keep getting more advanced, don't they?' She took a closer look at the machine. Like the others, it had a wheel and a speaker cone, this one angled to point at the mouth of the tube above. Beneath the wheel, she noticed that the vertical axle was wound with fine copper bands. 'I think this was designed to make copies of existing cylinders as well as recording voices. That'd explain why there was an echo on the cylinders we played in Australia – the recording cones were picking up sounds from other parts of the room.'

'So this is like a prehistoric iTunes?' Chase said. 'Pick your favourite track and they'll run off copies for you?'

Nina smiled at the comparison. 'In a way, yeah. Although it might have been more for religious purposes. Just think what it would be like to have an actual recording of, say, the Sermon on the Mount. You wouldn't need to interpret someone else's written account – you'd have Jesus's own words, exactly as he spoke them.' She bent down, removing a glove to rub the frost off what appeared to be text on one of the copper bands. 'Although it'd put a lot of religious scholars out of business if everybody could— *Ow!*'

She jerked back, clutching her finger. At the same moment, a mechanical *clunk* echoed through the chamber. The wheel of the central machine shuddered, straining against the ice before falling still.

'What happened?' Chase asked, hurrying to her. 'Are you okay?'

'I just got zapped!' Nina shrilled, more surprised than hurt. 'Like a static shock.' She rubbed her finger. 'Son of a bitch!'

Chase gingerly tapped the machinery. 'It's gone now.'

'Great,' Nina muttered. 'A static charge sticks around for thousands of years, and guess who gets hit by it?'

'Eddie, turn the wheel,' Sophia called to them from the machine she had been examining. Chase took hold of the wooden wheel and pulled at it. It only moved fractionally, still jammed by ice – but the wheel of Sophia's machine creaked in unison. The others did the same. 'They're all linked.'

Nina surveyed the room. 'Makes sense. If you're making copies, you want them to be identical. If each wheel was manually operated, they'd all be running at slightly different speeds.' She looked back at the axle. 'So what's making it work?'

'It can't be electric, can it?' asked Chase. 'No way this lot were *that* advanced.'

Nina looked back in the general direction of the statue, a puzzled frown crossing her face. 'I don't see how, unless . . . could they have used earth energy somehow? Those copper things outside the temple – they could be antenna.'

'Earth energy?' Sophia asked.

'That black project you said Callum was pissed off at us for wrecking?' said Chase. 'That used it.'

'It was a way to channel the earth's own magnetic fields into a weapon, using Excalibur as a superconductor,' Nina explained.

Sophia raised an eyebrow. 'Excalibur? Don't tell me you found that as well.'

'Yeah, kinda. Long story.'

'It can wait,' said Sophia, pointing her torch at an opening across the chamber. 'Whatever powered all this, it seems to have stopped working – and finding the tree of life's more important right now.'

Nina reluctantly had to admit they did need to move on from the fascinating chamber. The tilt-rotor had to return to the ship before nightfall, and they still needed to find another way back down to ground level. 'Let's see what's through there.'

On the surface, Trulli double-checked that the walkie-talkie was still working. It had been some time since he'd heard anything from the party below. But the green LED was lit; the radio was fine despite the cold. He was tempted to call for a status report, but resisted. Knowing Nina, she was probably so engrossed in exploration that she'd forgotten the outside world even existed.

He was stuck in it, though, and so were the others. Shrugging to circulate the warmth inside his thick coat, he slowly turned to take in the scene. The BA609 was now parked further away; Larsson had heeded the warning about the dripping ice above the fumarole. Bandra was plodding across the ice from the aircraft, no doubt to come and complain about something new. Rachel and Baker both sat on folding chairs by the winch, huddled together in their bulky clothing like nesting penguins. He noticed they were sharing the headphones of Rachel's iPod, and grinned. That was one way to start a relationship.

A faint noise, something other than the constant flutter of the wind across the plain. A low murmur. Powerful, mechanical . . .

And growing louder.

He turned again, scanning the sky. White haze on the horizon, the sun still crawling infinitesimally across the empty blue dome—

294

And something else, moving more quickly. Aircraft. Some way off, but heading towards him. He recognised the type immediately. C-130 Hercules transports, large, four-engined propeller craft. One painted in high-visibility red and white, the other a pale military grey.

The expedition wasn't expecting visitors. And in the Antarctic wastes, the odds of encountering anyone by chance were effectively zero. Whoever was aboard knew they were here.

Trulli could only think of one group of people who might be looking for them.

'Nina! Eddie!' he shouted into the radio, the urgency in his voice immediately catching the attention of Baker and Rachel, who looked at him in concern. No reply. 'Eddie, can you hear me? The Covenant are here!'

The radio remained silent, the warning unheard.

24

'I can see daylight again,' said Chase, leading the way.

'Yeah, but will we be able to get out?' Nina wondered. The crust of ice covering everything in the frozen city seemed to be thickening, icicles hanging longer and lower.

'Somehow I don't think so,' Sophia said, aiming her torch ahead. They had reached the end of the passage, the cold azure light illuminating the exit . . . and also revealing that it was blocked. Glassy ice covered the arched opening, angling claustrophobically down to the stone floor.

And even if the ice had not been there, getting out might still have been difficult. Nina could make out the silhouette of what appeared to be a barred metal gate inside the archway.

'Bollocks,' Chase murmured. 'End of the line.'

'We should have brought those gas cylinders with us,' said Sophia. 'We could have melted through.'

'Wouldn't make any difference. Look how thick it is. Take days to get through all that – even if we could open the gates.'

Nina was more interested in what lay to one side of the gate. 'There's something here, in the ice.' She directed her flashlight at it, trying to make out the objects. 'They look like bowls, metal bowls.' A word in the Veteres language appeared to have been painted on the side of the largest.

'Something here an' all,' Chase said from the other side of

the archway. 'It's another record player.'

'Weird. Why have one here?'

'Maybe it's the gate guard's iPod.' He turned his attention to the buried gate. 'Reckon this is the way to the tree of life?'

'Well, we had the tree of knowledge, so . . .' Nina tailed off. 'Huh. I just realised how biblical that is. In the Book of Genesis, the Garden of Eden contained the Tree of Life and the Tree of Knowledge.'

'The Tree of Knowledge of Good and Evil, actually,' Sophia corrected, moving back down the passage.

'Well, you'd know about the second one,' sniped Nina, before turning back to Chase. 'That's kind of a coincidence, though. If it *is* a coincidence.'

'So these people might have had something to do with the Bible?' Chase asked.

'I don't see how; the time gap is way too big. Even the oldest parts of the Torah only date back to around the tenth century BC. But . . .' She frowned, thinking. 'Some sort of race memory, maybe? An idea that passed down over a hundred thousand years . . .'

Sophia's urgent voice dismissed her musings. 'Over here! There's another room!'

Nina and Chase jogged to her. Behind one of the pillars was a narrow gap in the wall, a low passageway. 'Can you see what's inside?' Nina asked.

'Only that it's not very big. I can see the back wall.'

'Let's have a look,' said Chase. He began to break away the icicles obstructing it.

'Eddie, come on!' Trulli yelled into the radio. Still no response.

He looked up. The two Hercs had flown overhead, and were now circling back round.

'It's probably just a supply flight on its way to Vostok or Dome

Charlie,' Bandra said patronisingly. 'They didn't expect to see anyone here, so they're overflying us to make sure we're all right.'

'If they didn't know we were here, how come they were heading right for us?' Trulli shot back.

'Does it matter? Why, are you expecting trouble?' The Indian scientist's smirk fell when he registered Trulli's serious expression. '*Are* you?'

'Why do you think I'm trying so hard to get hold of Nina and Eddie?'

'Well – but why would there be trouble over an archaeological find?'

The Australian gave him a look of disbelief. 'Haven't you ever read anything about Nina? People are *always* trying to kill her!' He gave the walkie-talkie one last try, then glared at it in disgust. 'The radio in the plane's got more power – I'll try to hook this up to it and get through to them.' Another glance skyward. The C-130s had angled away, turning into the wind. They would pass a couple of hundred metres from the site. 'I don't know how they found us in the first place, though.' Bandra's expression became shifty. 'What?'

'That, ah . . . that may be my fault,' Bandra admitted. 'Last night, when we returned to the ship, I . . . I contacted UNARA.'

'You *what* ?' Trulli shouted.

'*I'm* the leader of this expedition, not Dr Wilde! I sent a detailed email to New York to complain about the way I'd been treated!'

'And did you tell them about the find?' Bandra's guilty countenance was all the answer he needed. 'Well, that's bloody marvellous! You've just led the bad guys right to us!'

'Bad guys?' Bandra snorted. 'This isn't some Hollywood movie!'

'Maybe not,' said Trulli, pointing at the approaching planes, 'but what do you call that?'

The rear cargo ramps of both aircraft had lowered. Men and

machines poured from them, white parachutes snapping open to send them drifting towards the frozen plain like a line of dandelion seeds.

'Get to the plane,' Trulli warned everyone. He ran for the parked tilt-rotor, clutching the radio.

The last icicles smashed on the cold floor. Chase crunched over them and emerged in the room beyond. He switched on the lantern as Nina came through the low opening, followed by Sophia. 'Another one?' Nina asked, seeing one of the primitive gramophones in a corner.

'Yeah. They really like their decks. But I don't think that's what the room's for.' He lifted the lantern higher, illuminating one wall.

Nina's eyes widened. 'My God!'

It was another inscription, blocks of text scribed into a layer of plaster. But this one featured something the one in Australia lacked.

A map.

It was not an accurate cartographical representation; instead, it was more like a linear account of the various places visited along a journey, what appeared to be coastlines strung out along its length between points labelled with more ancient writing. Nina recognised numbers and compass bearings: the direction and number of days' sail from each point?

'The land of cold sand,' said Sophia, pointing to the symbols at one end of the map. 'This is where we are now. Antarctica.'

Nina traced the route back. It was apparently a long voyage across open sea to another land – Australia? Then up the coast to . . . 'That might be the site north of Perth. If it is, then . . .' Her excitement rose as she continued. 'This could show the spread of the Veteres culture across the world – if these at the end are Antarctica and Australia, then these other coastlines would be Indonesia, Southeast Asia, India . . .'

'Which means,' Sophia said, looking at the other end of the map, 'this is their *origin*. The point they expanded from. Where it all began.'

'God, yes,' gasped Nina. Heart pounding, she ran her finger along the frosted wall. Westwards from India along the coast of what was now Pakistan, Iran, the mouth of the Persian Gulf . . . which at the time of the Veteres would have been closed off by the lower sea level, the Gulf itself nothing but an inland lake. Along the coast of the Arabian peninsula, another settlement there—

'Oman!' Sophia cried, stabbing a finger at the mark. 'That's the site I visited with Gabriel eight years ago, it must be. The Covenant had destroyed it.'

'Looks like they missed quite a few, though,' said Chase. There were at least a dozen places given as much prominence as the Oman site, and numerous smaller ones.

'They're still there to be found,' said Nina.

'Unless the Covenant has already found them,' Sophia pointed out.

Nina's finger moved faster across the map. 'They can't have got them all. Arabia, across the entrance to the Red Sea, up its coast . . . and then they go inland.' She looked at the others. 'Into Africa. That's where they came from. Africa!' The trail of the Veteres to the coast crossed a river, leading some distance inland back to its origin: three trapezoidal symbols, the topmost having four winding lines – more rivers? – running outwards from it.

'So that's why their statues look like that one you used to have,' Chase realised. 'Same people.'

'Different times,' Nina replied. 'These people had already moved out of Africa at a time when we thought early humans were only just starting to form the most primitive societies, in places like Ethiopia and Sudan.'

'That would fit with the map.' Sophia stood, regarding the text

300

above it. 'The first words here are something like "The journey of the people of God, from . . ." I assume that's a name. The name of their homeland, maybe. But the first line ends with "to the land of cold sand".'

Nina looked over the words with her. 'They left it in case their people ever returned – a reminder of who they were and where they came from. It's their whole history.'

Sophia read on. 'More mention of beasts, as well – the word appears quite a lot. They certainly seem to have had trouble with their animals.'

'Soph,' said Chase from behind them. 'That word you didn't recognise, you think it's a name, yeah?'

'Yes.'

'Well, it's here as well.'

Nina and Sophia turned to see him holding his torch over the icy gramophone. Next to it were two of the clay cylinders. 'So it is,' said Sophia, looking more closely at the one Chase had indicated. 'The other characters say . . . I think it's "the path from".'

'So that's the title of the recording?' Nina said. 'The path from . . . from whatever they called their homeland. If we could translate that as well as the whole inscription . . .' She peered at the second cylinder. 'What does that one say? Is that "prophet"?'

Sophia confirmed it. 'I can't read the other characters.' She pulled it free of the ice.

'What does it say?' Chase asked as she turned the cylinder in her hands.

She looked puzzled. 'I think it's "the song of the prophet".'

Nina examined it. 'That's the word for "song"? Because it's also what was painted on those bowls in the ice.' She turned to the gramophone, putting her hands on the wheel. Ice ground and crunched – then cracked, the wheel rotating more or less freely.

'These things were left here for a reason. I think we need to play them.'

By the time Trulli reached the tilt-rotor, the new arrivals were landing and collapsing their parachutes with well-practised skill. The Hercules in military livery had borne United States Air Force markings – but the men who emerged from it were not in American uniforms. The vehicles landing on pallets with them were not exactly standard US issue either: they looked like small hovercraft, glossy beetle-black bodywork bearing what appeared to be stubby, squared-off wings.

Five hovercraft in all, and about twenty men. *Armed* men.

He looked for the other expedition members. Rachel had initially hesitated before following him to the BA609, and was still clomping across the ice. Baker dutifully remained at the winch. Bandra, though, was moving to meet the paratroopers. 'Oh, you stupid bastard,' he moaned, before giving the walkie-talkie to Larsson. 'I need you to hook that up to the radio – and get this thing started!'

Chase delved into his pack to produce a flare, igniting it and holding the two cylinders beside the sizzling red flame to melt the ice off them. In the small room the light was dazzling and the sulphurous burning smell almost overpowering, but it quickly did the job. Once the cylinders were clear, he used the same trick to remove the ice crusted over the needle and speaker cone before tossing the flare into the passage outside.

Nina turned the wheel again. 'We'll have to work it by hand. Hope we can get it to the right speed.'

'The one you improvised wasn't turning that fast,' said Sophia, drying the cylinders and handing them to her.

Nina mounted the first cylinder, the one labelled 'song of the prophet', on the spindle, positioning the needle against the cylinder's groove. 'Okay. Here goes.'

She turned the wheel, spinning it at what she thought was roughly the right speed. An unpleasant scraping noise came from the copper cone. Chase winced. 'Sounds like the greatest hits of Fingernails and Blackboard.'

'Hold on.' She adjusted the needle and spun the wheel again. This time, she got a result. A slurred, uneven voice came from the cone.

'That must be the title,' Sophia told her. 'But you need to go faster.'

'Okay, okay.' Nina spun the wheel more quickly, waiting for the next words to emerge.

They didn't. What came from the speaker was a *chant*.

'"Song of the prophet"? You weren't kidding,' said Chase.

Nina kept the wheel turning. The music was a long, sustained note, distorted by the inevitable variations in speed of the turntable, but she imagined that, played as it had been intended, the singer would have maintained perfect pitch. The note rose an octave, then dropped two before rising again. Then it stopped. The whole was beautiful, yet somehow unsettling. 'What was *that*?' she said. Chase hummed the five-note theme from *Close Encounters of the Third Kind*. '*Not* that.'

'A ritual chant, maybe,' Sophia suggested.

'Of their prophet. Maybe even *by* their prophet,' realised Nina. 'Give me the other cylinder.'

Back straight, head held high to show a confidence that was rapidly draining, Dr Bandra strode towards the parachutists. Both aircraft, having disgorged their cargo, were heading away towards the coast. Most of the newly arrived soldiers were engaged in removing the hovercraft from their pallets, but there was a group of five men who appeared to be in charge, standing apart from the others.

He slowed as he approached the apparent officers. All but one had rifles slung over their shoulders as well as holstered pistols. Increasingly nervous, he stopped before the group. 'Good afternoon,' he began, the words catching in his throat. He cleared it and continued more authoritatively, 'I'm Dr Rohit Bandra of the United Nations Antarctic Research Agency, in charge of this expedition. I've been given no advance notice of any other activities – can you tell me what you're doing here?'

To his anger, they didn't even acknowledge him, most of them looking away as another soldier ran over to give a report. Only a white-haired man seemed to have any interest in his presence – and Bandra was already wishing that he didn't, finding his unblinking gaze increasingly unnerving.

'Look,' he said, trying to catch the attention of the others, 'I have authority here, as granted to me by the United Nations. So I insist that you tell me what's going on. After all, ha, I'm sure you remember that the Antarctic Treaty prohibits military operations.'

The white-haired man's stare didn't waver. 'We're not military,' he told Bandra . . . as he drew his pistol and shot him in the head.

The shot cracked across the plain, audible even over the rising noise of the tilt-rotor's engines. 'Shit!' Trulli yelled, throwing the cabin door open. 'Davo! Come on! Run!'

Baker stared as Bandra fell backwards, a slash of red spouting across the pristine white. It took a few seconds before his fight-or-flight instinct cut through his shock – by which time other soldiers were reacting to the unexpected gunfire, unslinging their rifles.

He started to run, weighed down by his heavy clothing. The soldiers were some two hundred metres from him – but the plane was almost as distant in the other direction. Rifle fire crackled across the gap.

'David!' cried Rachel. Trulli watched, appalled, as little geysers of ice spat up around the running man, a ragged pattern of bullet impacts.

The pattern rapidly tightened.

Baker stumbled. For a moment Trulli thought he had just lost his footing – then a puff of crimson spray burst through his padded coat. And another, blood gushing out as he crashed on to the ice, flailing to a stop at the head of a smeared trail of gore.

Rachel screamed. 'Take off!' yelled Trulli. 'Go, go, go!' The soldiers were already switching targets, directing their weapons at the tilt-rotor. Larsson pushed the throttle to full power.

A shot hit the tilt-rotor's side. Rachel shrieked again. 'Get down!' Trulli told her, ducking in his seat. Another bullet struck somewhere behind him. His view of the soldiers was obscured by a whirlwind of ice crystals as the Bell finally fought free of the ground. Larsson immediately tilted the stick sideways to slide the aircraft away from the soldiers, turning as he gained height.

More gunfire, this time a rattling burst on automatic. Trulli looked back. One of the hovercraft was slithering across the ice on a roostertail of snow and ice. Two Covenant soldiers were aboard, one driving, the other in the front seat with a rifle, flame spitting from its muzzle as he fired again—

More bullets hit home, ripping into the aluminium fuselage and penetrating the cabin. Larsson yelped as one struck the back of his seat – but didn't pierce the metal, the flattened round clanging to the floor. Other shots thunked round them, then the firing stopped as the aircraft transitioned to flight mode and sped out of range.

'Are we damaged?' Trulli asked. 'Can we still fly?'

Larsson hurriedly checked the instruments. 'I think so. But who were they? What the hell is going on?'

'Tell you in a minute.' Trulli turned his attention back to the walkie-talkie. 'First, I've got to get this radio working!'

★

Zamal watched the tilt-rotor retreat into the distance. 'They're getting away!' he yelled.

'It doesn't matter,' Callum told him, unconcerned. He looked at the hole in the ice. 'We've still got Wilde and Chase trapped. And Blackwood.'

'I want Sophia alive,' Ribbsley said firmly. 'If you want my help, that's the deal.'

Vogler smiled sardonically. 'Professor Ribbsley, do you know how far we are from the nearest ice station?'

He looked puzzled. 'No?'

'About two hundred kilometres,' said Hammerstein, lighting a cigar.

'Quite a walk,' Vogler continued. 'And since we only have enough seats in the paracraft to take us all back there,' he gestured at one of the four-seater vehicles, 'if we decided to bring Ms Blackwood with us, one person would have to give up his place and make that walk. And I assure you, that person will not be any of my men.'

'Nor mine,' said Hammerstein.

Zamal grinned. 'Or mine.'

'And I doubt Mr Callum will volunteer either. So, Professor, you may want to reconsider your position.' Vogler gazed into the distance. 'It really is quite a walk.'

Ribbsley turned away with an irritable, defeated growl. Vogler regarded him with brief amusement before calling to one of the soldiers. 'Situation report!'

'The paracraft are all ready, sir,' the man replied.

'And the ice-burners?'

The soldier indicated a pair of heavy objects the size and shape of oil drums, which were being lifted upright alongside two of the paracraft. 'Ready to be moved into position.'

'Then let us begin.' Vogler faced the other Covenant leaders.

306

'Hammerstein, take your squad down the shaft there,' he said, nodding at the winch. 'Zamal, get your men to set up the first ice-burner over the centre of the lake and proceed from there. My team will take the second to the southern end. Mr Callum, Professor Ribbsley, come with me.' He took his rifle from his shoulder, pulling back the charging handle to load the first round. 'Dr Wilde's search is over.'

The second cylinder was on the spindle. 'All right,' said Nina, 'let's see what this one has to say.'

'What was it called again?' asked Chase.

'"The path from . . ." whatever that name is,' Sophia said, pointing at the unknown word on the inscription, then moving her finger to the starting point of the map. 'Presumably this place in Africa.'

Nina turned the wheel. An ancient voice echoed from the speaker cone, reciting the cylinder's title. 'We'll take a look after we've played—' She stopped as she heard what it said.

Chase and Sophia were equally dumbfounded. Though the language was strange, one word stood out clearly from the others. A name.

A name they all knew.

Nina stopped the wheel. Chase jabbed a finger at the cone. 'Did that just say what I think it said?'

'Play it again!' Sophia ordered, but Nina didn't need any prompting, already moving the needle back to its starting position. She spun the wheel again.

Again, the unfamiliar words emerged from the speaker . . . followed by one they couldn't mistake.

Eden.

'"The path from *Eden*"?' Chase almost shouted. 'Are you telling me these buggers came from the Garden of fucking Eden?'

307

'It can't be,' Sophia protested, even as Nina reset the needle once more. 'The Garden of Eden is pure myth!'

'So was Atlantis,' Nina reminded her as the ancient recording played again.

Eden. The same word. Unmistakable. Undeniable.

'*That's* the Covenant's secret,' said Nina, stunned. 'The Covenant of Genesis . . . they took their name from the agreement, the covenant, between the three religions to protect Genesis, to protect *Eden*, and make sure nobody ever finds it.'

'Why?' Chase asked, mystified. 'If they say, "Hey, look, we found the actual factual Garden of Eden!" wouldn't that prove they were right all along?'

'Not if scientific analysis confirmed that what was written in Genesis is *wrong*. The story told in Genesis is the foundation stone of all three religions – kick it out, and they're all weakened. They can't allow that to happen.'

Sophia surveyed the map. 'So do they know where Eden is?'

'They can't, otherwise they would have dealt with it already.' She raised her hands to take in the room and its contents. 'But they don't have any of this. We do, and the Covenant don't know where we are – so we can find Eden first!'

Chase was about to say something when his walkie-talkie squawked. 'Matt? That you?' The only response was a stuttering electronic screech. 'Walls must be too thick for the signal to get through,' he said, ducking back through the passageway. 'I'll try it out here.'

He emerged in the ice-blocked hallway, where the red flare was still fizzing away. Trulli's voice became clearer, though still heavily distorted. 'Nina! Eddie! If you can hear me, for Christ's sake answer!'

'I'm here, Matt,' said Chase. 'What's up?'

'Eddie! Oh, thank God! Listen, they're here, the Covenant! They killed Davo and Dr Bandra!'

Chase was silent for a moment. 'Oh, *arse*,' he finally said.

'Eddie! Did you hear me?'

'Yeah, I heard you. Where are you?'

'We're in the plane. Listen, you've got to get out of there!'

'No shit, Sherlock,' muttered Chase as the women scrabbled through the passage, Nina clutching the cylinder containing the song. 'Nina, you know you just said that the Covenant don't know where we are?'

'Yeah?'

'Guess what?'

Nina's face fell. 'You gotta be kidding me!'

'Matt,' he said into the radio, 'we need to find another way back to the winch.' He paused. 'They're *at* the winch, aren't they?'

'Yeah,' came the crackling reply.

'Buggeration and fuckery!' Another moment of thought. 'Okay, then the only other way out's through the drainage shaft – if it hasn't frozen up. If we get out, I'll radio you so you can pick us up. But if you don't hear anything from us in . . .' he looked at his watch, 'in the next hour, then get the fuck out of here, because I don't think we'll be coming.'

'We'll land and wait for you,' Trulli assured him. 'Good luck.'

'Thanks.' Chase lowered the radio. 'Okay, we need another way back down to the ground – but first things first,' he said as an idea struck him, crouching and hurrying back through the passage.

'What are you doing?' Nina asked, pocketing the cylinder and following him.

'Give me your camera. Quick.' She extracted it from its pouch and handed it to him. He took several pictures of the African section of the map.

Sophia entered. 'What is it?'

'We're the only people who've seen this, right?' he said, closing the camera's cover and stuffing it into one of his inside pockets.

'Yeah?' said Nina.

'So nobody else ever will.' He raised the pickaxe – and smashed it repeatedly against the wall, obliterating the markings.

'Eddie!' Nina cried, horrified. 'What are you *doing*?' She tried to pull the axe from his hand.

'No,' Sophia said, 'he's right. We can't let the Covenant find this.'

Chase kept bashing at the wall until the African end of the map was nothing more than shattered fragments on the floor, then ground them to powder beneath his boot. 'Don't think they'll get much from that.' He went back to the passageway. 'Okay, now we need to find another way to the shaft – and we've got fifty-eight minutes to do it!'

25

Even through his sunglasses, Vogler had to squint to counter the glare of sunlight on snow as he looked across the ice field. In the distance he picked out Hammerstein and his team descending the winch line, and two hundred metres closer Zamal's men moved one of the black drums into position.

His own soldiers had done the same with the second. 'The ice-burner is ready, sir,' a man informed him.

'Then start it. Everyone, move back.'

The rest of the team, plus Ribbsley and Callum, retreated as the soldier inserted a long glass tube containing an amber liquid into an opening on the drum's top. Once it was in place, he pushed a button and quickly moved away. A faint crack came from within the heavy drum as a small explosive charge shattered the glass.

'Is that it?' Ribbsley asked, unimpressed. 'With something called an ice-burner, I was expecting jets of flame.'

'Just wait,' Vogler told him. Seconds passed . . . then the drum shifted, settling deeper into the surface layer of snow. Water pooled round its base.

Then bubbled, and boiled.

Steam swirled from the ground as the drum sank into the ice. Hot water gushed from the hole, displaced by the ice-burner's weight, and the hiss of escaping steam became a roar as the metal began to glow red-hot. Across the plain, a spewing plume of vapour shot up as Zamal's ice-burner disappeared into the frozen surface.

'Exothermic reaction,' said Vogler to the now somewhat more impressed Ribbsley. 'Two chemicals that produce an enormous amount of heat when mixed. Some sort of thermate derivative – I don't know what, chemistry is not my field, but I've been told the reaction will last long enough to melt through up to fifty metres of ice.' The drum dropped below the surface, steam and spray spitting out of the hole.

'How long will it take?' Ribbsley asked.

'Five minutes, perhaps less. As soon as it breaks through, we will secure ropes and climb down. Will you be able to manage?'

The professor gave him a scathing look. 'If I can manage a parachute drop, I can handle a rope climb.'

'Good. Then get ready.'

Nina, Chase and Sophia split up, hurriedly searching the unexplored areas of the library for other exits. Nina moved through the western side of the huge room, before long making a promising discovery. 'Eddie!' she called. 'I found another way out!'

Sophia was first to arrive. 'There's a doorway,' Nina told her. 'It's frozen up, but I can see light on the other side.' The azure glow of ice-filtered daylight was visible round the edges of the wood and metal door.

Chase reached them. 'What've we got?'

'A door,' Sophia said. 'Of the closed variety, inevitably.'

'I don't think it's frozen solid like that gate,' said Nina, 'but I can't get it open.' She tugged at the ice-caked handle. The door rattled, but didn't move.

'Let's have a go,' Chase said. He gripped the handle with both hands, pulling backwards as hard as he could. Ice cracked on the other side of the door. He grunted, then stepped back before charging and shoulder-barging it. There was a crunch, and as Chase reeled back the door swung open after him. 'Piece of piss.'

Nina hugged him. 'Nice job.'

'Yes, whenever you need nothing more than brute force, you can always rely on Eddie,' said Sophia.

Chase leered at her. 'Hey, you used to *like* some brute force. Ow,' he added as Nina hit him on his bruised shoulder. 'What was that for?' Her glare gave him the answer. 'Oh, right.'

'Enjoyable as it is to reminisce about our sex life,' Sophia sighed as she went to the opening, 'I really think we should move on.'

'Yes, we should,' Nina growled, giving Chase another reprimanding look as she followed.

They emerged on a slope leading down to the cliffs. Below, they saw the frozen city spread out before them – and uncomfortably close above, the icy ceiling. As the lake drained, millions of tiny icicles had formed where water dripped from the underside, giving the unpleasant feeling of a vast field of spikes hanging just over their heads. Not far up the slope, the ice arced downwards to meet the ground, entombing the end of the library – and the mysterious 'source of life' within.

Chase went to the cliff edge and looked down. 'Shit. It's too steep.' Part of the rockface had been dug away to accommodate the towering temple, the drop almost vertical.

'What about further along?' Sophia asked. 'If we can get to the side of the valley . . .'

He peered along the clifftop. 'Still a tough climb, but there might be a way down. Nina, you up for it?' She didn't answer. 'Nina?'

Her attention had been caught by a sound, but she couldn't work out its origin. It seemed to be all around them, a low rumble. 'You hear that?' she asked. 'Where's it coming from?'

'More to the point,' said Sophia, 'what is it?'

'Nothing good,' Chase guessed. He turned to hunt for the cause – before something made him look up. 'Oh, fuck.'

Nina followed his gaze. There was something in the ice almost directly above them, silhouetted against the blue glow from the surface. As she watched, she realised it was moving.

Descending through the ice. Fast.

The rumbling grew louder, a hiss rising behind it. Icicles fell round them like a rain of glass daggers. 'Get back inside!' Chase yelled. They ran for the door.

'What the hell *is* it?' Nina gasped. The cavern ceiling fractured explosively, the rumble becoming a roar—

A hole blew open, a huge cloud of steam shrieking out into the frigid air as thousands of gallons of boiling water cascaded down. The dark mass of the ice-burner hit the ground with a massive thud. The drum rolled down the slope, flying over the edge of the cliff amid a scalding waterfall to hit the ground outside the temple with a bang that echoed through the entire cavern.

No sooner had that noise faded than another reached them, a second black drum falling from the roof above the domed houses in another vast column of steam and melted ice.

Chase pushed Nina and Sophia through the door as the steam cloud whooshed past them, the sudden clammy heat a shock after the constant cold. 'Last thing I expected down here was a sauna,' he wheezed as he slammed the door. He waited for the steam to disperse, then opened the door slightly to look out. A mist hung over the slope outside, but it was clear enough for him to see a rope drop through the new shaft overhead. He hurriedly closed the door again. 'Guess who else wants a steam?'

'The Covenant?' Nina asked, already knowing the answer. 'Oh, man! That means somebody's now tried to kill me on every single continent on earth!'

'Shall I call the *Guinness Book of Records*?' Sophia snarked.

'We'll have to try climbing down that statue,' said Chase. 'Come on – it'll take 'em a minute to get down here and get their bearings.'

'But there are more of them in the city,' Sophia pointed out.

'Let's get out of the fucking Fortress of Solitude here first, then worry about them,' he said. Less than fifty minutes left, and they were no nearer finding a way down than before. They ran from the library, emerging at the top of the shaft behind the temple. 'Sorry, love,' he told Nina, 'but we're going to have to put that window through.'

She looked very unhappy. 'Oh God, it's absolutely priceless . . . but do it. I just won't watch.'

Taking out the pickaxe, Chase made his way as quickly as he dared round the ledge to the window. He glanced back. Nina winced and looked away. Taking that as a cue, he whacked the axe against the ancient window. The stained glass was already brittle from age and cold and shattered easily; the gold leading was tougher, needing several blows before he was able to bend the soft metal aside.

He clambered through the gap, finding himself on the statue's broad, squared-off shoulders. Ice covered the stone and the golden ornamentation. 'Is it okay?' Nina shouted across to him.

'Yeah, come on over. Just don't slip.' Now that he was up here, he realised the statue's left arm, raised as if giving a gift, wasn't at as steep an angle as he'd thought. It might be possible to climb down it . . . though that still left the problem of where to go next. The statue's hand was at least thirty feet in the air.

Nina rounded the ledge. He moved back to the window to help her through, then waited as Sophia negotiated the narrow path. 'All right,' he said as she reached him, 'we're still sixty feet up without any rope. Suggestions would be good. Even daft ones.'

Nina knelt to look over the edge of the statue's shoulders at the golden necklace reaching partway down its chest. 'Would this be strong enough to hold us? If we could climb down one of the counterpoises, we might be able to drop down – it looks like there's a ledge around its waist, where the belt is.'

Chase leaned out to see. 'You'd have to drop at least ten feet – and the ledge doesn't look all that wide. And you'd still be a long way up.'

Sophia directed her light down the back of the statue. 'Eddie, the statue's quite close to the wall here. We might be able to do a chimney climb down it.'

He went to her and checked. It did indeed look as though it would be possible to descend by pressing their backs firmly against the statue and using their outstretched feet to lower themselves down the wall – but there was one problem. 'We might,' he said, 'but Nina couldn't.'

'What?' Nina protested. 'Now she's some super-mountaineer, but I'm not, is that it?'

'No, it's that you got shot in the leg four months ago!' Chase replied. 'You might think it's okay now because it's stopped hurting, but if you try to do a chimney climb, you'll put a load of strain on it – and if the muscle tears, that's it, you'll fall. We need another way.' He returned his attention to the outstretched left arm. The hand's upturned palm was almost flat – and not all that far from the temple wall, where there was one of the tall, narrow windows . . . and a ledge just below it.

Nina had seen it too. 'How far's the jump?'

'Five feet, maybe six.' He tried to picture the temple's exterior. There had been similar ledges running round the *outside* beneath each row of windows . . . at the same level as the tops of the buttresses. 'If we can jump across to the window, we'll be able to slide down those supports on the outside!'

'*If* we can get to the hand,' said Sophia, regarding the route uncertainly. The shoulder was thick with ice, and apart from a pair of metal bands around the upper arm and wrist the statue offered almost nothing in the way of handholds.

'I'll go first,' Chase said. He cautiously stepped across the statue's shoulder. Ice squeaked and crunched under his weight. He dropped to all fours, turning to descend the arm feet first.

The first golden band was only a few feet below. Using it to brace his feet, Chase lowered himself until he was able to grip the edge of the metal and continue down. There was a depression in the statue's elbow, which had filled with ice; he rasped at it with his crampon spikes until he found grip.

Though terrified that he might fall, Nina couldn't look away – until she heard a noise behind her. 'Eddie,' she called, worried, 'they're in the library!'

Chase acknowledged her with a nod, then continued. There was less purchase on the forearm – not only was it narrower than the upper arm, but it was also longer, the stylised proportions not the same as a human body. The band round the wrist was nearly eight feet below the elbow, and there were no protrusions he could hold.

He put his hands on the cold stone, fingers splayed to maximise his grip, and edged downwards. Probing with his toes, he felt for the golden band. No luck. Looking down, he saw there was still over a foot to go.

No choice but to let go. He inched one hand down, then the other, moving them slightly further each time—

His left hand slipped.

He slithered down the statue's arm on his stomach, clawing for grip and finding only ice. Instead, he opened his arms and tried to wrap them round the stone, toes scrabbling for any purchase as he felt himself rolling over the edge—

His feet slammed against the top of the giant bracelet. Chase squeezed his arms round the statue, heart thudding as he arrested his fall. He wriggled sideways until he was back atop the arm, then lowered himself on to the stone hand.

'Eddie!' Nina shouted. 'Jesus, are you okay? Eddie!'

'I'm okay, I'm okay,' Chase panted, slowly getting to his feet. 'You just need to watch that last little bit there.' He looked at the nearest window, a vertical slash of backlit blue. It was further away than he'd initially thought, but still reachable.

He hefted the pickaxe. 'All right, here I go. If I make it, I'll break the window so I can get through and grab you from the other side. If I don't make it . . .' a glance at the shadowed floor below, 'then I hope I land on my head, 'cause that's a break-both-legs kind of fall.'

'Thanks for that reassuring image, Eddie,' said Sophia.

Nina unconsciously reached for her pendant as Chase prepared to make the jump, only realising what she was doing when she couldn't touch it – it was hidden under several layers of clothing. Hoping it was the thought that counted, she held her breath, watching as he psyched himself up, readying the axe, drawing back . . .

And hurling himself across the gap.

Chase swung the pickaxe just before he landed on the narrow ledge, smashing the glass. He hacked with the axe, trying to hook it on to something secure. Lead bent and glass broke, one of his feet slipping off the ledge as he overbalanced, toppling backwards—

A harsh clink of metal on stone. The pickaxe found the window's frame. Arm straining, Chase pulled himself upright, regaining his footing and reaching through the broken window to grip its sill. He used the pickaxe to knock out more of the glass, wrenching away the leading until the gap was large enough to fit through.

He poked his head through to check there actually *was* a ledge outside. To his relief, there was. One of the buttresses curved away to the ground a few feet to his right.

To his dismay, he also saw figures making rapid descents from the shaft cut by the second ice-burner. The Covenant were coming from two directions, maybe even three if they were also using the shaft Trulli had drilled – and he, Nina and Sophia were caught between them.

Spurred on by the sight, he climbed through, then leaned back into the temple over the sill. 'Okay, come on!' he called, seeing that Sophia was already descending. 'Jump and I'll grab you!'

She reached the hand with little trouble. Eyes locked on his, she made the jump, sailing across to land almost perfectly on the ledge. Chase seized her arms, holding on until she had fully recovered her balance, then shuffled sideways so she could climb through.

'Wait for me at the top of that,' he said, indicating the buttress. He returned to the window as Sophia edged along the ledge. 'Okay, Nina. Do what I did – no, wait, do whatever *Sophia* did and come down the arm. My way was a bit pants-filling.'

Nina gave him a small smile and stepped across the statue's shoulders.

She didn't even reach the arm.

The ice shrouding the stone, weakened by Chase and Sophia's footsteps, sheared apart. She stumbled, trying to regain her footing – and a spear of pain from overstressed muscle pierced the wound on her right thigh. Her knee buckled. She landed hard on her side, grasping in panic for anything that could stop her from going over the edge—

There was nothing.

She slithered down the statue's chest towards the sheer drop below.

26

'*Nina!*' Chase screamed.

She hit one of the necklace's long rectangular counterpoises.

And caught it.

But it didn't stop her. The metal was too thin to support her, buckling and swinging her across the statue's front. She slammed to a stop against a carved protrusion.

The counterpoise broke off. Nina plunged straight down—

Her feet hit the statue's gilded belt. Even as more pain exploded in her legs, she had just enough presence of mind to throw herself backwards against the great figure's stone stomach, collapsing on the small ledge at its waist. The long spear of the counterpoise plunged past, hitting the temple floor with an echoing clang.

Chase stared in horror, seeing Nina's face twisted in pain. 'Wait there!' he yelled. 'I'm coming!'

He started to climb through the window, but Sophia pulled him back. 'What are you doing?'

'What do you think?'

'Even if you manage to climb back up the arm, how are you going to get down to her?'

'I'll think of something!' He tried again to pull himself through the window.

Sophia jammed her arm across the frame, blocking him. His

mouth curled with cold anger. 'If you don't move, I'll chuck you off this ledge.'

She knew he meant it, but held her place. 'Eddie, the Covenant will be here any minute. They must have heard that noise. If they catch us, they'll kill us all.'

'I can't leave her!'

'You can't reach her, either. Eddie, we've got to go!'

Furious, frustrated, he looked back at Nina. She had managed to sit upright, and was clutching her leg. 'Nina!' he called. 'If you can—'

A noise from above: breaking glass. A man in snow camouflage was using his rifle butt to widen the hole in the window behind the statue.

He ducked through, looked round, saw Chase below—

Chase shoved Sophia away and darted sideways as the Covenant soldier fired, bullets pitting the ancient stonework and shattering the remains of the window. The gunfire stopped; Chase risked a look, seeing another man climbing on to the statue before being forced to jerk away from a second burst.

'Eddie, come on!' Sophia commanded, moving to the buttress. 'If we don't get out of here now, they'll cut us off!'

'*Fuck!*' Chase roared, thumping a clenched fist against the wall. He knew she was right – but that was absolutely no comfort. And if he tried to shout to Nina, even to assure her that he would come back for her, the Covenant members would know she was there.

And kill her.

Anguished, he followed Sophia to the buttress as she lowered herself over the edge . . . and let herself drop.

The buttress was wide enough for her not to slip off the side, but she still couldn't hold in a shriek as she hurtled downwards, boots grating on the frozen stone. The slope became shallower as it descended, but Sophia was still moving fast when she reached the bottom, shooting off the end and tumbling across the iron-hard ground. She came to a stop, unmoving for a moment – then gave Chase a dizzy wave.

With a last look back at the window, Chase plunged after her.

Jagged lumps of ice tore at his clothes as he hurtled down the buttress like a luge rider – *sans* luge. He tried to squeeze his feet against the edges to slow himself, but couldn't find enough grip, still picking up speed as he neared the bottom . . .

Chase was airborne for a moment as he flew off the end – then hit the ground arse first, taking a painful kick to his spine. He bounced over the frozen earth in a spray of ice crystals, skidding along on his back before coming to a halt.

'Are you all right?' Sophia asked, hobbling stiffly to him.

'Fine,' he grunted as he stood. Muscles ached and knives jabbed at various parts of his anatomy, but nothing seemed permanently damaged. He saw the sled nearby. 'Come on.'

'What are you doing?' Sophia demanded as he headed for it. 'If you go back in there, they'll shoot you before you get five feet across the room!'

'I know. That's why I'm not going back in – until I get a gun. If Nina keeps quiet, maybe they won't see her and they'll go.' He reached the sled, taking hold of the tow rope. 'Then I can climb up and get her.'

'We won't have time,' she insisted. 'And where are you going to get a gun, anyway?'

A shout reached them from the city, where another man in white had emerged from behind a building and seen them. 'He'll do.'

'He still seems to be using it!' Sophia warned as the man took aim. More men appeared behind him. Chase recognised Zamal's bearded face amongst the group.

'Okay, slight rethink!' There was no decent cover nearby, and going back into the temple would bring them into the sights of the men already inside. Instead, Chase grabbed Sophia and dived with her on to the sled. 'Hang on!'

He kicked at the ground – and sent the sledge racing downhill along the frozen road bisecting the ancient city.

Zamal's men opened fire, bullets spitting chunks of ice into the air around Chase and Sophia. But flattened on the sledge they were a tricky target – made the more so as they rapidly picked up speed. 'Get them! *Get them!*' shrieked Zamal, opening up with his SCAR on full automatic as he tracked the fleeing pair downhill.

Sharp-edged ice fragments bit at Chase's face as a line of bullet impacts snaked along the ground beside him, getting closer as the Arab refined his aim – one shot even exploded beneath him as it whipped between the body of the sled and its runner—

They hurtled through the arch and past the first buildings, cutting off Zamal's line of fire. Chase looked ahead. The road led all the way down to the edge of the city – and the drainage shaft cut through the dam. Their escape route.

But that would mean abandoning Nina, and he wasn't prepared to do that.

'Eddie!' Sophia yelled. Another group of Covenant troopers ahead. They must have come in through the original shaft, making their way up through the city to meet their comrades.

Either they had seen the approaching sled, or Zamal had radioed them. Whichever, they were lining up across the road, preparing to shoot . . .

Chase stuck one leg over the sledge's side, jamming his boot against the road surface. The sled slewed round, almost tipping over. He lifted his foot and it straightened out – now aiming for one of the side roads.

More gunfire, more cracking impacts around them as the soldiers realised they were about to lose sight of their prey—

Something blew apart with a crunch of shattered plastic. Chase took a blow to his side as one of the pieces of equipment strapped to the sledge was hit. The laser rangefinder had stopped a bullet for him.

But he had no time to reflect on his luck. They reached the side road, a domed wall looming ahead. He jammed both feet down, trying to slow the sledge, then lifted one to steer them round the obstruction.

Too fast—

The speeding sled scraped against the base of the curved wall in a spray of ice shards as it turned, teetering perilously on one runner before crashing down again. The gas cylinder rattled against its restraints, hitting Chase's leg.

Feet down, toes skittering over the ice. The sled slowed. Beyond the buildings ahead, he could see a roiling haze rising towards the ceiling – steam from the volcanic vent in the hypogeum.

He saw a route leading between the groups of houses and swung them into it. The path was tight, but it opened out ahead—

Over a drop.

'Shit!' gasped Chase, slamming both feet as hard as he could against the ice. Sophia did the same. The sledge juddered, slowing – but not enough. *'Roll!'*

He threw himself to the left, Sophia to the right as the sled fishtailed over the edge, crashing down on the frozen ground ten feet below. Chase hit a pile of broken wood, twisting round and bending his legs to absorb the impact. The wood shattered along with its prison of ice, pieces flying everywhere as he came to a stop at the very edge of the drop.

Sophia wasn't so lucky.

With nothing to stop her, she screamed as she careered over the edge—

One hand caught a knobbly chunk of ice. She jolted to a stop . . . and the ice cracked. Clawing for a hold that wasn't there, she fell, tumbling down a rocky slope.

Chase booted away the wood and looked down. Sophia lay below him, clutching her side. He hurriedly descended the little cliff, jumping the last few feet to land beside her.

'Sophia! You okay?' he asked. They had ended up fairly close to the hypogeum; he looked towards the road for any sign of the Covenant. Nothing yet, but it wouldn't take them long to track them down . . .

'Don't know.' She tried to sit up. 'Oh, God, that hurts!'

Short of opening her coat and feeling for broken bones, Chase had no way to know whether she was actually injured or just badly bruised – and no time, either. 'You've got to get up. They'll be coming.'

'I don't think I can.' Chase stood; through the pain, her expression became genuinely frightened. 'Eddie, don't leave me, please!'

'I wasn't going to.' He held out both hands. 'I'm just going to pull you up. It'll hurt, but . . . well, a bullet'll hurt more. Ready?'

She winced as she took his hands in hers. 'Okay.'

'On three – one, two, three!'

He pulled her upright. She let out a stifled gasp, holding her right side. Chase moved round to her left and supported her. 'Got you. Come on.'

'Where are we going?'

'Good question.' A shaft of light from the hole above cut through the air, the winch line still hanging from it, but even if Sophia could climb they would never reach the icy ceiling before being shot at. It would have to be the drainage shaft, then, but that presented another problem – it was straight, a perfect channel for bullets. Was there a faster way through it?

His gaze fell on the overturned sledge – but the idea that was forming was blown away by a shout. They had been seen. A man on the road waved to his comrades, then ran across the hard ground towards them.

He couldn't climb back up the slope while supporting Sophia. Instead, they headed as quickly as they could towards the hypogeum.

Nina curled up tighter, trying to squeeze as deep into the shadows as she could. The gunfire from outside had stopped, and she had overheard fragments of messages over the walkie-talkie of one of the men above; the frustration in Zamal's voice suggested that Chase and Sophia had got away, at least temporarily.

But that didn't help her. She couldn't even think about looking for a way down until the Covenant team left – and, if anything, more of them seemed to be arriving. She heard a faint crunch of glass overhead: someone else coming through the window. He spoke in German, and she recognised the voice – Vogler. She knew enough of the language to tell that their efforts to find something had been unsuccessful – then felt a cold shock at the sound of her own name.

They were looking for *her*.

Ribbsley's voice echoed across the shaft. 'What are you *doing* over there? We need to search the library – let Zamal and Hammerstein go after them!'

'Only Chase and Blackwood got out of the temple,' said Vogler, switching to English to address the professor. 'But I am looking at three sets of footprints. Either Dr Wilde doubled back into the library . . . or she is still in here.'

Fear rose in Nina as a flashlight beam lanced down, barely missing her hiding place. 'She did not fall to the ground,' Vogler continued, the beam playing over the broken counterpoise. 'But part of the statue did. I wonder . . .'

Nina heard ice cracking as he stepped right to the edge of the statue's shoulders, pieces falling past her. The torch beam slowly scanned across the giant figure's chest, down to its waist, creeping closer to her as Vogler leaned out further . . .

It touched her leg.

She tried to shrink away, but there was no more room.

'*There* you are.'

She let out a terrified breath as more pieces of ice fell past: Vogler moving across to the statue's outstretched arm. For a moment she held on to the hope that he might slip and fall just as she had, but he kept his footing, sliding down to brace himself in the crook of the elbow. He looked across at her. 'You do not look comfortable there, Dr Wilde.'

'How about we swap places?' she said, trying to mask her terror.

Footsteps echoed through the temple below: Zamal and his men entering. He looked up at the statue, impressed despite himself, before noticing Vogler. 'What are you doing up there?'

'I thought you were going after Chase and Blackwood,' Vogler said.

'The Jew and his men are closer. They—' Zamal stopped as he realised Vogler was not the only person on the statue. 'You found her!'

'Yes, I did. And maybe we would have found Chase and Blackwood as well if you had gone to help Hammerstein.'

Zamal ignored the rebuke. 'What are you waiting for? Kill her!'

'Yes,' said Ribbsley, coming through the window. 'If you've found her, then what's the delay?' A bitter tone: 'You certainly didn't hesitate to say you'd kill Sophia.'

Vogler gave him a stern look. 'Perhaps I am not in a hurry to kill an unarmed and helpless woman.'

'Then perhaps,' Zamal sneered, 'you are in the wrong profession.' He raised his rifle. 'If you do not, I will.'

'Very well,' said Vogler, shaking his head. He unslung his rifle. 'I am sorry, Dr Wilde. Unlike certain members of the Covenant, I do not take any joy in this. But it has to be done.'

'You murder people just to protect your secret,' Nina said accusingly. 'I don't think God would approve.'

'We are a necessary evil,' Vogler replied, almost sorrowful. 'We accept the burden of our sins – and will be held accountable for them in time.' He raised the weapon.

'It's a hell of a secret, though, isn't it?' The words came out more rapidly as Nina's fear rose, but she refused to surrender to it. 'The secret of *Eden*!'

Vogler froze. Below, Zamal stared up at her in surprise.

'Oh, yeah!' she shouted, sensing that something had changed. 'Yeah, I know what your secret is! Whaddya think of that, huh? I know you're looking for the Garden of Eden!'

There was silence in the temple for a moment. Then Ribbsley spoke, voice tinged with mocking sarcasm. 'Oh dear, Dr Wilde. Oh dear, oh dear. That was about the worst possible thing you could have said. Now they *have* to kill you.'

'Oh.' Nina's faint sense of hope melted away to nothing as she saw Vogler's expression, which confirmed Ribbsley's words. 'Well, that . . . sucks.'

He took aim—

'But I know how to *find* the Garden of Eden!' she cried as she shut her eyes tightly, expecting the only response to be a gunshot, searing pain, then nothing . . .

Silence.

She cautiously opened one eye to see Vogler, still aiming the gun at her, but now looking thoughtful.

'Just shoot her!' Zamal shouted.

'Wait,' Vogler ordered. He fixed Nina with an intense gaze – watching for any hint of deceit. 'Explain.'

Her mouth had gone dry. 'There's – there's a map,' she said. 'Up there, past the library. It shows the history of the Veteres, how they expanded across the world. But it won't help you find Eden. We destroyed that part of it.'

'Well then, you're wasting our time,' said Ribbsley. 'Vogler, get on with it.'

'I memorised it. I know where it is.' Nina stared back at Vogler, hoping her defiance would camouflage her bluff. 'So do Eddie and Sophia. If they get away – *when* they get away – they'll find it. They'll reveal it to the world.'

'They've got no chance of getting away,' said another voice. Callum. The white-haired man had also climbed on to the statue.

'Y'know, people have said that before about Eddie. And you know what? They've always been wrong.'

'Not this time.'

But Vogler, at least, appeared unsure. 'Can we take that risk? We should find out what she knows.'

'No,' Zamal said, 'we should just kill her!' He raised his rifle.

Vogler held up one hand. 'This is a decision for the Triumvirate.'

Zamal's face flushed with rage. *'What?'*

'Chase and Blackwood can't get away,' Callum added. 'So kill her.'

'I've called for a decision by the Triumvirate,' Vogler said firmly. 'Procedure demands that a vote must be taken. I will abide by the decision – but until it has been made, we will keep her alive.'

Zamal made an angry spitting sound. 'You're wasting time,' said Callum.

'It is my time to waste, not yours.' Vogler took out his radio.

'Hammerstein, this is Vogler. I have called a vote of the Triumvirate – I need you to meet us.'

'I'm busy right now,' came the sarcastic response, the Israeli sounding as though he was running. 'Blackwood and Chase just went into a building. We're going after them.'

'Then call me as soon as they are dead. Out.' Vogler turned to the men above. 'Lower a rope.'

Nina could do nothing but wait for them to capture her.

27

Chase and Sophia hurried across a bridge over the ice-filled hypogeum. Sophia was still in pain, but sheer adrenalin had forced her pace as the Covenant soldier gained on them. She glanced back. 'I can't see him.'

'He'll see us in a sec,' Chase said grimly. The elevated walkways and guard posts would give them some cover, but their tracks would give them away, crushed and cracked ice marking their footsteps.

Unless they could find somewhere there was no ice. The deeper they went into the hypogeum, the more water spattered down where the rising steam was melting the cavern's ceiling. It had worsened since they came through earlier, the drizzle now in places a full shower. And occasional bangs told Chase it wasn't just water coming down – chunks of ice were also falling. Small now, but they would only get bigger as more of the ice sheet was eaten away.

They reached an intersection – and Chase saw footprints. Three sets: his, Sophia's and Nina's. 'We've been this way before.'

'Is that good?'

'Hopefully.' He got his bearings and went left, looking back.

A flash of white amongst the grey and blue – the soldier entering the hypogeum—

'Down!' said Chase, pulling Sophia with him as he dropped. A shot smacked against the wall beside him; another sizzled just above his head. But the walls were high enough to provide protection. A third shot hit stone, then Chase heard the distant crunch of ice as the soldier ran towards them.

They reached the guard post, the gloomy interior just as Chase remembered – including the object hanging on the wall. 'Okay, you crawl along there and keep your head down,' he said, indicating another exit as he released Sophia.

She muffled a grunt, still clutching her side. 'What are you going to do?'

He pulled down the coiled whip, the ice coating it crackling as it broke loose. 'Live out my Indiana Jones fantasies.'

'What, you want to be a grumpy pensioner?'

'Just get going,' Chase said, gripping the whip's handle with one hand as he used the other to strip off the remaining ice. With luck, the cold of the lake would have stopped the leather from rotting too badly.

He backed towards the exit as Sophia crawled through it. The running footsteps came closer . . . then slowed to a cautious walk as the Covenant trooper approached the guardhouse. A light flicked on, the small but powerful spotlight mounted under the sights of his sleek, ultra-modern TAR-21 'Tavor' assault rifle probing the shadows.

Chase tensed as the man approached. The circle of light dropped to the floor, fixing on the boot prints in the ice. It moved one way, revealed that there were no more tracks in that direction, returned. Chase slowly drew back his arm, the whip creaking. The soldier was moving to the far side of the door to get the best viewing – and firing – angle into the building.

Chase would only have a moment to react when he came into view . . .

Another footstep, ice squeaking as it took the man's weight. He was just outside. The spotlight beam sliced across the interior, getting closer to Chase. Another step. Closer . . .

The gun came into sight, the intense light flashing into Chase's eyes—

The whip lashed out, its tip looping round the rifle's barrel. Chase was almost as surprised as the soldier that it had worked – but he was quicker to react, yanking back as hard as he could and tearing the gun from his hands. It flew across the room, slipping free of the whip and sliding over the icy floor away from both men.

Chase snapped back his arm for another strike, but the soldier was already reaching for his sidearm. Chase dropped the whip and charged at him.

The man pulled out the gun – just as Chase made a diving tackle and slammed him viciously against the wall. The pistol spun away. Chase punched him hard in the stomach, but the layers of cold-weather padding absorbed the blow.

He struck at the man's exposed head – only to take a blow himself, the soldier karate-chopping his shoulder. He reeled back—

And slipped. Before he could recover his balance, the Covenant soldier hit him in the chest. His coat deadened the impact – but it was enough to pitch him on to his back.

The soldier raised a foot high to stamp his spiked boot down hard on Chase's face—

A bright light flashed across the room and locked on to the trooper's crotch.

Which exploded, splattering Chase with blood as Sophia fired a single shot from the TAR-21 into the man's groin. He staggered backwards, screeching horribly. Sophia made a disgusted face – not at the blood, but at the noise – before firing a second shot between his eyes. At such close range, the force was enough to blow out the back of his skull, his hood bulging obscenely before he collapsed.

Wiping blood from his face, Chase looked up at Sophia. The rifle was still in her hands, her expression unreadable. He held his breath. Then—

She turned the weapon round, presenting it to him. 'As I said, my chances of survival are much higher with you than without you. Now get up, Eddie. His friends will be along any minute.'

Chase got up and snatched the TAR-21 from her. 'For fuck's sake, Sophia! You shot him in the balls!'

'What are you complaining about? It did the trick.'

'Shooting him in the chest would have been quicker! Why didn't you do that?'

Sophia gave him a feline smile. 'Curiosity.'

'Sadism, more like.' He noticed the pistol lying by the entrance and stepped over the body to pick it up, shoving it in a pocket.

And he saw something else: more men in white running across the hypogeum, having heard the shots.

Chase whipped the rifle up and fixed the glowing red dot at the centre of the circular sight on the nearest man. He squeezed the trigger twice, using the first shot to judge the recoil of the unfamiliar weapon before instinctively compensating and adjusting his aim with the second. Another red dot, this one dark, burst open in his target's chest. The trooper fell. The man behind him realised their prey was no longer defenceless and tried to drop behind the castellations, but Chase blasted off another three quick shots, the last catching him bloodily in the forehead.

But more men were following them, rapidly finding cover behind the stonework.

Chase ducked back into the guardhouse. 'Go that way,' he said, pointing at the doorway opposite. 'Go on, go!' As Sophia set off he stopped by the body, looking for extra magazines, but saw none. They were probably in the dead man's pack, and he didn't have time to search. Instead, he ran after Sophia, water dripping on to him from high above as he left the shelter.

★

Hammerstein looked at the two dead men, a twinge of fury twisting his lips. He had known them for years, trained them, commanded them on numerous missions for the Covenant . . . and now they were gone, cut down by a surprise ambush. Which meant that his third man was also dead – he would never have allowed his weapon to be taken as long as there was life in his body.

He briefly raised his head above the parapet, seeing that Chase had retreated, then turned to the two remaining members of his squad – like their late comrades, former members of the Israeli Special Forces or Mossad, true believers in the Covenant's cause. And like Hammerstein himself, they would want vengeance. An eye for an eye.

But with caution. They had underestimated Chase; he might have left active military service some years earlier, but he was clearly not out of practice.

Hammerstein spat out the stub of his cigar and raised his rifle, like those of his men a menacing black Tavor . . . but with an extra attachment. Beneath the barrel was the broad tube of an M203 40mm grenade launcher. He loaded it, pulling back the sliding barrel to cock it with a clack. 'I want them *dead*,' he hissed.

Chase quickly caught up with Sophia. 'Did you get them?' she asked.

'Got two, but there's at least three more. How's your side?'

'Still hurting – but I don't think anything's broken.'

'Good, 'cause you're going to have to keep up. I can't support you and shoot at the same time.'

'As sympathetic as ever.' She increased her pace, gritting her teeth. The swirling steam grew thicker, rivulets of hot water cutting channels through the ice in the pit below. 'Do you have a plan?'

Chase pointed at the steam cloud. 'If we can lose them in that, we can double back and get Nina. Then we'll head for the hole in the dam and get the fuck out of here.'

'That's not a plan,' Sophia complained as they crossed a bridge. 'That's an objective. Plans generally have some *how* amongst the *what*.'

'God, you're as pedantic as her! Okay, the *how* is that we kill these Covenant arseholes and don't get shot by them. That do you?'

'It's the best I'll get, I suppose.' She let out a faint laugh. 'This is rather like how we first met, don't you think?'

'Don't even start— Shit!' Chase pushed Sophia aside as a chunk of falling ice the size of his head smashed on the flagstones just in front of them. Another, larger lump landed with a splash in a steaming channel that had been melted through the ice beneath the bridge. 'Jesus, that was close!'

Sophia looked up, flinching as droplets of cold water fell on her face. 'It's turning into a bloody monsoon!'

'Hope the ceiling holds,' said Chase. He checked for their pursuers. 'Shit, they're coming! Leg it!'

They ducked into another guardhouse. Chase looked through one of the slit-like windows. Three men were coming after them, moving in a protective 'leapfrog' formation: two taking up positions to cover the third as he overtook them, then the rearmost man repeating the cycle.

He crossed to the doorway to the right of where they had entered. Off to the left was the arena-like area he'd noticed earlier, the icy expanse riddled with twisting trenches carved by hot water. Clouds of steam wafted over it, thick enough to obscure the view. A bridge ahead crossed over a broad passage divided by two deep, winding channels of glossy ice, more steam rising from them. On the bridge's far side was a larger building – abutting the hypogeum's outer wall. 'If we get across there, we can get outside and head back to the temple.'

Sophia shook her head. 'If they haven't killed Nina by now, they'll have captured her.'

'They might not have found her. I've got to look – and I don't want to hear any more fucking arguments,' he said as she opened her mouth to object. 'We're doing it.' He moved back across the guardhouse to observe the Covenant advance, then pointed along the bridge. 'Okay, you go first – keep down below the wall. I'll be right behind you.'

She got on her knees, sloshing through puddles. Chase looked through the narrow window, but saw no sign of the approaching men. 'Shit,' he whispered, moving to the doorway and glancing out. Now he saw them – or rather, two of them, a black gun barrel pointing towards the guardhouse round the end of a wall as the top of another hunched man's hood bobbed towards it.

If the last trooper was advancing, then where the hell was the man who had taken point?

He leaned out further, trying to find him—

Fire bloomed from the rifle's muzzle. Chase jerked back as bullets pitted the stone beside his head. But he had seen enough to know that the third man was not coming along the walkway towards him – which meant he had crossed the junction to another bridge parallel to the one Sophia was traversing.

He rushed to the other doorway, seeing that Sophia was just past the halfway point. Poking his head out, he finally spotted the third man. He *was* on the other bridge, kneeling at the parapet with his rifle at the ready.

He wasn't firing bullets. Chase recognised the attachment below the barrel, saw Hammerstein tilting the weapon upwards to give the grenade a perfect firing arc . . .

'Sophia!' he yelled. '*Grenade!* Run!'

He jumped out from cover, swinging his rifle towards Hammerstein as Sophia sprang forward like a sprinter off the blocks—

Hammerstein fired.

The grenade shot from the launcher – to explode against the bridge's central support.

The ancient civilisation had built its structures to survive the elements . . . but not high explosives. Pulverised rubble blew outwards, debris scattering over the ice.

The bridge fell.

Chase started shooting – just as the floor dropped out from under him. Flying stones pummelled his body. He glimpsed Sophia falling into one of the channels in the ice before he tumbled into the other one, sliding helplessly down its curved side to splash through the steaming water at its bottom.

The remains of the bridge crashed down behind him, blocking the channel. He staggered to his feet. Hammerstein was watching him from the other bridge.

Gun moving—

Chase fired first. Hammerstein ducked. But he was already shouting to his comrades. Chase tried to climb out of the channel, but the walls of recently melted ice were too slick.

No way out, no way to retreat. He was boxed in.

Hammerstein reappeared, another man running up to him, rifle ready—

Chase slammed the spikes on his boots into the glossy ice – and hurled himself into a headlong dive down the channel, skidding along almost frictionlessly as if on a waterslide.

Bullets tore into the ice, water spraying up – but behind him as he shot under the bridge.

Arms outstretched, spray in his face, Chase skidded down the channel. A curve rose ahead – he hurtled round it, flying up the wall like a human bobsleigh before landing back in the water and zooming onwards. More gunfire as the Covenant members ran to the other side of the bridge after him, but it quickly stopped as he swept out of sight behind the wall of ice.

Another channel shot past where a hot tributary had carved its own path. He was coming into a maze. Steam overhead, and shadows – the passage had taken him beneath one of the hypogeum's roofed sections.

The ice suddenly dropped away, the hot water having melted all the way down to the stone. Chase came to a stop in a foot-deep pool with a huge splash. Shaking water out of his rifle's barrel, he stood, quickly taking in his surroundings. He was in a roughly circular bowl in the ice, the surface over ten feet above him, out of reach. As well as the channel that had brought him here, there were several others; the widest, stone at its bottom rather than ice, was carrying the flowing water away. Most of the others were feeding it, streams running from them into the pool.

One, though, had dried up, crystalline sparkles along its floor. As far as he could tell, it headed back in the general direction of the collapsed bridge – and Sophia.

He sloshed out of the pool and hurried into the frozen channel.

One of Hammerstein's men ran back to him. 'No good, sir – I lost sight of him.'

Hammerstein glowered at the wrecked bridge. He had seen Sophia Blackwood trying to jump from it as it fell – but she had landed on the far side of the rubble, out of sight. For the moment, she was unreachable.

But not for long. 'Follow me,' he said, climbing over the wall and dropping on to the ice below, then climbing down into the nearest channel. 'We're going after them.'

★

Despite the cold, Chase was sweating, steam filling the darkened ice channel. The large building was, he guessed, where the volcanic vent emerged; the Veteres had presumably used it to supply this part of their city with hot water, an ancient form of central heating. Nina would be fascinated, he knew, but his concerns were more prosaic.

Foremost on his mind: *how the hell was he going to get out of this maze?*

The channel twisted and coiled, others splitting off it to form a confusing labyrinth. Unable to get his bearings from the cavern's ceiling, he was no longer sure if he was heading in the right direction to find Sophia – or even if the passage he was following joined up with hers. He had tried to climb out, but again the smooth, slippery walls defeated him.

He moved on. In places the walls between channels were thin enough to become almost transparent; in others, they were more like mirrors, his reflection rippling confusingly around him. The beam from his gun's light bounced off the glittering walls, making it seem as though there were dozens of men prowling through the ice around him . . .

He stopped, statue-still.

One of the lights was still moving.

Chase flicked off the spotlight. The passage plunged into near darkness, the all-pervading blue of the cavern coming faintly through the surrounding ice. The moving light paused, casting faint echoes of itself all around.

Chase took his best guess of the gunman's true position, then crept into the gloom.

The trooper looked cautiously round. He was sure he had seen a light – which had then disappeared – but the distortion of the surrounding ice walls made it hard for him to be sure of its exact location. Gun raised, he lifted his radio. 'This is Reiss,' he whispered. 'I'm in the eastern part of the covered section – are either of you near me?'

Hammerstein responded quietly. 'No – I'm at the south end, and Munk is north of me.'

'I just saw a light go out – he's here, close by.'

'We'll come to you. Be careful. Out.'

Reiss clipped the radio back to his belt, then moved step by step along the passage, his gun's spotlight illuminating the way. Steam curled past as he rounded a corner and entered an intersection, other channels twisting away in different directions.

He advanced, pointing the light down each passage in turn. Movement in one – he snapped the gun to it, before realising it was just the glint of his own beam. Tensing, he continued his sweep, moving onwards to check a second channel, a third . . .

A shadowy figure behind a translucent wall—

Reiss fired – and the thin wall burst apart, shattered chunks cascading everywhere to reveal . . .

Nothing.

He aimed his spotlight at the ragged hole, seeing another shiny wall of ice beyond it. His radio crackled. 'Reiss!' called Hammerstein. 'Did you get him?'

Reiss unclipped the radio. 'No, it was just a reflec—'

Chase stepped up behind him and snapped his neck with a brutal crack.

The soldier collapsed, head lolling horribly. 'Ice to see you,' said Chase in an Arnold Schwarzenegger voice, immediately wishing he'd thought of something better. He took the magazine from the dying man's TAR-21, then continued deeper into the maze.

★

'Reiss!' Hammerstein shouted. 'Reiss, answer!'

No reply. But the abruptness with which he had been cut off told Hammerstein his subordinate was dead. 'Man down,' he warned his remaining team member. 'Munk, watch yourself. These tunnels are like a damn hall of mirrors – don't fire unless you're sure it's him.'

'Roger,' replied Munk. He had increased his pace through the maze on hearing gunfire, but the sudden termination of Reiss's message brought him to a sudden stop. The echoes made it hard to judge, but the loudness of the shots suggested they had been no more than twenty metres away, to the east.

The channel he was traversing curved in that direction. He peered round the corner. No sign of anyone. He rounded the bend and moved warily along the frozen passage, his distorted reflections slithering along the glassy walls alongside him. The gun's spotlight beam flickered back at him, diamond-glints trapped within the ice. He stopped, listening.

A faint crunching. Boots on ice. Close by.

It couldn't be Hammerstein; the noise was coming from the wrong direction. And there was no sign of another spotlight.

Chase.

Munk brought his gun up to his shoulder, the scope's glowing dot a floating holographic point. Ahead, the channel he was in criss-crossed another. Another muffled crump, another step by his quarry. Getting closer . . .

He switched off the light, not wanting to give Chase any advantage. Reflections became sinister twisted shadows as he slowly advanced. He reached the intersection and looked round the first corner.

Movement. His heart thumped. A figure was creeping along the passage. But it rippled as it moved, merely a reflection. The channel twisted sharply; Chase was round the corner . . .

Munk stepped out, taking aim at where he would emerge, the red dot hovering at head height as the reflection turned—

Shots tore *through* the ice, ripping into Munk's head and chest. He fell, his dying thought the realisation that the reflection hadn't been a reflection at all – it was Chase's *silhouette*, the Englishman on the other side of the thin wall of ice . . .

Hammerstein heard the shots. Not far away. But had it been Munk firing, or . . .

'Munk,' he said into the radio. 'Munk, respond.' Silence. 'Munk!'

It had been Chase. Hammerstein spat a Hebrew curse and reloaded the grenade launcher. If it took overkill to bring him down, so be it.

28

Two down, one to go, but even with the improved odds Chase didn't feel like celebrating. The man he had just killed wasn't the leader, Hammerstein – which meant he still had to face the most dangerous member of the unit.

He moved on through the ice tunnels. The steam grew steadily thicker; the icy walls started to drip, water building up on the floor. Ahead, Chase saw the corner of a stone wall protruding through the ice – he had reached the building's entrance. From inside came an irregular rushing hiss that reminded him of a steam locomotive. Whatever it was, it was violent, and loud.

Water dripped on to him as he went through the entrance, feet splashing in puddles. The heat was rising to sauna-like levels.

There was only one other way out that he could see. He followed it, steam swirling as the hissing noise grew louder. The stench of sulphur hit his nose, and he realised the cause – heat from the volcanic vent was melting the ice, which was draining into the fumarole, flashing into steam and blasting back out again in angry spurts.

He heard another hiss to one side. The builders had apparently channelled the heat to different places; more steam huffed forcefully from a vent in the floor. Clambering over a slushy mound, Chase saw two more exits from the underground room. Both seemed equally dense with drifting vapour. 'Eeny, meeny, miney . . . *mo*,' he decided, pointing at the right-hand opening. Hefting the gun, he entered the billowing steam.

Hammerstein wiped his forehead. Being too hot in the Antarctic was the last thing he had expected, but the steam was getting thicker, corroding the maze around him. He saw he was approaching a wall, the clammy ice passage leading into a structure.

He switched off his gun's light in case it gave Chase advance warning, then moved inside.

The room Chase entered was already dark enough without the steam further obscuring his vision – but a diffuse blue glow told him there was an opening above. A chimney for the fumarole?

The noise was coming from below, loud enough to make the room tremble with each enraged blast. There was obviously some kind of larger vent in the floor through which the steam was escaping; he decided to give it a wide berth, free hand outstretched to grope for the wall.

Despite the heat, there was still plenty of ice in the room; his fingers brushed over icicles, water dripping from their tips. Something loomed out of the mist, a bench rising to waist height, more icicles dangling from its overhanging top. He sidestepped it, moving on—

He wasn't sure what made him stop – some sixth sense, the hairs on his neck rising as he got the feeling he had just passed uncomfortably close to something unseen. He looked round, another gusting jet of steam dissipating to reveal . . .

Hammerstein, barely two feet away, looking back at Chase with the same expression of jangled combat awareness.

They both whirled—

Their rifles clashed against each other like swords, too close to

THE COVENANT OF GENESIS

bring them to bear. Both men fired anyway, the shots forcing each
to flinch back.

Chase swept up his gun, trying to yank Hammerstein's weapon
out of his hands by using the magazine as a makeshift hook. He
succeeded – but the rifle's strap snagged on Chase's sights.

And by raising his arms, he had opened himself up to a different
kind of attack.

Hammerstein punched Chase in the stomach, hard enough for
the blow to hurt even through his coat. He lurched backwards,
fumbling to keep his hold on the TAR-21 – but slammed into the
jutting bench, the gun slipping from his hand. Both rifles clattered
to the floor.

Hammerstein ducked to grab them. Chase swept out one foot,
the guns spinning away into the humid fog. Snarling, the Israeli
pulled back and clawed at his holster. Chase grabbed for his own
pistol – but it was stuffed into a pocket, and would take too long to
pull out and aim.

Instead he whipped his hand back and snapped an icicle off the
bench, flinging it at Hammerstein's face like a glass knife. The
pointed end stabbed into his eye – but it had been blunted, rounded
off by dripping meltwater.

It still had an effect, though, the Covenant leader roaring and
instinctively bringing up a hand to protect his sight. The gun was
only halfway out of its holster. Chase saw his chance and sprang at
Hammerstein. He grabbed his right hand, trying to get the gun as
they grappled. The metal was already slick with condensation, his
fingers slithering over it. A punch to Hammerstein's jaw to
encourage him to loosen his grip—

It worked. Chase got the pistol – and immediately lost it again as
it slipped from his grasp. 'Shit!' It bounced across the floor, metal
clattering on stone – then the clank of metal on metal as it dropped
through the grating over the vent into the fumarole below.

Hammerstein recovered, two savage punches driving into Chase's stomach. Chase lashed out again, hearing a satisfyingly toothy crunch as blood spurted from the other man's mouth, but it didn't stop a steel-capped toe from smashing into his shin. He stumbled back, only for a second, harder kick to lash across his knee, spikes tearing his trousers and the skin beneath.

Pain slicing up his leg, Chase fell, landing on his back. The impact blew away the surrounding steam for a moment, revealing that he was very close to the edge of the vent. Another ferocious roar of hot vapour blasted past him.

He tried to roll away from the volcanic furnace – but Hammerstein drew a knife and dived at him.

Chase caught his hand just before the blade plunged into his throat, but the Covenant member was on top of him, pushing down with all his weight. The knife wavered, then descended, razor-sharp tip two inches from Chase's neck, one. Hammerstein leered bloodily, sensing triumph—

Chase spat into his scratched eye.

The Israeli flinched, just the slightest involuntary response – but the blink of distraction was enough for Chase to break his hold and ram the knife down point-first on the stone floor. It stabbed between two paving slabs, sticking out of the ground like a miniature Excalibur. Not the result Chase had expected – he had hoped either to jar the weapon from Hammerstein's hand or break the blade – but it would do. He headbutted the Covenant man, knocking him back, then grabbed his jaw and throat to push his head over the edge of the vent.

Another vicious hiss surged from below—

Hammerstein shrieked as a blast of searing vapour hit his face, exposed skin instantly blistering and reddening. But Chase couldn't hold him – the heat was biting at his hands and wrists, forcing him to let go. Thrashing and screeching, Hammerstein

347

rolled away, half his face a mottled patchwork of scabrous red and white, one eye clenched tightly shut.

But the other was still open, glinting with rage as it locked on to Chase.

Hammerstein kicked, one spiked boot landing squarely on target. Chase was flung backwards, grasping painfully at his chest. He landed hard near the wall, catching a glimpse of another exit through the swirling fog.

Hammerstein saw something else – one of the fallen rifles. He scrambled towards it as Chase groped in his pocket for the handgun.

The Israeli reached the rifle. *His* rifle. No thought of mere bullets as he snatched it up and twisted to face his enemy – instead, his hand went straight to the grenade launcher.

Chase spotted the tubular maw swinging towards him and flung himself desperately towards the half-seen exit as Hammerstein fired. He barely made it through the opening as the grenade smacked against the wall behind him. At such a short range the explosive hadn't even had time to arm itself, ricocheting off the stone and spinning past the doorway before detonating.

The explosion ripped apart a supporting pillar, a section of the floor above crashing down into the vent chamber, blocking the opening with tons of stone and shattered ice. Even shielded from the direct effects of the blast round the corner, Chase still felt as though a giant had flung him against a wall. He protected his head with his arms as chunks of broken stone pounded him.

The echoes of the detonation faded. Ears aching, Chase looked round. He was at the end of another frozen channel, stone walls giving way to glossy white ice. The channel led outside the building; he could see the cold blue light of the cavern.

He didn't have to worry about Hammerstein coming after him –

the collapsed ceiling had sealed the entrance. But after the maiming of his face, the Covenant leader would more than ever want him dead. And Chase was still no nearer to finding Sophia – or rescuing Nina.

He pulled himself upright and, gun in hand, went in the only direction he could – back into the ice maze.

Sophia slowly regained consciousness – then jerked upright as she realised she was lying in a puddle of lukewarm water.

She woozily looked round, seeing that she was in one of the ice channels. The ruins of the bridge blocked it in one direction, while the other coiled towards the large building. She dimly remembered Chase shouting something about a grenade . . .

Chase. She had to find him – if only to get the gun from his corpse.

But she suspected he was still alive. That she hadn't been found by now suggested that the Covenant troops had encountered more resistance than they'd bargained for from the Yorkshireman; she knew first-hand just how lethally efficient he could be.

Head throbbing, she sloshed along the icy passage. 'Eddie?' she called. 'Can you hear me?'

He could – and he could also hear Hammerstein's radio, sending a message that chilled him to the bone.

The Covenant had Nina.

Hammerstein had called for backup, which Zamal was providing, his men on the way – and Vogler had added that they had taken Nina prisoner. He made it clear that her fate rested in Hammerstein's hands, the other two Covenant leaders disagreeing about whether she should live or die.

The Israeli didn't sound in a merciful mood.

'I just heard Blackwood calling for Chase,' he snarled. Having exited the vent chamber by a different door, he was on the other side of an ice wall from Chase, close enough for the latter to hear every word. 'I'm going to kill her, then kill him, and *then* I'll decide what to do about Wilde.'

'Wait until Zamal's men get there,' said Vogler. 'We can't afford to lose you too.'

'I'm not waiting. I want that little shit *dead*.'

Chase almost shouted something mocking, but decided against it – if Hammerstein had any hand grenades, he could just lob them over the wall. Instead he hurried along the channel in what he hoped was Sophia's direction, out in the cold blue of the cavern once more. Water splashed under his feet, a chill rain spattering down from the ceiling.

'I hear him!' Hammerstein shouted. 'He's close – I'm going after him!'

'Hammerstein, wait—' began Vogler, but the Israeli cut him off and started running.

Chase quickly realised they were on parallel courses, the channels they were following almost side by side. 'Sophia!' he yelled.

'Eddie? Where are you?'

She wasn't far away – but was she on the same path? 'There's only one of them left, but I don't know if I can get to you before he does!'

The channel curved, taking him away from her. He could hear Hammerstein splashing along the other route – carrying on in a straight line. 'Shit! Sophia, he's gonna reach you first! Go back, try and hide!'

'There's nowhere *to* hide!'

'You didn't have to tell *him* that!' Another curve took him back towards her, but not quickly enough. Ahead, the wall of ice thinned, becoming translucent. A shape rushed along beyond it. Sophia. She was in the other channel.

And Hammerstein was behind her.

Chase reached the stretch of glassy ice just as the Covenant leader charged past on the other side. He looked ahead. The two channels didn't join up – if anything, they were diverging again, taking him further away from Sophia.

A ringing clang of metal – a crampon had come off one of Sophia's boots. She gasped in pain as she splashed down in the slush.

Hammerstein slowed, stopped. Chase could just barely see him through the wall, a blurred shadow – raising a rifle.

Chase brought up his own gun, but the ice was too thick for a handgun bullet to penetrate. He glanced at the top of the wall. Too high, too slick to climb.

He looked higher.

Water was still dripping from the ceiling. Almost directly above, a large icicle channelled a constant stream from its tip . . .

On to the other side of the wall.

He snapped up the gun and fired.

Hammerstein was about to fire his own weapon when he heard the rapid crack of gunfire. He spun to see a shape through the ice – shooting straight up at the ceiling. His confusion made him hesitate for a moment before he brought the TAR-21 to bear on the new target.

The delay cost him his life.

The bullet-riddled icicle broke from the ceiling with a splintering crunch. Hammerstein looked up at the noise – and froze in fear as a ton of dense, ancient ice speared downwards. He broke out of his paralysis, throwing himself backwards—

Too late.

The icicle hit like a bomb, exploding in a spray of crystalline white – and liquid red. The shock of the impact shattered the wall, knocking Chase to the floor in a storm of broken ice.

Sophia recovered her crampon and came to him, boots crunching over a billion ice cubes and the gory remains of Hammerstein beneath them. 'Eddie?'

'Yeah?'

'I think you got him.'

Chase jabbed a finger at the blood-stained heap of ice. 'Stop! Hammerstein.'

Sophia groaned. 'Your sense of humour survived intact, I see. Oh well.' She regarded the jagged gap in the wall. One side was somewhat stepped, leading up to the surface of the ice filling the pit. 'Think we can climb that?'

'Definitely. But there's more of them on the way – we need to get to that shaft.'

She lifted an eyebrow. 'You're not going after Nina?'

'They've got her,' he said, face emotionless. 'But this isn't over. One way or another, I'm going to fuck them up.'

'The best way to do that is to find Eden before they do. Come on.' She began to climb the ice.

Chase retrieved his gun and ejected the magazine. Empty, just one bullet left in the chamber. It would have to do. He replaced the mag and followed Sophia to the surface.

'Hammerstein, come in.' Vogler waited several seconds, but had no more response than on his previous attempts.

'Y'know,' said Nina, 'I think Eddie's put the hammer down.'

'Shut up!' barked Zamal. Vogler's men had lowered a rope so he could climb up to the library. He drew his gun and pointed it at her head. 'Where is Eden? Tell me!'

'The hell I will,' she said. 'You'll kill me either way – but at least this way you don't get what you're after.'

He ground the gun's cold muzzle under her jaw. 'You *will* talk, woman. And after you do, you'll *beg* me to kill you.'

'No one is going to kill her,' said Vogler, standing beside Nina and staring hard at Zamal. After a moment the Arab backed away. 'Not yet. The Triumvirate still has to vote.'

'That's going to be a tad difficult, isn't it?' said Ribbsley, striding through the endless stacks of the library towards them, Callum following. 'Hammerstein's obviously dead. That makes it one against one, and you're deadlocked.'

'Although,' Callum said with evident reluctance, 'keeping her alive might be a better option. For now.'

'Why?' Vogler asked. 'What did you find?'

Ribbsley regarded Nina with an aggrieved expression. 'We found the map. Unfortunately, part of it – the most vital part – has been destroyed. There was enough left to tell me that Eden is somewhere in eastern Africa . . . but I think we'd all come to that conclusion already.'

'What about the rest of the library?' demanded Zamal, waving a hand at the shelves. 'There must be *something* here that can help us!'

'Perhaps – but it would take months of study. And, unfortunately, Dr Wilde is probably right – the Veteres took the most valuable tablets with them. We might be able to locate some of the other sites on the map, but that'll take time.'

'Time we don't have,' said Vogler. 'If Chase and Blackwood get away . . .'

'They won't,' Zamal insisted. 'My men will stop them.'

'*If* they get away,' Vogler went on, 'we need to catch them.' He held up the empty pouch of Nina's camera. 'They have pictures of the map.' He turned to his men, gesturing at four of the five. 'Get back to the surface, take two of the paracraft and find where that shaft leads. If Chase and Blackwood make it out of the cavern . . . I want you to be waiting for them.'

★

'The shaft is that way,' said Sophia, pointing towards the dam as they emerged from the hypogeum.

'Yeah, but the sledge is this way,' Chase replied.

'So are the rest of the Covenant.'

'They're not here yet,' said Chase, with a glance towards the road. He reached the sled and righted it. Most of the gear was scattered over the ground nearby, but some pieces – including the gas cylinder – had stayed secured. He picked up the rangefinder's heavy tripod and tossed it aboard, then hurried back down-hill, tugging the sled behind him like a recalcitrant dog. 'Get a shift on!'

Sophia ran with him. 'Shit! Here they come!' Five men in snow camo barrelled round a building after them. 'You'd go faster if you let go of that thing!'

'We need it!' They reached the edge of the 'lake' at the base of the dam, where water had pooled below the bottom of the shaft. Chase was fairly sure it would have frozen thickly enough to support their weight, but the ice still creaked alarmingly as they rushed across it.

The troopers were catching up. Ahead, the sloping face of the dam rose to meet the flat ceiling of ice, the dark circle of the drainage shaft at its foot.

Sophia headed for it. 'Eddie, hurry up!'

'What do you think I'm doing?' The sled rasping over the ice behind him, he clomped towards the shaft entrance, heart pounding. A look back. The Covenant soldiers had split up, three of them still running, spreading out, the remaining pair stopping, crouching, taking aim—

'Incoming!' he warned as Sophia reached the hole and ducked inside. Chase dived after her as the soldiers opened fire, bullet impacts showering him with cold soil and stones. The bottom of the shaft was caked with ice that had frozen as the last dregs of lakewater flowed away. A tiny point of light shone in the distance.

The sled bumped to a stop against his legs. 'Okay, get on!' he told Sophia as he drew the gun.

She gave him a deeply dubious look, but obeyed. 'How many bullets have you got left?'

'One.'

'*One?*'

'It'll be enough.' *I hope*, he didn't add as Sophia climbed aboard the sled. He lay on top of her. 'This doesn't mean we're back together, by the way.'

'God forbid,' she sighed. 'What are you doing?'

'Giving us a kick-start!' Left hand gripping the frame, feet braced against the rear cross-member, he aimed the gun – not at the entry to the shaft, but at the gas cylinder taped to the sled. 'Threetwoone – *ignition!*'

Two soldiers sprang into view, rifles at the ready—

Chase fired, blowing the brass valve off the end of the cylinder.

Highly pressurised, highly flammable gas jetted out – and was ignited by the gun's muzzle flame.

A ten-foot-long lance of fire sprang from the gas tank, sweeping over the two men like a blowtorch – and sending the sled rocketing down the shaft.

Chase dropped the gun, struggling to grip the sled's frame as it hurtled down the passage. The roof of the shaft was less than a hand's-width above him, his clothing scraping against it with every bump. Sophia screamed, and he could understand why – the cylinder was straining against their legs, trying to rip free of its restraints.

If it came loose they would be dead, crushed as the sled flipped or incinerated as the tank shot past . . .

Blue light surrounded them – they were through the dam, into the glacier on the other side. But if anything, emerging from the darkness only made the ride more terrifying: now they could see just how fast they were going.

And they were no longer going straight, the sled lurching off course and riding up the side of the shaft—

Chase joined in the screaming as the sled corkscrewed up the wall, on to the ceiling – and dropped down again on the other side, having made a complete rotation. It reached the bottom again, snaking from side to side before straightening out.

The roar of the flame stuttered and died. The sled began to slow.

'J-Jesus!' said Sophia, voice quavering. 'You are a bloody *maniac*!'

Chase's only response was a whoop of something between exultation and terror. He let the massive kick of adrenalin start to disperse, then looked up to see how much of the shaft remained ahead.

Not much.

'Sophia?'

'What?'

'How high off the ground did this come out?'

'Oh, *God*!' she cried as they shot out into empty space.

29

Chase opened his eyes to find himself in an alien landscape. It took a few seconds for his mind to process what he was looking at, strange gnarled and twisted columns rising all round him like the bones of some giant glass monster. He realised where he was; the jet of water from the drainage shaft, coming out under enormous pressure, had carved a great cave out of the other side of the crevasse, the water then flowing away to leave a collection of bizarre blasted shapes as the ice refroze.

And he and Sophia had ended up in the middle of it, slamming down on the ice and skidding into the surreal amphitheatre before crashing to a halt.

He staggered upright. The sled's journey was over; one of its runners had been torn off, the frame bent around the lump of ice that had brought it to an abrupt stop and catapulted its passengers into the weird cave. He took a step, wincing at a sharp pain in his shin. The sled's contents were strewn all around. He picked up the tripod to use as a makeshift crutch, its spiked metal feet digging into the ice as he turned.

'Sophia!' She was sprawled about twenty feet away in a pile of fragmented ice. He limped over to her. She was still breathing, little clouds drifting from her nose. Blood ran from a deep cut on her chin. 'Sophia? Come on, wake up.'

'Eddie, not now,' she mumbled in complaint, before her eyes

snapped open and she clutched at her jaw, her glove coming away with a Rorschach patch of blood on the palm. 'Ow, oh God! My face, Eddie, you've wrecked my bloody face!'

'If that's all you're bothered about, you're probably fine,' Chase growled. 'You should put some ice on it.' He looked at their frozen surroundings, then gave her a theatrical shrug. 'Dunno where we're going to find any, though.' He smiled as he turned away from her look of fury and raised the walkie-talkie, hoping it had survived the beating. 'Matt! Matt, it's Eddie. Are you still there?'

Silence for a long moment, then: 'Eddie! Christ, mate, you're cutting it fine – your hour's almost up! Where are you? Are you okay?'

'We're in the crevasse, where the drainage shaft came out. How long will it take you to get here?'

'We're about eight clicks away, so . . .' A pause as he consulted Larsson. 'About five minutes.'

'We'll be here.'

'Okay, on our way.'

'Make it quick. Out.' He turned back to Sophia, who had scraped up some loose ice and pressed it to her face. 'Think you can stand up?'

She jabbed both feet at him. 'If you were any closer I'd kick your arse.'

'For fuck's sake, stop moaning,' he said, lifting her. 'I've had my face bashed up tons of times, and I never worried about it ruining my looks.'

'Yes, but you were hardly starting from a high baseline, were you?'

'Bloody hell, shallow much?' They picked their way across the cave, using the tripod for support. 'It didn't bother you when we were married.'

'I can only put that part of my life down to temporary insanity.'

'What, as opposed to the permanent insanity you've got now? You're not a bunny-boiler, you're a bloody bunny-*nuker*!'

'If you have such a problem . . .' Sophia tailed off as they heard a low buzzing. 'Is that the plane? That was quick.'

They emerged in the ice-slathered crevasse, the high walls casting everything into deep, cold shadow. 'It's not the plane,' Chase said, looking south. The noise grew louder, echoing off the walls – revealing two distinct engine notes. 'Shit! They've found us!'

A pair of gleaming black shapes swept over the top of the crevasse and wheeled round under their blood-red rectangular parachutes, heading straight for them.

Chase had seen similar machines before. Invented in New Zealand, home of crazy and dangerous leisure activities, the paracraft were a mutant combination of paraglider and hovercraft, the latter's main fan used to inflate the fabric wing at takeoff and provide forward thrust like a propeller. The differences between a paracraft and an ultralight were that the former was larger, the squared-off, stubby wings protruding from its sides giving it much greater lift at low altitudes through ground effect – and that its hovercraft base meant it could not only take off and land on almost any terrain, but travel overland at speed by releasing the 'chute.

Making them ideal pursuit vehicles for the Antarctic wastes.

He saw two men in each paracraft: one pilot – and one gunner. The gunner in the lead paracraft was carrying a sniper rifle, while the man in the second aircraft had a Swiss SIG assault rifle.

Sophia started to back into the cave. Chase grabbed her wrist. 'No, get between those.' He pointed at several huge boulders of ice that had fallen from the ravine walls.

'I don't think we'll be any better off,' she said as they hurried down the slope.

'If they land and trap us in the cave, we're fucked. At least this way we've got some room to manoeuvre.' The paracraft were three hundred feet away, closing fast. The lead paracraft dipped its nose, descending into the canyon. *Good*, Chase thought – in the relative confines of the walls, they wouldn't have enough room to turn, meaning it would take them time to swing about and make another pass.

Assuming they missed on the first one.

'Down!' Chase yelled, dropping the tripod and pulling Sophia behind the fallen boulders. The SIG's harsh bark filled the crevasse, a three-shot burst blasting chunks from their cover. But the bullets didn't penetrate it, the millennia-old blue ice compressed almost as densely as stone.

'Come on!' He crawled into a narrow gap between two larger blocks. Another burst of gunfire, ice cracking and splintering. He pushed Sophia under the overhang, peering upwards as the rasp of the first paracraft's engine grew louder – and part of the ice above exploded, hit by a high-power bullet from the sniper rifle. Fist-sized chunks of ice bombarded him. The paracraft roared overhead, a flash of black. The second followed a few seconds later, another burst of bullets pounding their hiding place.

'Wait there,' Chase told Sophia, shaking off the shattered ice and scuttling along the narrow passage until he reached a spot where he could see down the crevasse. Keeping low in case the sniper was still aiming back at him, he looked out. The second paracraft, higher up, was rising to breach the top of the crevasse and turn about for another attack, while the first had been forced to continue flying along the ravine.

It wasn't trying to gain height, though. Instead it was descending rapidly. 'One's landing!' he called to Sophia.

'I don't know why you sound so happy about that.'

'Because as long as they're in the air, we can't touch 'em. If they're on the ground, at least we've got some chance of fighting back.'

'With what? Snowballs?'

The lead vehicle touched down in a cloud of spray, having inflated its rubber skirt just before landing. The parachute collapsed, a huge red flag drifting to the ground as its lines were released. The second paracraft, meanwhile, had reached the top of the ravine, briefly disappearing from sight before swinging round.

Chase quickly unfastened his coat and shrugged it off, ignoring the numerous aches in his upper body. Sophia watched, puzzled. He found a chunk of ice the size of a football and stuffed it into the coat's hood, bundling the rest of the garment up tightly and holding it below the neck.

Another glance down the crevasse. The first paracraft was making a great skidding turn with a huge feathered trail of ice crystals blowing out behind its main fan. The second dropped towards him.

He ducked back into cover. 'Okay, stay under there until it goes overhead!' he shouted. 'Soon as it's gone past, throw me the tripod!'

'The tripod?' Sophia asked, looking at the metal frame lying nearby. 'What for?'

'Just do it!' Still holding his coat, the cold already biting through his damp clothes, Chase turned back to the opening. The engine note grew steadily louder. Keeping himself behind the frozen boulder, he raised his coat, slowly moving it into the open . . .

The hood blew apart in an eruption of pulverised ice and shredded quilting. Chase yanked the ruined coat out of sight, shaking out the ice and pulling it back on.

The paracraft roared overhead, rasping back up the crevasse. 'Now!' Chase shouted, but Sophia was already tossing him the tripod. He grabbed it, then looked down the valley. The first paracraft was racing along the icy surface. Thirty seconds away, less—

THE COVENANT OF GENESIS

He leapt up, jamming one spiked boot against the ice boulder opposite and ascending the narrow gap in a rapid chimney climb until he reached a jagged ledge. Another scramble over a broken outcropping and he was almost at the top.

Engine noise from two directions. The second paracraft had also landed, dumping its parachute. Its gunner thought he had made a kill, and was eager to see the results of his marksmanship. Ahead, the first paracraft was closing. Chase hefted the tripod. He had only one chance, and even that was a long shot. If he failed, then the only weapon he would have really *was* a snowball.

Closer, closer, the sniper aiming at the base of the boulders, closer—

Now!

Chase sprang up and hurled the tripod like a javelin.

It arced through the air, spearing down over the top of the paracraft's windscreen – and hit the driver, the spiked metal feet stabbing into his face.

He screamed, clawing at the tripod. His hands off the controls, the paracraft charged onwards at full speed, heading straight for the giant boulder. The gunner tried to grab the throttle lever, but by the time he reached the control it was too late.

The paracraft smashed into the wall of ice. The tripod had ended up wedged between the dashboard and the driver's chest; he was instantly impaled upon it as he was hurled forward by the sudden stop. The gunner fared no better, whiplashing face first through the windscreen. The engine kept running despite the crash, blindly grinding the vehicle against the ice.

Chase slithered down the frozen mass, landing beside the paracraft and reaching in to pull back the throttle. The engine note dropped to a dull rasp, just enough to keep the skirt inflated. 'Sophia, come on!' he shouted as he dragged the two bodies from the vehicle. 'I've got us a ride!'

362

Sophia emerged from the boulders. 'The other one's still coming.'

'Yeah, but we've got guns now – that should even things up a bit.' The scope of the sniper rifle had been broken in the crash, but the driver's weapon, a SIG SG-551 assault rifle, seemed undamaged. 'It's not like hunting pheasants, but you remember how to shoot, don't you?'

'Yes, but I may be a little rusty – for some strange reason, they never let me use the practice range at Guantánamo.' Chase pulled the floating craft round to face down the crevasse. 'Do you know how to drive this thing?' she asked.

'Not really. You?'

'Not at all.'

'In that case, I'll drive, you shoot.' He climbed into the driver's seat, the paracraft wallowing with the extra weight. The steering column dipped as he brushed it, hinged to act as a flight control. Sophia sat beside him, hefting the SIG. Over the engine's grumble, they could hear the buzz of the other paracraft. 'Ready?'

'Hardly, but—'

Chase rammed the throttle forward.

The engine screamed, a freezing backblast whipping round them from the wall of ice behind. The paracraft leapt forward, slewing almost sideways before Chase managed to redirect the steering vanes behind the fan and straighten out.

'—I doubt that makes any difference,' she finished.

Chase looked back, his view partly obscured by the cloud of ice particles the paracraft was kicking up in its wake. They were leaving the boulders behind with surprising speed – but their new ride was already showing its weaknesses. Hovercraft had very little grip at the best of times, only the friction of the thick rubber skirt against the ground, and on newly frozen ice it was practically zero. 'Jesus!'

he gasped. 'It's like trying to steer a bar of soap along the bottom of the bath!'

'*They* don't seem to be having any trouble,' Sophia said. The second paracraft had rounded the barricade and was sweeping after them in a long, carefully controlled drift.

'Bloody show-offs!'

They burst out into the sunlight, the crevasse's walls falling away as they reached an ice plain. In the distance, Chase saw the tilt-rotor heading in their direction. Holding the wheel with one hand, he raised the radio. 'Matt! We're moving – we're in a hovercraft!'

'Hovercraft, huh?' Trulli's voice crackled. 'You know, nothing you guys do surprises me any more. I see you.'

'But we've got company – hold back until we get rid of them!'

'How're you going to do that?'

Chase gave Sophia a pointed look. 'Shooting at them would be a good start.'

'I was waiting for a decent shot,' she sniped. 'But I can just hose them with bullets if you like. It's not as though I only have one magazine or anything.'

'Just shoot them!'

Sophia fired, keeping the SIG on single-shot to improve her aim. It didn't make much difference, the buffeting of the paracraft throwing both her shots wide.

The new threat spurred on their enemies, however. The gunner fired back – on full auto, bullets cracking the fan's fibreglass casing. Sophia gasped and ducked. 'Shit!' Chase yelped as a piece of debris spun past him. He looked over his shoulder to see the other paracraft change course and fall in behind them – so that Sophia's line of fire would be blocked by the fan.

He tried to bring the vehicle back into her view. The paracraft turned – too fast, spinning round its centre of gravity while still racing across the ice field in a straight line. He attempted to compensate, but they had already made a half-turn so that they were facing their pursuers . . . and with the fan pointing backwards, they were rapidly slowing.

'Oh, nice driving!' Sophia sneered as she squeezed off a pair of three-round bursts at the approaching paracraft. She and Chase both ducked as the gunner returned fire. The windscreen shattered, bullets plunking through the hull. There was a flat *whap!* and a shriek of escaping air as the skirt was punctured, the paracraft's nose dipping as the bullet hole widened and split the rubber.

Chase steered one way, the Covenant driver the other as the two paracraft whipped past each other. Sophia tracked the other vehicle, still firing and scoring hits – but only to the bodywork, not its occupants. She glanced at the SIG's magazine, which was made from a translucent plastic, showing how many bullets she had left. It was half empty. 'Running low!'

'So make 'em count,' was the only advice Chase could offer her as he fought with the controls. The damage to the skirt had made the paracraft even more unwieldy, the nose pitching downwards. 'Get in the back. I need to balance this thing!'

The other paracraft turned with considerably more grace, performing a sweeping ballet across the ice compared to his duck-on-a-frozen-pond manoeuvring. He searched for anything that might help him. The BA609 was circling, holding back out of rifle range. There were some ice ridges that might provide partial cover, but everything else was smooth and glossy where the lake water had frozen over the past day.

There had been a hell of a lot of water, though. The plain wasn't *that* big – some of it must have drained away elsewhere . . .

Sophia dropped on to the rear seats, the shift in weight raising the paracraft's nose slightly. She reacquired her target and fired another burst, this time hitting only ice. Chase clutched the radio. 'Matt! I need a spotter – can you see any crevasses or cliffs?'

'Yeah, about ten o'clock from you,' came the reply. 'There's a cliff – a *big* cliff.'

'Thanks!' He changed course, making a quarter-turn to the left to see the cliff edge in the distance, a thin bite out of the horizon. Quickly getting closer.

He adjusted his heading, the second paracraft disappearing behind the fan. The spray would obscure its view of what lay ahead, hopefully until it was too late. He looked over the paracraft's other controls, finding a lever that might prove helpful . . .

'They're catching up,' Sophia warned.

'Get down,' Chase told her, reducing the throttle. The paracraft's engine, mounted beneath the fan, would give them both some protection. But not much.

'Why are you slowing down?'

'I need to get them closer.'

'*Closer?*'

'I'm going to turn so they'll come round on our left.' The cliff was now clearly visible ahead, the absence of any landscape beyond it suggesting quite a fall. 'Shoot if you get the chance – otherwise just hold on tight!'

She braced herself across the rear seats as Chase kept driving. One hand on the wheel, the other on the control lever, he readied himself for the inevitable gunfire. The Covenant men were gaining fast, moving in for the kill—

Shots hit the back of the paracraft, splintering the bodywork and ripping into the engine bay. Chase flinched as a bullet whipped past him and punched through the dashboard. The engine noise became raw, ragged.

More shots—

'Now!' Chase shouted, slamming round the wheel.

The paracraft spun – and Sophia blindly fired the SIG's remaining bullets on full auto as it swept round. The gunner was hit in the shoulder, blood and shattered bone spraying into the air. He fell back, screaming.

Chase's paracraft kept spinning, pirouetting about in a half-turn—

He pulled the lever.

The paracraft switched from ground to flight mode, all power being transferred to the main propeller as the smaller lift fans under the body were shut off. The rubber skirt instantly deflated, dropping the paracraft down hard on to the ice. It grated along, the combination of friction and the rearward blast from the fan rapidly slowing it. The other paracraft shot past, zooming out of the obscuring spray to see the cliff edge dead ahead—

Chase's paracraft ground to a stop less than two feet from the drop. The other vehicle wasn't so lucky, shooting over the edge of a vast frozen waterfall and arcing towards the ground hundreds of feet below.

Chase watched it fall, Sophia sitting up behind him. 'Nice of them to *drop* by, eh?'

She made a disgusted noise. 'Eddie, even Roger Moore would think that joke was—' Her eyes widened as the plunging paracraft sprouted a second parachute, the scarlet canopy snapping open to arrest its fall. Engine roaring, it spiralled back up towards them. '—premature!'

Chase revved his own engine, yanking the lever back to re-inflate the skirt. The paracraft slithered away from the cliff. 'Matt!' he said into the radio, seeing the tilt-rotor changing direction. 'It didn't quite work out like I'd hoped – how long'll it take you to land and pick us up?'

'About a minute,' said Trulli. Too long, Chase realised – the gunner might have been hit, but the driver was probably a good shot in his own right, and if he damaged the tilt-rotor they would be doomed.

'You'll have to pick us up on the move,' he decided. 'Lower a line from the winch. We'll grab it and you can pull us up.'

'You think that's a good idea?'

'No, but it's the only one I've got!'

Ahead, the Bell descended, engines now in hover configuration, and Chase made out a black cable descending from one side. He looked back. A red slash rose above the edge of the cliff, the paracraft following it a moment later – and dropping amidst a huge cloud of blown spray, the parachute flapping away behind it. But the black vehicle didn't hit the ground, instead gliding along less than a foot above it, the stubby wings trapping air beneath them and providing just enough lift to support it in wing-in-ground effect mode.

And without the drag of the fabric 'chute, the paracraft could go much faster.

'We haven't got time.' The Covenant craft was rapidly gaining, and he had no idea how to make his own paracraft lift off and do the same. 'Matt! We'll come to you – just fly in a straight line and I'll aim for the cable!'

The BA609 dropped to around a hundred feet and slowed, the cable skittering over the ground. Chase turned the paracraft towards it, checking the other controls for anything that might help. A black button turned out to be the release for the backup parachute, but that was no use to him now, as it would just act like a giant airbrake and slow them even more.

All or nothing. He lined the paracraft's battered nose up with the tilt-rotor, seeing Trulli looking out of the door. 'How close are they?' he asked Sophia.

'A hundred and fifty metres, less – they're catching up very fast.'

'Get into the front,' he told her. 'When I say, grab the line. Soon as you've got it, I'll tell them to climb – they'll pull you with them.'

'What about you?'

'Still working on that part!'

Sophia climbed back into the front seat. They were gaining rapidly on the tilt-rotor, which tipped forward to match their speed. The end of the cable was a hook, part of the winch system they had used to recover Trulli's submersible. It bounced along the ice, kicking up chips with each impact. 'Go up,' Chase told Trulli. 'About two feet.'

The Bell ascended slightly, the heavy hook rising with it until it was wavering in the wind just above the ground. Chase adjusted course to follow it, the freezing spray kicked up by the tilt-rotor slashing at his face. 'Where are they?'

'Fifty metres.'

The cable danced just ahead of the paracraft. 'Get ready to grab it!'

The engine noise of the second paracraft changed sharply. A moment later there was an oddly muffled bang from behind. 'What happened?' Chase demanded, unable to risk looking away from the cable.

'They just landed.' The Covenant craft had dropped back on to the ice, the air cushion absorbing most of the impact. The gunner, face filled with pain, had nevertheless managed to prop his SIG on the windscreen, swinging it towards his target. 'Eddie, he's going to shoot at the plane!'

Chase said nothing, grimly urging the paracraft forward . . .

The hook clunked against fibreglass. Sophia grabbed the line and pulled it to her, shoving a foot into the hook.

A burst of gunfire. Two shots missed, the third clanging off the tilt-rotor's fuselage. The gunner adjusted his aim—

'*Climb!*' Chase roared.

Larsson responded immediately, the Bell's engines whining as he increased power. The cable snapped taut and whisked Sophia out of the paracraft.

The gunner's finger tightened on the trigger—

Chase hit the black button and leapt from his seat, kicking down the steering column and clamping one outstretched hand round Sophia's ankle as she soared away.

The paracraft's reserve 'chute burst from the back of the hull. The backblast from the fan immediately snapped it open and it shot into the air, pulling the empty paracraft with it.

Chase's last kick to the controls had moved the wing flaps to their limit, pitching the paracraft into a steep climb – too steep. It backflipped into a stall, falling back to earth . . .

On to the other paracraft.

Fibreglass shattered, shards tearing flesh, then the fuel tanks of both craft ruptured and exploded, scattering ragged hunks of burning debris across the pristine ice.

Chase felt the heat of the explosion. He looked up, seeing Sophia clinging to the line, the underside of the tilt-rotor spinning above her. He tried to bring up his other hand to the hook, but in the gale from the rotors couldn't quite reach. His other hand was slipping, inexorably losing its grip on Sophia's boot. He looked pleadingly up at her . . .

She looked back, but her expression was one of *annoyance*. She pointed at the ground. Chase lowered his gaze – and saw he was hanging only a foot above the ice, Larsson having slowed and descended. Sheepishly, he let go of her foot and dropped. Sophia jumped down beside him. The tilt-rotor moved off, Trulli giving them a thumbs-up as it turned to land nearby.

'All right,' said Sophia, 'can we go now?'

'Yeah,' Chase replied. 'We need to get back to Australia . . . and then on to Africa.'

★

'We've found the paracraft,' said one of the remaining Covenant members over Vogler's radio. 'Both destroyed.'

'What about Chase and Blackwood?' Vogler asked.

'No sign. But there are marks from landing gear nearby. They must have got away.'

Vogler's normally impassive face revealed frustration. 'Understood. Get back here. Out.'

'Wow,' Nina said. 'Not your day, huh? That's, what, eleven guys and two hovercraft?'

'Luckily for you, Dr Wilde, we still have enough seats in the other paracraft for you. Otherwise this,' he indicated the library around them, 'would be your permanent residence. For as long as it remains, at least.'

She regarded him sourly. 'You're still going to destroy it?'

'When we have what we need, yes.' He glanced across the huge room. An impromptu production line had been set up, two of the Covenant troopers bringing over stacks of clay tablets that Ribbsley had decreed of interest, so that a third could take high-resolution photographs of them.

'We shouldn't take her at all,' growled Zamal from nearby. 'We should kill her right now.'

'Not this again,' Vogler sighed. 'You know procedure.'

'Procedure doesn't count now Hammerstein is dead. And he would have voted to kill her as well.'

'You don't know that,' he said. Nina was certain Zamal was correct, but decided it best to keep it to herself. 'And I will not allow anyone to take action against her until the Triumvirate has reached a majority verdict.'

Zamal laughed sarcastically. 'Which will be hard, since there are only the two of us left. Or were you thinking of granting a field promotion?' He looked across at the three men working with the tablets – all Arabs. 'One of my men, perhaps? I have three to your one. The odds are in my favour.'

Vogler shook his head. 'I was thinking of someone we both trust, whose opinion we respect.'

Another harsh laugh. 'Not Ribbsley, surely? Or *Callum*?'

'The Cardinal.'

Zamal looked surprised. 'The Cardinal? He is no longer a member of the Covenant.'

'Nobody leaves the Covenant, Zamal. Not really. And I know you value his opinion. And trust him.'

'I do,' Zamal said with reluctance. 'But since he was your mentor, I don't think his decision will be unbiased.'

'He'll decide based on the facts. And I think he is just as likely to vote with you as with me. Until our Jewish comrades appoint a new member to the Triumvirate, this will be the fastest way to reach a decision. And since Chase and Blackwood have the location of Eden, we *need* to move fast.' He looked at Nina. 'You will come with us.'

'So I get to stay alive, huh?' she said.

His hard smile did not reassure her. 'For now.'

30

Vatican City

It is the smallest independent state in the world, less than a quarter of a square mile in area. A city within a city, completely surrounded by the Italian capital of Rome. Yet for all that, it is also one of the most *powerful* states in the world, transcending boundaries of nationality and race and politics to hold influence over more than a billion people across the globe: the followers of the Roman Catholic Church.

Both Rome and Vatican City were places that Nina had long wanted to visit. But she had planned to do so as a tourist, not as a prisoner. And especially not with the threat of death hanging over her.

A threat that would be dismissed – or carried out – based upon the word of one man. A man she was about to meet.

Once Ribbsley had all his photographs, the Covenant moved out, making a long and cold flight in the remaining paracraft. Their destination was the bleak Wilkins ice runway some forty miles from the Australian Casey research station, the only place for hundreds of miles able to support aircraft capable of crossing the Antarctic Ocean. Two Hercules transporters waited there, one of them taking Nina, the two surviving Covenant leaders, Ribbsley and Callum to Hobart on the Australian island of Tasmania, from where a jet carried them on the lengthy journey to Europe. It was night when, exhausted and jet-lagged, she was finally brought to the Vatican in an Audi Q7 SUV with blacked-out windows. Zamal and Callum flanked her, each holding a gun. The Audi passed through a side entrance, Nina catching the barest glimpse of the majesty of St Peter's basilica before being driven to a nondescript building near the tiny city-state's railway station.

The guns were put away, but Nina felt no less threatened as she was taken inside, Vogler leading the way. Men in dark suits stood guard within, with the same cold, hard faces as Vogler's team at the frozen city. Former Swiss Guards, now tasked with a more secret objective. Was this the headquarters of the Covenant, right inside the Vatican itself?

The building's interior was elegant yet austere. This was a place of work, not worship. Though it was quiet, their footsteps echoing through the polished hallways, Nina got the sense that a lot went on behind each of the closed doors she passed. There was a feeling of *power*, understated yet undeniable.

Vogler took her up a flight of steps to a door at the end of a long hallway. He opened it. 'Go inside.' Nina hesitated, then steeled herself and went through. Vogler followed her, the others remaining outside.

The room was a mix of office and study, two walls lined with book-filled shelves and tall filing cabinets, high windows in the third giving a view of the dome of St Peter's. The fourth wall was dominated by a beautiful marble fireplace, flames crackling gently in the grate. Before it were two armchairs of time-polished red leather.

An elderly man dressed in black sat in one of them, gazing into the fire. Vogler stood beside him, respectfully lowering his head.

'*Cardinale*,' he said. The man looked up, replying in Italian. Nina didn't know the language well enough to understand what they were saying, but from their tone it was clear they knew each other well.

Vogler handed the old man the cylinder containing the recording of the song. He examined it, then carefully placed it on a small table and stood to face Nina, revealing that his clothes were the robes of a cardinal. There was something unusual about them, however, and it took a moment for her to realise what: they were devoid of any kind of colour or decoration, even a crucifix.

'Dr Wilde,' he said, gesturing to the empty armchair. 'Please sit down.'

She eyed it suspiciously. 'Not until I know what's going on.'

He shrugged. 'As you wish. I simply thought that after your long journey you might want to be comfortable. I hope you don't mind if *I* sit.' He lowered himself back into his chair, the leather creaking. 'I am Jonas di Bonaventura, and I'm sure you have many questions. But the question that has brought you all this way is a simple one: should you live?' He fixed her with a piercing, crystal-clear gaze that belonged on a much younger man.

'You want me to answer that?' Nina replied. 'Because in that case: a big fat yes!'

Di Bonaventura smiled. 'You live up to your reputation, Dr Wilde. Do, please, sit down. It will make my neck ache if I have to keep looking up at you.' The smile darkened. 'And you would not want that to affect my decision.'

Nina paused, then perched on the edge of the chair. Vogler moved to stand behind her – in a position, she realised, that would give him the easiest shot should he choose to draw his gun. 'So,' she said, trying not to let that intimidate her, 'this is the headquarters of the Covenant of Genesis, huh?'

'The Covenant has no headquarters,' said di Bonaventura. 'It does not even exist. Officially, at least. It is a shadow, a phantom, its work known only by a few.'

Nina looked through the windows towards the great floodlit dome of St Peter's. 'Including, you know . . . *him*? The man in the hat?'

Vogler made a faint sound in his throat, enough to indicate his displeasure at her disrespect. Di Bonaventura, however, merely leaned back in his chair. 'Of course not. That is our firmest rule – he must *never* know. That would make His Holiness a hypocrite, and that cannot, must not, be allowed to happen. What we do, we do in secret. I am a *cardinale in pectore*, a secret cardinal – but not in the way most people would use the term, even His Holiness. Popes are chosen from the ranks of the cardinals, but simply by knowing of the existence of the Covenant I am disqualified from ever being nominated. I am, you might say, an *agent* of the Church, just as governments and corporations have their agents who work to protect them. And keep their secrets.'

'Like the secret of the Veteres. Yeah, I know all about them,' she said, catching a slight upward twitch of the cardinal's white eyebrows.

He smiled again. 'You do? I think not.'

'Well, let's see now,' said Nina. 'They date back to well over a hundred and thirty thousand years ago, they expanded across the world all the way from Africa to the Antarctic, they built cities that wouldn't be equalled in scale for over a hundred millennia, they had a complex written language, a numerical system that would be adopted by the Atlanteans, they worshipped a single god . . . and something else too, what was it?' She pretended to search her memory. 'Oh, and they came from a little place called the Garden of Eden, that was it,' she finished. 'I think that about covers it.'

Di Bonaventura regarded her silently . . . and then, to her growing dismay, laughed long and hard. It wasn't sarcastic, or mocking – he was genuinely amused, in the same way that a parent might be at a display by a precocious child. 'My apologies, Dr Wilde,' he finally said, still smiling broadly. 'You do indeed know a great deal about the Veteres, some of which, yes, the Covenant did not. So I congratulate you on that. But despite everything you have learned, there is one thing you have not – the secret of the Veteres themselves!'

'What?' Nina demanded, realising that he had just effortlessly manipulated her into revealing part of her hand – the limits of her knowledge. 'What secret?'

Di Bonaventura merely smiled again, infuriating her. 'None of what you have discovered matters to the Covenant. If that were all it was, the Covenant would not even need to exist.'

'So what's the secret?' He said nothing. 'Okay then, it's something you think is such a threat to the Abrahamic religions that all knowledge of it has to be suppressed and all evidence destroyed. Am I right?'

He nodded. 'Go on.'

It struck Nina that if she did deduce the truth, she could be signing her own death warrant. But something drove her on: she *had* to know. 'But it's not just that this civilisation existed long before Abraham. There's something about it that contradicts Genesis – that can be *proved* to contradict Genesis,' she realised. 'That's the threat, isn't it? And you know what it is.'

'But do you, Dr Wilde? Do you have that knowledge?'

'Why?' She glanced at Vogler. 'Are you going to have him shoot me if I do?'

Di Bonaventura chuckled. 'Certainly not in here – the carpet would have to be cleaned.' He regarded her with another intense look. 'And perhaps not at all. But that depends on you.'

'So if I give you the right answer, you might not kill me?'

'It is not the answer that matters, but the beliefs that lead to it.'

'Thanks for that, Yoda,' she scoffed, before frowning in thought. 'So what could contradict Genesis so much that the Covenant would kill to stop it becoming known? Genesis has been contradicted by science often enough in the past, in everything from geology to zoology to astrophysics, but you didn't send out commandos to assassinate Stephen Hawking. So it must be something huge . . .' She tailed off. 'It's . . . it's not *aliens*, is it?'

A long silence, only broken by the snapping of the fire. Then: 'Of course it's not aliens!' said di Bonaventura, somewhere between mirth and disbelief that she could entertain such a ridiculous suggestion. 'And I thought you were a serious scientist. Aliens!'

'Hey!' Nina protested. 'I *am* a serious scientist! I found out more about the Veteres in two weeks than that jerk Ribbsley did in fifteen years, or however long he's been working for you. How long *has* the Covenant been around, anyway?'

Di Bonaventura was still amused. 'Subtlety is not one of your investigative tools, is it, Dr Wilde?'

'And it's not one of the Covenant's methods, either. So how long? If you're going to kill me anyway, there's no harm in telling me.'

'And if I decide to let you live?'

'Then you need me for something, and I might be more inclined to co-operate if you give me something in return.'

'So you're saying you are willing to co-operate with the Covenant?'

'I said *might*. But that's a pretty small might. Tiny.'

'You may surprise yourself, Dr Wilde. But to answer your question, the Covenant, in its current form, has existed since the 1950s. But a similar secret organisation has existed within the Church for over a hundred years, since the first discovery of the Veteres.'

'So Judaism and Islam weren't always part of it?'

'No, though they had their own equivalents.'

'It must have been something big to unite them. I mean, Christianity, Judaism and Islam aren't exactly noted for their mutual co-operation.'

'There have been examples,' said di Bonaventura. 'Have you heard of the Declaration of Alexandria?' Nina shook her head. 'It was an agreement between the faiths signed in 2002, to end their mutual hostilities in an attempt to bring peace to the Holy Land.'

'Wow, it's been a roaring success so far, huh?'

For the first time, di Bonaventura betrayed a hint of defensiveness. 'You may mock, Dr Wilde, but the intentions of its signatories were sincere. They were all men of God, working for a common goal. Just like the Covenant.'

'The Covenant – men of God?' Nina cried. 'After all the people you've killed, you've got the nerve to say you're doing it in God's name? Yet you daren't even tell your own leader that the Covenant exists? That certainly makes *you* a hypocrite.'

'It does,' he admitted, his face revealing a long-held shame. 'And when the time comes, we will all be judged. Perhaps we will even be damned. But for now, protecting the faith seems the right path to follow.'

'Protecting the faith? Or protecting the Church?' Nina fixed him with her green eyes, a look as intense as the one he had earlier given her. 'Is that what this is about? You're afraid that what I've discovered will destroy the Church? And not just yours, but the Jewish and Islamic ones too?'

'You over-estimate yourself,' he replied. 'The Church has survived Copernicus, Galileo and Darwin. It will survive Nina Wilde as well. As will the other faiths. If anything, your discovery of Eden will strengthen them, by turning the story of Genesis from an allegory to historical fact.'

'*My* discovery?' said Nina, feeling an odd spark of triumph. 'So the Covenant didn't actually know for sure?'

'We . . . suspected,' said Vogler. 'Finds at other sites, Ribbsley's translations, they were leading in that direction. But it wasn't until you found the audio recording in Antarctica that we had proof of its existence.'

'But you don't know where it is,' she said. 'And Eddie and Sophia do. And they're probably already on their way there – I mean, I haven't heard anyone saying they're dead.' A glance at Vogler. 'Gonna set me straight?'

He shook his head. 'They seem to have escaped Antarctica.'

'Good for them. Well, good for Eddie. I don't really care what happens to Sophia.'

'Perhaps you should,' said di Bonaventura. 'Do you really want *her* to find the Garden of Eden? A murderer, a terrorist, a blackmailer . . . yes, I know why your president is so afraid of her,' he went on, seeing Nina's surprised look. 'It is my job to know such things.'

'To protect the Church, I guess.'

'Yes. We rarely use such influence directly, but because of Gabriel Ribbsley's lust we were forced to make a . . . *request* to President Dalton, to give him what he wanted in return for helping us.'

'Release Sophia or we end your presidency with the scandal of the decade?'

'Something like that. But Gabriel was already greedy, and this has proved he can no longer be relied upon. So we need someone else to uncover the secrets of the Veteres.' His intense gaze returned. 'Perhaps you.'

'Me?' Nina gasped. 'What, are you nuts? First you try to kill me, and now you're offering me a *job*?'

'Not a job, exactly. An arrangement.'

'Find Eden for you and not get killed, right?' He nodded. 'And if I turn down your generous offer?'

Di Bonaventura gazed into the fire. 'Now that we know it exists, we must find Eden. One way or another, we will know what you know. You can tell us willingly . . . or we can give you to Mr Callum.' He turned back to Nina, eyes hard. 'There is an empty cell at Guantánamo Bay, formerly occupied by Sophia Blackwood. He could see that it becomes occupied again.'

Nina's mouth went dry at the threat, but she tried not to let her apprehension show. 'But by the time I talked, Eddie might already have found Eden.'

'Which is why I would prefer your co-operation. Dr Wilde, I have made my decision, which both the surviving members of the Triumvirate have agreed to accept. I believe it is in the current interests of the Covenant for you to . . .' He paused. 'Live.'

'Great,' said Nina, understandably relieved. 'Pity Zamal wasn't here to hear that. I'd have loved to have seen his face.'

'I would not be so smug,' said Vogler. 'Zamal may find some other reason to end your life. And perhaps next time, I will agree with him.'

Di Bonaventura waved him down. 'I think she understands the threat. I hope she also understands the opportunity she is being given.' He stood to address Nina. 'Agree to help us find Eden, and you will go too. You will be the one to *discover* Eden. Imagine it, Dr Wilde – it would be the single greatest archaeological discovery in history. Not even Atlantis compares.'

'You might be right,' she replied. 'But discovering Eden isn't much use to me if I'm dead five minutes later.'

'There may be no need to kill you. If you find Eden, and if it contains what we suspect, then you may understand why the Covenant was created. You may even agree with its purpose.'

'Somehow I doubt that. But why don't you just tell me what the big secret is, right now?'

The cardinal smiled. 'Because then you would have no incentive

THE COVENANT OF GENESIS

to find out for yourself. I know what kind of person you are, Dr Wilde. I understand you. You are driven by the need to *know*, to discover that which is hidden. You have an urge to expand the boundaries of your knowledge – of all knowledge. I understand you, because I am the same.'

'We are *not* the same,' Nina insisted vehemently. 'I'm a scientist, I deal in fact – the tangible, the provable, things I can hold in my hand and show to the world. You're doing the opposite, you're trying to *suppress* knowledge. To protect your faith.'

'My faith is strong enough not to need protection.'

'Then why are you trying to destroy all trace of the Veteres?'

'Because not everyone's faith is as strong as mine.' As Nina took in the implications of that, he continued, 'Dr Wilde, science and faith are not mutually exclusive. The Church is not opposed to science, far from it. Astronomy, cosmology, genetics, evolutionary biology . . . the Church has embraced them all.'

'After long battles,' Nina pointed out.

'Sometimes, yes. Controversial theories cannot become accepted overnight. But in the end, only a fool denies the undeniable. And that is when science and faith come together. They are two sides of the same coin – the search for *truth*. Through science, you can answer the question: what is this? And then through faith, you can answer the other: what does this *mean*? Only when you know both answers can you find the ultimate truth.'

'The ultimate truth being . . .'

'The purpose of the Covenant. The secret of the Veteres. And the hope . . .' he looked away, at the ceiling – or something beyond it, 'the hope that one day, we will understand how it fits into God's plan.'

'*Cardinale*,' said Vogler – and this time there was a warning tone to his voice. The balance of power in the room had subtly shifted from the Covenant's former leader to his protégé. Had di

Bonaventura said too much – or was he expressing another long-withheld regret over his actions?

His words at least confirmed to Nina that whatever the secret of the long-dead civilisation might be, it did indeed conflict strongly with the words of Genesis – so much so that the Covenant was afraid of the damage it could cause to all three Abrahamic religions. But what could that secret be?

One thing was clear. For now, her only chance of survival was to accept di Bonaventura's offer – and hope she could string out the meagre amount of information she could remember from the destroyed map long enough to escape.

And there was something else. What if . . . what if she actually *did* discover the Garden of Eden? The cardinal was right – it *would* be the greatest discovery of all time. And if she were the one to make it . . .

'All right,' she said, standing. 'Cardinal? I accept your offer.' She held out her right hand.

For a moment he seemed almost surprised. But then he took her hand, shaking it. 'Very well. Killian,' he said, turning to Vogler, 'it was good to see you again, and I hope I was of one last service to the Covenant.'

Vogler bowed his head. 'You were, *cardinale*. Thank you. Though I suspect Zamal will not be pleased with your decision.'

'Zamal will see the wisdom of it. In time. He always does.'

'Yes, he does. In time.' The two men shared the smile of a private joke, then shook hands. '*Cardinale*,' Vogler said again; then he led Nina to the door.

'Dr Wilde?' di Bonaventura said as they reached it.

'Yes?'

'Good luck.'

Her surprise at his apparent sincerity was such that all she could think to say was, 'Thank you.'

★

As Vogler had predicted, Zamal was less than pleased about the cardinal's decision.

'He is *wrong!*' he bellowed, slamming a fist down on the table. The group had left the Vatican and gone to a large house in Rome, the dome of St Peter's still visible in the distance through its windows. 'I knew he would side with you!'

'You agreed to abide by his decision,' said Vogler. 'And now the deadlock has been broken, we have a new objective. Dr Wilde will guide us to Eden.'

Ribbsley snorted. 'I doubt that very much. Even if she knows its location, which is unlikely, she'll just try to delay us to give Chase a chance to get there first.'

'She knows the risks of wasting our time,' said Vogler, looking to where Nina was sitting apart from the others, her face stony. 'And surely,' he continued, turning to Callum, 'the intelligence resources of the United States have been able to track down Chase and Blackwood by now?'

The white-haired man sat up stiffly, bristling at the challenge – but unable to respond to it. 'Unfortunately, not yet.'

'Not yet?' echoed Zamal. 'Satellites, computers, spies, trillions of dollars – and you have *nothing*?'

'No, not nothing,' Callum said through tight lips. 'The *Southern Sun* arrived at the French ice station of Dumont d'Urville about five hours ago. The surviving members of the UNARA expedition are going to be flown back to Australia from there. But Chase and Blackwood weren't aboard – and the ship's tilt-rotor was missing. It wouldn't be able to reach land from off the Antarctic coast, so either the ship headed north to the limits of its range and then turned back to Dumont, or they stripped out the plane and turned it into a flying gas can. Even so, the only place it could have reached is Tasmania – but so far it hasn't been found.'

'Maybe they crashed in the sea,' muttered Zamal.

'I doubt we are that lucky,' Vogler said. 'But there's been no trace of them? Nothing at all?'

Callum shook his head. 'Either they're still in Australia, or they've used false IDs to get out of the country.' He glowered at Nina. 'I don't suppose you'd know anything about that.'

Nina leaned back and put her hands behind her head. 'Law-abidin' citizen here.'

Zamal banged his fists on the table. 'I can make her tell us.'

'It's not important,' said Vogler. 'We have far more resources – we can still beat them.'

'If she co-operates,' Callum said.

'I believe she will.'

'You have a great deal of faith,' rumbled Zamal.

'Isn't that the reason we are here?'

'It's not the reason *I'm* here,' said Ribbsley, going to a window to gaze out at Rome. 'And if you think I'm going to trek across the bloody deserts of Sudan, you can think again. Khartoum's a backwater hellhole, but at least the hotels have air conditioning and room service, even if you can't get a drink. I'll fly myself to the site once she finds it.' He turned, giving Nina a suspicious sneer. 'If she *can* find it.'

'I'll find it,' she snapped back, partly to maintain the fiction that she had both memorised and translated the map, but also out of affronted professional pride. 'I've been doing better than you so far, haven't I?' He huffed and turned away. 'Hah!'

'In which case,' said Vogler, 'it is time you gave us a starting point. Sudan, you said, but you will need to be more specific. Since it is the largest country in Africa.' He slid a map across the table to her. 'So. Shall we begin, Dr Wilde?'

31

Sudan

'So, do you actually know where you're going?' asked Tamara Defendé, 'TD' to her friends, as she guided her battered Piper Twin Comanche to a landing on the dusty runway.

'More or less,' said Chase, taking in the landscape. The desert surrounding El Obeid in central Sudan looked as desolate as the surface of Mars. 'Okay, maybe less than more.'

The plane touched down, wheels squawking. Chase jolted forward in his seat. 'Sorry,' said TD, braking. 'I'm not exactly thrilled to be here. Hardcore fundamentalist Islamic state on one hand, independent African businesswoman on the other – not the best mix.'

'Do you have a problem with the Sudanese?' Sophia asked from the Piper's second row of seats.

'Yes, if they're paying the Janjaweed to rape and murder African women,' TD said with angry sarcasm. 'Maybe you hadn't heard in your cell, but there have been some problems here. A little place called Darfur.'

'We're not going to Darfur,' Chase said, trying to head off any further conflict between the two women. TD was an old friend, who at first had been happy to fly to meet him at Nairobi in Kenya – but she became less keen when she learned his intended destination, and outright appalled on discovering the identity of his travelling companion. He got the feeling that TD disliked Sophia more for betraying him personally than for any of her crimes.

'Close enough. That part of the desert you showed me on the map, it might look empty, but it's still Janjaweed territory.' She mimed spitting. 'You should stay well away.'

'We don't have a choice, unfortunately.' TD turned off the main runway. Several planes were parked on the dirt, white-painted trucks and Land Rovers lined up nearby. 'Those are UN trucks. What's all this?'

'Relief effort,' TD told him. 'It's supposed to be going to Darfur. But *quelle surprise*, it has stopped here.' Her attractive face took on an uncharacteristic hardness. 'I hate this country.'

'Just another African basket-case,' Sophia said dismissively. 'The entire continent was much better off in the colonial days.' TD gave her a look suggesting that had she not been occupied with the controls, she would have reached back and hit her.

'Soph, shut up,' Chase said, tired. The last few days of travelling on false passports using bogus credit cards had been long, and tense, the possibility that they might be identified and captured – or killed – constantly hanging over them. And with Sudan being run by Islamic fundamentalists, there was a danger that the Covenant, at least Zamal's branch of it, had influence. He patted TD's shoulder. 'Thanks for doing this for us.'

'I'm doing it for *you*, Eddie,' she replied pointedly. 'And Nina. I hope she's okay.'

He put on a stoic front. 'So do I. But they took her prisoner when they could have just killed her, so hopefully she's stringing them along about the map. The further away she tells them Eden is, the longer we'll have to find it.'

'You really believe that?' TD asked. 'The Garden of Eden, the actual one from the Bible? Here, in Sudan?'

'That's what Nina thought, so yeah. No idea what we're going to find, though. If there's some magical oasis out in the desert, I'm pretty sure it'd have showed up on Google Earth by now.'

'There are only two things you can be sure of finding out there,' said TD, bringing the plane to a stop. 'Sand, and death.'

'I can cope with the first one, even if it's a pain when it gets in my arse crack,' said Chase, the deliberate crassness of the comment producing a hint of a smile from his pilot. 'Second one, though, I'd rather be the one causing it. Will your mate be able to sort something out?'

TD switched off the engines, the silence unsettling after the continuous buzz of the flight. 'I spoke to him before I met you in Nairobi. He's got you a jeep, and some guns. I don't know what state they'll be in, though.'

'So long as the wheels turn and bullets come out when I pull the trigger, they'll do. Thanks.' He kissed her cheek. 'What're you going to do now?'

'Personally, I'd like to fuel up and get as far from here as possible. But . . .' she tipped back the bill of her baseball cap, 'I might stay around for a couple of days. Just in case you need me.'

Chase grinned. 'Appreciate it.'

'Try not to get killed, Eddie. I hope you find what you're looking for. And Nina.'

They climbed out and headed for the rundown terminal building.

A hundred and fifty miles to the north, a convoy of five Humvees pulled off a rough dirt road and came to a stop. Painted black rather than in camouflage colours, the oversized 4x4s appeared to be civilian vehicles. But beneath the paint, its gloss dulled by dust following the westward drive from the Sudanese capital of Khartoum, they were ex-military M1114 models, armoured and powerful.

Despite their size, each Humvee only had four seats. Nina rode in the lead truck, accompanied by Vogler and two of his men, more former Swiss Guards replacing the ones killed in Antarctica. She had noticed, however, that Vogler's contingent consisted of only four men, rather than the five he had had before. Did the Covenant only have limited manpower remaining? The absence of a new leader to replace Hammerstein, despite the presence of another group of six hard-faced Israeli troopers, suggested that was the case; if so, then the Covenant had its limits, and was far from the omnipotent organisation it had once seemed to be.

Zamal's squad was at full strength, however. They emerged from their Humvees, forming an armed cordon as the Arab strode across the sand to meet the four horsemen waiting for them. 'So who are those guys?' Nina asked. 'The apocalypse?'

'Our guides,' said Vogler. 'The Janjaweed.'

Nina knew the name: the United States government had declared the militia group to be guilty of genocide in Darfur. 'The Covenant sure is friends with some really nice people,' she said, not concealing her disgust.

'They would not have been my first choice. But this is their territory; we will need their support. Get out. They want to see you.'

'I don't want to see *them*,' she said. But Vogler had already exited, rounding the Humvee to open her door. She reluctantly left the cabin.

The Humvee's interior was air conditioned; opening its door was like opening that of a furnace. She hurriedly donned a floppy-brimmed hat to protect her pale face and neck from the sun's searing glare, tugging her sleeves as far down as they would go. The occupants of the other Humvees also emerged, all in desert camouflage except for Callum, who was wearing civilian khakis. He regarded her from behind the blank quicksilver of his sunglasses.

Zamal was talking to the riders in Arabic. All wore thick headscarves and layered clothing to protect themselves from the sun, the top layer military fatigues in green and brown camouflage patterns. Their guns were AK-47s, the near-universal rifle of the Third World. One man had a rocket-propelled grenade launcher slung from his saddle; brand-new military equipment in the hands of a purportedly civilian militia. Despite the heat, there was one cold thing in the desolate landscape – their eyes, the narrow, unblinking gaze of men who expected to be feared, and had done much to justify it.

All four pairs of eyes locked on to her.

One of the riders said something to Zamal. He replied, his sneering smile directed at Nina. The four men all laughed malevolently.

'These are the Janjaweed,' Zamal said, turning to stand imperiously before her. 'I can tell from your expression that you have heard of them.'

'Yeah, you could say that. At the United Nations. Usually in connection with words like "mass murder", "gang rape", "genocide" . . . Real good company you keep for a supposed man of God.'

'They serve a purpose. They will take us across the desert to where you say Eden will be found.' His lips curled back, exposing his teeth in a sadistic grin. 'And if it is not there . . . I will give you to them.'

'I've heard it all before,' said Nina, outward defiance not quite concealing her dread. The horsemen were still watching her, leering. 'And it'll be there.'

'Perhaps you should show them where we are going,' said Zamal, producing a map. 'Before we meet the rest of their group.'

'There's more of them?' she asked nervously. Four Janjaweed – the name literally meant 'devil on horseback' – were ominous enough, but an entire militia group . . .

'Oh, yes. Many more.' He placed the map on the Humvee's hood, Vogler and Callum coming to look. 'So. We crossed the Nile at Khartoum . . .'

'So they crossed the Nile,' said Chase, holding a digital print of the map from the frozen city. 'Then if we backtrack west, they started from an oasis between three mesas.' He looked at one of the satellite images Sophia held. 'I don't see an oasis, but they can come and go in a couple of years, never mind a hundred thousand. But the mesas . . . it's got to be these.' He tapped at a trio of formations on the printout.

Sophia gazed into the shimmering desert to the northwest. 'We're at the end of the road, then. Literally.'

'If you call this a road.' Chase looked back along the rutted track they had followed after heading northwards from El Obeid. 'Going off road's not going to be any worse for the truck.' He banged the bonnet of the rusting, sand-scoured, 1980s-vintage Toyota Land Cruiser that TD's contact had acquired for them.

'Or our spines. So how far have we left to go?'

Chase swapped the Veteres map for a considerably more recent representation of the area. 'About a hundred miles.'

'How long will it take?'

'Over this terrain? No way we'll get there today. We'll have to camp for the night.'

'And we only have one tent,' Sophia said with a playful smile. 'Cosy.'

'One tent and one truck,' he reminded her. 'I'm not bloody telling Nina that I slept with my ex-wife.'

'Your loss. Do you have a preference, or shall we toss for them?'

'You can have the tent.'

'Then you can put it up. What?' she said as Chase shook his head in exasperation. 'You got to choose where to sleep. It only seems fair.' She looked into the truck. 'And what about the guns?'

'They'll be sleeping with me,' he said firmly. As well as the truck and some survival gear, they had been furnished with a pair of weapons: a battered Browning High Power automatic that Chase guessed was a couple of decades older than he was, and an even more ancient Lee-Enfield rifle, its wooden body chipped and scarred, that almost certainly dated back to the Second World War.

'Yes, I thought they might be.' She smirked. 'Sleeping with something cold, hard, inflexible, with awkward knobbly protrusions . . . it'll be as if you've got Nina back.'

'Har fucking har. Just for that, you can put up your own tent.' Ignoring her look of displeasure, he gathered up the sheets of paper and got back into the Land Cruiser. 'Coming?'

'A long journey through a hot desert over awful terrain in a truck with worn-out suspension to spend the night in a tent? I can't wait.' She climbed in and slammed the door.

They picked their way northwest for hours, slowing over the harsh, rocky plains littered with sharp stones that threatened to rip through the Land Cruiser's tyres, then speeding up to avoid getting bogged down in mile after mile of soft sand. Despite Chase's best efforts, they still had to stop and dig themselves out a couple of times, further slowing their progress. By the time the sun neared the horizon, the Land Cruiser's milometer told him that they had barely covered two-thirds of the distance to their destination.

The sunset itself was something to behold, though. The dust and sand in the air turned the western sky a lurid, dripping-blood red, swathes of orange running through it as though the heavens had caught fire. 'Look at that,' Chase said. 'That's a hell of a sunset. Wish we'd brought the camera.'

'This isn't going to become your new "night sky in Algeria" story, is it?' Sophia yawned. Chase spotted a rock poking from the sand and swerved the Land Cruiser so that the wheels on her side slammed over it, jolting her hard. 'Ow! Did you do that on purpose?'

'Don't be daft,' said Chase, suppressing a smile as he looked back at the splendour of the setting sun.

He spotted something else, though: a column of black smoke rising into the sky two or three miles away. 'Soph, check the map – the proper one. Were there any villages near the route we were going?'

She had seen the smoke too, and consulted the map. 'Not for a long way. Are you off course?'

'Don't see how; I've been following the compass.' He tapped the compass ball attached to the dashboard, which showed them to be heading northwest. Looking at the distant smoke, he saw a second column starting to rise beside it. 'We'd better take a look.'

'Are you sure that's a good idea?' Sophia asked, her tone making it clear she thought it was not.

'There's not supposed to be anyone out here. Someone might be in trouble.'

'Which is hardly our problem. And if it's the Janjaweed?'

'Then I want to know where they are before they know where *we* are.' He aimed the Land Cruiser towards the smoke.

Fifteen minutes later, Chase stopped the truck. They were close to the base of a rocky rise. The smoke was coming from the other side, more dark stalks having sprouted during the drive. He wound down the window, listened for a moment, then took both guns from the back seat. 'Come on.'

'What is it?' Sophia asked as he got out.

'I heard shouting. Keep your voice down, and stay low.' He clambered up the shadowed face of the dune. Sophia followed.

The shouts became clearer as they approached the low summit. Men, the yelling of a mob. And others cutting through it, higher-pitched: the screams of women.

And children.

Chase crawled the last few feet to peer over the top of the dune. 'Shit,' he hissed when he saw what lay below.

He'd seen similar scenes in different countries: Afghanistan, Iraq, half a dozen others where the rules of civilisation had been broken down by war. Over the dune was a rocky hollow, a small pool of rancid water at its heart, round which had been built a pathetic collection of shelters. A makeshift village, a camp for refugees fleeing the violence in Darfur to the west. A few dozen people at most, most of them women and children, trying to find safety.

They had failed.

The shelters were on fire, bodies strewn around them. Some had been shot, but most had been hacked down by machetes, or simply bludgeoned to death with clubs and rifle butts. Some of their attackers were on horseback, circling the doomed encampment and forcing back those of the dwindling group of survivors who tried to flee, laughing and shouting abuse as they rode to block and strike at them.

Those who had dismounted were in groups, three or four to each of the refugee women. They too were laughing, egging each other on.

Chase watched, a seething rage rising, as one of the women was thrown to the ground, the men holding her down and ripping away her clothes. She screamed, begging for mercy that would never be given as the Janjaweed leader, a man in a white headscarf

394

and teardrop mirrorshades, tugged at his own clothing, belt flapping from his waist. More laughter, a cheer from the others as the screams rose into hysteria.

Chase brought the rifle to his shoulder, locking the cross hairs on the back of the man's head—

Sophia shoved the barrel down. 'What the hell are you doing?'

'The world a favour,' he replied angrily. 'Let go of the gun.'

'There must be fifteen of them, and they've all got AKs. If they realise we're here, they'll kill us.'

'We'll see how many I get first.'

'This *isn't your fight*, Eddie. We have to find Eden before the Covenant. And we've got no chance of doing that if the Janjaweed know we're here.' She looked him in the eyes. 'You want to save Nina? Then we need a bargaining chip we can use against the Covenant. Being a white knight here will get us killed, and it will get *her* killed.'

Chase's face tightened with fury . . . but he lowered the gun. '*Fuck!*'

Below, the screaming woman managed to pull one arm free, flailing it in panic – and knocking off her attacker's sunglasses. The other men holding her laughed mockingly, but he punched her brutally in the face once, twice, blood spurting from her mouth and nose – then pulled back, drawing a gun and shooting her twice in the chest. He adjusted his clothing, then picked up his sunglasses and spat on the corpse.

Then the group moved on to another woman.

Sophia was already sliding back down the slope. 'We should go,' she said. 'Wait for them to leave – and hope they're not going the same way as us.'

'They'd fucking well better not be,' he growled as he descended after her.

Behind him, the screams stopped, one by one.

★

The horsemen led the convoy of vehicles through the empty desert. The sun was a fat, shimmering semicircle on the horizon by the time they stopped. Nina saw on the Humvee's GPS screen that they were still at least thirty miles from the possible location of Eden, but the break in the journey was being called by their escorts.

They had arrived at the Janjaweed's camp.

Nina watched nervously through the tinted window of armoured glass as the five vehicles pulled into a circle like a wagon train. There were at least fifty men in the camp, mostly young, all with the same predatory eyes as the horsemen as they watched the 4x4s come to a stop in their midst. The Janjaweed had trucks of their own, though they were the antithesis of the military vehicles in terms of sophistication – half a dozen 'technicals', elderly pickups stripped to the bone with machine guns affixed to mounts welded into the rear beds.

Zamal was the first out of the Humvees, the waiting horsemen now joined by a man whom Nina assumed to be the group's leader. White headscarf, mirrored sunglasses, AK-47 over his shoulder and a machete across his back . . . and a face of cold, merciless stone. After a minute of discussion, Zamal gestured for the vehicles' other occupants to emerge.

Nina was even more reluctant than before to do so, but had little choice. 'This is Hamed,' said Zamal of the Janjaweed leader. 'He and his men will escort us to where we are going tomorrow. But tonight we are their guests. We are invited to share their shelter.'

'Thank him for his generosity,' said Callum, sarcasm creeping into his voice. Nina could see why; the collection of shabby, patched-up tents looked anything but inviting. 'But we brought our own tents. Thank God,' he added under his breath.

'He also invites us to join them for their evening meal. Hamed has just returned from a successful mission, and wants us to share in the celebrations. Especially you, Dr Wilde. He is particularly keen for you to join him.' Behind Zamal, Hamed's face showed expression for the first time: a sadistic lust.

'I'd rather sit in the Humvee's trunk and eat dog food,' she said.

Zamal smirked. 'It can be arranged.'

To Nina's surprise, Vogler came to her defence. 'It would be best if Dr Wilde were kept apart from our . . . hosts. To avoid any unfortunate incidents.' The two Covenant leaders stared at each other, an unspoken challenge.

'A shame,' said Zamal after a moment. 'The Janjaweed will be disappointed not to have the pleasure of her company.'

'I don't want to be a part of *any* kind of pleasure these guys have,' Nina said in revulsion.

'Nor do I,' Vogler told her. He issued orders to his men. They unpacked large quick-erect tents, kicking aside stones and deadwood in the wide circle formed by the parked Humvees to make space for the dome-shaped shelters.

Zamal turned back to Hamed, apparently telling him that he would be having one guest fewer for dinner. The Janjaweed leader scowled, before launching into a discussion of something else . . . but his eyes never wavered from Nina.

Despite the heat, she shivered.

'Well, shit,' muttered Chase, scanning the firelit encampment through the rifle scope.

'What is it?' Sophia asked from beside him. It was night; they lay just below the crest of a low dune, observing the activity in the distance.

'It's not just the Janjaweed. I don't think they could afford five new Humvees.'

After returning to the Land Cruiser and driving to a safe distance from the ravaged refugee camp, they had waited to see in which direction the Janjaweed left. With a certain inevitability, they had gone northwest – the direction in which Chase and Sophia needed to head.

Chase had waited longer to give the horsemen time to open up the gap between them, then followed on a parallel course, hoping to skirt round them before night fell. But then he saw more smoke silhouetted against the dying light of the dusk sky – ahead of them. A Janjaweed camp. They would have patrols watching the desert, so the Land Cruiser's lights would be spotted from miles away if he tried to drive round it – and driving without lights in this terrain was a recipe for disaster.

'The Covenant?'

'It's not tourists, that's for bloody sure.' He panned across the camp, seeing horses, pickup trucks, tents, far too many armed men for his liking . . . and a familiar face. 'Ay up,' he muttered. 'It's the Covenant all right. There's Zamal – and he's talking to that rapist fucker from the refugee camp.'

'Well, that's marvellous,' said Sophia. 'You know what Nina's done, don't you? She's given the Covenant the directions to bloody Eden!'

'She can't have done,' Chase said defensively. 'She didn't know. Not accurately enough.'

'She didn't need to. She saw the general location in Antarctica. If we could figure it out from modern maps, so could they.'

'She wouldn't have helped them,' he insisted.

'Then they tortured it out of her, if that makes you feel any better. But it doesn't change the fact that they're here. Even if they don't know the exact location, they've got enough manpower to search the desert until they find it. Damn it!'

'We can still beat 'em,' said Chase, continuing to scan the encampment. More Janjaweed men, pushing the number to over fifty, sitting in groups round the fires; Covenant troopers in desert camo; dome tents inside the circle formed by the Humvees—

'Buggeration and fuckery,' he whispered.

'What?'

He adjusted the focus, picking out some very familiar red hair through the half-open flap of one tent. 'They've got Nina.'

'She's *there*?' Sophia said in disbelief. 'They actually brought her with them?'

'They must need her to work out where Eden is.' He shifted the sights, pinpointing her exact position.

'Or,' Sophia countered, 'she made a deal with them. Her life for the location of Eden.'

Chase glared at her. 'She'd never do that.'

'Are you sure? For all she knows, you're dead. She might have thought she had nothing else left.'

'Bullshit,' Chase snapped, looking back through the sight. There were a couple of Covenant men patrolling inside the circle of Humvees . . . and more Janjaweed on the outside, the two sides regarding each other with clear mutual suspicion. He surveyed the camp's perimeter. Away from the fires, everything was in flickering shadow.

He sat up and handed the rifle to the surprised Sophia. 'Here.'

'You're giving me a gun?' she asked, as if expecting some trick.

'Yeah. I need you to cover me.' He had donned his black leather jacket when the temperature fell after nightfall; now he removed it and gave it to Sophia as well. For what he was planning, he couldn't allow the creak of leather to give him away.

'Why?'

''Cause I'm going to rescue Nina.'

'From *there*? There must be at least sixty men!'

'Not for long.' He drew the Browning. 'I'm going to get a knife from the truck, then I'm going in.'

399

Sophia shook her head. 'Do you seriously think you can just stroll in there, get Nina and walk back out without anyone noticing?'

'No. I don't.' He flicked off the automatic's safety. 'Let's start the violence.'

32

Chase crept across the sand, hunched low. He had watched the camp from the dune long enough to get an idea of the routes of any patrols – and their attitudes to their job.

Both were sloppy. There were only two men strolling the perimeter, clearly bored and annoyed at missing out on the loud, macho camaraderie going on round the fires. They didn't expect anyone else to be out here. Even obvious hiding places – behind rocks, among gnarled and scrubby bushes – were being ignored.

Their loss.

Chase dropped into a dip, lying flat as he heard plodding footsteps pass. Raising his head, he saw one of the guards heading away, spending more time looking longingly towards the fires than into the darkness of the desert. Nobody in the direction the man had just come. He crawled along the shallow ditch until he reached a long-dead bush, and lay behind it. The nearest tent was about fifty feet away, a pair of horses tethered beside it.

One of the Janjaweed came round the tent – and walked towards Chase.

Chase very slowly lifted his gun. Even in the low light the man would be able to pick out sudden movements.

He was still advancing, one hand hovering near his holstered pistol. Had he seen him? Chase couldn't imagine how, but he was striding right for the bush. He brought the Browning up, ready to fire.

The man stopped, less than six feet from him, only the twisted branches of the bush between them. He looked down . . .

And opened his fly.

Chase forced himself not to flinch away from the spray as the man unleashed a splattering stream of urine on to the bush. Which just kept coming. How much had the bastard drunk?

Finally, the torrent eased off . . . then started again, a second wind before it finally trickled to nothing. The man made a satisfied sound, then fastened himself up and turned away. By now, the other guard had come round the camp; the two men exchanged a few words before the urinator went back to join his fellows and the patrol trudged on.

Chase disgustedly wiped his face, then peered round the bush. Pisso's little excursion would work to his advantage: he could follow the new set of tracks straight into the camp without the guards wondering where they had come from.

He waited for both men to move out of sight, then quickly crossed the sands to the nearest tent. He was uncomfortably aware as he traversed the open space that Sophia was almost certainly tracking him through the rifle scope – if for any reason she decided that he had outlived his usefulness to her, he could be dead before he even heard the crack of the Lee-Enfield.

But he reached his destination. Glancing round the tent, he saw the circle of Humvees not far away. He also saw reflections of flames in their windows; they were close to one of the Janjaweed campfires.

Giving the horses a wide berth in case his presence spooked them, he hurried to another tent, then into cover between two of the parked technicals. One of them, a Toyota Hilux pickup, was missing its cab. The bent stubs of metal poking up from behind the gaps where the doors had once been suggested it had rolled over at some point, and rather than waste a still-working engine the Janjaweed had simply sawn off the flattened roof. He glanced inside, seeing the key still in the ignition – with a plastic Hello Kitty key ring dangling from it. He almost smiled at the incongruity, then moved to the front of the truck.

The nearest Humvee was not far away. The men round the fire nearby mostly had their backs to him. Nobody in sight in the other direction. He rose to his full height, looking for signs of movement inside the circle of Covenant vehicles—

One of the Janjaweed emerged from a tent – and saw him.

For a moment, neither man moved. Chase's gun hand was hidden from his view behind the Hilux. He slowly raised it . . .

The man stared at him disdainfully, then turned and walked away towards one of the other groups of loud, whooping thugs. Chase realised what had happened. The militiaman had assumed he was one of the Covenant troopers – in the shifting orange half-light, his pale, dusty clothes could easily be mistaken for their camo fatigues.

He held back until the man moved away, then strode to the Humvee. He made sure nobody was watching, then dropped and rolled underneath it. The Covenant men inside the circle wouldn't be as gullible.

He could see one of them approaching. He waited for the patrol to pass, then rolled out from under the Humvee and scurried between two of the domes. He knew where Nina's tent was, and stayed low as he headed for it.

He stopped as he saw another Covenant trooper sitting on a folding chair outside Nina's illuminated tent. A TAR-21 rifle lay across his lap. 'Bollocks,' Chase whispered. There was enough open space between the tents for the soldier to see him and bring up his gun before he could get close enough for a knife attack, and if he fired a shot the entire camp would be alerted.

He needed another way . . .

He backed up, weaving between the tents as he followed a circuitous route to bring him round behind Nina's tent, watching for the men on patrol. One passed; Chase darted to his destination and took out the knife. He wouldn't have long before the other man came round – if he didn't make it inside in time, he would be in plain view. Jabbing the knife through the fabric at the base of the curved frame, he quickly drew it across to cut a slit. When it was wide enough to fit through, he ducked inside—

The heavy base of a battery-powered lamp came within an inch of smashing down on his head.

'Eddie!' squeaked Nina, just barely arresting the blow.

'Shh! Chase hissed frantically, a finger to his lips. He glanced back through the hole, seeing the patrolling trooper walking past.

Nina put down the lamp beside the slit and hugged him. 'Oh my God!' she whispered. 'You found me, I can't believe you found me!'

'I can't believe it either – we didn't expect the Covenant to be out here ahead of us.'

'We?' She made a face. 'Oh, so Sophia's alive too?'

''Fraid so. But what about you? Not that I'm complaining, but why'd they bring you along?'

'They needed me to find Eden, since I was the only one who'd seen the map.'

Chase frowned, noticing a map, several pages of notes and the cylinder she had taken from the frozen city on a folding table. 'And you *told* them?'

'Not . . . exactly,' she answered hesitantly. He stared at her. 'What? I don't know where the damn place is. I was stringing them along!'

'Yeah, and you strung them along to thirty miles from it!'

'It's a big desert!'

'They're a big organisation!'

'Actually, I don't think they are – they've started running out of goons . . . and can we discuss this later? Once I'm, y'know, out of here?'

'Yeah, I think we ought to,' he snapped as he went to the door flap. The zip was slightly down, giving him an eyehole through which he could see the back of the sitting guard's head. He hadn't heard anything – yet.

He moved back to Nina as she gathered her belongings, including the cylinder, and stuffed them into a backpack. 'Okay, once the patrol goes past, go out and hide under one of the Humvees.' He realised she wasn't looking at him, but the door. 'What?' He turned his head to see—

'Shadows!' hissed Nina, just as he realised what was wrong. The lamp was casting their silhouettes like shadow puppets across the fabric.

Two silhouettes.

And he heard the chair creak as the man outside stood and began to tug down the door's zip—

Chase hurled his knife as the Covenant trooper looked inside. The blade stabbed deep into his neck with a wet *thuk*. The man let out a choked, gargling gasp, then toppled through the door. The entire tent shook.

'Get ready to go,' Chase told Nina as he pulled the trooper inside and picked up his assault rifle.

Nina dropped to all fours, lifting the cut fabric and peering through.

She saw a pair of boots. 'Uh-oh.'

The guard outside yanked up the slit, revealing Nina behind it. She looked up at him as he pointed his gun at her face—

Chase fired the TAR-21, sending a sweep of bullets through the tent's wall above Nina. The Covenant soldier screamed and fell backwards.

'Get under the Humvee!' Chase shouted, rushing to the door to locate the other patrolling guard. Nina scrambled through the slit, vaulting the fallen soldier and diving beneath the nearest 4x4. Shouts rose all around, Janjaweed and Covenant responding to the gunfire.

Chase spotted the remaining guard ducking behind a tent. Another burst of fire from the stolen TAR-21, the taut nylon puckering as bullets slashed through it, and the soldier tumbled back into view with several bloody wounds across his chest.

More movement, beyond the Humvees. A group of Janjaweed running to investigate, AK-47s raised.

Chase fired again. Blood puffed from the head of one of the running men, who fell. The others scattered, taking cover behind the armoured vehicles. One militiaman looked round a Humvee and recognised Chase – it was the man who had ignored him earlier, assuming he was a member of the Covenant.

He wasn't ignoring him now, ducking back and yelling. More men were coming. Chase fired a last couple of shots, felling another Janjaweed, then retreated into the tent and exited through the hole.

Sophia heard gunfire from her vantage point atop the dune. She had been tracking Chase through the Lee-Enfield's scope until losing sight of him amongst the tents; now, she swept her sights back and forth, hunting for targets.

She found one. 'Well, well,' she said as she lined up the crosshairs on the white hair. 'Goodbye, Mr Callum . . .'

Callum stood with Vogler and Zamal, the latter engaged in a shouting match with Hamed. Covenant troops had moved to protect their leaders, facing off against the militiamen. 'One of your men shot at us!' the Janjaweed leader yelled in Arabic.

'I don't know what's going on,' Zamal replied, 'but it wasn't us.'

One of Hamed's lieutenants, the man who had seen Chase, ran to them. 'I saw him! It was a white man, like him!' He shoved Callum in the chest, knocking him back a step—

Half the man's head blew apart in an explosive shower that splattered across the crowd of Janjaweed.

For a moment, nobody moved, frozen in shock.

Then the guns on both sides came up.

The Covenant forces, better trained, fired first, taking down eight men in an instant.

But there were more than eight men facing them. AKs blazed, the Janjaweed firing wildly on full auto. Three Covenant troopers went down, spouting blood.

Vogler, Zamal and Callum ran, their remaining soldiers covering them as they fired into the crowd. Hamed dived the other way, using his men as shields. 'Defensive positions!' Vogler yelled. 'Get to the Humvees!'

Sophia humphed at the results of her shot. She tried to track Callum, but the scene below was too chaotic. 'Arse,' she muttered, searching for other targets.

Chase joined Nina beneath the Humvee. 'Not quite what I planned, but it'll do,' he said, hearing the thudding bark of AKs against the crisp chatter of the Covenant's more modern weapons.

'Great, they're fighting each other,' said Nina, 'but we're still right in the middle of them! How are we going to get out of here?'

He looked over at the parked technicals. 'We'll nick one of those.'

More gunfire and shouting from behind. The Covenant survivors were forming a protective circle, using the Humvees for cover. 'If we can get to them.'

Chase saw another Janjaweed run from a tent, carrying a rocket launcher. 'Now's a good time to try!' They crawled out and ran for the pickups.

Shots whipped past as a Janjaweed saw them. Chase grabbed Nina and dived behind a tent as more bullets tore through the tattered material. 'Stay down!' he told her, switching the gun to full auto and twisting to return fire. The spray of bullets carved across the gunman's stomach.

A sound, close by, the clack of a rifle's charging handle. Chase rolled to see another Janjaweed run out from behind the technicals, the fear and confusion on his face replaced by anger as he saw the Englishman.

Chase whipped up his gun, pulled the trigger—

It clicked.

Empty.

The Janjaweed gave Chase a sadistic smile – and a ragged hole blew open in his chest, the impact of a .303 rifle bullet slamming him to the ground.

The echoing crack of the Lee-Enfield reached Chase a moment later. 'Cheers, Soph,' he said, dropping the empty TAR-21 and drawing the Browning. 'Okay, Nina, we—' He saw one of the Janjaweed hoisting a rocket launcher on to his shoulder, lining it up on the Humvees. '— *need to get the fuck down!*'

He threw himself on to her as the rocket-propelled grenade streaked from the tubular launcher.

It slammed into one of the Humvees, the explosion tearing off the wheels and flipping the whole vehicle end over end amongst the Covenant's tents. One trooper was torn apart by shrapnel, another crushed under the massive 4x4. It came to rest with its smouldering underbelly pointing into the air at an angle, nose half buried in the sand.

Whoops and cheers came from the Janjaweed. 'Jesus!' Nina gasped. 'Glad you didn't decide to take *that* truck!'

'Didn't like the colour,' said Chase. He helped her up, then picked his way towards the technicals, pistol at the ready. Gunfire sounded all around as the Janjaweed moved in on the Covenant, bullets clanking off the Humvees' armour. Screams pierced the firelit night.

Chase crouched lower, coming round a half-collapsed tent to reach the technicals. He indicated the one with a key in its ignition. 'That's our ride.'

'It's pointing the wrong way.' The Hilux was facing into the camp, towards the Humvees.

'That's why they invented steering wheels. Come on.'

The militiamen's attention was focused on the Covenant, nobody watching the fringes of the camp. They reached the first technical, a rust-pocked old Ford pickup. Chase moved round the truck's rear, seeing one of the campfires, now abandoned, not far away. Waving Nina on, he headed for the decapitated Hilux—

A Janjaweed jumped from the back of another technical near the fire, carrying a case of RPG rounds. He saw Chase – and yelled a warning, dropping the box and clutching for his AK.

Chase snapped up the Browning and fired, hitting the man's arm and spinning him against one of the petrol cans strapped to the pickup's side. He reeled back, shrieking, before falling on to the fire in an explosion of flying embers. The shrieks became much louder as he leapt back up, clothes and hair aflame.

Half a dozen Janjaweed ran round the first pickup, guns raised.

Chase fired again – not at the militiamen, but at the petrol can.

A jet of fuel spurted from the hole – and splashed over the burning man as he staggered in blind agony. Flames surged back along the gushing petrol—

The can exploded, liquid fire sluicing out. The screaming man was consumed, as was a second, larger can, which blew up and bowled the pickup into the approaching gunmen inside a roiling fireball.

Chase reached the Hilux, shielding his face from the heat, and looked round to see if there were any more Janjaweed posing an immediate threat.

There were. A man on the edge of a group near the Humvees pulled the pin from a grenade, about to throw it at the Hilux—

His wrist was blown in half by one of Sophia's bullets. The severed hand plopped to the ground at his feet, still clutching the grenade . . . which exploded, lacerated Janjaweed flying in all directions.

But there were still plenty more left, and the Covenant troops to worry about as well. Chase looked at the pistol in his hand – then up at the weapon in the pickup's rear bed. It was an old Kalashnikov PK, a light anti-aircraft gun being used here as a heavy machine gun, a belt of ammunition already loaded.

Definitely more firepower than the Browning.

'You drive,' he told Nina as he climbed into the back of the Hilux. 'I'll shoot.'

Nina entered the open cab, searching for the key. 'Cute,' she said, finding Hello Kitty. 'Drive where?'

'I'll tell you when I've shot a big enough hole to fit through!' He swung the gun round towards the Humvees – and pulled the trigger.

The machine gun roared, the recoil threatening to rip the makeshift mount from the pickup's floor. Chase held on and swept the PK back and forth. Every fifth round was a tracer, green lines from the Russian ammunition streaking across the camp like lasers, but Chase was barely able to see them through the staccato flames erupting from the muzzle. The flanks of the Humvees cratered, tyres bursting and dropping them with a crash on to their run-flat steel inserts. The onslaught was enough to shatter even the armoured windows.

A Covenant soldier aimed at him over the bonnet of a Humvee; he hauled the gun round and hosed him with lead. More movement, outside the circle of 4x4s – another group of Janjaweed, realising that the machine gunner wasn't a militiaman. Chase turned the barrage on them before they could act on that realisation, bullet-riddled bodies tumbling.

The ammo belt reached its end, the thunder stopping abruptly. There were more ammunition boxes in the pickup bed, but he didn't have time to reload. Nina was bent almost double in her seat, hands pressed against her ears to protect them from the deafening noise. 'Start the truck!' he said.

'What?'

'I said start the – never mind!' He jumped into the cab and turned the key. 'Go!'

She raised her head. 'Which way?'

'Left.'

Nina released the clutch, the Toyota kicking sand from under its tyres as it lurched into motion. She turned left – only to see a group of Janjaweed running towards them. 'Maybe not,' she said, spinning the wheel to the right.

'I said go *left*!' Chase shouted.

'Yeah, and there's a bunch of guys with guns that way!'

'Have you seen what's *this* way?'

She looked. 'Oh, shit!'

The man who had destroyed the Humvee had reloaded his rocket launcher, lining up a second RPG round – not at the Covenant vehicles, but at the Hilux.

Nina tried to turn, but found nowhere to go, armed men on both sides and the burning wreck of the upturned Humvee directly ahead . . .

'Go straight!' Chase shouted. He shoved his foot down on hers, jamming the accelerator to the floor.

'Eddie, what—'

'*Straight!*' he said, pointing forwards. The Humvee's broad underside rose out of the sand like a ramp.

'Are you out of your—'

The RPG leapt from its launcher, hurtling across the camp.

'— fucking—'

The Toyota hit the inverted Humvee, shot up the slope—

'— *miiiiiind!*'

The grenade slammed into the upturned Humvee just as the Toyota cleared the top of the makeshift ramp. It exploded, blasting the wrecked 4x4 into the air. It cartwheeled out of the swelling fireball to smash down on top of one of the other Humvees, ripping it in half – along with the Covenant trooper in cover against it.

The Hilux landed in a massive spray of sand, demolishing the dome tents as it ploughed through them. Every bone jarred by the impact, Nina looked up – to see another Humvee directly ahead. She yelped and spun the wheel, narrowly missing Vogler as the pickup swerved. Flaming debris rained down behind the Toyota.

She aimed the truck out of the encampment and switched on the headlights. 'Where now?'

'Northwest,' said Chase, pointing. 'Towards Eden.'

Sophia tracked the fleeing Hilux with the rifle, picking out the person at the wheel. Nina.

She lined up the crosshairs, finger hovering over the trigger . . . then lowered the gun. 'Not just yet.'

Movement – much closer than the camp. She snapped her head round to see one of the Janjaweed running towards her. He had heard the rifle shots, worked out her position, and was coming for her.

The Lee-Enfield came back up. 'Not tonight,' Sophia said, looking through the scope again. The man was so close that his face entirely filled her magnified field of view – then suddenly there was a large hole in the middle of it. 'You have a headache.'

She cycled the bolt, then ran back to the Land Cruiser.

Hamed struggled upright. An explosion had knocked him down, his head hitting a rock, but he had fared better than his men. Many had been massacred, the rest fleeing into the desert to escape the Covenant's superior firepower.

He looked round. One of the technicals was barrelling out into the desert. *The woman*, he remembered – he had seen her at the wheel just before the blast threw him to the ground.

Anger surged inside him.

He grabbed an AK from a dead man and hurried to where his horse was tied. It was struggling to break free, frightened by the noise, but he quickly took control and mounted the animal, turning to pursue the retreating tail-lights into the desert.

Vogler bent low and moved along the side of one of the surviving Humvees to reach Zamal. The Arab unleashed a burst of automatic fire, then ducked back into cover. 'What's our status?' he asked.

'The Janjaweed are running,' Vogler told him. 'We've lost at least half our men, though.'

Zamal let out an angry breath. 'Why did they turn on us?'

'They didn't. It was Chase.'

'*What?*'

'He was in that truck – and Wilde was driving it.'

Zamal swore loudly in Arabic. 'If Chase is here, Blackwood must be as well – the sniper!' he realised, looking towards the dark dunes. 'It must have been her.'

Both men turned as Callum ran to them, firing a burst from a SCAR and taking down a man with a rocket launcher. 'Wilde's escaped!'

'Yes, we noticed,' said Vogler acidly. 'With the help of Chase – and your former prisoner.'

'Don't try to pin this on me,' Callum growled. 'I didn't turn this whole goddamn thing into a slaughterhouse. Your psycho friends did that, Zamal.'

Zamal's face tightened, but Vogler interrupted before he could reply. 'We need to secure this situation. How many Janjaweed are left?'

'Forget the Janjaweed, we need to get after Wilde,' Callum said. 'Are the Humvees still driveable?'

Vogler looked at the vehicle they were crouched behind. Its bodywork was scarred with bullet holes, windows cracked and broken, and a tyre had been blown out. 'Two destroyed, and the rest all damaged. Repairable, but I doubt we will be able to leave before morning.'

'They could be fifty kilometres away by then,' said Zamal. 'We'll never find them.'

'I'll take care of that,' said Callum. 'Just find me a satellite phone.'

'Slow down, slow down!' Chase yelped as the Hilux crested a rise and briefly took off, ploughing back with a suspension-straining crash.

'Are you crazy?' said Nina, grinding the pickup into a lower gear to keep up its speed. 'I want to get as far away from them as possible!'

'We need to wait for Sophia.' He looked back. A pair of headlights was bounding across the desert towards them – not from the Janjaweed camp, but from the surrounding dunes. Sophia, in the Land Cruiser.

'Do we really?'

'Yeah, really. She's got an extra gun, if nothing else.'

'Right, and how long before it's pointing at us?'

'Not as soon as that one,' Chase said with alarm, seeing something pursuing them, silhouetted against the fires. A man on a horse, AK-47 on his back.

Catching up fast.

Chase climbed into the cargo bed. 'Okay, forget slowing down, go faster!' He found one of the ammo boxes and pulled out the heavy belt of bullets. A glance behind: the horseman was still coming, but had veered to one side, moving to intercept the approaching Land Cruiser.

Sophia was slammed forward as the Land Cruiser hit another bump. The elderly vehicle only had a lap belt rather than a full seatbelt, and a threadbare one at that. She spun the wheel to straighten out, aiming for the tail-lights ahead. Nina was charging through the desert like a maniac, far too fast for the terrain.

But she wasn't the only one.

Movement in her peripheral vision – a man on horseback galloping parallel to the Land Cruiser, a hundred feet away and closing as he swung an AK from his back and aimed it at her.

She tried to swerve away, but too late.

Only a few bullets from the wild spray of fire hit her vehicle – but one found a vital spot. The front tyre blew out, the wheel hub digging into the sand. The Land Cruiser skidded to a stop in a huge cloud of dust, almost rolling over before dropping heavily back on to its remaining three wheels.

Dazed, Sophia sat up – to see the horseman flash through her headlight beams, still pursuing the other truck.

★

'Shit!' said Chase as he saw Sophia's 4x4 slew to a halt. The Janjaweed rider was still gaining – and now had his gun at the ready.

He struggled to load the machine gun, having to rely almost entirely on touch to figure out the unfamiliar mechanism in the dark. He managed to open the ammo feed's cover, hinging it up and trying to load the first round—

The AK-47 spat fire. A bullet hissed past Chase's head; he dropped, the ammo belt chinking down beside him as more shots hit the back of the Hilux. Nina ducked in her seat.

The gunfire stopped. Chase risked a look over the tailgate. The rider was a blood-red demon in the rear lights. He shouldered the AK – out of ammo.

But he had another weapon.

A machete. He raised the long, brutal blade high like a sword.

Chase retrieved the ammo belt and jumped back up to reload the machine gun, glancing at Nina to check she hadn't been hit. She was only just sitting up . . .

And hadn't seen what was rushing at them in the headlights.

'Look out!' he started to shout – but the Hilux had already reached the edge of the ditch.

The empty stream bed was shallow, the steep bank no more than eighteen inches deep – but it was enough to tip the Toyota over as its right wheels dropped into the depression. Nina braked hard and tried to stop the truck overturning . . .

Too late.

Chase threw himself out of the cargo bed as the truck rolled, landing hard in dry stream. The pickup hit the far bank and crashed to a standstill on its side.

He crawled towards it. Only one headlight was still working. No sign of Nina. He stood—

And was smashed to the ground as something huge and heavy hit him from behind.

Hamed pulled the reins to slow his horse and wheel round for another attack, preparing to trample Chase into the sand.

Chase dived into the ditch as the horse thundered at him, then scrambled clumsily back to his feet. The rider turned again, his horse jumping down into the red-lit arena of the stream bed.

They faced each other for a moment. Then the Janjaweed leader extended his arm, pointing his machete at Chase – and spurred the horse into a charge.

Chase grabbed for the Browning. It wasn't there – he had lost it when he jumped from the truck. He turned and ran for the pickup, the pounding hooves closing fast, almost on him.

A swish—

Pure instinct made him dive and roll as the machete swept over his head. Hamed pulled up. The horse turned and reared, front legs swiping at Chase. He threw up his arms to protect his head, taking a savage kick and falling on his back.

Hamed jumped from the horse, slashing the machete at Chase. He rolled as the blade smacked down where his shoulder had just been. Another roll, springing up as the blade hacked again, narrowly missing his legs.

Behind Hamed he saw Nina crawling from the Hilux's open cab. The machine gun was pointing towards him. If she could reach it—

No good. It wasn't loaded, the ammo belt a coiled snake in the ditch.

Hamed advanced, jabbing the machete. Chase ducked back, the two men slowly circling.

Nina groaned, catching the Janjaweed leader's attention. He leered. Chase had no doubt what his intentions were: kill him, then . . .

'No you fucking don't,' he growled. Hamed might not have understood the words, but still knew what Chase was saying, and grinned malevolently as he lunged. Chase dodged the heavy blade as it whipped past. He tried to knock it from the Janjaweed's hand, but Hamed anticipated the move and twisted the machete to rip through his sleeve, the blade's ragged edge drawing blood. Chase jerked away, realising too late that the horse was right behind him.

Hamed shouted a command. The horse reared again, knocking Chase down.

The Janjaweed leader moved in for the kill, raising the machete high to cleave it down through Chase's spine—

The tip of the ammo belt lashed across Hamed's face as Nina swung it, tearing bloody gashes in his skin. He staggered back.

Chase jumped up. 'Here!' Nina tossed him the belt. He caught one end with his left hand, whirling it – and snagging it round Hamed's machete arm. He cracked the belt like a whip. Hamed's arm shot up, the machete flying out of his hand.

Chase yanked hard, pulling Hamed towards him – and delivering a nose-crushing punch.

The Janjaweed leader reeled, but didn't fall, held up by the ammo belt as Chase caught the falling machete with his right hand . . .

And swung it.

Hamed's body collapsed, blood squirting from the stump of its neck. His head bounced away down the stream bed, rolling to a stop – at Sophia's feet. She eyed it. 'This is no time for football, Eddie.'

Chase didn't reply, instead going to Nina. 'You okay?'

'I think so . . .' She saw the cut on his arm. 'What about you?'

'It's not as bad as it looks. Just hope he washed his machete after he used it last.' He crouched and unwound the ammo belt from Hamed's arm.

Sophia reached them, the rifle over one shoulder, a backpack on the other. After exchanging looks of mutual loathing with Nina, she went to the horse, which had taken its owner's death with a complete lack of concern, and patted the animal's neck. 'You found another ride, then. Although it might be a little cramped for three of us.'

'Dobbin wasn't what I had in mind. Give me a hand.' He spotted and retrieved the Browning, then went to the pickup to push it back on to its wheels. The two women joined him; after a few seconds of effort, it toppled back down. He dropped the ammo belt into the rear bed, tossing other spilled items after it, then hopped into the cab and turned the key. To his surprise, the engine started first time. 'Wow, these things really *are* indestructible.'

Sophia held up the bubble compass from the Land Cruiser as she and Nina climbed aboard. 'And I've got the perfect dashboard accessory.' She looked northwest. 'That way.'

'The gang's all here,' Nina said sarcastically, giving Chase a pointedly questioning glare when she realised Sophia was wearing his leather jacket. He took it back, to Sophia's annoyance, and put it on.

'Okay, then,' he said. 'Next stop . . . the Garden of Eden.'

33

They drove through the night, Chase guiding the Hilux across the desert. There was no sign of pursuit, by either the Janjaweed or the Covenant. Even so, the going was slow, with treacherous terrain and only one working headlight to guide them. More than once, they had to dig the truck out when it became bogged in soft sand.

The hours passed, Nina managing to doze fitfully despite the bumpy ride. By the time Chase was forced to stop to refuel from one of the battered cans in the rear bed, the eastern sky had started to brighten. At this low latitude, sunrise came quickly.

'Okay,' said Chase, throwing the empty can back into the truck and waking Nina with a start, 'now we can see, let's work out where we are.' He surveyed the surrounding desert for landmarks. 'Give me the rifle.'

Sophia handed him the Lee-Enfield. He peered through the scope, scanning the horizon. Distant shapes resolved themselves into flat-topped islands of stone rising above the sands. 'Okay, I see one, two, three mesas.'

'Let me see those,' said Nina, taking the photo blow-ups of the Antarctic map from Sophia. The word that had been pronounced as 'Eden' on the ancient cylinder lay at the beginning of the Veteres' long trail . . . between three trapezoidal symbols. Truncated mountains. 'You think . . . ?'

Sophia examined the modern map. 'It matches the terrain. Three bluffs – and these dry riverbeds. Four of them.'

Nina looked more closely. Four faint lines wound outwards from the centre. 'Eddie, how far away are they?'

'Five or six miles,' said Chase. 'It shouldn't take too long to get there.' He put down the rifle, regarded the machine gun for a moment, then started to reload it. 'Just in case,' he told Nina. 'The Covenant'll probably be able to fix some of those Humvees.'

'But they won't be able to follow us, will they?' She looked back. The desert wind was already scouring away their tyre tracks.

Chase's expression didn't reassure her. 'Like I said, just in case.' He chambered the first round, then climbed back into the driver's seat and restarted the engine.

'Of course, Nina,' said Sophia as they set off, 'we wouldn't have to worry about the Covenant if you hadn't teamed up with them in the first place.'

'I didn't "team up with them",' Nina protested. 'I was their damn prisoner, I didn't have any say in the matter!'

'All the same, they didn't have the map.' She held up one of the photos. 'Without this, you could have told them Eden was in Ethiopia, or Egypt, or bloody Timbuktu, and they couldn't have contradicted you. But no, you not only bring them to Sudan, but you even bring them to the right *part* of Sudan! What did they do, offer you a deal?'

'All right, that's enough,' said Chase, giving Sophia a warning look. She made a dismissive sound and turned away. His gaze moved to Nina, holding on her for slightly too long before returning to the landscape ahead.

'What?' Nina said defensively, correctly guessing what he was thinking. 'I *didn't* make a deal, not like that. "Tell us what we want to know or we'll kill you" isn't really a deal.'

'But you still brought 'em here.'

'I told you last night, I didn't have much choice. What was I going to do, say no and get killed?'

'But why didn't you give them the wrong location?' Chase asked.

'Because – because I . . . Look, they were going to *kill* me, all right?' Nina drew her arms tightly around herself. 'I thought that once we were out here, I might be able to get away.'

'And then find Eden all on your own,' Sophia said. 'Since you conveniently brought them right to its doorstep. You used your friends, then you used your *enemies* to get here. You really are quite the little glory-hound, aren't you?'

'Jesus, shut up!' snapped Chase. 'Fucking non-stop snideyness, it's like still being married to you!'

Sophia frowned, but fell silent. Nobody spoke for several seconds.

'She's got a point, though,' Chase said quietly.

Nina's response was louder. *'What?'*

'I know you get obsessive about archaeology, but Christ, this is taking it to a new level! You've never voluntarily worked with people who want to kill you,' a glance at Sophia, 'to find something before. And I know Matt's a soft touch, but you still walked all over him to get to Antarctica. He was lucky to get out of there alive – and Bandra and that other guy, David, didn't.'

'You're blaming me for their deaths?' asked Nina angrily.

'No, the Covenant killed them.'

'But you think it was my fault, right?'

'I think this is a side of you I hadn't seen before, is what I think,' snapped Chase. 'Remember on the *Pianosa*, when I asked you how far you were willing to go for this stuff?' He looked at her. 'Looks like now I know.' Nina couldn't meet his eyes.

She *hadn't* made a deal with the Covenant, she told herself. She had just done what she had to in order to stay alive.

Hadn't she?

There was no conversation for the rest of the drive. The bluffs drew closer. Still no sign of pursuit. The Hilux bumped over the last dunes surrounding the mesas to find traction on harder, stonier ground, the landscape already shimmering as the sun heated it.

Nina looked up. The steep sides of the first mesa rose a couple of hundred feet above the surrounding desert, the others slightly higher. But the plain between them was devoid of anything but rocks.

'So is this it?' Chase asked, turning the Toyota towards the plain's centre. 'Not much of a garden spot.'

'Not now, but it would have been, over a hundred thousand years ago,' said Nina. 'Even the Sahara was green once.' But the area was so desolate it was hard to imagine *anything* growing here, never mind a garden worthy of God himself.

She looked at the photograph again. The text for 'Eden' was, she noticed, closest to the northernmost of the huge rocky outcroppings. 'Head for that one,' she said, pointing.

They drove across the plain, the sun beating down. The whole place seemed utterly lifeless . . . until Nina noticed a lone bird above the mesa ahead. It glided in a lazy circle, then dropped out of sight behind the flat summit. She waited for it to reappear, but it didn't.

The technical jolted. 'Sorry,' said Chase, slowing as the Toyota descended a slope. 'I think we found one of your riverbeds, though.'

'It's only narrow,' said Sophia, speaking for the first time since Chase had snapped at her. 'We must be near its source.'

'Yeah, but where is it?' Nina wondered. The shallow channel led to the rising cliff walls of the bluff . . . and stopped abruptly at its base.

'Must have been a spring here once,' said Chase, bringing the technical to a stop near the cliff and climbing out. Nina and Sophia followed, gazing up at the wall of grey and orange stone.

'Maybe the Garden of Eden was on *top* of the mesa,' Sophia suggested. 'It would have been a good defensive position, especially if they were worried about animal attacks.'

'Maybe,' Nina replied, but the idea didn't feel right. Shading her eyes, she slowly turned to take in the plain, the other mesas, the surrounding desert . . .

Something in the sky, a pale dot. 'Is that a plane?'

Chase whirled. 'Where?'

'There.' She pointed.

Chase ran back to the pickup and took out the rifle. 'What is it?' Sophia asked as he stared through the telescopic sights.

His reply, when it came, was a horrified whisper. 'Buggeration . . .'

Nina grimaced. 'If the next words I hear are "and fuckery", I'm going to be very unhappy.'

'And fuckery,' Chase finished. 'It's a fucking Reaper!'

'That . . . doesn't sound good.'

'It's not. You know on the news, when the White House or the Pentagon show those videos of missiles zooming right at some terrorist and flying down his throat before they explode?'

'Yes?'

He stabbed a finger at the approaching grey spot. 'That's what fires the missiles!'

Nina gawped at him. 'It's an *American* plane? Where did it come from?'

'There's a US Air Force base across the border in Uganda, at Entebbe. Either that, or a carrier in the Red Sea.' He shouldered the rifle and picked up the rucksack, tossing it to Nina. 'Doesn't matter – it's here, and in about five seconds some nerd in Las Vegas is going to try to blow us up!'

'What do you mean, Las—' Nina began, but was cut off as Chase hustled her away from the technical, Sophia hurrying after them. A dot detached itself from the Reaper and fell away – then lanced towards them at the head of a line of smoke.

An AGM-114 Hellfire missile, homing in at almost a thousand miles an hour.

'*Run!*' Chase yelled, but Nina and Sophia were already racing away from the pickup as the Hellfire streaked across the plain and arced down to its target—

The missile struck, nine kilograms of high explosive detonating on impact to gouge a crater twenty feet across out of the rock and sand. The front half of the Hilux disintegrated in a storm of torn metal, the remains of the pickup cartwheeling through the air to smash against the cliff wall. A shockwave of dust and stones tore past the trio as they dived to the ground.

Nina raised her head. What was left of the Toyota slid to the foot of the slope on its one remaining wheel, the machine gun nodding on its bent pole. 'Son of a bitch!'

'Get up,' Chase said, already on his feet. 'It'll fire another one in a minute.'

'How many missiles does it carry?' Sophia asked.

'Fourteen.'

'*Fourteen?*' Nina gasped, looking nervously at the Reaper. It was still heading for them, less than two miles away.

'Yeah – and now it's taken out the truck, it'll probably switch to an anti-personnel warhead to take out *us*.' No cover on the plain, and against the steep face of the mesa the Reaper's targeting laser would pin them like butterflies on a board . . .

'Split up,' he ordered. 'Nina, go that way; Soph, go the other way.'

'What about you?' Nina asked.

He pointed at the mangled remains of the technical. 'That way. Go on, run!'

Nina was about to object, but Sophia was already sprinting away. Chase shot Nina a 'Move it!' look, then ran for the wreck. Out of options, Nina took off.

Chase rushed through the field of blackened debris, glancing at the closing Reaper. The aircraft was a remote-controlled drone, its operator on the other side of the world in Nevada, watching on a screen. Warfare as videogame.

But unlike in a game, the targets could shoot back.

He reached the smouldering back end of the technical and swung the Kalashnikov round. The Reaper's operator would already have seen him reach the gun, making him an immediate threat. Another Hellfire would be launched any moment—

Chase took aim – and pulled the trigger.

The PK still worked, a testament to its rugged design. Bullets roared from the barrel, the green lines of tracers shrinking to burning dots as they arced into the sky. He adjusted his aim, trying to 'walk' the tracers on to the Reaper—

Hellfire!

It dropped from beneath one of the long, slender wings, rocket motor flaring.

The tracers closed on the aircraft. Chase kept firing, knowing he had only seconds before the missile hit. Almost out of ammo, the last section of the belt clattering through the feed—

Smoke puffed from the Reaper's fuselage.

A hit!

Chase didn't know how much damage he had caused, and wasn't going to stand and watch. Instead he jumped out and raced along the foot of the cliff, seeing a boulder part buried in the scree.

He flung himself over it.

The missile hit the remains of the technical, striking with such force that it punched straight through the wreck and into the cliff face before exploding. A huge eruption of sand and rock burst outwards, shattered stone smashing down in the dry stream bed.

The boulder had shielded Chase from the worst of the blast, but the shockwave had still felt like being hit by a bus. He groaned, squinting up at the sky. The missile's smoke trail led back to its starting point, the Reaper . . .

It was no longer there.

'Yes!' he gasped triumphantly, seeing the crippled robot aircraft spiralling towards the distant dunes. The orange flash of a fuel explosion, a rising pillar of oily black smoke . . . and, after a few seconds, a thump as the sound of the detonation finally reached him.

Sophia and Nina came back to him, Nina limping. 'Are you okay?' she asked.

'Just about,' he grunted, finding several new sources of pain across his battered body. 'But the Blue Oyster Cult were right.'

'Let me guess,' said Sophia tiredly. 'Don't fear the Reaper.'

'Tchah! You spoiled my joke.' He turned to Nina. 'How's your leg?'

'Sore. But I can still walk on it.'

'That's good,' Sophia said, gloomily regarding one of the Toyota's burning tyres, 'because you're going to have to.'

'We'll nick a new truck from the Covenant,' said Chase.

'What do you mean?'

'Callum must have called for that Reaper to look for us – they probably told the pilot we were high-ranking terrorists or some bullshit to justify crossing into Sudanese airspace. But it found us, which means they'll have told Callum where we are. The Covenant'll be on their way.'

Sophia swept a hand through her blonde hair. 'Marvellous. But at least they won't have any more luck at finding Eden than we have.'

'I'm not so sure,' Nina said quietly. Chase and Sophia turned to see what she was looking at.

'Bloody hell,' they said in unison.

The missile hadn't merely blown a crater out of the side of the mesa. It had blown a hole. Through the drifting dust and smoke, a cave entrance was now visible.

'There *was* a spring here once,' Chase realised. The dry stream bed began its journey across the desert directly beneath the opening. 'It came out of there. But . . .'

'Somebody blocked it up,' Nina finished. A simple landslide would have piled debris outwards from the cliff, but the remaining rocks covering the entrance were *inside* the cave mouth. They had been deliberately placed to seal it.

'From the outside – or the inside?' wondered Sophia.

Nina started towards the entrance, the pain in her leg forgotten. 'Let's find out.'

'If there isn't another way out, we'll be trapped in there when the Covenant arrive,' Chase pointed out.

'You'd rather wait for them out here?' She climbed over strewn rocks to the opening. It was roughly five feet across and four high, dusty darkness beyond. 'Is there a flashlight in that pack?'

Sophia produced a torch and tossed it to Nina. She caught it and switched it on, leaning through the opening. The drifting dust made it difficult to see, but beyond the broken rubble the cave went back into the rock for some distance.

Not a cave. The shape was too regular. A *tunnel* . . .

'It's man-made,' she announced, excited. She bent to duck through the hole. 'Come on, there's a way through!'

'Wait,' Chase called, but she had already scrambled inside. 'Oh, for fuck's sake.'

By the time he reached the opening, Nina was already picking her way down the heaped debris on the other side. 'Check it out,' she said, shining her light round the tunnel. It was oval in cross-section, taller than it was wide, some twelve feet at its broadest.

While the walls had clearly been carved by hand, it had been done to widen an existing channel, the floor grooved by once-flowing water. She directed the beam down the tunnel, which curved away out of sight. 'It must go right into the mesa.'

Chase traversed the opening, Sophia following, and jogged after Nina as she started down the tunnel. 'Slow down, will you? You don't know what's down there.'

'And I won't until I see for myself, will I?'

'You won't see anything if a big fucking rock falls on your head,' he chided. 'You're so mad keen to find the Garden of Eden that you're rushing things.'

She waved her hands in a mixture of enthusiasm and exasperation. 'That's because it's . . . it's the *Garden of frickin' Eden*, Eddie! If it's real, if it's down that tunnel, then it changes *everything*! And I'll have found it!'

'*We'll* have found it,' said Sophia, giving Chase a pointed look.

'All right, *we'll* have found it, whatever! But this is our only chance to reach it before the Covenant. Unless you want to block up that hole behind us?' She read his expression. 'Yeah, I thought not. So come on!' She set off again.

Chase blew out a long, frustrated breath. 'Don't look at me,' said Sophia as she strode past. 'You're the one who wants to marry her.'

The remaining dust soon cleared, the tunnel curving back and forth as they progressed along it. The daylight from the entrance faded. But the torch beam wasn't the only light . . .

Nina stopped, Chase and Sophia flanking her. She switched off the flashlight. Another source of illumination became clear – ahead. 'It's daylight,' she whispered. 'And listen – can you hear something?'

Chase strained to pick anything out over the residual ringing in his ears from the two missile explosions, but Sophia cocked her head curiously. 'It sounds like running water.'

'In the middle of a desert?' said Chase dubiously. But now he could hear it too.

Nina relit the torch. 'It's not far away.' She set off again, quickly stepping up to a jog in her eagerness to see what lay ahead. Chase had little choice but to keep pace.

They rounded another curve in the tunnel . . . and emerged into a vastly larger space, stopping in sheer amazement at the sight that greeted them.

'My God,' Nina whispered. 'We found it.'

34

The Garden of Eden

'Jesus,' said Chase. 'This can't be real. Can it?'

'It's real,' Nina replied, awed. 'It's really real.'

The cavern was huge, a massive space within the mesa, the walls sloping inwards to form almost a dome of rock overhead. But it was not complete; there were holes in the stone ceiling through which sunlight poured, great beams slanting down to illuminate the ground below.

To give *life* to the ground below. The tunnel emerged by a slight rise in the southwestern corner, giving them a view across the colossal chamber – and the lush green jungle filling it. Steam rose from the trees where sunlight touched the leaves, swirling as it rose . . . to condense on the rocky ceiling and drip back down on to the vegetation below. The source of all the water was easy to see, a large lake occupying most of the cavern's southeastern corner, streams leading from it. The sound of running water came from a small waterfall dropping into a giant chasm that split the entire chamber seemingly in two, just east of their vantage point.

Sophia arrived behind them, for a moment also overcome by the incredible sight. 'That's . . . that's incredible.'

'You're not kidding,' said Chase. He walked to the edge of the chasm, looking down into it. And down. And *down*. The bottom was out of sight, lost in darkness. Only the distant rumble of churning water told him that there was any end to the fall. His gaze tracked along the opposite edge of the jagged canyon, a great tear in the ground that had even ripped a hole in the chamber's southern wall. It narrowed as it cut through the jungle to the north, but the tree cover meant he couldn't see if it extended all the way to the far wall.

Nina's attention had been seized by something rising above the trees at the cavern's eastern side, however. 'Oh, my God . . . Eddie, give me the gun.'

'What, you going to shoot something?'

'I want to *see* it.' She took the Lee-Enfield and looked through the sights at the shape in the far-off shadows.

A face stared back at her.

She stiffened in momentary surprise before the object in the cross hairs resolved itself. It was another statue, a representation of the Veteres' god, like the one they had seen in Antarctica. Although it was unmistakably the same figure, the design of the giant sculpture was different, in some odd way simultaneously more primitive yet more refined. More naturalistic. Yet for all that, the shape of the skull and the facial features were just as elongated and stylised as on the statues in the frozen city.

Beyond the statue was a plateau, the top of a domed structure just visible on it. She moved the sights down, seeing that the statue had one hand held out, palm up as if scattering seeds, just like its counterpart at the South Pole. This one, however, was not within a temple – instead a circular wall, reaching almost to the lake's shore, surrounded its feet.

'It's another statue of their god,' she told Chase and Sophia, passing him the rifle so he could see for himself. 'Looks even bigger than the one in Antarctica.'

'The original?' Sophia suggested.

'Could be. And if it's anything like the other one, there might be another library there – another Tree of Knowledge.'

'Of Good and Evil,' Sophia added. 'We're in the right place, after all. Watch out for snakes.'

Nina gazed across the jungle at the towering statue. 'We need to get over there.'

Chase lowered the gun, pointing it into the chasm. 'Bit of a jump.'

'Maybe it's narrow enough to cross further along. Come on.' She walked down the small rise into the dry stream bed, which was abruptly truncated by the ravine, almost directly across from the waterfall. 'Must have been a pretty big earthquake to cause a rift that deep.'

Ahead, several large boulders lay on the rocky ground, moss clinging to their sunward sides. Chase looked up. Directly overhead was a hole in the ceiling. 'Probably made that too.' The other holes above ranged from car-sized to easily large enough to fit a helicopter, some sections of the roof Swiss-cheesed with openings. 'One more big shake and the entire ceiling'll come down.'

'It's survived for well over a hundred thousand years,' said Nina. 'Why would it collapse now?'

'Because we're here? Stuff does have sort of a habit of going *buh-koom* around you.'

'That's *so* not true,' Nina said, annoyed. 'It only happens when idiots deliberately try to destroy things.'

Sophia cleared her throat. 'Far be it from me to name the person who brought down the roof of the Tomb of Hercules . . .'

'Oh, shut up.' They continued, reaching the edge of the jungle. Condensation pattered down as they moved into it. 'It's incredible,' said Nina, scientific wonder quickly overcoming her irritation. 'A perfectly balanced ecosystem.' She stopped, turning to the shafts of sunlight. 'Look how the vegetation's densest underneath the sun's path during the day. Enough light gets in to sustain photosynthesis.' They moved on through the thinner vegetation along the edge of the chasm.

The ravine narrowed as they progressed. On the far side, another large boulder had dropped from the ceiling, a great wedge of stone half buried in the earth and protruding out over the incalculable fall below. 'Ay up, that might be handy,' said Chase, pointing ahead. A tree had fallen, its trunk spanning the gap.

'It looks a bit slippery,' Nina noted dubiously as they reached it. The wood was slick with moisture and entwined with creepers.

Chase examined the broken end of the log, then the ground beneath it, before testing the wood with his foot. 'Feels solid.'

'You first, then,' Sophia said.

Chase gave her a sarcastic look, then climbed on to the log. He began to walk across, arms outstretched for balance, then thought better of it and dropped to all fours, progressing at a slower – but safer – crawl. 'You were right,' he called from the other side. 'It is a bit slippy. Come on over.'

Nina still didn't like the look of it. 'Y'know, I might see if there's a longer way round instead.'

'It's fine. Trust me.'

Nina unwillingly got on to the log. The wood was damp, the bark squishing under her hands. But if it could support Chase's weight, then . . . 'Okay,' she said to herself, eyes fixed on the trunk ahead rather than the vertiginous drop to either side. 'It's safe. It's just like a bridge.' She started across. 'A wet, rotten, really narrow bridge . . .'

She edged along, dislodging patches of moss as she went – and trying not to watch them tumble into the darkness below. Instead she concentrated on the log, and Chase's encouraging face at its far end. She could feel the wood bowing beneath her, but kept moving, advancing inch by inch, until she reached the other side.

'Oh, thank God,' she said, hopping back on to solid ground with relief.

Chase patted her shoulder. 'Told you it'd be fine. Okay, Soph?'

Nina looked round as Sophia began to cross the log. As well as the constant splash of the waterfall, she heard another sound, a rustling in the treetops. Birds, she realised, flitting through the foliage. She saw one circling near the ceiling, soaring through a hole into the sunlight before swooping back down into another. 'Look at those birds,' she said to Chase. 'I wonder if they live here permanently, or found it while they were migrating?'

'So long as they don't crap on my head, I'm not that bothered,' Chase replied. 'How you doing, Soph?'

'Fine,' Sophia replied. 'I don't know why Nina was so scared.' She put one hand on the stump of a broken branch for support – and it snapped with a wet crack.

She lurched sideways. Her leg slithered off the log in a shower of mouldering bark, other hand clawing for grip as she fell—

Her fingers caught a knot of creepers, the thinner vines stretching and snapping as she swung from the makeshift bridge.

Chase ran to the edge of the chasm, gripping one of the log's exposed roots and stretching an arm towards her. She struggled to bring up her free hand, but couldn't quite reach. 'Eddie!' she cried. 'I'm slipping!'

'Hang on!' Chase climbed on to the log. He gripped her wrist and tried to pull her up, but in his kneeling position couldn't get enough leverage. 'Nina, help me!'

She hesitated, then ran to him. 'What do you want me to do?'

'Hold that root,' he said. 'Then grab my arm so I can pull her up!'

Nina did so. The root creaked unsettlingly when she pulled it. Rotten. 'I don't think it'll hold!'

'It'll have to! Come on!'

She gripped it, reaching out with her other arm to Chase. Their hands closed tightly. Chase took Sophia's weight, Nina his as he strained to lift her. More of the knotted vines snapped, Sophia's handhold breaking away—

Nina pulled, groaning at the strain on her shoulder muscles. The root groaned too – but held. Chase got to his feet, hauling Sophia up with him. She found purchase with one boot and leapt to the safety of the cliff edge, Chase jumping after her. 'Oh, God!' she gasped, holding him tightly as she fought for breath. 'Oh, thank you, thank you . . .'

'Ahem,' said Nina, deciding their clinch had gone on long enough. Chase got the hint and pushed Sophia away.

'And thank you too. I suppose,' Sophia said to Nina, the words sticking distastefully in her mouth.

'You're *welcome*,' Nina replied, taking the 'compliment' in kind. 'Come on, let's get moving.'

She set off in the direction of the statue. Chase caught up. 'Can't *believe* I just saved her life,' Nina muttered.

'I can,' said Chase. 'Because you're not her.'

'Y'know, that might be the nicest thing you've ever said to me.'

Chase let out a muted laugh, then picked up a stick and swatted aside plants as they moved deeper into the strange little jungle. After walking for some time, at one point splashing across a stream, they were directly beneath one of the largest openings in the ceiling. The varieties and colours of the vegetation multiplied in the daylight, various fruits and berries ripening on the trees. 'It really is beautiful, isn't it?' Nina said, pausing to smell an unfamiliar purple flower. 'I can see why it was passed down through memory as a paradise.'

'Prefer something a bit more open, myself,' said Chase. 'You know, with actual sky rather than just little patches of it overhead . . .' He tailed off.

Nina picked up on his suddenly cautious stance. 'What is it?'

Chase used the stick to bend back the branches of a bush. 'There's something here.'

Beyond the bush were the remains of a building, a tumbledown ruin barely standing beneath layers of vines and lichen. 'It's brick,' she said. 'Like the other Veteres structures.'

'It's the wrong shape,' said Sophia. 'It's not round, it's square.' Nina saw she was right; what was left of the walls displayed right-angled corners. 'And the bricks have just been stacked on top of each other – they're barely even straight.'

'Cowboys,' joked Chase.

Nina moved past the crumbled walls, seeing more ruins amongst the plants. 'There's a curved wall, though – or what's left of one.' The reason struck her. 'Of course! It's like the site we found in Indonesia – the original Veteres structures were scavenged for materials by later settlers. They didn't have the skills to build something as complex as a dome, so they used the bricks to make something simpler. That means someone was here *after* the Veteres left. But who?'

'Who was in the Garden of Eden after Adam and Eve?' asked Chase.

'Nobody,' Nina told him. 'They were banished – and God made sure they wouldn't come back by setting cherubim armed with flaming swords to guard it.'

Chase raised an eyebrow. 'Flaming swords? Sounds familiar.'

'Mm-hmm.'

'Flaming swords?' Sophia asked. 'Am I missing something?'

'Excalibur glowed under certain conditions because of earth energy,' Nina explained. 'An early culture could easily have interpreted it as a kind of fire.' She gazed at the ruins. 'This must have been part of the Veteres settlement – where they lived. Where their civilisation started.'

'So why did they leave?' asked Chase. 'They didn't just expand across the world – they upped sticks and completely left this place behind.'

'They were driven out,' Nina remembered. 'By "beasts".'

He shook his head. 'I don't get it. They must have been pretty advanced to have built all the stuff we've seen – so why couldn't they master pointy stick technology and just kill these beasts? I mean, lions and tigers and bears—'

'Oh, my.'

'— are nasty predators, but they didn't have a chance in the long run 'cause of the whole "opposable thumbs, motherfuckers!" thing.' He raised his hands, thumbs aloft.

'Charmingly put, as ever,' said Sophia. 'But you have a point – tools and weapons are great equalisers. Unless the beasts also had opposable thumbs, of course.'

'The inscriptions did say that the Veteres tried to train the beasts, though,' said Nina. 'To give them the gift of knowledge. Maybe not a great idea to teach a gorilla how to use a spear.'

'Gorillas didn't build this,' Sophia said, pointing at the wall. 'And they didn't build that giant statue, either.'

'You're right.' Nina looked to the eastern wall. 'If the answers are anywhere, that's where they'll be.'

The three Humvees, their black flanks pock-marked by bullet impacts, stopped near the base of the mesa.

Callum, riding in the lead vehicle with Vogler, checked the truck's GPS. 'We're at the position where the missiles hit.'

'You didn't need the GPS to know that,' said Vogler. Ahead, a crater had been gouged out of the ground, mangled metal scattered round it. A short distance away, more debris surrounded another hole – one that went much deeper into the towering mass of stone than anything a missile could have caused. 'This is it. We've found Eden.'

'In there?' Callum said sceptically.

Vogler didn't reply, instead climbing out and regarding the surroundings. The only sound was the wind, the plain desolate and lifeless. It didn't seem possible that the end of their quest could be here. But then, he had never imagined that his missions for the Covenant would take him to a city frozen beneath the Antarctic ice either.

The doors of the other Humvees opened. Zamal emerged first, mood as black as ever. 'No bodies? So much for the wonders of UCAVs.' He made a disapproving sound, regarding Callum caustically. 'War by remote control, using robots to do your killing? A cowardly way to fight. A true warrior of Allah looks his enemies in the eye.' Issuing orders to his men, he started for the cave entrance.

'Where are you going?' Vogler called.

Zamal paused as the men went to the hole. 'To look my enemies in the eye.'

'We should wait for Ribbsley – he'll be here in less than an hour.'

'You should know by now, Killian,' Zamal said with a thin smile, 'I am not a patient man.'

One of his men reported that there was a wider tunnel behind the opening. 'Wide enough to fit the Humvees?' Vogler asked. The trooper nodded. 'We should clear it. We don't know what's in there – they might be useful.'

'I *do* know what's in there,' Zamal countered. 'Wilde, Chase and Blackwood. It is time for them to die.'

'We had an arrangement with Dr Wilde.'

'Which was cancelled the moment she betrayed us. *You* can wait for Ribbsley,' he said, turning away. '*I* am going to carry out the Covenant's purpose – to kill anyone who threatens our faith.' He unslung his rifle and gave Vogler an even colder smile as he prepared to climb through the opening. 'God is great.'

★

Nina, Chase and Sophia emerged from the jungle on to the lake's muddy shore. 'There's the statue,' said Chase, seeing it towering over them to the east.

Nina looked up at it. 'It's bigger than I thought. Must be at least a hundred feet tall.' It was higher than the small plateau behind it, the head rising above the edge of the steep cliff. The rockface itself, she now saw, was covered with a network of similar copper 'branches' to those they had seen atop the temple in Antarctica. And from this angle, she could see a feature behind the statue, seemingly cut out of the rock. 'Eddie, give me the gun.' She took a closer look through the rifle's sights.

'What is it?' Chase asked.

'It's a path to the summit. Stairs, carved out of the stone.'

'Like that spiral one in Antarctica?'

'This is open on one side – it's more of a zig-zag. A long zig-zag. There's a hell of a lot of steps.'

Chase sighed. 'Great. More climbing.'

'At least it's not covered in ice this time.' She glanced across the lake. 'Hello, what's that?'

'Another tunnel,' said Sophia as Nina peered at it through the scope. 'It looks flooded, though.'

'It is,' Nina confirmed. 'Almost to the roof. And the water inside doesn't look to be flowing – it must be blocked at the other end.'

'Like the one we came in through,' said Chase.

'Yeah . . .' She slowly turned clockwise, pointing across the lake at the near-submerged tunnel entrance. 'One.' Then to the waterfall falling into the chasm, and the opening beyond it. 'Two.' Further round, another stream running roughly northwest into the jungle – the one they had crossed earlier. 'Three.' And finally, turning back to face along the lakeside, a wider waterway between them and the statue. 'And four. Four rivers, all fed from the same source – and I bet that at one time they flowed into the desert.'

'Four rivers,' echoed Sophia. 'Pishon, Gihon, Tigris, Euphrates . . .'

'The four rivers that according to Genesis flowed from the Garden of Eden. But they don't any more – because the Veteres blocked them off.'

'Hang on a minute,' said Chase. 'The Tigris and the Euphrates are in bloody Iraq! That's not even on the same continent.'

'Names get re-used. Paris, Texas isn't the same as Paris, France. It could be another case of a memory being passed down through generations.' She looked back up at the plateau. 'We need to get up there. If this place is anything like the temple in Antarctica, then whatever's at the top of those stairs will be the place that we couldn't get into because of the ice – the Source of Life.'

'Or the Tree of Life, if you use the alternative meaning,' Sophia said. 'Another reference to Genesis.'

'And if there's another library, then we've got our Tree of Knowledge.'

'If there's an apple tree in there,' Chase said, staring up at the statue's impassive face, 'I might have to apologise to Nan for skiving out of Sunday school.'

They headed along the lake. Crossing the fourth stream, they splashed over to the far bank close to the wall surrounding the statue. The high stone barricade at first appeared to have no entrances, but then they saw that a huge lump of rock had fallen from the ceiling, demolishing a section of it.

'Good job that happened,' said Chase as they approached. 'We'd have had a job getting over that wall.'

'It's not just a temple,' said Nina, realising its purpose. 'It's a *fort*. The Veteres built it to protect something, just like they blocked off the tunnels into the cavern. Another line of defence.'

'So did they block everything off from the outside . . . or the inside?' Chase said. He pointed at the plateau behind the statue. 'Are they still up there?'

'Let's go see.' Nina led the way up the pile of broken stone to the damaged wall. She peered over it at what lay below. 'Oh . . .'

It was another library, rank after rank of clay tablets and cylinders containing the knowledge of the Veteres. But unlike the carefully arranged archive in the Antarctic, this was chaotic, thrown together. Some of the tablets, those nearest the base of the statue, were carefully stacked, but the majority were simply piled up, increasingly randomly the closer they were to the outer wall. Some had fallen – or been knocked – over, smashed pieces littering the narrow pathways through the crammed collection. The whole place was covered with dirt, damp with dripping water, creeping plants laying claim to every surface.

'God, what happened to it?' Chase asked.

Nina felt a pang of sadness, recognising the growing desperation of the people who had made it. 'It was their last stand,' she said. 'They wanted to preserve all of this, just like they did in Antarctica . . . but they were running out of time. They must have been building the wall around it even as they brought everything in.' She indicated the stacks closest to the statue. 'When they started, they tried to keep everything organised, but at the end, all they had time to do was just dump the tablets and hope not too many of them broke. Once they had as much as they could, they finished the wall. The knowledge of an entire civilisation, sealed in here . . . for ever.'

'Presumably they took the most important records with them,' said Sophia. 'Like the audio cylinders, the voices of their prophets. As long as they had those, they knew they could eventually make copies.'

'But they must still have lost so much.' Nina contemplated the remains of the library for a long, quiet moment. Then she climbed through the wall.

Through binoculars, Zamal watched the three figures drop out of sight into the temple. After entering the vast cavern and overcoming his initial awe, the first thing he had done was get a sense of the topography of his new battle zone – and while surveying the landscape from a rise near the tunnel mouth, he had spotted the fugitives moving along a lake, heading for the enormous blasphemy that was the statue at its far end.

He and his men gave chase, running along the edge of the ravine splitting the chamber until they found a log bridge. Quickly traversing it, they moved as swiftly as they could through the jungle to the lakeshore – now only minutes behind Wilde and the others.

'We have them,' he said with a malicious smile.

Like its smaller counterpart in the Antarctic, the statue had a low passageway at its base, requiring anyone going through to prostrate themselves at the feet of their god. Unlike the ice-encrusted opening, however, this was teeming with life, insects scuttling out of the way as Nina crawled through the layer of filth that had built up over thousands of centuries. 'It's a pity you didn't bring that machete,' she said to Chase, behind her, as she ripped vines aside to reveal a taller, wider passageway beyond. Holes in the arched ceiling let in an indirect twilight cast, creepers hanging through them. 'There's a corridor, and what looks like a bigger room at the end of it. It must lead to the stairs up the cliff.'

She stood and brushed off the muck as Chase and Sophia emerged, then shone the flashlight down the passage. The sheen of copper and gold reflected back at her. 'That's new. There wasn't anything like that at the other site.'

She moved down the corridor, directing the beam round the

walls of what was revealed as a large circular chamber. 'There was something like those, though. *Exactly* like those.' The light fell on four metal bowls of different sizes arranged in a line directly across from the entrance – beside the spindle and copper horn of one of the primitive gramophones.

'Is that a door next to it?' Chase asked, walking past her, about to enter the chamber – before freezing in astonishment at what came into view. 'What the hell are they?'

Nina and Sophia were equally amazed. The objects greeting their gaze were three statues – but unlike the other Veteres sculptures they had seen these were metal, not stone. They stood close to fifteen feet tall, elongated figures with their arms held out from their bodies, reminding Nina of the pose of the giant statue behind them . . . but where that had its hand open in generosity, these held a long, dangerous blade in each.

It was not the weapons that made the statues so startling, though. It was their *faces* – plural. Each figure's head had four faces around it, looking in different directions. The one facing forward was similar to the long, stylised features of the Veteres' god figure, though with its almond-shaped eyes narrowed threateningly. To its right was what seemed to be the face of a lion, teeth bared in a snarl; opposite this was the horned head of a bull. One of the statues was angled away from the entrance, revealing that the remaining face was an eagle, beak open, ready to attack.

Sprouting from each figure's back were what looked like wings, formed from copper plate and gold filigree, stretching straight up to touch the metal-plated ceiling. Another set, similar in design but smaller, extended downwards from the statues' chests to the floor between their four feet, which resembled the hooves of a cow. The legs themselves were wrapped in narrow bands of copper.

Chase was the first to speak. 'Just to check that I haven't just gone completely mental – those wings . . . they're meant to be angels, right?'

'They're more than just angels,' said Nina. 'They're *cherubim*. "And he placed at the east of the garden of Eden Cherubims . . ." '

' "And a flaming sword which turned every way, to keep the way of the tree of life",' continued Sophia. 'If I remember correctly.'

'Genesis, chapter three.' Nina turned her light to the metal floor. There were scrapes and indentations, as though something heavy had moved across it.

'Okay,' said Chase, taking out the Browning, 'why am I suddenly getting a really bad we-just-walked-into-a-deathtrap feeling?'

'Probably because we just did.' The torch beam settled on something lying on the floor. It was little more than dust, decayed fragments giving a hint of its former shape.

A human shape.

'There's another one,' said Sophia. Nina illuminated a second long-crumbled form. People had once entered the chamber . . . and somehow fallen to its guardians.

'Oh, great,' Chase snorted. 'I always thought cherubim were little fat angel kids playing trumpets, but now you're telling me they're like God's bouncers?'

'Those are *putto*,' said Sophia. 'They appeared a lot in Renaissance art. You can blame Donatello and Raphael for the confusion.'

'What, the Ninja Turtles?'

Both Nina and Sophia sighed as one. 'A lot of traditional art – not just in the Abrahamic faiths, but earlier ones like Babylonian as well – portrays cherubim as having four faces and four wings,' said Nina. 'And often the legs of an animal as well.' She lit the nearest statue's feet. 'Although I've seen some medieval illustrations that show them standing on a wheel . . . or a *bearing*.' She crouched, seeing that the hooves didn't quite touch the floor; the bottom of a sphere was visible in the narrow gap.

'They move?' Sophia exclaimed sceptically.

'Don't sound so surprised – you've seen similar things yourself, in the Tomb of Hercules. The traps that were used to protect it from robbers.'

'Don't remind me,' Chase muttered.

'I don't see how,' said Sophia. 'Those had machinery moving them. These are just sculptures. Even if those swords somehow turn, there's plenty of room just to walk around them.'

'Dusty there probably thought that too,' said Chase, gesturing at the nearer of the remains.

'Maybe he did – a hundred thousand years ago. Do you seriously think anything could possibly still be in working order after all this time?'

Nina extended a hand towards the statues. 'You want to test that? Be my guest.'

'I think I will.' With a dismissive shrug, Sophia stepped through the entrance on to the metal floor. Nothing happened. 'You see?' she said, turning to face Nina as she backed off a low step circling the room's perimeter. 'Absolutely nothing to—'

The chamber flooded with light.

Lightning bolts flashed across the room, crackling round the wings of the cherubim where they touched the copper-plated ceiling. Sparks crackled from the statues, a sharp ozone-like tang filling the air. With a hideous grinding noise, the blades began to move. The sculpted hands of the statues were actually part of the swords, turning at the wrists and rapidly picking up speed to form a circle of death like an aircraft propeller – and then the statues' arms moved too, swinging back and forth in scything arcs.

Another metallic groan, a great weight shifting—

One of the statues jolted out of the indentations its bulk had pressed into the floor over the untold centuries and advanced on Sophia. The others did the same, swords whirling.

446

Sophia gasped, about to run back to the entrance – when she saw something at the other end of the passageway. 'Eddie!'

Chase whirled – to see silhouettes crawling through the low tunnel beneath the colossal statue.

The Covenant had found them.

35

'Get inside!' Chase shouted, pushing Nina into the chamber. She resisted, even as she saw the danger behind. 'What about the statues?'

'They're slower than bullets! Go on!'

They ducked round the corner of the entrance, Sophia running to the other side. The statues continued their grinding advance, sparks cracking from their wings where they brushed along the floor and ceiling, but at less than walking pace.

Their slowness didn't make Nina feel any safer, though. There was an inexorability about them, a feeling that they would keep on coming until their targets were dead.

But how were they moving? What was making them work?

Chase leaned round the corner, firing the Browning. The first Covenant soldier, movement restricted by the confined tunnel, had no chance to dodge, the bullet hitting his forehead. He slumped into the dirt, dead. The figure behind him rapidly scrambled backwards, pulled out by one of his comrades.

'Eddie!' Sophia called, holding up both hands. He tossed her the Lee-Enfield. 'How many are there?'

Chase saw movement on both sides at the other end of the bottleneck. 'At least three.' All it would take was one of the soldiers to fling a grenade into the chamber to kill them all.

And there were other dangers, getting closer. 'Uh, I think we should move,' said Nina, tugging his arm. Two of the statues were bearing down on them, the third angling towards Sophia.

Chase fired another shot at the nearest statue's head. There was a ringing clang, a dent appearing between its frowning eyes as the bullet bounced off, but it was otherwise unaffected.

'Eddie, can you not waste bullets trying to kill the inanimate objects?' Sophia chided.

'They look pretty fucking animate to me!' He followed Nina as she ran round the outside of the room. The cherubim changed direction, tracking them, but did so without turning, the heads of the bulls now facing in the direction they were moving.

'They're like dodgems,' Nina said, looking up at the ceiling. Chase regarded her as if she had gone mad. 'The way they work, I mean. The floor and ceiling must have different polarities – the wings complete the circuit and make them move.'

'How? And where are they getting the power?'

'"Earth sky-fire" – that's what that inscription meant. It's earth energy, it must be! All those things made of copper above the statue? They're antennas, energy collectors – just like the ones we saw in Russia.' The Veteres had been able to harness the lines of energy running through the earth itself, using them to power crude – but effective – electric motors, in Antarctica working the recording devices, here both moving the statues and spinning their swords. The blades themselves were aglow with an eerie blue light, suggesting to Nina that they had the same nigh-unstoppable cutting edges as Excalibur. 'Keep away from the swords!'

'How *ever* would we manage without your advice?' said Sophia with understandable sarcasm.

They were almost at the chamber's rear doors, and the metal bowls. Chase looked at the entrance. The Covenant were still holding back on the other side of the tunnel, but he was sure they would be trying to find good sniping angles.

He saw Sophia crouch and lean round the corner to search for targets through the rifle's scope – and the third cherubim's blades getting dangerously close to her. 'Soph! Watch out!'

Fear flashed across her face as she saw the threat and dived out of the chamber to land on the stone floor outside. The cherubim shuddered, then reversed direction, now heading for the nearest other person – Nina.

But Sophia was still in danger. Gunfire echoed up the passage, bullets chipping the floor as she rolled. She reached the opposite wall and threw herself back into the chamber – only for the retreating cherubim to change direction once more and head back towards her.

'They're homing in on us!' Chase yelled. 'How the fuck are they doing that?'

'I don't know,' said Nina, seeing familiar symbols painted on the bowls, 'but I know what to do with this!' She reached into her pack for the clay cylinder she had taken from the map room in Antarctica and pointed at the inscription round its top. 'It's the same words – "the song of the prophet"! We need to play it.'

'I don't think it's going to charm those things to sleep – and if you stand at that record player, you'll be right in the Covenant's line of fire!'

She quickly took in the positions of the cherubim, the speed at which they were moving . . . 'Eddie, go back round to Sophia.'

'What? Why?'

'Just do it!'

He reluctantly turned and hurried back round the room. 'What about you?'

'I'm . . . gonna run right through the line of fire,' she said, trying to psych herself up. 'Nothing to worry about!'

'*What?*' Chase stopped. 'Nina, don't—'

But she was already breaking into a fear-driven sprint across the chamber, passing in front of the closed metal doors. A volley of shots tore through the room as one of the Covenant troopers opened fire. Bullets smacked into the doors just behind her as she ran, fragments of metal spitting from the impacts. A piece hit one of the bowls, causing it to ring with a deep, sonorous note. Nina now knew exactly what the bowls were for, but put it to the back of her mind as she tried desperately to stay one step, half a step, ahead of the spray of gunfire . . .

It stopped. She was out of the shooter's sight.

But the cherubim was still following her, screeching along on its giant ball-bearing 'feet'. All she could think was that they were electrically charged, somehow in opposition to the human body. Like poles repel, keeping the similarly charged cherubim from demolishing each other with their spinning blades – and unlike poles attract. As long as a person was in the room, the statues would be drawn towards them. It wasn't magic, or malevolence: just magnetism.

Individually, the heavy, sluggish cherubim weren't hard to avoid. But between the three of them, and their swinging, whirling blades, it became all too easy to become hemmed in. Spend too long in one place – such as at the doors – and you would be dead.

Chase reached Sophia. 'What the hell are you doing?' he shouted to Nina.

'Wait, wait . . .' she called back. Her cherubim was still moving across the room . . .

It crossed in front of the entrance.

Nina ran back towards the doors. The colossus haltingly changed direction to follow her, animal faces leering. More gunfire came from the tunnel—

It hit the statue, bullets clanking against its legs and body.

She raced to the bowls and put the cylinder on the spindle, taking advantage of her new cover. As long as the cherubim kept moving in a straight line towards her, it would shield her from the Covenant's fire.

But every second she stood there brought the whirling swords closer.

A shout from outside: Zamal issuing an order. With Chase and Sophia forced away from the chamber's entrance, the Covenant soldiers could advance through the tunnel.

Chase backed round the perimeter, followed by Sophia. The purpose of the small step was now clear – it was just high enough to stop the cherubim from hitting the wall. 'We've got to get back to the entrance.'

'Easier said than done,' Sophia replied.

'If we can stop 'em from moving . . .' He paused, staring at the top of the wings where they sparked against the ceiling – then aimed the Browning at one of them and fired. The bullet went straight through the copper sheets. More sparks flew, an electrical bolt sizzling angrily across the room, but the wing stayed in contact with the metal above.

'What are you doing?'

'Nina said they're like dodgems – so we need to cut their power poles.' One of the cherubim was close to the step, the other coming from the centre of the chamber. He watched the nearer one, judging the grinding swing of its arms, the distance between the tip of the blade and the wall . . .

The cylinder was in place, the needle positioned at the top of the groove. Nina hunted for a clue as to what to do next. Simply spinning the turntable by hand wouldn't work: if the bowls served the purpose she thought, the ancient recording had to be played at precisely the right speed. She looked back; the cherubim was getting closer.

And behind it, she saw shadows playing across the wall of the passage. Covenant soldiers were crawling through the tunnel.

'Crap, crap, crap!' She tried to remember how she had released some residual spark of earth energy in the frozen city . . .

Metal gleamed through the dust and cobwebs. A contact—

She touched it.

With a reluctant creak, the turntable rotated, picking up speed. The copper cone amplified the clicks and hisses, the strange voice reciting the name of what was to follow . . .

Then the song began.

The haunting voice echoed through the chamber, holding a note in perfect pitch for several seconds . . . and one of the bowls began to hum as well, the same note ringing out with increasing volume, shaking off the covering of dust. It was responding to the singer's voice, *resonating*. For a moment, Nina forgot about the danger, entranced by the purity of the sound.

Another sound reached her. A click.

Part of a lock. The sound of the bowl, vibrating at a very specific pitch and frequency, had caused something else to resonate, shaking loose.

'It's a key!' she cried. 'A musical key!' The note from the cylinder changed, the singer's voice rising an octave – and the next bowl, smaller, also hummed with the same wondrous sound.

Music was not the first thing on Chase's mind, though. 'Nina, move!' he yelled. The cherubim was almost upon her.

She shrieked and leapt away from the bowls, running round the edge of the room. The moment she took her finger from the metal contact, the turntable wound down, the song's note dropping and dying. There was another click from the door – but there were still another two bowls, two more locks to open.

'Oh, fuck this,' said Chase, glaring at the nearest cherubim. He had timed the movement of its arms – he thought. 'Give me the gun!' He and Sophia swapped weapons. She looked puzzled. 'On three, run across the room! One, two, *three*!'

Sophia skirted the statue coming for her and ran across the chamber – as Chase threw himself into a diving roll against the curving wall.

The blade whipped past, barely missing him as the statue's arm swung around – but he was clear, gripping the Lee-Enfield by its barrel and swiping the wooden stock at the cherubim like a baseball bat.

It hit the bottom of one of the wings. Sparks spat up – but the metal was bent back by the blow, no longer touching the floor. Cutting off part of the current.

The other wing was still in contact, though, and Chase was forced to jump clear as the sword swooshed back towards him.

But it was slowing, and the cherubim itself seemed to be moving more haltingly . . .

He ran to the entrance, seeing one of the Covenant troopers pulling himself clear of the tunnel, a second man not far behind. He flipped the rifle back over and fired. A bloody rosette exploded across the wall directly behind the first man's head, and he collapsed. The two corpses now blocked more than half of the low tunnel. The other man fired a burst from his SCAR in response, the bullets sizzling past Chase as he retreated.

Nina's cherubim was still grinding after her. She kept moving, trying to repeat the same trick as before. 'Eddie! I need to run across the entrance – can you give me cover?'

Chase pulled back his rifle's bolt to load the next cartridge, aware that the sparking cherubim was getting uncomfortably close. He backed away. 'Not with this thing coming at me! Sophia?'

She was edging away from her own statue, the Browning raised. 'Do it fast.'

'Okay, get ready,' said Nina. The cherubim drew closer, off to one side of the line of fire. 'Ready, ready . . . now!'

Sophia whipped round the corner as Nina ran across the entrance behind her. She saw the man in the tunnel raise his SCAR, and fired – but the bullet hit only the corpse he was sheltering behind. Sophia jerked back as another burst splintered the stone wall.

One of the cherubim was almost on her – and the only way she could get clear of its blades was to run across the opening.

Into the trooper's sights.

Nina paused, waiting for the cherubim to cross the room's centreline – then sprinted back towards the doors. The metal figure jerkily changed direction to follow. She had her shield.

But would she have long enough to play the rest of the song?

She slapped her hand on the metal contact. The turntable rotated again, the unearthly voice rising in pitch as it reached full speed. Again, a sustained note filled the chamber, the third bowl starting to hum in sympathy . . .

Chase saw that Sophia was about to be pinned down. His own cherubim was blocking the way to the entrance: he couldn't give her any cover without making a wide circle round it. 'Sophia, move!'

One of the statue's arms swung at her, the blade slicing through the air at chest height. She hesitated – then dived towards it.

She rolled, passing just beneath the quicksilver slash to land at the cherubim's feet. She swung the gun at one of the copper wings—

Crack!

A blue spark burst from the metal as she touched it. Chase had been insulated by the rifle's wooden body; the Browning's metal frame gave Sophia no such protection. She was thrown away from the cherubim, sprawling across the metal floor several feet away. Unconscious. Her gun skidded away to stop in front of the entrance.

Nina looked round, but couldn't move, her fingers pressed against the contact. A clunk from the wall as the harmonic vibrations released another lock – but there was still one more note to play . . .

The cherubim advanced on Sophia. Chase swore: no choice but to run across the room to save her. He dropped the rifle and grabbed Sophia by one limp arm to drag her away from the lethal circles of steel.

The damaged cherubim was still following him, more slowly than Sophia's statue. Chase dragged her in a curve, trying to guide them into a collision.

The blades almost clashed together – and then the two statues lurched apart, repelling each other.

The damaged one was in the lead. A sword tip clipped the Lee-Enfield, slicing it in half and sending the pieces spinning across the chamber.

The fourth note began. Nina didn't take her eyes off the advancing cherubim as it drew closer.

Behind it, she saw more shadows on the walls as the Covenant members advanced.

Chase was running out of room, backing towards the wall, pulling Sophia with him. Whether he went left or right, the undamaged cherubim would round its slower companion to form a wall of spinning death. With Sophia down it was three against two. He needed to even the odds.

A way came to him.

He pulled Sophia against the wall, then rapidly shrugged off his leather jacket, holding it up like a matador's cape . . . then tossing it to the floor directly in front of the lead cherubim.

It landed flat, the swords scything over it as the statue rolled on. The bent wing passed over it, the tip of the other for a moment snagging on the leather and pushing it along—

Then running it over.

The result was instantaneous. The cherubim stopped abruptly, the circuit broken, the earth energy feeding the crude motors cut off.

And with the power removed, so was the statue's electrical charge.

With nothing to repel it, the second cherubim lurched forward, heading straight for Chase and Sophia – and its blades smashed into the inert statue with a horrendous clash of metal. The recoil sent the moving cherubim spinning back across the chamber, while the dead figure was thrown to the floor in pieces. One of the blades stabbed a foot deep into the wall beside Chase. The statue's severed head came to rest at his feet, the lion face glaring accusingly at him.

He lifted Sophia. She was starting to recover from the electric shock. 'Nina! How much longer?'

'Not goddamn much, I hope!' Nina cried. The fourth note was still playing, the bowl humming, but the final piece of the lock still hadn't opened – and the cherubim was almost upon her.

Scuffling footsteps in the passageway. The Covenant were through the tunnel—

A click.

'Eddie!' Nina shouted as a crack appeared between the doors, the metal panels slowly swinging apart. 'It's opening!' She kept her hand on the contact until it was just wide enough to fit through. The moment she lifted her fingers, the doors jolted to a stop. 'Come on!' She yanked the cylinder from the spindle and leapt through the gap just ahead of the cherubim's glowing blades.

She was clear – but now that she was out of the room, the statue immediately changed direction towards new targets.

Chase pulled Sophia up. 'Can you run?'

'I'm not sure,' she mumbled.

'*Get* sure!' They could go to either side of the cherubim near the door – but one way would put them dangerously close to its swords, and the other would expose them to gunfire.

He made his choice, and pulled Sophia with him towards the blades.

The cherubim rumbled towards them. One of its arms swung round to block their path.

'Duck!' Chase dropped beneath the blade as the other sword, a blur of cold light, slashed through the air behind them.

Almost clear . . .

One of the cherubim's feet bumped against the little step round the chamber's edge.

The statue jolted, throwing off the timing of its swinging arms. Sophia saw it coming and dropped lower, but Chase barely had time to react.

He flattened himself against the wall – but the very tip of the sword caught the side of his shoulder. A fine spray of blood splattered the wall behind him, though the pain of the cut was nothing to the burning as a fat electrical spark spat from the point of contact.

The glowing blade swung back at him—

Sophia shoved him forward, throwing herself flat against the floor where it met the wall. The spinning sword buzzed over her head, lopping off a clump of bleached hair. 'Eddie, go!' she shouted, pushing at his legs. Clutching his shoulder, he staggered upright as Sophia crawled beneath the arc of the blade.

The door was not far away. He could see Nina's worried face on the other side. A glance at the entrance: the Covenant forces were not yet in sight, but he could hear them cautiously advancing, not knowing that their prey was now unarmed.

But they would realise any moment . . .

Sophia was on her feet. The cherubim was already reversing course, the eagle face sneering. The other statue was also grinding back across the chamber. 'Run for the door!' Chase told her. She didn't need any prompting, rushing past him before he'd finished speaking.

He followed, looking down the passageway. Three men in desert camouflage, Zamal in the lead, recognition then anger crossing his bearded face.

Sophia was through the gap. Chase dived after her, clothes tearing on the door's edges as a fusillade of bullets clanged against the thick panels just behind him. He landed hard on the stone floor and rolled away.

The moment he cleared the room, the flashes of earth energy across the ceiling ceased. The two cherubim stopped moving, their swords winding down.

'What happened?' Chase demanded, sitting up. Nina peered through the opening to see Zamal running into the chamber, his two men behind him.

The cherubim remained still.

'Oh, crap,' she gasped. The act of getting safely through the door had deactivated the trap – which meant Zamal and the others had a clear run at them. 'Shut the door, quick!'

She shoved one of the doors. Chase braced himself and pushed the other, Sophia joining him. The mechanism moaned in complaint, offering stiff resistance on top of the sheer weight of the metal panels. The gap narrowed, inch by sluggish inch, as Zamal sprinted past the cherubim, yelling in Arabic, about to hurl himself against the bullet-dented doors—

The doors closed. Something clunked; a fraction of a second later came a bang as Zamal barged against them, but the lock had re-fastened.

And as the lock closed . . . the trap came back to life.

The two troopers reached Zamal, flanking him as they tried to force the doors open – then all three looked up in surprise as crackling energy bolts flashed across the ceiling. Sparks spat from the wings of the two cherubim, their swords glowing with the unnatural rippling blue light as they started to spin once more. The massive figures ground towards the soldiers, terrifying angels straight out of ancient mythology, a sight fearsome enough to freeze even Zamal for the briefest moment before he fired his SCAR at the nearest behemoth.

To no effect. The bullets punched straight through the thin copper plate of the wings, unable to do anything more than dent the thicker metal of its body.

The other troopers also fired, but with no more success – and now they were trapped against the doors as both cherubim closed in, fiery swords turning every way . . .

Nina heard the men's screams, which were cut off abruptly by a series of wet *thunk*s as pieces of their bodies splattered over the doors. The cherubim bumped against the step, shifting back and forth in inanimate confusion as the objects to which they had been drawn were suddenly spread out over a much larger area.

But the electrical charge generated by living bodies quickly dissipated, and without it the trap shut down. Silence and stillness returned to the chamber.

Nina recoiled from a trickle of blood running under the doors. 'I don't think we want to go back out that way.' In the light of her torch, she saw Chase's face tight with pain as he held his shoulder. 'Eddie, are you okay?'

'Won't be going to the world juggling championships.' Wincing, he opened his fingers slightly to examine the wound. A three-inch slash had been cut through his shoulder muscle, blood seeping from it.

'I'll get some bandages,' she said, opening her pack.

'Work on the move,' said Sophia, striding past her. 'There'll be more of them on the way. And I think,' she announced, looking up, 'we have quite a climb ahead of us.'

Around them rose the steep face of the plateau. Part of the cliff had been cut away by the statue's builders; a stepped a stone path zig-zagged precariously up to the summit, doubling back on itself multiple times before finally reaching the top.

For a moment, Nina forgot about the bandages as she stared at the clifftop above.

Whatever the Covenant had been fighting to keep from them, whatever the secret of the Veteres . . . it was waiting up there.

36

Two Humvees emerged from the tunnel into the enormous chamber and stopped near the edge of the ravine. Vogler, at the wheel of the first vehicle, struggled to contain his astonishment. Even as a devout, lifelong Christian, a true soldier of God, he had been forced to admit that in an age where new scientific discoveries pushed the boundaries of human knowledge further on a daily basis, there were aspects of the Book of Genesis that seemed more likely to come from the fallible interpretations of ancient man than to be the flawless word of the Almighty.

But *this* . . . this reaffirmed his faith in a moment. The Garden of Eden was *real*. Undeniable. And if the stories of Eden were true, then so too were all the other events of the Bible.

The question was, he thought as he spotted the vast idol: what did the Garden of Eden hold that was *not* in the Bible?

Callum was less impressed by the wonder of their surroundings. 'So where's Zamal?'

Vogler picked up the radio handset. 'Zamal, this is Vogler. Zamal, come in.' No response but the faint hiss of static. He repeated the call, still with no result.

'They're dead,' the American said bluntly. He let out a dismissive snort. 'Muslims. Huh. If they spent less time praying and more training . . .'

'Be quiet,' Vogler ordered. Muslim or not, abrasive and arrogant or not, Zamal had still been a comrade. He scoured the surreal landscape of the pocket jungle with binoculars. His adversaries would almost certainly have headed for the statue . . . 'I see them,' he announced at the sight of three small figures slowly picking their way up a narrow path behind it. 'Chase, Dr Wilde . . . and Blackwood.'

Callum took out his handgun. 'Time for a reunion, don't you think?'

'I do.' Vogler turned the wheel and set off, driving the big 4x4 into the jungle.

Nina reached yet another hairpin twist and stopped, leaning exhaustedly against the rock wall. 'I think I'm gonna throw up.'

Chase, ahead of her, paused in his ascent of the path. 'Ah, come on, this is nothing. You walked up more stairs than this when the lift broke down at our old apartment, remember?'

'Yeah, but I hadn't been chased and shot at and blown up then, had I? And I almost threw up that time, as well.'

'If you're going to be sick,' Sophia said as she caught up, 'at least have the courtesy to let me get above you first.'

Nina irritably brought up a hand as if about to stick a finger down her throat. Sophia sneered, but still quickened her pace as she passed. 'How much further?'

Chase peered upwards. 'Looks like another six zig-zags.'

Nina groaned. 'Six?'

'Maybe seven.'

'*Seven?* Oh, great. And I thought—' She broke off, hearing a distant sound over the dripping of condensation.

Sophia heard it too. 'Trucks. It must be those Humvees.'

Chase looked past the statue's outstretched arm across the jungle, but saw no sign of movement. He could hear the noise, though: powerful engines revving. 'They're racing Humvees through the bloody *Garden of Eden*? Who's driving, Jeremy Clarkson?'

'Will they be able to get them across the ravine?' Nina asked.

'Even if they can't, they can still get out and use that log,' said Chase. 'Either way, it won't take 'em long to get here. We need to shift.' He moved back to Nina and took her hand. 'If you're going to hork, just don't do it down my back.'

They set off again, increasing their pace as much as they dared along the precarious winding path. It took close to fifteen minutes before they finally rounded the last hairpin, the path curling up to the top of the plateau. To one side, a narrow stone bridge led across the gap to the statue's shoulders.

'Finally,' Nina gasped. Both her legs ached, a rod of hot pain through the wound in her right thigh.

'Better be something good up here after all that,' Chase said, the bandage on his shoulder damp with sweat.

Sophia blew out a dry breath. 'I could certainly use a source of life right now.'

Nina overtook Chase, the pain subsiding beneath her urge to find out what awaited them. The Source of Life, the most sacred, best-protected part of the Veteres civilisation; entombed in ice in the Antarctic, guarded by 'angels' here. But what *was* it? She broke into a clumsy jog, hurrying up the last few yards of the path to see . . .

Beauty.

The summit was a swathe of glorious colours, a field of wild flowers. White, red, yellow, purple, sunset orange, vivid blue, all gently swaying in the breeze circulating round the cavern. The floral carpet spread across most of the plateau – leading Nina's gaze to something at its centre.

A building.

Like much of the ancient civilisation's architecture, it was a stone dome, but it seemed older, heavier, built to last for all time. And there was something else, almost hidden beneath the dazzling petals. Small stone markers rose from the ground, arranged in concentric circles around the building.

She moved to the nearest, pushing the flowers aside to reveal a rectangular slab about eighteen inches high. Letters were carved into the surface. The Veteres language.

'They're gravestones,' she realised. 'This whole place . . . it's a cemetery.'

'What?' said Sophia, sounding almost outraged. 'This is what we came to find? A *graveyard*? How can a graveyard be the source of life?'

'It's obvious, innit?' said Chase. 'They die, they're buried, they go back to the earth . . . and new life comes from them.' He flicked a hand at the flowers.

Nina smiled at him. 'Right. All life comes from death, in a manner of speaking. Life forms feed off other life forms. And every single atom in our bodies was created by the death of a star.' She stood, facing the building. 'It's another piece of metaphorical language. The source of new life . . . is the death of the old. And if they believed in an afterlife, then this – being buried according to religious ritual – could have been where they thought it started.'

'So if this is a cemetery,' said Chase, indicating the dome, 'what's in there?'

'Or who,' Sophia added. 'It could be a mausoleum, for rulers or important families.'

Nina regarded the structure thoughtfully. 'If the Veteres buried their dead in the earth, there'll be nothing left in these graves after all this time. But if that's a mausoleum, and they used stone rather than wood or cloth to contain the bodies . . .' Her heartbeat quickened. 'There might be remains.'

'Of who?' asked Chase. 'Adam and Eve?'

Nina nodded enthusiastically. 'Yeah. Maybe!' She set off for the stone dome, leaving a trail through the flowers as she weaved between the gravestones. Chase and Sophia exchanged looks, then followed.

The light level fell as she approached: this close to the edge of the cavern, the reason was simply that less daylight was coming through the holes in the ceiling, but it still felt disturbingly ominous. As she got closer, she saw an entrance, a single tall, thin opening with blackness beyond. She lit her flashlight and slipped inside.

'Nina, wait— Why do I fucking bother?' Chase muttered. He went through after her.

The interior was divided into three rooms. The first and largest was a pie-slice shaped chamber with the entrance at the centre of the curved outer wall, two smaller rooms leading off diagonally from the straight sides. Several stone benches were arranged within, on which dirt and fungus had built up over the millennia. The walls were also grubby – but Nina was already brushing away the filth of time to reveal the inscriptions beneath. 'Sophia,' she said, 'look at this.'

'It's the same language,' said Sophia, examining the ancient text, 'but some of the characters are different.'

'If this is where the Veteres originated, that'd make sense – this is the primal form of their alphabet. How much of it can you read?'

'Enough to think that you were probably right about this being their entrance to the afterlife.' She indicated one particular section. 'This is something about their god – "the source of all things". And he's mentioned again here, and here . . . it's a god-heavy room.'

'Maybe it's a chapel,' Chase suggested.

'Could be.' Nina moved to one of the other doorways, shining her light into the room beyond. 'There are more inscriptions in here . . .' She stopped as she lowered the torch beam.

There was more in the room than mere inscriptions. At the

centre of the dark inner chamber was a long stone object raised off the floor on carved blocks. A sarcophagus.

The last resting place of one of the Veteres.

'So what do we do now?' Chase asked, after a silent moment had passed. 'When we found that Atlantean coffin, you weren't happy about it being opened—'

'We open this one,' Nina interrupted. He gave her a questioning look. 'I know, I know. Normally I'd never do anything like that without a proper survey, but if we at least know what's inside the sarcophagus, it might give us a bargaining chip when the Covenant get here.'

'Good point.' Circling the sarcophagus, he saw that the lid was hinged at the back. 'Here, give me that bag.' He came back round the coffin and took the backpack from Nina, pulling out a claw hammer. 'Okay, I'll try to lift up the lid a bit. If you two can hold it up for a couple of seconds, I'll prise it open more. Give me some light.' Nina aimed the torch at the side of the sarcophagus. He ran his fingers along the edge of the lid before finding a slight imperfection and jiggling the claw end of the hammer into it. 'Ready?' The two women moved into position and nodded. 'Okay, here goes . . .'

Straining, he pulled the hammer's shaft back and down with all his weight. The lid rose about half a centimetre as the hammer's head crunched against the stone. Nina pushed up as hard as she could. Sophia did the same; the gap widened to over two inches, a slit of blackness visible beneath. Chase quickly jammed the hammer in deeper and pushed down again. 'Push it, *push!*'

Nina and Sophia both strained to lift the lid higher. A rasp of stone from the sarcophagus made Nina cringe, but she somehow found an extra ounce of strength, and with an involuntary cry was able to open it wider. The hammer slipped, spitting stone chips into Chase's face, but the women held the lid up long enough for him to grip its edge and shove it upwards. It swung past the vertical, then came to a stop with a bang, just beyond the tipping point.

Chase and Sophia stepped back as Nina shone the torch into the sarcophagus. Inside was a figure, tightly wrapped in a surprisingly well-preserved cloth shroud. The stone coffin must have been practically airtight; once the body's decomposition processes had run their course, the remains had stayed more or less intact, no weather effects or organisms to disturb them.

She waited for the dust to settle before taking a closer look. The figure inside the shroud was tall. *Very* tall – at least seven feet.

'So I guess they were great at basketball,' said Chase.

Sophia wafted dust from her face. 'Some African tribes are very tall. Maybe these people were their ancestors.'

'We'll find out in a second,' said Nina. 'If someone's got a knife, that is?'

Chase produced a penknife and snicked open the largest blade before handing it to her. Hesitantly, she reached down, the blade's tip hovering just above the cloth as Chase held the torch. 'Let's find out what the big secret is.'

She made the first cut.

The blade slipped easily through the shroud as she carefully moved it in a sawing motion down the figure's chest. Once she had opened it to roughly waist level, she moved back to where she started and began cutting upwards, slicing more delicately along the long neck and round the side of the head to the top of the skull.

She pocketed the knife and took hold of the edge of the cloth. Very slowly, very carefully, she lifted it away, gradually peeling the covering off the corpse's face to reveal . . .

'Oh, God,' she said in a quiet voice, free hand to her mouth as she saw the exposed features.

They were not human.

37

'I told you,' said Chase, somewhere between shock and vindication. 'I fucking *told* you they were aliens!'

The skull was close to human – two eyes, a nasal cavity, a mouth with a few small teeth still remaining – but nevertheless different enough for it to be instantly obvious that it was not a member of the species *Homo sapiens* . . . and also to be somehow disturbing. The forehead was higher, the top of the skull noticeably larger than any human's, while the lower jaw was narrower and more protruding. The nasal cavity was longer and thinner. The eye sockets, empty but for desiccated shreds of tissue, were higher on the face and distinctly almond-shaped, slanting upwards. Nina had no choice but to admit that it looked like the popular image of a 'Grey' alien, the black-eyed, expressionless face of otherworldly life from over half a century of UFO mythology.

But she knew this was no extraterrestrial.

'For the last time, Eddie, they're *not* aliens,' she said, taking back the flashlight and holding it closer to the ancient corpse.

'You're kidding, right?' he said in disbelief. 'I mean, look at it!'

'I *am* looking at it. And what I see evolved right here on earth. It's just that . . . it evolved before humans did.'

'A different species?' Sophia asked.

'Exactly. A species that was *related* to humans, just as humans are related to *Homo rhodesiensis* or *Homo neanderthalensis*. But they weren't humans. They'd established a civilisation at a time when *Homo sapiens* had only just evolved into its current form. *They* were the first people to spread across the planet – not us. *That's* why the Covenant of Genesis was created, and why they're so determined to destroy any evidence of this. The Veteres were monotheistic, they worshipped a single god . . . which means that by definition they worshipped the same god of the Torah, the Bible and the Koran, because they all say there is only one god. But we've seen the Veteres' god, in the giant statues – and he looks like *them*. Not like us.'

'So much for God creating man in his own image,' said Sophia.

Chase shook his head. 'Hang on. The Veteres lived here in the Garden of Eden, yes?' Nina nodded. 'So how come they're not in the Bible?'

'Maybe they were,' said Nina. 'Right there in Genesis, all along. "There were giants in the earth in those days . . ."' She swept the torch beam down the seven-foot-plus length of the body. 'Maybe they were the origin of the stories about the Nephilim.'

'So then what happened to them? They were advanced, they were smart – so why'd they disappear?'

'The beasts killed them,' Sophia said.

'What beasts?' Chase demanded. 'What *are* these beasts?'

Nina now knew, and the realisation chilled her to the core. 'We are.'

Chase was confused. 'What?'

'*We're* the beasts. Humans.' Images flooded Nina's mind as she imagined the African plains of two hundred thousand years earlier, at the very dawn of *Homo sapiens* as a species. A new creature spreading across the lands that had been home to the Veteres for millennia, in every way genetically identical to modern man, but feral, still animalistic in thought and action, no language or laws or culture to restrain them. Until . . . 'Oh, my God.'

'What is it?' asked Sophia.

'I just realised what the inscriptions in Antarctica meant. About their god punishing the Veteres for giving "the gift" to the beasts. The gift was *knowledge*. They thought they could train the early humans, domesticate them, turn them into servants. But they were wrong. They screwed up. What they really gave them was the means to destroy their masters. They taught them how to build, how to grow food, use medicine, a thousand and one other things . . . including how to use weapons. And once they had that knowledge, the humans used it. We drove them from their lands, chased them across the world, and eventually wiped them out. Completely.'

'They must've been able to put up a fight, though,' objected Chase. 'Look how big he is.'

'Size doesn't necessarily mean strength. All the statues we've seen of the Veteres are tall and *thin*.' Nina brought the torch closer to the skull. 'They had the advantage in intelligence – look how much bigger the brain must be than a human's. It's like comparing our brain to a chimp's. But his teeth are small, the incisors are blunt – the Veteres were probably omnivorous, like us, but these teeth are closer to a herbivore's.'

'So they had the brains,' said Sophia, 'but we still destroyed them.'

'We had something they didn't – or they didn't have enough of it,' Nina realised. 'Aggression. They were smarter, but we were more vicious.' She gave Sophia a cutting look. 'More willing to kill.'

'Spare me the sanctimony,' Sophia replied. 'If they hadn't been, none of us would be here. It was survival of the fittest, Darwinism in action.'

Nina couldn't deny that. But she still felt sadness as she regarded the shrouded corpse. Whether their motives had been selfish or altruistic she would never know, but the Veteres had still given the knowledge of their civilisation to the early humans . . . and in so doing, brought about their own destruction as surely as if they had handed a gun to an angry child. Forced to flee, the Veteres had used part of their knowledge that they hadn't passed on to their attackers – shipbuilding and sailing – to cross the seas and set up new homes, but eventually the cycles of climate change had lowered the waters and opened the way for the humans to pursue.

And kill.

'Wait a minute,' said Chase. 'If the Garden of Eden and the cherubim and all this were made by these guys, why are they in the Bible?'

The answer was now clear, but at the same time Nina had to struggle even to contemplate it. Although her own upbringing in New York by scientist parents had been anything but evangelical, the seed of religion had still inevitably taken root within her psyche simply through cultural osmosis. But the evidence before her had to be acknowledged. 'Because . . . because the Veteres taught the humans *their* beliefs. Our religions are based on theirs – one god, one creator. And the story of Genesis is a distorted race memory of what once happened here. Some of the Veteres must have made a last stand to protect what was most holy to them. This place.' She gestured at the walls around them. 'Their sacred ground. And the library, their "tree of knowledge" – which the humans "ate" from. And they were cast out of Eden for it.'

'So they chased the Veteres all the way to Australia? Bloody hell, talk about holding a grudge.'

'Darwinism again,' Sophia said. 'If you have two species competing for the same ecological niche, eventually one of them will destroy the other.'

'Maybe they weren't entirely destroyed,' said Nina. 'They survived as memories, at least – they might have lived on at a genetic level too. Maybe there was some interbreeding, just as there was between humans and Neanderthals. It might explain why I could affect the earth energy fields and you couldn't. Like I could with Excalibur.'

Sophia sneered. 'Oh, are you also saying your *superior intellect* comes from you being a descendant of these creatures?'

'No,' Nina replied tightly. 'But there's obviously some connection between the Veteres and the Atlanteans, because they used the same numerical system. And I *am* descended from the Atlanteans. So in answer to your question: bite me.'

Chase moved between them. 'Okay, so what do we do now?'

'This is our proof,' said Nina, indicating the body. 'DNA and carbon-dating tests will provide absolutely irrefutable evidence of an intelligent species that pre-dated humanity. If we can get this out of here and keep it out of the Covenant's hands, then we still have a chance to expose them to the world—'

'It sounds,' said a Swiss-accented voice, 'as though you are going back on our deal, Dr Wilde.'

Nina, Chase and Sophia whirled to see Vogler in the doorway, a gun in his hand.

'I thought you *didn't* make a deal with them,' Chase said accusingly.

'Not the time or the place, Eddie,' Nina replied as she raised her hands.

Vogler stepped into the room, regarding the sarcophagus and its contents with interest. 'So they really were another species.'

'You knew?' Nina asked.

'After the structure of DNA was discovered in the 1950s, the Vatican secretly had the remains obtained by the Covenant's predecessor organisation analysed. Even though the tests at that time were primitive, the evidence pointed towards it – which led to the creation of the Covenant itself. But they were only small samples; we never found a complete body – until now.'

'And now that you have one . . . what are you going to do with it?'

Vogler stared at the corpse. 'A good question. But for now, come with me.' He waved them towards the door with his gun. 'Professor Ribbsley is about to arrive.'

Vogler took them back into the field of flowers, where Callum was waiting, along with two more Covenant troopers. Trampled trails led to the edge of the plateau, where Chase saw several carbon fibre hooks on the rocky edge. Rather than running the gauntlet of the temple, Vogler's team had fired grappling hooks up the cliff and scaled the lines attached to them. 'This all you've got left?' he asked mockingly. 'The Covenant's goon platoon must be pretty short-staffed by now.'

'There will be more to replace them,' said Vogler. He looked at Nina. 'But . . . there may be no need.'

A loud noise caught everyone's attention: a helicopter hovering above the largest hole in the ceiling. The gap was tight, at one point little more than a metre's clearance to each side of the blades, but the pilot skilfully brought the aircraft through. As it turned towards the plateau, a flash of white clothing in the cockpit revealed the pilot's identity: Ribbsley.

Petals whirled like a scented snowstorm as the helicopter descended, settling near the top of the cliff path. Ribbsley emerged and walked through the flowers as if out for an afternoon stroll. 'I must say,' he called as he approached the waiting group, 'this is rather impressive. The actual Garden of Eden, an entire self-contained ecosystem, right in the middle of one of the most awful wastelands on the planet. Remarkable!' He gave Vogler a quizzical look. 'Your numbers seem to be rather thinned, Killian. And where's Zamal?'

'Dead,' Vogler told him.

'Ah. Terrible shame.' There was not even the pretence of sincerity in Ribbsley's voice. 'Good job I decided to stay in Khartoum until you found this place, then.' He turned to Nina. 'Or, I suspect, until *you* found it, Dr Wilde. Congratulations.'

Nina's reply was equally insincere. 'Why, *thank* you, Professor. That makes it all worthwhile.'

He smiled, barely giving Chase a glance before moving on to Sophia, his relieved response now genuine. 'Sophia, thank God. Are you all right?'

'A little bruised,' she said with a smile, 'but still alive and kicking.'

'Thank God,' he repeated, taking her hands in his and gazing into her eyes with a mixture of longing and lust before embracing her tightly and whispering something into her ear. She replied in kind; Nina couldn't make out what either had said, but as they moved apart she caught a flicker of expression on Sophia's face.

Anticipation?

Nobody else had noticed, Ribbsley blocking their view. He turned back to Vogler. 'So, I understand that we have an interesting find. Show me.'

'This way,' said Vogler. He gestured for his men to bring the prisoners before heading back to the mausoleum. Ribbsley followed, Callum at the rear of the line, briefly reaching into his jacket.

While the soldiers watched over Nina, Chase and Sophia in the main room, the others went into the burial chamber to examine the body, emerging a few minutes later. Ribbsley turned his attention to the inscriptions on the walls. 'So the story of the expulsion from Paradise in Genesis really was true . . . from a certain point of view. I suppose we'll never know how much of the distortion of events was deliberate and how much was down to Chinese whispers, but it's not important right now. What *is* important,' he said to Vogler, 'is what the Covenant plans to do about it. You're the only member of the Triumvirate still alive, so it seems to be entirely your decision.'

'So it does,' said Vogler. He stared through the doorway at the body before turning away – not to Ribbsley, but to Nina. 'In the past, things would have been very simple. The Covenant had a specific purpose: to locate and destroy all evidence of the Veteres and their civilisation – anything that could undermine the creation story in the Bible and the other holy books. We would simply have obliterated this entire place.'

'So what's stopping you now?' Nina asked, challenging.

'I think you know.' Vogler pointed at the doorway. 'Out there is the greatest, the *holiest* place in history. The Garden of Eden, Dr Wilde! Paradise on earth, where God himself once walked! Destroying it would be . . . *blasphemy*. A mortal sin.'

'What, worse than all your others?'

He prickled at the barb, but didn't respond to it. 'The discovery of the Garden of Eden doesn't undermine Genesis,' he said. 'It confirms it. If Eden is revealed to the world, then it will show the faithful that they were right to believe.'

'You might be right,' said Nina. 'Except for one minor inconvenience.' She indicated the ancient body. 'The Garden of Eden was *his* paradise, not ours.'

'Which is why I have a dilemma – and why you may be the one to help me solve it.'

'Why her?' Ribbsley demanded. 'In fact, why is she even still alive?'

'A good question,' Callum added. His gaze fixed on Sophia. 'Why are *any* of them still alive, Vogler?'

'Because she will be believed,' said Vogler. 'The world's most famous archaeologist, the discoverer of Atlantis, and the tombs of King Arthur and Hercules? If she is the one who reveals that Eden has been found, everyone will accept her story.'

Nina gave him a humourless half-smile. 'But if I tell the world about finding Eden, I'd tell the whole story – including the part about the Veteres being its original occupants. It'd be kind of hypocritical otherwise.'

'But you're *already* a practised hypocrite, Dr Wilde,' Vogler countered. 'You lied to the world about the real reasons behind Kristian Frost's search for Atlantis. And I'm sure you lied in your official report to the UN about Excalibur being lost at sea.'

'That – not telling the whole story about Atlantis was for security reasons,' said Nina, wrong-footed, and trying to avoid Callum's accusing stare. 'If I'd announced that the discovery of Atlantis led to the world coming *this* close,' she held her thumb and forefinger a bare inch apart, 'to having a plague unleashed on it, there would have been total chaos!'

'And what do you think will happen if you tell the billions of people who follow Christianity or Islam or Judaism that you have undeniable proof their beliefs are wrong?'

'I—' Nina began, before stopping as she considered the question. 'Wait, *you've* seen the proof, and your beliefs haven't changed,' she said, changing the subject to avoid having to give an answer.

'My beliefs are unshakeable. I would not be able to do what I do if they were not. Accepting the existence of the Veteres does not mean denying the existence of God. But there are many who will feel angry and afraid at having their beliefs challenged. And when people are angry and afraid . . . that is when order breaks down.'

'Order, and *obedience*,' Sophia said cuttingly. 'Which is what religion is really all about, isn't it? It wouldn't be good to have people questioning what they've been told to believe.'

'Mr Callum, if she speaks out of turn again, you can shoot her,' said Vogler. Callum's expression made it clear that he thought the decision was long overdue. Ribbsley watched the American closely, face tight. 'Dr Wilde, do you remember what Cardinal di

Bonaventura told you about the way the Vatican dealt with controversial scientific theories?'

'Yeah. It accepted them.'

'Over time. The Big Bang, evolution . . . the Church now accepts such things as fact. But that acceptance took years, even decades. Not because those within the Vatican resisted the ideas, but because the faithful *would* resist them if they were thrust upon them all at once. But if they are gradually introduced . . .'

'. . . they're believed,' Nina concluded.

'Yes. They eventually become part of catechism, and cannot be denied. But when the truth will seem so controversial, so *dangerous*, that truth needs time to be accepted.' He looked back at the entrance. 'You have found the Garden of Eden. I . . . I cannot allow it to be destroyed. It must be revealed to the world. But the Veteres are an integral part of Eden – yet I cannot reveal *them* to the world without risking chaos. Do you see my dilemma?'

'Yeah. But I'm starting to see what you've got in mind for a solution.'

'And do you approve?'

'No. But I approve of the alternative even less.'

'Mind filling the rest of us in?' Chase asked.

'He's giving me two choices,' Nina told him. 'I tell the world about finding Eden, but don't mention anything about the Veteres – for years. In the meantime, the Covenant gradually introduces the *idea* of them into the public consciousness, while they get theologians to work out ways to explain their existence that don't contradict Genesis. Then, by the time their existence is actually revealed, the idea's been around long enough to neutralise the shock value. Am I right?' Vogler nodded.

'And option B?'

She glanced at Vogler's gun. 'Bang, aargh, thud.'

'Yeah, I thought so.'

'So what is your decision, Dr Wilde?' said Vogler. 'One way or another, Eden must be revealed to the world . . . but whether by you or by someone else is entirely your choice. Make it now.'

Nina turned to Chase. 'Eddie? This affects you too – what do you think?'

He shrugged. 'Either cave in to these arseholes and lie to the world, or be dead? They're both crap options, but the second one's definitely crappier.'

'I know.' She squeezed his hand sadly, then reluctantly turned back to Vogler. 'I don't have much choice, do I? I . . . I accept your offer. At least this way, *some* truth will come out. Eventually.'

'A wise decision,' said Vogler.

'Hardly!' Ribbsley spluttered. 'Do you really think she'll go along with it?'

'I think she's a person of her word, yes.'

'It doesn't matter what you think,' said Callum. 'It's the wrong choice.'

Vogler rounded on him. 'That is not for you to decide, Mr Callum.'

'Actually, it is.' He drew his gun – and shot Vogler.

38

Nina gasped as Vogler fell to the floor, blood gushing from his abdomen. Before anyone could react, Callum unleashed a rapid-fire spray of bullets at the remaining Covenant troopers, felling them.

Vogler's rifle landed near Chase. He was about to drop and grab it, but Callum had already seen the danger and was jabbing his gun at him. 'Don't even think about it!' He gestured for Chase, Nina and Sophia to move towards the doorway.

Ribbsley retreated to the other side of the room. 'Some explanation, please, Mr Callum?'

'I'm correcting the Covenant's bad choice.' He reached into his jacket, flicking a switch on something within. 'Mr President, did you hear all that?'

'Loud and clear, Mr Callum.' The voice was rendered hollow and metallic by the radio's small loudspeaker, but it was still unmistakable: Victor Dalton, President of the United States of America. 'Report your situation.'

'All remaining Covenant forces are dead or,' he glanced at Vogler, who was weakly clutching the bullet wound, 'disabled. Still here are Chase, Professor Ribbsley, Dr Wilde . . . and Sophia Blackwood.'

'Hello, Victor,' said Sophia, almost chattily. 'It's been a while.'

There was a pause before Dalton spoke again, choosing to ignore her. 'Mr Callum, I take it that the Garden of Eden contains what we feared?'

'Yes, sir. Definitive proof of a non-human civilisation pre-dating mankind – which influenced the story told in the Book of Genesis.'

Another pause. 'I see. In that case, Mr Callum – codeword: *Revelation.*'

'Understood, sir,' said Callum. Still covering Nina, Chase and Sophia, he adjusted a setting on the radio. 'Abaddon, Abaddon, this is Archangel. Do you copy?'

'Roger, Archangel,' came a distorted Texan voice, 'this is Abaddon. I read you.'

'Abaddon, you have authorisation to proceed with the operation, these co-ordinates. Give me estimated time to initiation.'

'Archangel, I estimate fifteen minutes to initiation. Will that give you sufficient time to egress area?'

'Affirmative, Abaddon. Begin operation now. Archangel out.'

'Confirmed, Archangel. Commencing operation. Out.'

Callum flicked the switch back. 'Mr President, the operation is under way.'

'What operation?' Nina demanded.

Dalton sounded faintly amused. 'Abaddon, Dr Wilde, is the codename of a B-2 stealth bomber that took off from our base in Uganda about an hour ago and is now circling over Sudanese airspace at sixty thousand feet. Mr Callum just gave the order for it to drop two MOPs on what the pilots have been told is a high-value terrorist target.'

'MOPs?' Nina suspected she wouldn't like the meaning of the acronym.

'Massive Ordnance Penetrators,' said Callum. 'Thirty-thousand-pound bunker-busters.'

'Earthquake bombs,' added Chase.

'Ah. But – but why? What do you gain from destroying Eden?'

'That's not your concern any more, Dr Wilde. Mr Callum, I'll let you get moving. But one last thing – you know your orders. Carry them out . . . starting with Sophia Blackwood.'

'My pleasure, sir. Callum out.' He switched off the radio, then stepped forward, shifting his gun from Chase to Sophia.

'Kill me, and Victor's career is over,' she said. 'The recording of us together will be released.'

'You're already officially dead,' he reminded her with a cold grin. 'Nothing happened. The president's position is secure.'

'Oh, nice job with the blackmail,' Nina muttered as Sophia's face fell. 'You didn't think of that?'

'Actually, I did. But I was rather hoping nobody else had.'

Callum's smile widened as he took aim at Sophia's heart—

Blam!

The gunshot echoed round the chamber – but it hadn't come from Callum's gun, which flew from his hand to land inside the burial chamber. The white-haired man yelled in pain.

'Sorry, old chap,' said Ribbsley, his own smoking pistol tracking Callum. 'But I can't let you do that.'

'Good shot,' Chase said in sarcastic admiration.

'Before I entered academia, I was an officer in the Rhodesian army. Not a skill-set I draw on very often, but it can be useful.'

Sophia gave him a relieved smile. 'You cut that rather close, Gabriel.'

'I knew I could trust you when you gave me back my laptop in Australia, so you could trust me too.'

'You gave him back his laptop?' Nina said, angry.

'Just hedging my bets,' said Sophia, joining Ribbsley. 'After all, my long-term prospects for survival with you and Eddie weren't really any higher than with the Covenant.'

'Well, you're safe now,' said Ribbsley as she picked up a dead soldier's rifle. 'Everything's worked out very well. We found Eden, we have a surprisingly intact Veteres body, and Callum even took care of the Covenant for us.'

'We also have a stealth bomber bearing down on our heads, and less than fifteen minutes to get clear.' She looked at her watch. 'Less than fourteen, in fact.'

'Once we reach the helicopter, we'll be out of here in two. Keep them covered.' He picked up Vogler's SIG, then entered the burial chamber, reaching into the sarcophagus and tearing at the shroud.

'What are you doing?' Nina asked.

'An insurance policy. And a retirement policy,' Ribbsley told her as he ripped away the last of the cloth, then gripped the corpse by its neck. 'The Covenant may have lost its leaders, but it still exists. With this – or rather, with the threat of the DNA evidence it'll provide – I'll be able to renegotiate my terms with the new leaders.'

'Trade the proof for money?' said Nina in disgust.

'Something like that.'

Everyone reacted in momentary surprise as Vogler spoke, his quavering voice revealing the intense agony he was suffering. 'Not . . . the deal . . . we made . . .' He went limp.

'The deal you made is no longer relevant,' Ribbsley told him, straining at the skeleton. 'Because soon you'll be dead, and so will Dr Wilde, and this entire place will be a smoking hole in the ground. A shame, a waste, but one has to make the best of changing circumstances.' With a last grunt, he tore the skull from the body with a dry crack. He looked into its decayed face, then wrapped it in the torn piece of shroud and returned to the larger chamber. 'Time we were going.'

'One minute, Gabriel,' said Sophia. She smiled again, this time with a cat-like malice. 'There are some people I've waited a long time to deal with. And so many choices! Who should I kill first?' She pointed the gun at Callum. 'My charming chaperone, perhaps? I'm really going to enjoy watching your boss squirm. Or . . .' the weapon came round to Chase, 'the last – and least – of my ex-husbands?'

'Hey!' said Chase, offended.

The muzzle settled on Nina. 'Or you, Nina?' Sophia fingered the scar on her cheek as she moved closer. 'You've already given me so much to remember you by.'

'Glad I won't be forgotten,' said Nina.

'Oh, I won't be giving you much thought. The media will, though, what with such an ignominious end to your career. The discoverer of Atlantis, fired from her post in disgrace before disappearing and dying in anonymity. Unmourned. Sad, really.'

'At least she won't have people lining up to piss on her grave,' Chase said.

'They can do whatever they like to my grave, as long as I'm not in it. Unlike our religious friends here,' said Sophia, 'I believe that you only get one life, and all that matters in it is winning. I'm legally dead – a spot of plastic surgery, a deal with the Covenant, and Gabriel and I will be free to do exactly as we please. The best revenge, as they say, is living well . . . and I intend to live *very* well.'

Ribbsley walked towards the main door, looking back impatiently. 'Neither of us will be living if we don't get out of here, Sophia. Just kill them and let's go.'

'Oh, very well,' sighed Sophia, for the briefest moment glancing at him—

Chase's hand lashed out, trying to knock the gun from her grip.

He wasn't quite close enough, only catching the weapon a glancing blow. Sophia instinctively fired, the bullet slicing past Chase to hit the wall behind him. Startled, then enraged, she whipped the gun round at his chest, about to fire at point-blank range—

Nina whipped the penknife from her pocket and stabbed its blade deep into the back of her wrist.

Sophia shrieked and jumped away, trying to fire – but the blade was jammed between the bones of her forearm, paralysing the tendons.

Chase was about to lunge at her, until he saw Callum diving for one of the dead troopers' rifles. Ribbsley was also bringing up his own pistol. He immediately changed tactics, grabbing Nina and leaping with her into the burial chamber. He shoved her away from the entrance as he searched for Callum's fallen gun.

Sophia had also seen Callum snatching up the rifle. She hurled herself over one of the stone benches and took cover behind it, pulling the blade from her wrist. 'Bitch!' she hissed as she tossed the bloodied penknife away and painfully flexed her fingers.

Callum was about to fire at her, but Ribbsley got off the first shot as he found cover behind another bench near the entrance. Callum was left with no choice but to throw himself into the second, unexplored, burial chamber, disappearing into the darkness.

Chase found Callum's gun, a Smith and Wesson Sigma 40P, and snatched it up before pressing his back against the wall beside the entrance. He examined the weapon. Ribbsley's shot had dented the slide, the steel buckled forward of the ejection port. He racked it experimentally, hand over the port to catch the unfired bullet. The slug plopped coldly into his palm as he pulled the slide fully back – but it was extremely stiff, not moving smoothly along its rails. If he fired, there was a very high chance of a jam. He would have to rack the slide manually for each shot. Quickly ejecting the magazine, he clicked the stray bullet into its top before slapping it back into place.

'Sophia!' Ribbsley shouted. 'Are you okay?'

'That bitch stabbed me!' she yelled back.

'Get over here, I'll cover you!' Crouching, the professor looked round the side of the bench, gun fixed on the entrance to the second burial chamber.

Chase risked a look round his own doorway. He caught a glimpse of Sophia as she shuffled quickly between two of the benches, but not enough of her to take a shot. He leaned out slightly further, trying to spot Callum – and jerked back as Ribbsley changed targets and took a shot at him, the bullet pitting the stone beside his head.

Another gunshot – but this was closer. Callum darted out to take a shot at Ribbsley, forcing him to duck. The American was about to make a run for the cover of another bench when Chase fired at him. The bullet went wide, but the startled Callum still flinched back into the dark room.

Chase looked at his gun. The spent casing had ejected, but the slide was stuck in the locked-back position, even though there were still bullets in the magazine. Cursing, he forced it forward until he felt the mechanism chamber the next round.

Sophia took advantage of the distraction to hurry to Ribbsley's position, picking up another SIG assault rifle from one of the dead men en route. Ribbsley looked in dismay at her blood-soaked wrist. 'My God, you're—'

'Never mind that,' she snapped. 'Get to the chopper and start it up – I'll keep them pinned down here until you're at takeoff speed.' He looked about to object, but her barked order of 'Go on, go!' silenced him. Instead, he waited until she was ready to fire, then made a run for the exit as she blasted two shots at Callum's position and a single one at Chase's before dropping down again.

Nina jumped as the bullet hit the burial chamber's back wall. 'What's happening?'

'Got a bit of a Mexican stand-off,' said Chase, peering cautiously round the doorway. 'I've got Callum pinned, he's got *us* pinned, and Sophia's got a good angle on us both.' He could see Sophia's shadow in the light coming through the mausoleum's entrance, but she herself was in full cover.

'How long have we got left?'

'Twelve minutes, give or take.'

'How are we going to get out of the cave in twelve minutes?'

'Let's worry about getting out of this *room* first.' He peered round the doorway again; the brief glance revealed a rifle pointing at him from inside the second chamber and he pulled back as Callum fired, the bullet slamming a chunk of stone from the wall. A moment later, Sophia took a shot at the American. Chase took another look to see Callum retreating into the shadows. He fired at him, the Sigma's slide jamming again. 'This is fucking ridiculous!' he growled as he reloaded. 'None of us can move!'

'Sophia will in a minute,' said Nina, hearing a rising sound from outside. The helicopter's engine.

'Great, and we won't be able to go after her because Callum'll shoot us, and he can't go after her because I'll shoot *him*!'

Callum had reached the same conclusion. Nina and Chase heard him speak urgently into his radio. 'Abaddon, Abaddon, this is Archangel, urgent! This is a code alpha hold, repeat, a code alpha hold order.' The response was too muted for them to make out.

'What's he doing?' Nina asked.

'Telling the stealth not to drop its bombs,' said Chase.

'Well, that's great! Isn't it?'

'Yeah, until he tells 'em to start the clock again. It's still on its way.' Another glance; Sophia had raised the SIG. She fired two shots at Callum's position, and Chase unleashed one at hers, the bullet cracking stone as she dropped.

He racked the slide again. The helicopter sounded almost at takeoff speed – which meant Sophia would be about to move. With nobody to give her covering fire, he could guess her tactics: switch the SIG to full auto and spray both doorways with bullets as she retreated.

If he could catch her as she rose to fire . . .

He moved back into firing position, saw Sophia jumping up from behind the bench, took aim—

And was forced to throw himself back into cover – Callum was fixing his sights on *him*!

Grit sprayed into his face as another rifle bullet cratered the stone. 'Twat!' Chase snarled, a rattle of automatic fire and a hailstorm of lead against the walls telling him he'd missed his one chance.

The firing stopped. Sophia had made it out of the mausoleum.

Which still left Callum to deal with.

The only thing stopping him from escaping was Chase, and vice versa. They would have to face off against each other—

Now!

Chase sprang round the doorway at almost the same moment Callum came into view in the other chamber. The Englishman had the advantage that his Sigma was quicker to aim than the assault rifle, but the other man had firepower on his side . . .

Chase fired first – but his damaged gun's sights were slightly off. The shot zipped past Callum to impact inside the other burial chamber. Callum returned fire as Chase pulled back, struggling to cycle his recalcitrant weapon. 'Come on, you fucking thing—'

The next bullet was chambered. He whipped back out, instinctively compensating for the misaligned sights as he fired, a moment too late to catch Callum.

The American reappeared – but not lining up another shot. Instead he ran out into the open. He had realised Chase was having trouble with the gun, and used the vital few seconds to reach one of the dead troopers and snatch a hand grenade from his webbing as Chase fumbled with the Sigma.

The slide cycled; bullet loaded.

Too late.

Callum had pulled the pin, lobbing the grenade through the doorway.

Chase instantly forgot about shooting him. He had less than four seconds to find cover before the grenade exploded, filling the room with a storm of shrapnel.

He pulled Nina with him.

Three seconds.

Hiding behind the sarcophagus wouldn't be enough to save them.

Two seconds.

The only protection was *inside* it.

One—

Nina half jumped, was half thrown into the ancient stone coffin as Chase leapt in on top of her and pulled the edge of the heavy lid.

Zero.

Sophia heard the explosion as the helicopter took off, dust and smoke swirling from the mausoleum a second later. Either Chase or Callum had got hold of a grenade and used it against the other – but who was still standing?

Not that it mattered. Callum might have ordered a postponement of the bombing, but since Dalton wanted Eden destroyed, it wouldn't be long before the attack resumed, whether Callum was clear or not.

She still had the rifle, keeping it fixed on the entrance as Ribbsley manoeuvred the chopper towards the cavern's ceiling. Seconds passed. No sign of anyone. Beside her, Ribbsley frowned in concentration as he watched the narrowing gap between the rock and the tips of the rotor blades.

Movement in the entrance. White hair. Callum.

Sophia fired a burst, forcing him back inside. Ribbsley winced at the noise, but held the chopper steady, guiding it into position directly beneath the hole. Callum reappeared, trying to bring his own rifle to bear, but Sophia's last bullets made him retreat again.

Ribbsley brought the helicopter to full power. Backwash from the rotors against the rocky ceiling buffeted them, and then they were clear, emerging into the bright desert sunlight.

Sophia took a final look down at the Garden of Eden as the helicopter turned east, towards Khartoum. A brief glimpse of the statue and the plateau, the mausoleum at its heart amidst the carpet of flowers – then it was gone as they moved away.

Ribbsley let out a relieved breath. 'We did it. We did it!' He glanced at the wrapped skull in Sophia's footwell. 'I think that should give us plenty of leverage over the Covenant. We'll be able to get a new identity for you . . . and a substantial sum of money, of course.'

'Can you trust them?'

'If di Bonaventura becomes the acting head of the Catholic contingent, which I'm sure he will, then yes. If I pitch it to him as a business opportunity rather than full-on blackmail, I think we'll get what we want.'

Sophia smiled. 'Marvellous. And then, I think a little petty revenge on Victor is in order.'

'I thought it might be,' said Ribbsley with a grin. 'Who were you shooting at, by the way? Chase or Callum?'

'Callum.'

'So Chase is dead? And Dr Wilde too, presumably. Not before time.'

'I know. Although I would have preferred to kill them myself . . .' She looked back at the retreating mesa.

'What is it?' Ribbsley asked.

'Something I once said to Eddie. That I wasn't going to make the mistake of assuming he was dead until I actually saw his body.'

'Even if Callum didn't kill him, he's still going to be blown to bits when the bombs hit. There's no way he'll get out of that cave in time.'

'Let's hope.' All the same, she stared back at the mesa until it was obscured from view by the fuselage as the helicopter turned. 'Goodbye, Eddie,' she said quietly.

Callum glared up at the opening, then shook off his anger at Sophia's escape. He had more immediate problems.

He looked back into the mausoleum. Dust was still swirling, but the air was clear enough for him to tell that there had been no movement from the burial chamber, no sounds of life.

Shouldering the rifle, he ran across the plateau, feet decapitating flowers as he headed for the grappling lines. Below, the two Humvees were parked beside the lake almost underneath the giant statue's outstretched hand, their tracks leading back into the jungle. The 4x4s had flattened most of the obstacles they encountered on their way round the far end of the ravine and through the jungle; by retracing the route, he could reach the tunnel before the bombs hit.

He tossed all but one of the grapnels over the edge of the cliff, taking hold of the remaining line and rappelling down it. Once at the bottom, he shook the line until the grapnel came loose, clanking down the rockface. On the extremely slim chance that anybody was still alive, they now had no way down except by the long and precarious path behind the statue.

They wouldn't even have time to get halfway. He reactivated the radio. 'Abaddon, Abaddon, this is Archangel.'

'Archangel, we copy,' the B-2 pilot answered.

'Give me your current estimated time to initiation.'

'Estimate ten minutes, Archangel. But we are still in a code alpha hold. Do you wish to resume operation?'

Callum ran to the nearest Humvee. 'Confirm, Abaddon. Resume operation. Take this place out.' He started the engine, and set off in a spray of soil.

39

'Well,' said Chase, 'this is cosy.'

'Three's a crowd, though,' Nina replied, horribly aware despite the total darkness that she was lying on top of a headless corpse.

The crack of the grenade explosion and the boom as the sarcophagus's stone lid slammed down had come simultaneously. The body's ribcage had collapsed beneath them with an unpleasant crunch, stubs of bone poking at Nina's chest.

'Depends who the third one is. But it's definitely not this bloke.' Chase shifted, trying to arch his back against the stone slab. 'Let's get this open.'

He strained, pushing himself up. There was a faint rasp from the lid, but no light entered the sarcophagus. 'Bollocks,' he muttered. 'Shift over a bit, I need more room.'

Nina tried to move, but to one side was nothing but solid stone, and on the other a rattling collection of dry bones. 'Sorry . . .' She instead attempted to push herself up underneath Chase to give him an extra boost.

'Yeah, that's hot,' he said, pushing again, 'but . . . *nnrgh!* Not much help. Can you turn on your back?'

'Eddie, I can barely turn my *hands* over in this space.' She tried anyway, but was unable to do more than twist a little.

'Have to make do, then. When I say, push up against me as hard as you can. Ready?'

'Just a sec, I've got a bone stuck in me.'

'That's my job.'

'*God*, Eddie!' She fidgeted until the offending fragment dropped away. 'Okay, ready.'

'All right . . . *Push!*'

They both forced themselves upwards. The rasp was louder this time, the heavy cover moving slightly, but still not enough. Chase leaned as far as he could towards the side opposite the hinges and pushed even harder. The lid grated again, for a moment a thin line of pale light appearing along its edge . . . before the sheer weight forced him down again. In the confined space, he couldn't get enough leverage.

'Buggeration and fuckery!' he spat. 'I almost had it.'

'It took three of us to open it before,' Nina pointed out.

'Maybe we can call Callum back,' replied Chase, pain flaring in his knees as he pushed again. The faint line of light reappeared, widening slightly before wavering, then narrowing once more. 'Shit, come on, come *on!*'

The light became a razor-thin slit, then vanished . . .

And suddenly widened again.

Nina and Chase both gasped as some of the pressure on their bodies was released, the lid rising by several inches. Chase slid one knee forward, able to brace himself and push harder. He shoved an arm through the gap, working his head and shoulders after it . . . to see Vogler, face twisted and sweating, holding up the stone slab.

He didn't have time to ask for an explanation. Instead, he pushed up with all his might. Vogler cried in agony and slumped against the sarcophagus as the lid passed the tipping point – but instead of coming to a stop as before, kept going. There was a nerve-scraping

493

crunch as the hinges broke, and the lid crashed to the floor, one corner breaking off.

Chase slumped, breathing heavily. 'Nina, get out.' She clambered from the sarcophagus, looking at Vogler with puzzlement – and suspicion. Chase did the same. 'All right, I'll bite – why'd you help us?'

Vogler pressed a hand against his bullet wound, the agony on his face easing slightly. 'Dalton betrayed the Covenant,' he said, voice little more than a choked whisper. 'So did Ribbsley. Somebody's got to tell the Cardinal what happened. I don't think I'm going to make it out of here.'

'I don't think *we* are, either,' Nina said, looking at her watch with dismay. 'Nine minutes! It'll take us longer than that just to get down to the temple!'

'We need a quicker way,' said Chase, climbing out. 'Those grappling lines – no, shit, Callum'll have chucked them.'

'Could we jump into the lake?' Nina suggested.

'We wouldn't be able to jump far enough.' His eyes widened. 'Unless we get a boost!' He rushed round the sarcophagus to the fallen lid. 'Vogler! Are you going to die any second, or can you help us kick Callum's arse?'

Vogler gave him a strained rictus grin. 'What do you want to do?'

'This lid – we need to get it to the statue, fast as we can!'

Nina looked at the cracked slab. 'What for?'

'Quick way down. Nina, give him a hand.'

'He's . . . he's kinda got blood squirting out of his stomach, Eddie.'

'I can do it,' Vogler rasped, moving stiff-legged to the lid.

'Okay,' said Chase. 'I'll lift this end; Nina, get that end as high as you can so he doesn't have to bend down too much. Soon as you've got it, we move and don't stop until we get to the statue!'

Nina, still uncertain what he intended, crouched and took hold of the broken corner. Neck muscles bulging, Chase let out a strangled roar as he lifted the slab. Her end lighter because of the missing corner, Nina managed to do the same, but it was still heavy enough to hurt. 'Can't – hold it!' she gasped.

Vogler stepped forward and gripped the slab – and screamed in pain.

'Put it down, put it down!' Nina begged, seeing more blood gush from his wound.

'No!' Vogler croaked. His whole body shuddering, he twisted to push one of his elbows against his abdomen. Another noise of agony escaped from his mouth – but he kept hold of the slab.

'Okay, go!' Chase shouted. Step by clumsy step, they swung the lid round and carried it through the doorway into the outer chamber.

'You holding up?' Chase called. Vogler gurgled something that might have been an affirmation, but Nina could tell that he was close to breaking point.

They couldn't stop, though. They were running out of time.

They reached the entrance and moved out amongst the flowers. No chance to appreciate their beauty one last time as they trampled them, weaving to avoid the gravestones. The back of the statue loomed ahead, the little bridge leading to its shoulders. 'Okay, get it across,' Chase grunted.

Nina looked down. The switchback cliff path dropped vertiginously away below. 'Hope it can take the weight.'

Chase went first, shuffling on to the narrow stone crossing. Nina shifted position at the other end of the slab so she and Vogler could both fit on the bridge at once. Her arm and shoulder muscles were ablaze, but she tightened her grip and moved step by step after Chase.

He was halfway across. Two-thirds. The surface of the bridge was covered in dirt and bird droppings. Detritus fell from the edges as he advanced, some dislodged by his feet – and some shaken loose as the stone blocks rocked under his weight.

'Oh, shit,' he said. 'Come on, faster, faster! I don't think it's gonna hold!'

Nina tried to move more quickly, but Vogler gasped and spat out blood. The movement of the stone lid had momentarily pulled his arm away from his body, releasing pressure on his wound. 'Oh God, I'm sorry!' she cried, slowing again.

Vogler forced an unconvincing smile, his face a ghastly white. 'Not a problem . . . just get us across . . .'

Chase reached the far end, the last block dropping half an inch with a clunk as he stepped on to the statue's shoulders. He brought the slab round towards its outstretched left arm. 'Just a couple more feet, come on!'

Nina and Vogler followed, bumping against each other as the slab turned. Nina made footfall on the statue, the Swiss Guard a step behind—

The stone block beneath his foot gave way.

It slipped sideways, smaller blocks ripping loose and falling away. Unsupported, the rest of the bridge broke apart and tumbled down the cliff to smash on the ground far below.

Vogler fell. The heavy slab dropped from Nina's hands, the broken end barely missing her feet. The impact jarred the other end from Chase's grip, sending him reeling backwards. He caught the statue's carved ear, just stopping himself from going over the edge.

Vogler dangled by his fingertips from the broken stub of the bridge. Even as Nina watched, one of his straining fingers lost its grip. 'Eddie! He's going to fall! Help me!'

'No!' Vogler gurgled as she grabbed his sleeve, blood bubbling from his mouth. 'No – time! You have to – tell the Cardinal!' He looked Nina in the eye, fear and panic and pain suddenly replaced by the serenity of self-sacrifice. 'Tell the Cardinal,' he repeated.

He closed his eyes.

And let go.

Nina couldn't keep hold, already weakened by the effort of carrying the slab. Chase seized her from behind to stop her from toppling after him as Vogler plunged, not even screaming. A wet thump echoed up the cliff face.

Chase pulled Nina upright. 'Oh, Jesus,' she whispered as she saw Vogler's twisted body below.

'We've only got six minutes,' said Chase, drawing her away from the edge. 'We've got to get that stone to the top of the arm. Now!' He moved to the slab's unbroken end and pulled it inch by inch across the statue's shoulder, gouging a furrow through the dirt.

Nina pushed the other end. 'How's this going to help us?'

'We can ride it down the arm like a sledge!'

She regarded him as if he'd gone mad. 'What?'

'Trust me! I've done it before.'

'*What?*'

'Well, not *exactly* like this. But I once went down the side of a skyscraper in Shanghai on a sort of sledge, and that was a lot steeper.' He looked down as he reached the top of the arm. 'Although the drop at the end was only about five feet, not fifty,' he added, biting his lip. 'But the principle's the same!' He jumped over the slab to land beside Nina, helping her push it over the edge.

The statue's arm was dirty and moss-covered, its open palm overflowing with dangling creepers and spindly plants. Beyond it stretched the lake. Nina heard the roar of an engine; in the distance, she saw trees swaying as Callum ploughed his Humvee through the jungle, taking a long, dogleg route to pass round the end of the ravine near the cavern's northern wall.

She looked back at Chase as she felt the slab shift, teetering on the edge of the slope. 'If by some miracle we survive this, to hell with waiting until May – we are going to get *so* married.'

Chase grinned, and they kissed. 'First things first, though,' he said as they parted. 'Kneel on the back end.' Nina did so, bringing the see-sawing slab back to the horizontal. He straddled the stone in front of her, lowering himself until he was almost touching it. 'Now grab my waist – and *don't let go.*'

'I'm not gonna enjoy this, am I?' Nina said as she took hold of him.

'Nope – but it'll be a really good bit for your autobiography.'

'If I get to write it.'

'You can start after the honeymoon. Okay. Here . . . we . . . *go!*'

He dropped on to the slab, grabbing its edges – as his weight tipped it over the edge.

Stone rasped angrily against stone, a terrible grinding assaulting their ears. But the moss and dirt acted as a strange form of lubricant. The slab quickly built up speed, throwing up a spray of soil from its front edge. They hit the slight bend at the giant elbow with a crash, the slab slithering sideways, threatening to fall off the carved arm – but they were moving too fast for gravity to claim them, already at the hand—

There was a colossal explosion of soil and vegetation as they ploughed across the statue's palm, shooting up its splayed fingers and flying out into open space . . .

Nina screamed as the slab fell away – and she lost her grip on Chase. The lake whirled below. They had been flung past the shore, falling towards deeper water – but too fast, gravity eagerly reclaiming its prizes.

She saw Chase twist in mid-air, trying to hit the water feet first. She did the same.

They hit the water.

The impact felt to Nina like landing on concrete – but it was nothing to the much harder blow a moment later as she hit the lake's muddy bottom. The stone slab smashed down behind her, a shockwave pounding her back. Her breath was knocked from her in a froth of bubbles as silt swirled round her, obscuring her vision.

How deep was she? Her feet brushed the bottom, sending a painful bolt through her legs. She tried to swim upwards, but seemed engulfed in quicksand, her waterlogged clothes slowing her movements to the pace of a nightmare.

A sound. A voice, muffled, muted. Chase, calling her name.

Nina still couldn't see, surrounded by mud – and he couldn't see her. She brought her arms as high above her head as she could, but they didn't breach the surface. He could be just feet away, but it might as well be miles.

With her last dregs of air, Nina screamed. Bubbles roiled up her face – then stopped. Water filled her mouth. She tried to scream again, but there was nothing left . . .

A hand clutched at her hair, her face – then grabbed her collar and pulled as Chase swam down to scoop her up. They broke the surface, Nina spitting out brown water and gasping for air. To her shock, she realised she had been on the verge of drowning less than fifteen feet from the shore.

Chase kept swimming until he was able to put his feet down, then carried Nina the rest of the way. 'Are you okay?'

'Hurt my legs,' she panted. 'Couldn't swim . . .'

They splashed out of the lake, Nina in Chase's arms. 'Can you walk?'

She tried to move one leg, the result making her wince. 'I dunno.'

'Okay, just hang on. I'll get you to the Humvee.' The 4x4 waited at the foot of the cliff, the tracks of its sister vehicle disappearing into the trees. Streaming with water, Chase carried Nina to it. She opened the passenger door for him, and he placed her inside. 'Oh, cock,' he said as he checked his watch.

'How long?'

'Four minutes.' He climbed into the driver's seat, starting the engine. The 6.5 litre turbo-diesel growled as he made a U-turn to face along the shore.

'We'll never make it,' said Nina, a chill running through her. 'Callum had that much of a head start on us, and he hasn't even got round the end of the ravine.'

Chase pushed down hard on the accelerator. The Humvee's wheels spun, slipping sideways in a spray of mud and earth before finding grip and surging forwards. 'We're not going round the ravine.'

'We're not?'

They charged through a stream, kicking up a massive shower of crystalline droplets. 'Taking a short cut.'

Nina gripped her seat as the Humvee bounced back on to dry land. 'I don't think this thing's gonna fit over that log!'

'I'm not going for the log.' Chase swerved round a tree, wheels carving through the water before he straightened out and smashed the 4x4 through some bushes on to a small hill.

'What *are* you going for?'

Despite the rockier terrain, Chase kept the pedal down, building up speed as they approached the top of the rise. 'You remember *The Dukes of Hazzard*?'

Nina blanched. 'You're going to *jump* the ravine?'

'If we go the long way round, we'll never make it!'

'And we'll never make it if we jump! We're not in an action movie, and this thing must weigh five tons!'

They reached the top, the western side of the Garden of Eden opening out before them. Verdant jungle lit by shafts of sunlight to the right, the dark crack of the ravine slashing across the landscape ahead—

'There he is!' Chase yelled, catching a flash of reflected light on the far side of the ravine. Callum's Humvee was bounding along the edge of the cliff, squeezed between the trees and the near-vertical drop. He pushed the pedal to the floor, the engine surging. 'How long?'

'Three minutes!'

The log bridge was off to the right; almost directly ahead was the large, slanted rock Chase had noticed earlier, protruding over the side of the chasm. Callum was still short of the log, but would reach it in seconds. 'Soon as we stop on the other side, no matter what happens, you run for the tunnel!' he told Nina.

'And if we don't reach the other side?'

The Humvee picked up speed as it descended the rise, flattening everything in its path. Chase aimed for the rock, then looked at Nina. 'Then this is your last chance to say I love you!'

'I love you,' Nina said, grimacing. 'But I hate the way you *driiiiiive!*'

The Humvee hit the rock at over fifty miles an hour and shot up the impromptu ramp—

And flew across the ravine.

40

Callum glimpsed movement to his left as he passed the log. He looked round – and froze at the sight of the black colossus arcing across the gap at the head of a trail of dust and dirt from its still-spinning wheels.

Fear snapped him back to life as he realised that the other Humvee was not only going to make it over the ravine, but would collide with him if he didn't stop—

He slammed on the brakes. His Humvee slewed on the damp ground as the other vehicle smashed down in front of him.

Even with the soft earth absorbing the impact, its suspension collapsed, one wheel ripping away. Amidst a whirlwind of churned soil and shredded creepers, the Humvee tore through the tangled net of vines hanging from the trees before slamming sidelong into the trunks and bouncing back towards the cliff . . .

Smashing into Callum's skidding vehicle.

Glass shattered and metal tore with a banshee screech. The colliding 4x4s swept over the edge, teetering on the brink before starting to fall—

And abruptly jerking to a stop.

The wrecked suspension of Nina and Chase's Humvee was entangled in vines and creepers. It hung sideways over the edge of the cliff at a forty-degree angle – as Chase discovered when he opened his eyes to find that the steep tilt of the world around him wasn't solely down to his dizziness.

He saw blood on the steering wheel where he had banged his head against it. Below him, Nina was crumpled in the footwell.

Pulling himself upright, Chase forced open his door, immediately seeing how perilous their position was. Even as he watched, the vines holding them vibrated like plucked guitar strings, the weaker creepers twisting . . . and snapping. The little pops and cracks sounded like someone stepping on bubblewrap – but each break put more strain on the others. It was only a matter of moments before the Humvee fell.

'Nina, get up,' he said, reaching down to take hold of her arm.

She raised her head, looking dazedly at him. 'Did we make it?' she asked absently. He nodded. 'Oh, good.'

'We're not safe yet. We've got – shit, two and a half minutes.'

'Until what again?'

He pulled at her. 'You know? The bomb?'

'What bomb?' Her eyes finally focused on him. 'The bomb! Oh, shit, the bomb!' She tried to stand, only to gasp in pain. 'Oh, God, my leg still hurts!'

'Think you can walk?'

'I'm gonna have to! No, wait,' she added as she forced herself up, 'I'm gonna have to *run*!'

A much louder snap from outside was accompanied by a jolt. One of the thicker vines had just given way. 'This thing's going to fall! Come on!' Chase put both feet against the high transmission tunnel between the seats and straightened his legs, lifting Nina up. 'Climb over me!'

'But—'

'Quick!' He shoved her through the door. More snaps. The Humvee lurched.

Nina scrambled clear. Chase gripped the door frame and pulled himself upwards, using the steering column for a step as he dived out—

Several vines snapped at once. The battered Humvee swung round, tipping over the edge – and plummeted into the ravine, bouncing off the rockface and cartwheeling into the darkness below.

Nina hobbled to Chase, who lay at the lip of the chasm, both legs hanging out over nothingness. Despite the pain, she pulled him clear. 'Jesus! Are you okay?'

Chase could hardly speak, his heart slamming in his chest. He managed a thumbs-up, before seeing they were not alone.

Callum's Humvee hung almost vertically over the cliff edge, nose down at what seemed like an impossible angle until Chase saw it was suspended from a pointed rock, its tip wedged under the 4x4's rear axle. The engine was still running, and its front doors were both open, extended like stubby wings – revealing Callum slumped over the wheel inside.

Unconscious.

'Get to the tunnel,' Chase said, standing.

'Not without you,' Nina said. 'What are you doing?'

'I can use his radio to delay the strike – I remember the code. Look, go!' he said, seeing that she was about to object. 'There's only two minutes left!' He waited until she reluctantly turned and began a limping run towards the exit, then bunched together several creepers and used them to climb down the cliff.

Not sure how much weight the passenger-side door could take, he kept hold of the creepers as he gingerly put his feet on it. The hinges creaked. Wincing, he eased himself into the cabin. The armoured windscreen was cracked, loose gear strewn across it. Not sure if it would support his weight, Chase instead stood on the dashboard and looked more closely at Callum.

The white-haired agent still seemed out cold, a deep cut

across his cheek. His jacket hung open. There was no sign of a radio in the equipment on the windscreen, so it was probably still in his pocket.

Chase edged closer, alert for any noises or movements warning that the Humvee was about to fall. It swayed as he crossed the cabin, but the rock supporting it seemed solid – for now.

He reached Callum. The American was still breathing. Chase hunched lower, carefully slipping his arm through the steering wheel to reach Callum's inside pocket. His fingers touched the fabric; something hard and heavy inside. He edged his hand up, feeling plastic, switches . . .

Callum's eyes opened.

He grabbed Chase's outstretched arm and slammed it against the wheel, sweeping his other hand across to deliver a crunching backhand blow to the Englishman's face. Chase tried to pull back, but Callum bent his wrist backwards over the wheel's rim until the joints crackled, pinning him as he swung at Chase's head again, catching his jaw.

Chase retaliated with a punch of his own, then gouged Callum's eye with his thumb. Callum jerked away, releasing his grip on Chase's arm.

Chase stumbled back, one foot slipping off the dash on to the windscreen. Fractured glass squealed, cracks spreading out from beneath his boot like thin ice. He hurriedly lifted his foot—

Callum hit him in the chest. Caught off balance, Chase staggered . . . and fell backwards.

He landed on the open door – which buckled, one of the hinges snapping. With a yelp of 'Oh, *shit*!' Chase slid down it and was pitched into the chasm below—

His hand clamped round the window frame.

The jolt as he stopped his fall almost wrenched his arm from its socket. He slammed against the Humvee's mangled front wing, swinging helplessly. More cracks came from the door's overstressed hinge as it was bent past its limit.

Callum crossed the cabin. He saw Chase's hand gripping the frame, knuckles white. A nasty smile crossed his lips as he edged closer – and smashed his heel down on the door. The hinge groaned. Another strike, and another. Metal strained, split—

Snapped.

The door dropped into the ravine – just as Chase caught the Humvee's wing with his free hand. He slammed face first against the wheel as the door fell past him, hitting his shoulder and almost tearing him loose. Blood seeping from his fingers where he clutched torn metal, he kicked and flailed before finally finding a second handhold.

Callum leaned out of the doorway above him. Their eyes met. For a moment Chase thought he was going to lower himself out and stamp on his hands, but then he retreated into the cabin.

He knew why. The Humvee was hanging from a single rock; a couple of kicks would send the entire vehicle plunging to its doom. If Callum reached the top of the cliff before he did—

The thought spurred him to action. He pulled himself up, climbing hand over hand until he managed to get a foothold on the bumper.

Callum heard him moving as he was about to climb out through the driver's-side door. He halted, spotting something in the footwell. A pistol.

Chase kept climbing. He reached the doorway, looked inside—

To see Callum bringing up a gun.

He ducked as Callum fired. Two shots zipped just above his head, a third striking the door frame. The Humvee shook as Callum climbed across the cabin, coming to finish the job.

Nowhere to go . . .

Except down.

Chase released his grip – and dropped.

He caught the front wheel, hands slipping over the mud clogging the tread before finding purchase. Without a pause, he swung himself underneath the Humvee, grabbing the front axle and clambering along it like a monkey bar.

Callum returned to the doorway and looked down again. No sign of Chase. With a satisfied smirk, he peered up the cliff, comparing the vines Chase had used to climb down to the ones on the other side of the vehicle. Deciding that the latter appeared stronger, he turned back across the cabin.

Reaching the other end of the axle, Chase hauled himself round the wheel and pulled himself up beneath the open door. Through the window, he saw Callum negotiating the steering wheel, not wanting to stand on the damaged windscreen.

Chase grabbed the dangling vines beside the door and rapidly climbed upwards. Callum, halfway through the door, heard the noise – as Chase pulled up both legs and booted him back into the cabin. The gun clattered on the windscreen. Chase dropped on to the door, the hinges screeching. He grabbed the door frame – and smashed a nose-breaking punch into Callum's face.

The American fell, sprawled over the dashboard. Chase stepped inside and plucked the radio from Callum's jacket. He pulled back, reaching for the vines outside.

Callum's hand closed round the gun. Eyes narrowed to pain-filled slits, he brought it up, taking aim—

Chase stepped on the accelerator.

The Humvee's wheels spun, finding grip even on the cliff face – and wrenching the rear axle off the pointed rock.

Clinging to the vines with one hand, Chase yanked his leg out of the cabin as the Humvee fell. Callum's scream echoed up the canyon as the vehicle disappeared into shadow – then was cut off by a huge crash of metal on stone.

'Fuck you, whitey!' Chase gasped, shoving the radio into the waistband of his jeans before gripping the vines with both hands and climbing. He could feel the plants straining under his weight. Only six feet to go, five, the edge of the cliff tantalisingly close—

A loud snap. One of the larger creepers gave way, the smaller vines bunched with it in his hand also ripping. He snatched at others, but they had been damaged by the Humvee when it ground over the edge and broke instantly. He swung, the vines in his other hand tearing . . .

Hands gripped his flailing wrist. Startled, he looked up.

Nina.

'I got you,' she said.

She pulled. Toes scrabbling against the rocks, Chase forced himself upwards until he was able to get one hand over the edge. He dragged himself on to solid ground, staring up at Nina as he panted in relief. 'I told you to get out!'

'Like you say, I never listen to you.' She helped him sit up. 'I wasn't going to leave you here.'

'Thanks.' He examined the radio. He didn't recognise the type – some kind of spook special, he guessed – and hoped Callum hadn't changed the frequency. 'Okay, let's give this a try.'

'You're not going to do your John-Wayne-with-brain-damage voice, are you?' said Nina as he switched it on.

'Shh.' He put on his best attempt at an American accent, trying to remember the codes Callum had used. 'Abaddon, Abaddon, this is Archangel, urgent. Code alpha hold, repeat, this is a code alpha hold!'

Silence. Nina and Chase looked at each other in concern. Then: 'Archangel, this is Abaddon.' Chase pumped his fist in silent triumph. The B-2 crew thought he was Callum, and would stop the drop—

'We, ah . . .' The pilot's hesitant tone vaporised his jubilation in an instant. 'We released the bombs five seconds ago.'

'*What?*' Nina yelped. She looked up at the cavern's ceiling. 'Son of a *bitch*!'

'Say again, Archangel?'

Chase jumped up, grabbing Nina's hand and pulling her after him. '*Leg it!*'

'Ow, ow, *ow*!' Nina gasped with every step on her injured leg. 'How long have – aah! – have we got?'

'Not long!' From sixty thousand feet it took a person in freefall over five minutes to reach zero altitude – but the GPS-guided Massive Ordnance Penetrators each weighed fifteen tons, and their terminal velocity would be supersonic. They would hit the ground in a fraction of the time.

They reached the edge of the jungle, emerging on the dry river bed. The tunnel was a dark arch directly ahead. They entered it, running footsteps echoing through the curving passage. Light ahead. The Covenant had cleared the entrance to accommodate the Humvees. 'Come on, we can do it!' Chase cried, running faster. Nina responded, increasing her pace as they sprinted for the open desert, and safety—

The bombs hit the cavern.

The first MOP speared through the roof as if it were wet paper, hitting the ground just outside the temple walls. The combination of its weight and speed punched the reinforced bomb casing almost a hundred and fifty feet into earth and solid rock.

The second bomb went deeper, by fluke dropping through one of the holes in the ceiling and plunging into the ravine.

Body broken, organs ruptured, Callum was nevertheless still alive, lying in the Humvee's mangled wreckage. Through pain-racked eyes he could see a circle of sky high above – in which a black dot appeared, rushing at him before he even had time to scream—

The MOP hit the Humvee, utterly disintegrating it and its occupant as it slammed through them and dug deep into the ground – before detonating.

Each bomb carried three tons of high explosive. The power of the blast added to the sheer kinetic force of the impact was enough to pulverise solid rock, sending out a massive shockwave that acted like a localised earthquake.

The whole mesa shook as the ground *pulsed*, bulging upwards beneath the impact points before smashing back down again in two huge craters. The temple walls collapsed, the stacked archives shattering. The statue's outstretched arm broke off and exploded into stone shrapnel as it hit the ground, the rest of the enormous figure toppling into the jungle.

But there was worse to come. A tsunami surged from the lake, sweeping away everything it touched and causing a huge swathe of the southern wall to fall. For a moment, the whole of the Garden of Eden was lit by bright daylight – before the rest of the great chamber collapsed.

Chase and Nina were almost at the exit when the subterranean shockwave blew them off their feet, a vaporous wall of compressed air surging down the tunnel and blasting them out into the open. They tumbled across the sand, the ground reverberating with more enormous impacts as the mesa fell in on itself. Nina couldn't even hear herself scream as she curled into a ball, trying to protect her head from the noise and debris.

Finally the tumult faded.

Nina risked opening her eyes. Dust and sand swirled round her, but even through the haze she could see that the entire shape of the mesa had changed, the high walls and flat top replaced by ugly, jagged peaks and mounds of boulders.

The Garden of Eden had been destroyed.

She slumped in defeat, barely able to believe the sheer *pointlessness* of the devastation. The most significant archaeological find in history, to say nothing of the world-shaking anthropological revelations it had contained . . . and now it was gone, wiped from the face of the earth. Not by the wrath of God, but by the will of man. One man: Victor Dalton.

Why? She couldn't even begin to think of a reason. Why had Dalton suddenly turned on the Covenant? How would he benefit from Eden's destruction?

Coughing nearby. Chase. 'Eddie?' she called. 'Where are you? Are you okay?'

'Tip fuckin' top,' Chase grumbled, crawling to her. 'You?'

'I've . . . been better.' She slumped against him. 'Jesus, Eddie, this is, this is . . . I can't even begin to describe it. Everything's . . . it's all *gone*. The greatest find ever, and it's gone. And it's my fault.'

'How's it your fault? You didn't drop the bomb.'

'But I gave them the target. They never would have found it without me. If I hadn't been so obsessed, if I hadn't been so determined to prove how goddamn great I was . . .' She put her head in her hands, voice quavering with exhaustion – and misery. 'Rothschild was right. And so was Sophia. And you. I *was* doing all this for myself, for my own glory.'

'Yeah,' said Chase. 'You were.'

'Oh, thanks, Eddie,' Nina replied, despondency deepening.

'But so fucking what? Why does any explorer do anything? Columbus didn't discover America for shits and giggles – he did it for fame and fortune. And I bet Rothschild didn't take the IHA job for the benefit of all humanity either.' He put an arm round her shoulders. 'At least when you go looking for this stuff, you're doing it because you want to show it to the world, not because you want to steal all the treasure or blow everything up.'

She lifted her head. 'What you said on the way here, about me going too far . . . do you still think that?'

He glanced back at the ruined mesa before looking into her eyes. 'I think that, yeah, sometimes you go overboard. But other times . . . the stuff you find is worth it. You found the *Garden of Eden*, for Christ's sake.'

'And lost it again. It's all been destroyed. And we've got nothing.'

'Not all of it's gone,' he reminded her. 'Sophia and Ribbsley've still got that head.'

'Yeah, and they're going to trade it with the Covenant – who'll destroy it. And we haven't got a chance of catching up to them.'

'Hey, hey,' said Chase, resting his head against hers, 'it's not over yet. We're still alive, aren't we?' He pointed; the last of the Covenant's Humvees was parked not far away. 'We've got a ride out of here – and if it's got a satellite phone, we can call TD and get her to pick us up.'

'And then what?' Nina asked gloomily. 'We still have to find Sophia and Ribbsley. They're probably halfway to Khartoum already, and after that we don't even know where they'll be going.'

Chase didn't answer at once, but Nina could tell from the movement of his facial muscles against her head that he was smiling. 'What?'

He leaned back, grinning. 'I think *I* do . . .'

41

Switzerland

Moonlight glistened on the snow-capped peaks above the valley, the constant rumble of a waterfall rolling through the clear Alpine air.

Sophia looked over the edge of the viewing platform as the churning waters dropped away into a lake hundreds of feet below. The scenic point she had selected for the meeting was some thirty miles from Zürich, a popular tourist spot during the day, but now, at night, completely deserted. The nearest village was in the valley below, over two miles away by winding road, and past the surrounding trees she had a clear view of the route to the top of the waterfall. Nobody could approach without being seen.

'Someone's coming,' said Ribbsley.

Headlights were moving along the road. 'Is it him?'

Ribbsley watched the car through binoculars. 'I think so.'

'Is he alone?'

'As far as I can tell.'

That wasn't as much of an assurance as she would have liked, but there was certainly nobody else in sight. They had only told di Bonaventura that the meeting place would be in Switzerland that morning, and given him the exact location less than forty minutes earlier. There was still the possibility the Cardinal might try to take what they possessed by force, but with the Covenant's forces seriously depleted, the odds of that seemed long.

Besides, she thought as she fingered the revolver in her coat pocket, the weapon having been kept in the same safe deposit box as the object she had come to Switzerland to collect, she and Ribbsley were prepared for trouble.

She stood beside him as the car got closer. At his feet was an unassuming leather case the size of a bowling bag. Inside it was the skull: the last piece of proof that an intelligent, but non-human, civilization had existed on the earth before man. In whose hands it ended up depended entirely on whether di Bonaventura was good to his word.

The car, a sleek silver Mercedes, turned on to the short spur leading to the beauty spot and stopped beside Ribbsley's rented BMW. Di Bonaventura stepped out. He was alone.

The Cardinal approached them, giving Ribbsley a baleful look. 'Gabriel.'

'I'm sorry this means the end of our friendship, Lorenzo,' said Ribbsley, 'but it isn't the first time a woman has come between two men.'

'Perhaps so. But *that* woman, Gabriel? You know what she has done.'

'I believe that sins are traditionally forgiven upon death. And officially at least, Sophia Blackwood *is* dead. With the Covenant's help, we can ensure nobody ever knows that's not the case.'

Di Bonaventura regarded Sophia sourly. 'There is one quick and simple way to make certain of that.'

'Our way is better for everyone,' said Sophia, sliding the gun from her pocket and making sure di Bonaventura saw it. 'Except Victor Dalton, of course.'

'You have it?' asked the Cardinal.

She took something from another pocket and held it up: a small white plastic stick. A flash drive. 'Video proof of the President of the United States not only committing adultery, but doing so with . . . well, you know my reputation. Only eight minutes long – Victor was another short-term politician – but it should be more than enough to have 1600 Pennsylvania Avenue sending out change-of-occupier cards.'

'And . . . the other item?'

Ribbsley nudged the bag with his foot. 'Physical proof of the true nature of the Veteres, ready for DNA testing. Or incineration. As long as you agree to our terms, I don't care which.'

'Your terms,' said di Bonaventura with distaste. 'Ten million euros, a new identity for her, and the Covenant's . . . protection.'

'We won't need your protection if you use this,' Sophia said, turning the flash drive in her hand. 'It's the only copy – but I'm willing to give it to you. It'll take down Dalton, and all his cronies like Callum will go down with him.'

'Actually, Callum's dead,' said a new voice.

All three whirled to see Nina emerging from the nearby trees. 'Oh, for God's sake!' said Sophia in exasperation as she raised her gun. 'She's more resilient than a bloody cockroach!'

'Ah-ah,' Nina warned, waving a finger. 'Try anything and Eddie'll blow your head off. He's in the trees with a sniper rifle.' Sophia reluctantly returned the pistol to her pocket, but her hand remained hanging over it like a Wild West gunslinger. Ribbsley raised his hands.

'I'm surprised to see you again, Dr Wilde,' said di Bonaventura. 'I'd been told you were dead.'

'Your man Vogler saved us. He wanted to save Eden too – he decided that its value to the faithful, to the *world*, would outweigh any damage that the truth about the Veteres might cause. As long as that truth was revealed gradually.'

He nodded. 'I would probably have reached the same conclusion.'

Nina came to a stop facing the trio. 'It was kind of a least-worst option, but I agreed to go along with him. Until Callum decided to blow up Eden on Dalton's orders. And then Ribbsley took the opportunity for a little blackmail. So here we all are.'

'How did you find us?' Ribbsley asked.

'Because Eddie knew Sophia,' she replied with a small smile. 'When she "died" and he got all her paperwork, he saw she had a Swiss deposit box. After she told us about the recording,' she glanced at the flash drive, 'we figured that must be what she kept in it. So we got out of Sudan by persuading the head of the UN relief effort in El Obeid to fly us to Egypt, then came here, and staked out the bank until you turned up. Then we followed you and waited to see what happened. As Eddie would say, doddle.'

'So now, what *does* happen?' said di Bonaventura. He indicated the bag. 'I assume you want that.'

'That depends on you. You said you would probably have done the same as Vogler – is that still the case now Eden's been destroyed? Because if it is, I'm willing to make the same deal with you that I did with Vogler.'

'How very mercenary of you,' Sophia sneered.

'I'm not asking for money,' said Nina. 'I just want the truth to be revealed . . . however long it takes. And, y'know, I'd prefer to be alive when it happens.'

'And President Dalton?' asked di Bonaventura.

'Screw him,' said Nina after a moment. 'Although not in the way that Sophia did. But he betrayed everyone – including the Covenant – and tried to kill us. Callum's dead, but I bet there's a dozen more like him. The only way Eddie and I can be safe is if Dalton's removed from office.'

The Cardinal stood in thoughtful silence for several seconds before speaking again. 'Until now, it was easy for the Covenant to suppress any discoveries of the Veteres. But now that we know the scale of their civilization . . . sooner or later, they *will* be revealed, and the Covenant will not be able to stop it.' He looked at the bag, then back at Nina. 'Vogler was right. If this is to become known, then it should be on our terms. We have to prepare the world for it. Dr Wilde . . . if you agree to work with us towards that goal, then I will grant you protection.'

'And Eddie, too,' Nina said.

'And Mr Chase, yes. What do you say?'

'Excuse me,' Sophia snapped, 'but we were here first.'

'Sophia,' Ribbsley said tersely, 'we're not arguing over a parking space here. Your ex-husband has us in his gunsights.'

Sophia gave Nina a suspicious look. 'Does he, though?'

'You want to find out the hard way?' said Nina.

'I think I might. Gabriel, take out your gun.'

'You must be joking!' Ribbsley protested. 'You know that I'd do almost anything for you – but getting shot is definitely one of the exceptions.'

'You won't get shot. I'm sure Eddie's here somewhere, but he doesn't have a gun. And nor does she.' Sophia fixed her eyes on Nina's, calculating. 'You can't have arrived in Switzerland much before we did – we didn't come directly from Khartoum, but we weren't stopping for picnics en route either. I know Eddie has friends all over the world, but I find it hard to believe they could furnish him with a sniper rifle – but not get you a gun as well.'

Nina put a hand in one pocket. 'I assure you, I'm armed.'

'Then Gabriel won't have to feel guilty about shooting a defenceless woman, will he?' She turned to Ribbsley. 'Gabriel, take out your gun. Nothing will happen, I promise. I know Eddie – and I know Nina as well.'

'Your call,' Nina said.

'Your bluff,' Sophia replied. 'Do it, Gabriel. Now!'

Ribbsley hesitated, eyes scanning the dark forest – then pulled out his gun and pointed it at Nina.

Nothing happened. No gunshot came from the trees, the only sound the endless thunder of the waterfall.

'Well,' said Sophia, 'I told you.'

Ribbsley let out a relieved breath. 'I wish you could have found a less stressful way of proving it.'

Sophia nudged the bag. 'Cardinal, our original offer still stands. I recommend that you take it. Otherwise we'll have to fall back on Plan B – blackmailing the President of the United States. Which would be messy for everyone. As for you, Nina . . . I think it's time we said goodbye, once and for all. Gabriel, shoot her.'

Nina tensed. 'Don't you want to know where Eddie is?'

The question was enough to give Ribbsley pause, though the gun remained locked on Nina's heart. 'All right,' Sophia sighed impatiently, 'where's Eddie?'

'Right behind you.'

Sophia looked annoyed at the attempted distraction, but Ribbsley turned his head—

To see Chase vault over the railing and smash a fist into his face.

Ribbsley crashed nervelessly to the ground, the gun spinning away. Soaked by the waterfall's spray while he climbed round the viewing platform's supports, Chase whirled to face Sophia—

She shot him.

'*Eddie!*' Nina screamed as he fell, blood splashed across his chest. He let out a strangled moan, convulsing before falling still.

'Hold it!' said Sophia as Nina ran to him, pointing the smoking .38 at her. Nina stopped. 'Gabriel, are you all right?' Her concern went unanswered. 'Gabriel!'

Nina was unable to take her eyes from Chase's motionless body.

'Oh, Jesus, Eddie!' she gasped, shocked tears streaming down her cheeks. 'Oh, please, get up, get up . . .'

Sophia cast a dismissive sidelong glance at him. 'I think,' she said, 'that marks the end of the Chase.'

Hatred exploded inside Nina. 'You fucking bitch,' she snarled, all fear vanishing in her fury, 'I'm gonna fucking *kill* you!'

'No,' said Sophia, with a smile of malicious pleasure, 'you're not.'

Di Bonaventura jumped forward, arms held wide as if pleading. 'No! You don't have to—'

Sophia fired just as the Cardinal moved in front of Nina. The bullet caught him high on his chest. Sophia froze as he collapsed, realising she had just shot the only person with whom she could make a deal.

Nina leapt at her.

Driven by rage, she smashed the gun from Sophia's hand before slamming a brutal blow into her face. Sophia shrieked in pain, the flash drive in her other hand dropping to the ground, but Nina was already striking again, and again, fists crunched tight like blocks of stone. Blood smeared her knuckles as Sophia staggered.

Nina pulled back her arm, winding up for a final punch, swinging—

Sophia caught it.

'*Whore!*' she hissed as she gripped Nina's hand in both her own, twisting. A spear of agony shot through Nina's wrist as the Englishwoman pulled her closer, wrenching harder as she raised an elbow, ready to smash it into the back of Nina's arm to break it at the joint—

Nina struck first. One of Chase's moves: crude, savage – but effective. Sophia's nose broke with a snap of cartilage as Nina headbutted her, spraying both women with blood.

She tried to pull free, but Sophia still had a solid grip on her arm despite the pain. Gasping, Nina raked her fingernails at the other woman's eyes.

Sophia jerked her head back – and kicked Nina hard in the stomach. Choking, Nina stumbled, the wound in her leg searing with resurgent pain. Sophia tried again to break her arm, but the kick had thrown her off balance, forcing her to let go to avoid falling.

But Nina was already past the point of no return. She fell heavily beside di Bonaventura. For a moment their eyes met, the Cardinal's gaze full of pain and regret, before an almost infinitesimal relaxation of the tiny muscles around his eyes marked the moment when life became death. Di Bonaventura was about to find out if his beliefs were true.

Clutching her aching stomach, Nina got to her knees and looked up.

The gun was pointing at her head.

Sophia's enraged face was behind it, rivulets of blood running from her nose. Her finger tightened on the trigger—

A terrifying roar made both women whirl.

Chase had staggered upright, one hand clutched to his bloodied chest. He launched himself at Sophia, tackling her as she fired again and slamming her back against the railings.

They toppled over them, and were gone.

Sophia's piercing shriek of terror vanished beneath the waterfall's rumble as she fell. Chase made no sound as he plunged into the darkness with her.

Nina stared at the railings in stunned disbelief before running to the spot and looking down. The waterfall was a silver streak in the moonlight, the lake at its base a pool of pure black speckled with froth. Of Chase and Sophia there was no sign.

'Eddie!' She couldn't accept that he was gone, leaning out to look beneath the platform. He *must* have managed to grab its supports or a rocky outcropping as he fell, she told herself, was dangling just below her, saving himself at the last moment yet again . . .

But he wasn't. There was nobody there.

She had lost him.

Nina stumbled away from the railing with a moan of despair, tripping and landing by the bag. She didn't feel the pain of the fall, a far greater agony overpowering it.

Chase was dead.

'No,' she whispered. 'No, no, *no* . . .' She couldn't accept it. She *wouldn't*. He couldn't be dead. It wasn't possible.

Click.

A mechanical noise: a gun's hammer being cocked. Ribbsley had recovered, had found his gun, was pointing it at her with his bloodied face twisted by rage—

A hole exploded in his chest as a high-velocity bullet blew right through him in a bloody shower. The force of the impact sent the professor rolling over several times before coming to a stop, leaving a ragged red trail like a child's hand painting.

Some fearful instinct made Nina grab the bag and clutch it to herself as she scrambled back against the railings. There was nobody in sight. Who had fired the shot?

And was she the next target?

She looked in panic across the valley. The distant lights of the village glowed below, but she couldn't see any sign of the sniper . . .

A dazzling blue-white light pinned her from above. A helicopter – but she couldn't hear any rotor noise, or see anything except the blinding spotlight as it approached.

'Dr Wilde,' said a man's voice, American-accented but unfamiliar. It didn't seem to be coming from the helicopter, but from all around her – or inside her head. 'Do not move, remain still. I repeat, do not move, or you will be killed.'

'I'm not going anywhere,' she whispered, frozen with fear. Some remaining rational part of her mind dredged an explanation from her memory: a few years earlier, an advertiser had experimented with a hypersonic loudspeaker in New York, only people standing in a small area able to hear the commercials it played while others just feet away heard nothing. She had even gone to experience it for herself. This was something similar, the helicopter's occupants not wanting to rouse the entire valley.

But who were they?

The light came closer. Nina could now feel the downdraught from the rotors, but still couldn't hear any noise until it was almost upon her, when a low-frequency thrum filled the air. The light flicked off as the helicopter swept overhead and moved to land behind the cars, cutting off her escape route.

Not that she was planning to move. A strange numbness rolled through her body, as if something within her had switched off to escape the pain. She watched the helicopter almost with disinterest, noting that it was a very strange-looking aircraft, unlike any chopper she had seen before: a flat matt black with a sharply pointed, seemingly windowless nose and an odd rotor assembly within a ring that rose above the fuselage like a halo. Some kind of stealth prototype? Whatever. She didn't care.

A hatch opened in the helicopter's featureless side, several men in all-black combat gear jumping out and rapidly securing the area. Two more men, faces hidden behind black masks and night-vision goggles, advanced on her, silenced compact rifles flicking between her and the two bodies nearby. Once it was clear that neither Ribbsley nor di Bonaventura would be moving again, they came to a stop ten feet from Nina and fixed their guns on her, laser spots dancing over her chest.

Another man emerged from the helicopter. No mask, no camouflage; she saw he was wearing a suit and tie as he passed one of the lamps illuminating the platform, the light catching his face.

A face she knew well.

Victor Dalton. The President of the United States.

He stopped between the two men in black. 'Dr Wilde, hello again. You probably won't believe me, but I'm glad to see you.'

'Go to hell,' Nina growled.

'No, really – I've been watching what was going on down here. I didn't think you'd be the last person standing, but it's worked out fairly well.' He walked to the railing near where Chase and Sophia had fallen and picked up a small white object – Sophia's flash drive. 'I even heard Sophia say this was the only copy.' He looked back at the helicopter. 'It's a hell of a machine, by the way. One of DARPA's latest toys. Full array of surveillance gear, almost totally invisible to radar, and ninety per cent quieter than a normal chopper. Lucky for me it was in Germany for NATO evaluation, or my trip would have attracted a lot more attention – officially, I'm on vacation at my estate in Virginia. I wanted to keep this whole thing quiet.' He took a step towards her. 'Personal.'

Nina crawled away. 'Stay back! What do you want?'

'This, for one,' he said, holding up the memory stick. 'For another, what you've got in that case there. May I see it?' She didn't respond immediately; one of the soldiers flashed his laser sight over her face. 'Don't expect me to ask twice, Dr Wilde. For anything.'

Reluctantly, she opened it and took out a large plastic ziplock bag – inside which, still wrapped in the remains of its ancient shroud, was the skull. 'Open it,' ordered Dalton. 'Let me see.'

'Why do you want it?' she demanded as she unfastened the seal and began to peel away the cloth.

Dalton didn't answer at first, watching as she carefully removed the shroud. The skeletal face was revealed beneath. She turned it towards the President. To her surprise, he appeared visibly discomfited. 'So, it's true,' he said. 'The Covenant was right.'

'Yeah, it's true,' said Nina. She got to her feet. Both soldiers tensed, rifles tracking her. A nod from Dalton and they eased off, slightly. 'So why did you turn against them? And why did you destroy Eden?'

'Because it was in *Sudan*. Do you really think I'd let a group of backwater barbarians lay claim to it? Especially when it would give the foundation of the Christian faith to the Muslims.' He sneered in distaste. 'Better no one has it than they do. As for the Covenant, every politician has skeletons in their closet, and the Covenant has taken advantage for decades. It was time that situation ended. I should thank you and Chase for that much, at least – between you, you've decapitated the entire organisation.' He glanced at di Bonaventura. 'There'll be others to replace them, but right now the Covenant's in total chaos. It'll take a while for them to recover – and by then, it won't matter.'

'What do you mean?'

'You were making a deal with him,' said Dalton. 'Well, now you get to make that same deal with me. Only there won't be any pussyfooting around, gradually preparing the world for the Veteres. As soon as the DNA analysis confirms what that thing really is, you'll be back at the IHA announcing what you've discovered – a non-human race that was the basis of the Book of Genesis.'

Nina regarded him with growing suspicion. 'So . . . what's the catch?'

'Catch number one is that if you don't agree, you die right here and we find someone else to do it. But we'd prefer it to be you; you've got the credibility.'

'Who's "we"?'

'Catch number two,' he went on, ignoring her question, 'is that in making that announcement, you'll become the most hated person on the planet.'

Some of her old defiance returned. 'What, even more than the President of the United States?'

A brief smirk. 'Presidents are hated for political reasons. With you, it'll be *personal*. You'll be telling billions of people that their deeply held beliefs are wrong, that the basis of their entire religion is false, and you can prove it. They won't like that.'

'If I can prove it . . .' Nina began, before realising where he was heading.

'There are people who believe the earth was created in 4004 BC, that fossils are fakes put there by God to test their faith, that there were dinosaurs aboard Noah's Ark, that they can talk to ghosts, that a UFO crashed in Roswell. It doesn't matter what "proof" you show them otherwise: they have their beliefs, and they won't change them. These are the people who will consider the revelation of the Veteres as a personal attack on their faith. Not just in America, but all over the world.'

'And what does that gain you?' she asked. 'Sounds like you want to stir up the Danish cartoon riots, times a thousand.'

'More than that. We want to stir up the entire *world*. Religion against science. Religion against religion. Believers against atheists. Individual countries against the United Nations. And the outside world against the United States. And you, as a scientist, a part of the UN, an *American*, will be the lightning rod for it all.'

'I don't think I like your deal,' Nina said quietly.

'You don't have a choice. Either you do what we say, or you die.'

'But *why*?' Nina cried, the numbness swept away by a resurgence of emotion. 'This is insane! Why would you *want* to turn the world against America?'

'To protect it!' said Dalton, a flash of fervour in his eyes. 'There are too many people pulling in too many different directions, and in the end they're going to tear the country apart. But this will splinter the outside world – and bring America together. The silent majority will finally speak with one voice. A God-fearing, American, *Christian* voice. Not Catholic, not Jewish, and certainly not Muslim.'

'Last I heard, Catholics *are* Christians.'

'Who give their loyalty to Rome, not their country. It's time America was unified against threats from inside and out. One voice, one God, one people.'

'You actually have the *arrogance* to say you speak for every Christian in America?' Nina held up the skull. 'And you think all that will happen just because of this? You think the American people are that frightened and gullible?'

Dalton looked smug. 'The people believe whatever they're told because they have faith in something else – the system. They want – they *need* to believe it works, that their faith is justified. So what the leaders say, the followers accept.'

'Because it's easier and safer than having their beliefs challenged, huh?' said Nina. 'Well, you know what *I* put my faith in? I put my faith in *the people*. To be *better* than that.'

'You're going to be sorely disappointed, Dr Wilde.' He took another step towards her. 'But enough philosophical discussion. You're either with me or against me. And believe me, you don't want to be against me.'

'I sure as hell don't want to be with you.'

'Your choice.' He nodded at the soldiers. Their rifles came back up, laser spots rock-steady over her heart.

She whipped out one arm and held the skull over the edge of the platform. The shroud fell away into the spray below. 'If I drop this, you've got nothing. No proof of the Veteres, so no way to set the world on fire.'

Dalton shook his head. 'I'll be in exactly the same place as before. The Covenant's been crippled, and I've got Sophia's recording. And what I've told you will happen, *will* happen, one way or another. This was just an unexpected bonus, a way we can advance our timescale.'

'There's that "we" again,' Nina said. 'Who are "we"?'

'As I said, there are leaders and there are followers.'

'So which are you?'

That seemed to sting him, his superior expression turning to irritation. 'I warned you I won't ask twice, Dr Wilde. Face it: you've lost everything. Your job, your *fiancé* . . . Do you want to lose your life as well?'

The laser points moved up to her face. She closed her eyes – and just for a moment saw Chase, smiling at her from the darkness. Everything they had shared over the past three years flowed through her mind: the adventures, laughter and tears, exhilaration and fears, the highs and lows of the roller coaster ride that had been their relationship. And through it all, the love underpinning it all. Whatever differences they had, in the end he had always been there for her. A friend, a lover . . .

A guide.

She knew what she had to do. What *he* would do.

Nina opened her eyes, and met Dalton's. Her gaze was unwavering, resolute. Fearless.

For the briefest moment, his eyes flickered with the realisation of failure.

She opened her fingers.

The skull dropped into the void. There was a faint *crack* as it hit a protruding rock and shattered, the fragments caught by the wind and vanishing into the empty waters.

Nobody moved. The soldiers still had their guns fixed on Nina, who stared unblinkingly at Dalton. He looked back, until finally turning away with a small grunt almost of amusement. A gesture, and the two men lowered their weapons.

'Well?' Nina demanded, breathing heavily.

One of the soldiers turned questioningly to Dalton. 'Sir?'

'Leave her,' said Dalton. He met Nina's eyes again. 'You've got nothing, *Nina*. No concrete proof, just a few photographs – and they'll be debunked as fakes, I can guarantee that. The news networks will make you a laughing stock before you even open your mouth. You'll just be another crank, a has-been who had her moment – then went off the rails.' The smug smirk returned. 'Living with that will be worse than killing you.'

'This isn't over,' Nina insisted.

'Oh, it is.' He spoke to the nearest soldier. 'Get rid of these bodies and clean up.'

'And her?' the man asked.

'Like I said, leave her.' He started towards the helicopter, before delivering a parting shot over his shoulder. 'There's a two-seat F-15 waiting for me in Germany – I'll be back in Virginia before breakfast. As for you . . . I wouldn't be in any rush to get home. You won't enjoy the reception. Goodbye, Dr Wilde.'

He disappeared into the black helicopter's red-lit interior. The soldiers quickly scooped the two corpses into body bags, one man using a high-pressure spray of some pungent chemical to disperse the blood. The guns were retrieved, even the leather case and ziplock bag taken away. The whole process took barely two minutes before the last soldier boarded the chopper, which left the ground before the hatch had even fully closed. The aircraft swung over Nina's head, blasting her with a hot wind before being swallowed by the dark sky, the thud of its rotors fading within moments.

She stared after it, left alone.

Completely alone. Dalton was right. She had nothing. No proof. No Chase.

Slumping against the railing, she began to weep.

Epilogue

New York City

Nina blankly watched the endless bustle of Manhattan passing the coffee shop's window with a feeling of complete disconnection. Even though she was surrounded by crowds, she was isolated, alone. Hollow.

It was now three weeks since she faced Dalton at the waterfall, two weeks and six days since she had endured a hostile interrogation at JFK and an unpleasant confrontation with a press pack of mocking jackals as she emerged from the gate, all prepped with questions about her suspension – now permanent – and the deaths she had caused and her crazy theories that were an insult to every decent American. Dalton's people had done their job well, a pre-emptive smearing to make her look a fool, a dangerous crank, a joke.

She didn't care. About anything. Nothing mattered any more.

The media interest died down quickly, simply because she had nothing to say. Cable news pundits still reviled her every so often, but the mainstream media had moved on. Disgraced scientists were less of a draw than drunken actors or pregnant singers or the contestants in the latest talent show. It had been two days since anyone had recognised, or insulted, her in the street. Dr Nina Wilde was old news. Forgotten.

She stared into her coffee cup, swirling the last dregs around its bottom. Her reflected face looked back at her without expression.

That, she knew all too well, was just a façade, a shell. She couldn't *allow* herself to feel anything. Because if she did, she knew what emotion would consume her.

Despair.

She had thought her anguish would fade over time. She had been wrong. Instead it had mutated, a cancerous tumour in her psyche, poisoning every moment. It took all her willpower not to give in to it . . . but in moments of loneliness, she couldn't stop the awful darkness from rising.

She gulped down the final mouthful of coffee, then summoned the strength to return to the apartment. The empty apartment. Sometimes she kept walking the streets of Manhattan for hours to avoid having to go back to it, but in the end she always had . . . because she had nowhere else to go.

Nina was walking to the door when something made her pause. Dalton's name.

It was hardly the first time she had heard it since returning, loss and loathing flooding back at each occurrence. But there was something different about it now, a buzz as it spread through the customers. She turned. People were talking on phones, scanning news pages on laptops, spreading the word. She tried to pick out details through the growing hubbub.

'– the President –'

'– he slept with –'

'– terrorist –'

'– might have to resign –'

'– a video –'

'– all over the Internet –'

'– I found it, I got it here!'

People clustered round one man, who tilted his laptop's screen so they could watch. Nina hesitated, then joined them. She could barely see the screen through the throng, but a glimpse was enough.

She turned away, heading for the exit as the grainy video of Sophia Blackwood and Victor Dalton, faces and naked bodies clearly visible, played.

'Where did it come from?'

'I dunno, but it's all over the place. YouTube already pulled the original, but there's hundreds of copies up, it's on the torrents, everywhere!'

'Is that – that's her, isn't it? The bitch who tried to nuke us?'

'Is that really the President? It can't be. Can it?'

'It's him, it's really him!'

The voices faded behind Nina as she left the shop and stood on the street. The word was here too, a verbal virus leaping from person to person. Shock, laugher, disbelief, intrigue – everyone had a different reaction.

But *everyone* had a reaction. Everyone knew.

Nina hurried towards her apartment, the tiniest seed of an emotion she hadn't felt for some time taking root inside her.

Hope.

By the time she reached home, every shop window TV, every radio blaring from a passing cab, every overheard cell phone conversation was about the same thing.

The President of the United States had been filmed *in flagrante*. That he hadn't been president at the time was immaterial; that the woman with him not only was not his wife, but had almost succeeded in detonating a nuclear bomb in New York, most certainly was. The video had spread across the Internet in a matter of hours, a digital hydra spawning new heads exponentially. A news story so big that whatever a network's political biases, it could not be ignored.

Nina rushed to the TV. She had avoided the news channels since her return, but now sought them out. There was only one story.

A caption told her she was watching a live broadcast from the White House press room, the familiar blue curtains behind a flustered man in a suit: the White House press secretary. Questions were being shouted at him, voices overlapping. 'One at a time, one at a time!' he cried, almost pleading. 'You, Pete. One at a time.'

'Is the President going to resign?' someone yelled.

'The Pres – the President will make a statement concerning this – this fabrication later today,' the press secretary stammered. 'That's all I can say right now.'

'That's the official line, that it's a fabrication?'

'It is, yes.'

'It's a fabrication, or it's the official line?'

Another voice chipped in with a loud aside of, 'If it's a fake, it'll win the Oscar for special effects.' Laughter erupted around the room.

'Will the President resign?' someone else boomed. The question was repeated with minor variations from what seemed like the entire press corps. The man visibly quailed.

Nina stepped back from the TV. 'Gotcha,' she whispered as she switched it off. If Dalton had Sophia's recording, then the only way a copy could have been made was . . .

A reflection in the blank screen told her she was not alone.

'Ay up,' said a familiar voice. 'Don't I get a kiss hello?'

'*Eddie!*' Nina screamed in delight as she spun to see Chase sitting casually on a chair in the corner, looking as if he'd just come back from the 7-11 rather than the dead. She ran to him. 'Oh my God, oh my God! Is it really you?'

'Course it's bloody me! What, you think I'm a zombie? Ow, don't hug me there, ow!' He grimaced and pushed her off his chest. 'I've got a bust rib and a fucked-up lung, so don't go poking at 'em!'

'What happened?' Nina asked, emotions whirling. 'I thought you were dead!' Tears rolled down her cheeks. 'Oh, God, I thought you were dead . . .'

'Yeah, I did too, for a bit. When Sophia shot me she hit a rib, but I still got a fragment in the lung. I don't remember too much, just trying to keep my head above the water, but I think I ended up a couple of miles downstream where someone found me. Got taken to hospital, and they patched me up.'

'What happened to Sophia?'

'Now that I *do* remember. I, ah, used her as an airbag. She hit a couple of rocks on the way down.'

'Is she dead?' Nina asked hopefully.

'Dunno. After we hit the water, I lost her. But if she isn't, I doubt she'll be running any marathons for a while. I definitely heard a couple of bits of her go snap. See, I told you there weren't any feelings left between us.'

'Throwing your ex off a cliff's kind of an extreme way of proving it. So when did you get back to New York?'

'Couple of days ago.'

'*And you didn't tell me?*' she shrilled.

'First thing I did was check you were okay!' he said, holding her arms so she couldn't hit him. 'But I had something to sort out first.' He glanced at the TV. 'Looks like it worked.'

Her outrage faded. 'But how did you get the recording? Dalton took the only copy.'

He grinned. 'He took *Sophia's* only copy. You know when I went into that bank in Zürich to check if she'd already been there?'

She nodded. 'Yeah?'

'Well, it occurred to me that seeing as she was legally dead and she'd named me as her next of kin or whatever, that'd mean I had the right to open her deposit box. Took a bit of wheedling, but they eventually let me look inside. And there it was. So . . .'

'You made a copy.'

'Yup. Had to buy a memory stick off some clerk, but I made a copy. And it even survived falling off a cliff into freezing water.' He held up a small orange flash drive. 'Might have it framed, actually.'

'So you put a copy of the recording on the Internet.'

'I put *lots and lots* of copies of the recording on the Internet. Got in touch with some old mates. Then this morning, all at the same time, they sent it out to every news agency, all the TV stations, papers, YouTube, all of those places. Spammed the world so everybody'd see it. And it looks like they did.' Another smile. 'Ain't technology grand?'

'Why didn't you tell me you'd made a copy?'

'I didn't have time. Sophia and Ribbsley turned up at the bank right after I left, remember? If I'd been another couple of minutes farting about, she'd have caught me.'

Nina raised an eyebrow. 'And they didn't tell her that you'd just been rifling through her safety deposit box?'

'Well, you know those Swiss banks. Very discreet.'

She laughed, for the first time in three weeks, then kissed him, long and hard. 'So now what?' she asked.

'Well, we can sit back and watch Dalton get fucked in slow motion.'

'Eddie, that's gross.'

'I don't mean with Sophia!' he hastily qualified. 'I mean on the news. There's no way he'll be able to slime his way out of this one. He'll *have* to resign, otherwise he'll get impeached. That's something I always found funny about you Yanks. Your politicians can lie, cheat, steal, kill, and they'll still probably stay in office. But one whiff of dodgy sex, and bam, they're up shit creek! You're such bloody puritans.'

She huffed in mock offence. 'Oh, you think I'm a puritan, do you?'

'Well, not so much since I bought you that book . . .'

They both laughed, Nina taking his hands in hers and lifting them – then looking at her engagement ring. 'You know what?'

'What?'

'I think a ring'd suit you too.'

He considered, then a broad smile spread across his square face. 'I think it might. What, right now?'

Nina could hardly contain her rising excitement. 'Yeah, right now. Come on!' She jumped up, helping Chase stand. He winced at the pain in his chest – but it didn't take the smile off his face.

They hurried down to the street. 'Taxi!' Nina yelled, waving down a yellow cab.

'Where are we going?' Chase asked.

'Oh, crap, good point. New York's got a twenty-four-hour waiting period on marriages. Oh, I know!' The cab stopped and they climbed in. 'Take us to Connecticut!'

The driver, a Central Asian man with a stubbly beard, gave her a dubious look. 'Where in Connecticut?'

'The nearest place with a Justice of the Peace!'

'It's your dollar,' said the driver with a shrug, starting the meter. 'Hey, you heard about the President?'

Nina and Chase smiled at each other. 'Yeah, we have,' Nina said, laughing.